JUSTICE
BETRAYED

A Novel

JUSTICE BETRAYED

A Novel

Jeffrey David

SUNSTONE
PRESS

SANTA FE

This is a work of fiction and any resemblances between persons living or dead is purely coincidental.

Sunstone books may be purchased for educational, business, or sales promotional use. For information please write: Special Markets Department, Sunstone Press, P.O. Box 2321, Santa Fe, New Mexico 87504-2321.

Book and Cover design › Vicki Ahl
Body typeface › Californian FB
Printed on acid-free paper

Library of Congress Cataloging-in-Publication Data

David, Jeffrey.
  Justice betrayed : a novel / by Jeffrey David.
    p. cm.
  ISBN 978-0-86534-893-6 (softcover : alk. paper)
  1. Judges--Fiction. 2. Trials (Murder)--Fiction. 3. Murder--Investigation--Fiction. I. Title.
  PS3618.E9754J87 2012
  813'.6--dc23
                    2012024399

WWW.SUNSTONEPRESS.COM
SUNSTONE PRESS / POST OFFICE BOX 2321 / SANTA FE, NM 87504-2321 /USA
(505) 988-4418 / ORDERS ONLY (800) 243-5644 / FAX (505) 988-1025

*For Esther and Michael Sutin
in loving gratitude*

Acknowledgements

*T*he author would like to thank the following people who made this book possible: Barbara Bloy, Ph.D., for her unflagging enthusiasm and mentoring during the entire writing and rewriting process and for her devoted editing. Joanne Rubin, attorney at law, former president of the Lucas County Bar Association (Toledo, Ohio) for her technical assistance on some of the finer elements of the law. Sylvia Judith Scharf, Krystal DuBose, and Cheryl Gotthelf for wise counsel, tenderness, and gentle prodding when needed. Finally, James Clois Smith, Jr., president of Sunstone Press of Santa Fe, New Mexico and his dedicated staff for taking a chance on a fledgling writer.

Doing nothing is an active decision: the easiest decision of all, and a bane upon the soul.

Prologue

Out West lies sleepy, old New Mexico with her grassy high plains. On the eastern slope of the state the silver and brown silt colored Pecos River meanders out of the lower fingers of the Rockies spreading southward, flowing in turns like an Arab scimitar—a moving oasis in the parched arid land, the river brings green fertility where the earth is dry and the soil rocky; yet where the Pecos flows the land tastes the sweet cool waters and lush irrigated fields flourish on both banks, while just a short distance away rock formations, mesas, and mountain ranges pierce the sky.

There are contrasts among the people as in the land: Native Americans, Spanish, and Anglos each adding a layer of texture and cadence, each contributing vibrant cultures and artifacts: Indian jewelry and pottery, the Spanish Catholic faith, and an Anglo system of government and laws. For the most part these people co-exist with civility and cordiality, but sometimes the centuries old grudges and ancient resentments break through and there is violence. These deep contrasting currents run deep in the land, the people, the river. And as the Pecos River gathers speed and broadens, it flows southward and curves back on itself away from the oil-rich Permian Basin, and toward the edges of the Chihuahuan Desert in New Mexico and its capital, Santa Fe.

Santa Fe was named by the Spanish conquistadors who explored northward from Mexico City bringing civil government and their religion to the land. The city's high elevation makes for short, mild summers, a colorful fall, long winters, and brief springs when the mountains north and east of the city come alive in greens of various shadings from the mountain aspen and pine forests. Santa Fe reflects its diverse history and successive political leadership in the architecture of its government buildings and homes. The city has its plaza and stately cathedral, narrow lanes and art galleries, and the aesthetic ambiance of the Old World. It is a place unto itself, a city that thinks of itself as a major artistic capital of America, proud of its past and aware of the possibilities of its rich future. No building in Santa Fe shows these contrasts more strikingly than the Supreme Court of New Mexico.

On the outside, the building's Spanish motif and contours combine in synthesis with the simple and austere lines of the Anglo territorial style—just as the history of the state had. The building has an elegant portico entrance and two enormous polished brass doors: the "Portals of Justice." The doors' bas relief panels cite the law from the Holy Scriptures and the New Testament, including Moses giving the Ten Commandments to the ancient Israelites, Solomon rendering judgment upon the infant and two mothers, Abraham before God asking mercy for the righteous of Sodom and Gomorrah, Nathan accusing King David of killing Bath-Sheba's husband, Jesus giving the sermon on the mount, and saving the woman accused of adultery. The doors are protected from Santa Fe's long winter by the portico and are polished daily by the all Hispanic maintenance crew who proudly keep the building and its grounds immaculate.

The building has four stories and a basement level where the administrative staff members who manage the district courts throughout the state have their offices. The first floor houses the dark paneled courtroom and the private robing room of the justices just behind the courtroom's bench. The rest of the first floor houses the court clerk's office and the entrance to the huge, four story law library with law books from all regions of the nation as well as New Mexico's territorial past. There is an acrid, almost rich smell of unsmoked aging tobacco, making the law books not unpleasant, but distinctive. The browning pages of law reports, some more than a century old, filled the shelves. New technology is also accommodated: computers are placed throughout the library. Adjoining the library are the chambers of the justices.

1

He sat behind his desk, a desk belonging to the past, alone in his spacious chambers surrounded by years of mementos reflecting a long and successful career. Chief Justice Big Jim Richards had photographs of himself with governors and United States senators, an inscribed picture of himself with Lyndon Johnson, and one with Willie Nelson.

He rarely looked back; his focus was the future with its challenges. While he sat at his large desk, he did not feel alone; something else was in chambers with him, something larger than himself: the law. He thought of himself as a servant of justice for the people, the combined will of all the citizens of New Mexico and the majesty of the law before which they must all bow. The law he upheld dispensed practical wisdom and discipline with impartiality and was sometimes tempered with compassion.

The chambers were sunlit from the south all day and in the afternoon from the west also. White light streamed into the austere office, brightening the texture of the dark woods.

Bookcases filled with law books, state statutes, and treatises lined much of the walls. On their pages were the living history of New Mexico and her long proud past: annals of ranching, farming, oil, natural gas, and mining. She was a potentially rich and fertile state.

On his desk a computer—the new way of practicing law, replacing law books. He knew that the next generation of justices will have all the issued decisions of New Mexico on two discs or a flash drive. The wizardry of the computer will give lawyers and judges access to all the written decisions of the United States Supreme Court, the federal courts, and all the state courts in a flash. The law has been revolutionized by the computer, he knew.

In front of his desk were two sturdy dark-stained wooden arm chairs. They too were relics of the past, the kind of chairs that were used in lawyers' offices and courtrooms across the nation sixty years ago. He favored them as reminders of other days.

On the east wall was a comfortable dark brown leather couch capable of sitting three lawyers easily.

Behind his desk, in the southeast corner of the chambers stood the state flag of New Mexico and in the opposite corner the American flag.

On the wall facing the desk stood a bookcase strewn with law books and family photographs. Scraps of yellow legal pad paper served as bookmarkers for important decisions in the case reports. Despite modernization, he was still a captive of the law book.

On occasion he would look up at a photograph from twenty five years before when he was a young magistrate judge in Curry County, just a few years out of law school with everything before him, and little law practice behind. The photos showed him tall, trim and athletic with dark brown hair, not the judicial gray he had come to earn on the bench as the years passed. In one photo he stood beside an older Hispanic man both wearing black judge's robes. The older man was much shorter, but had an impressive, dignified aura, as if size didn't count at all. Jim looked at the picture and he remembered.

Those were days of sheer joy, sitting as a magistrate judge fashioning justice for his townspeople, sentencing petty criminals, holding arraignments and bail hearings for more serious offenders, or handling minor civil suits between Curry County citizens.

In those early days, he worked closely with his mentor and the local sage, Judge Reuben Fuentes, an older magistrate judge who had decades of experience in the courtroom with all kinds of men and women and had learned from them. After the days' hearings Judge Reuben studied and applied the law. He had become a keen observer of human nature and a wise dispenser of justice.

Judge Fuentes treated Jim like a son and Big Jim loved and respected the older man. Out of respect for his older colleague Jim rarely called him Reuben, but instead referred to him as Judge Reuben. These golden, halcyon days were filled with excitement, happenings and learning about the law and human nature. Jim greeted each day as a new adventure, arriving early and staying late. He was an apt pupil and was learning much under the tutelage of Judge Reuben about the practice of judging.

At home, his children were growing and going about the doings of family life. His wife Karen, his college sweetheart, had proved to be a good companion, and a competent, cool-headed advisor. She had married a man with ambition, and she knew and wanted that. Life made no sense to her if you were just going to stand still; she wanted to move ahead. Karen was a tall woman with warm brown eyes that provided reassurance and acceptance, but that were tempered with intelligence and strength. She wore her hair shorter now, not the luxuriant length down to her shoulders that she'd worn in college, neat and easier to tend to, but not unattractive. She had a smile that shone from her young fresh face and a beautiful figure: full joyous breasts and long shapely legs. She was altogether an attractive woman and a good wife. She proved to be the best decision Big Jim had made in his life.

Karen taught the fifth grade, and like everything else in her life, she was good at it. She called her students "her children." She loved them, and their adoring young faces loved her right back. Each new school year was spirited and fun-filled with the exception of grading papers nearly every night, "But all work has its burdens," she would say to herself. She was content in her life—her husband, her children, her career.

Big Jim stood 6'4"and 245 pounds. He was always trying to keep his weight down. In college years he had played second string linebacker at Texas Tech. where he saw some playing time, but mostly rode the bench. Now circumstances had changed—he sat behind the bench. His dark eyes and face still retained some of his youth, but his forehead had begun to show the furrows of thought and deliberation. His jaw was firm and tight and marked by determination and ambition. He was a hail-fellow-well-met when away from the concerns of the court. He could work a room or meet with lawyers amiably, and all came away with the feeling they had been heard. He was a good listener.

Jim had remained honest, and aloof from entanglements in Curry County, where the political scuffles for state contracts in road resurfacing and new school construction were fought over like a fresh kill by lions on the savannahs of Africa. Big Jim had wisely used his judicial office and its impartiality to steer clear of competing factions and local controversies, but remained a good and true friend.

The intercom rang, bringing Jim back from his Curry County past to the present.

"Judge, Mr. Arnold's on the phone."

Vance Arnold and Jim went way back. Arnold had been a police officer in Clovis, the county seat of Curry County, when Jim was an assistant DA and then sat as a magistrate judge. They saw a lot of each other in court back then, advancing on parallel careers, and had become good friends. Jim was responsible for bringing Vance to the new Children's Department fifteen years ago, and it was Big Jim's prestige as a justice of the supreme court and his well placed phone calls that secured Vance's position as chief of the Children's Department for the entire state some years later.

Vance Arnold's voice came across the phone, "Can you meet me in the Village Inn parking lot out on Cerrillos Road at noon?"

The restaurant was busy with the lunch time crowd. Jim saw Vance sitting in his parked car and walked over and got in. If anyone had noticed they would have seen two men in shirt and ties talking in the front seat of a car for about fifteen minutes then the passenger getting out carrying a black laptop computer bag, got into his own car, and drove away.

Jim unlocked his chamber's door, walked inside, locked the door behind him, and went to his inner office. The staff would not be back from lunch for another half hour. He laid the computer bag on his desk, inside tightly belted packets totaling $150,000 in fresh green bills. This was not his first rendezvous with Vance at various spots in Santa Fe. He could do a lot of things with the cash, but he had no foolish fantasies: the money was for a fixed purpose—his campaign for United States senate. He looked at it again, and then put the bag safely under his desk where it would not be visible. Theresa, his secretary, and the law clerks would be back soon. He unlocked his chamber's door.

2

*S*teve Light may have been the Legal Aid lawyer in the small, quiet town of Clovis, the county seat of Curry County, but in the course of his practice he had handled some sophisticated, complex cases well beyond the ordinary. On his desk currently was an Agent Orange death benefits case before the Pentagon for review.

In that case the facts were undisputed. Airman Stan Emery worked on the flight line nightly at Tan Son Nhut Air Base in South Vietnam. His duties included servicing and washing down the planes that had sprayed the jungle during the day with Agent Orange, the chemical defoliant that stripped the jungle trees of their leafy canopy to make bombing runs from above more accurate for United States pilots.

Night after night Airman Emery hosed down the planes and the back splash soaked his clothes with Agent Orange.

When he returned to the states he fell sick, was hospitalized, and diagnosed with pancreatic cancer. There was no history of cancer in his family, but Agent Orange by that time had been determined to be a highly toxic cancer causing chemical. His weight dropped from 186 to 118 pounds before he painfully died at the V.A. Hospital in Albuquerque 43 days short of having served 20 years in the military, thus depriving his family of retirement benefits. He left five children all trying to get a college education. At issue was whether or not the one semester he took of college R.O.T.C. would count towards his years of service thus putting him over 20 years of duty. The military argued no, but Steve Light contended that the R.O.T.C. counted towards Airman Emery's active duty.

Emery's widow had been up and back, down and 'round with the Pentagon, trying to secure survivor's benefit status to help her and his kids, but the military was adamant. Nineteen years 322 days were not 20 years of military service and Stan Emery had died 43 days short of fully vesting in military survivor benefits for his family.

Steve Light waged this battle month after month: filling out forms, speaking with Pentagon officials, and filing appeals. He turned every stone.

Emery's two eldest sons—living at home—took low paying full time jobs to help support the family and attended university at night, taking a course or two every semester. The other children had taken part time jobs and attended school around their work schedules. There was no help from the military.

Steve Light was angry. Stan Emery did not duck military duty, or protest the war. He enlisted, and did his assigned duty for 19 years and 322 days as a military man, exposed to the element that killed him, and now that military abandoned his surviving children and widow.

Steve's anger in this case drove him to make calls and question officials about remedies available to military families, and class action settlements for Agent Orange victims and their survivors. He encountered wall upon wall of concerted resistance and each negative call or letter of denial only intensified Steve's determination to help this family. He remembered what Justice Susan Waters had told him when he was her judicial law clerk at the New Mexico Supreme Court fresh from law school: "If you feel strongly about the facts of a case there is probably a rule of law that supports your position." It was wise counsel from a wise judge.

After nearly two years of wrangling, document filing, letter writing and endless phone calls the appeal had reached the highest level of the Pentagon and Steve knew that the solution he sought lay in the vale of the federal courts in the District of Columbia, at the next level of appeal where he hoped he might get a full and fair hearing that would take into account the R.O.T.C. course that Stan Emery took in college before enlisting. He would have to marshal his facts, get expert witnesses. "Where will I get the funds to pay for experts," he worried. "Maybe I can find an expert or two who will donate their time. We'll cross that bridge when we get there."

In another extraordinary case that Steve had at this time he filed a writ of prohibition against the governor and the New Mexico Department of Health, asking the courts to stop the governor from discharging from the state children's hospital a profoundly developmentally challenged, bedridden child who couldn't walk, speak, or feed herself, and needed 24 hour nursing care, because in two weeks she would be 18 and no longer be considered a child.

The parents, plain people of ordinary income, were frantic in their efforts to secure a facility to care for their daughter within their limited financial means. They had no medical insurance that would pay for a private nursing home. The child was entitled to benefits, but the benefits were not sufficient to cover the costs. The children's hospital director was adamant about terminating the child's stay and treatment at the hospital.

Steve went to the courts filing the writ prohibiting the state from discharging the child from the hospital until satisfactory new arrangements could be made. News of the story makes the *Clovis News Journal* and would be in the other state papers in the morning.

At 4:50 p.m. on the day the writ was filed Steve got a call from the governor's office.

"Mr. Light, my name is Bob Riley. I'm special counsel to the governor."

"How can I help you," Steve asked.

"The governor is aware of your writ of prohibition filed today and is in full sympathy with your client's family. He has instructed Dr. Stockton, the medical director of the Children's Hospital, to give your client's family six additional months to find a suitable facility for their child. Will that be satisfactory, and will you withdraw your writ hearing for later this week?"

"Bob, the governor's offer is very generous. Let me talk to my clients and see what their reaction is and I'll get back to you within twenty-four hours. Will that work for you? The writ is scheduled to be heard Friday morning at ten before the supreme court in Santa Fe."

"Steve, that's fine. If the family needs more than six months the governor is willing to be flexible. He has taken a personal interest in this child."

"That's good to know. The family will be happy to hear the good news. Thanks Bob, you'll hear from me tomorrow."

Steve's caseload also included the run of the mill: divorces, landlord /tenant matters, and such simple transactions that filled a lawyer's day in small town practice. But the work was rewarding and Steve liked the people. He felt satisfied that he was doing some good. He had his favorite clients, of course, and there was lots of humor among his staff to relieve the stress of the day's work.

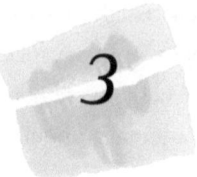

3

*A*fter putting the laptop bag under his desk and opening his chamber's doors Chief Justice "Big Jim" Richards returned to his desk and glanced at the photo of Judge Fuentes. Big Jim reflected on his mentor of days past. Jim thought back to the start of his judicial career and the tutelage he received from Judge Reuben Fuentes and what made Reuben Fuentes a great judge. And the memories flooded his mind and carried him back.

Reuben Fuentes was a man of wondrous, delightful contours and shadings. He could be serious and judicially-minded when on the bench or discussing the law, but off the bench he had an impish, mischievous sense of humor and was a constant practical joker. His sense of humor was displayed only to those within the court family of Curry County.

Judge Fuentes, five foot seven inches, had a swarthy, olive complexion, and a medium build that he kept trim by his daily walks to and from the magistrate courthouse two miles from his home. He drove only on Thursday when he had his weekly Kiwanis Club luncheon. His once black hair had now gone all gray, adding to his distinguished look, but his raven black eyes still held the flash of youthful vigor and strength. His mustache—now also gray—would rise in a smile when he heard a good story or played a joke on someone. He wore his black framed glasses, but only to read a decision in a law book, or some statute. Otherwise they sat on his desk or on the bench when he conducted court. He had a way of fixing his eyes upon a defendant or plaintiff, listening deeply to the testimony, and trying to garner all his wisdom in resolving the conflict before him—and that wisdom was considerable. He wore dark conservative suits and striped ties and always a crisp white dress shirt. Judge Reuben had become vigorous with age, as if each year strengthened both his physical and mental prowess. Reuben loved the law, becoming more and more impressed by its practicality and wisdom with the passage of his years. He was a humble man, without false piety, and his streak of humor made him even more lovable. He dispensed the law fairly, and like the apothecaries of old he'd fashion the elements and compounds of his decision making—taking from here and there—based upon the evidence and reaching the desired result after carefully grinding and shifting through the testimony and elements of the law in the pestle and mortar of his mind before dispensing his remedy.

While his work was only in the magistrate court, "Judge Reuben," as Jim called him, read widely in the law, including United States Supreme Court Justice's Cardozo's seminal work, *The Making of a Judicial Decision* and other learned works on jurisprudence. He worked to distill all that he had learned from the cases that came before him daily at the magistrate court, but he had never gone to law school. He had been elected to the position when lawyers were hard to find in the outback of New Mexico, and had taught himself the ways of the law so that now he had become a scholar of sorts. Yes, Judge Reuben was a man of contours and shadings.

When Big Jim was elevated by the governor to the magistrate court he was in his thirties and Judge Reuben was approaching sixty-five. At the swearing in ceremony, after Jim had sworn allegiance to the Constitution of the United States and the Laws of New Mexico, he donned the black robe of the judiciary for the first time and made a few remarks to friends and relatives who had gathered for the ceremony. Big Jim felt a certain pride mixed with humility. He had been set apart now, and the black robe signified that he was no longer just "one of the boys." A new standard of conduct was now expected of him, even though it was just magistrate court. Jim had reverence for the symbols of office.

Reuben Fuentes had been a magistrate judge for over 30 years when Jim was elevated to the bench. Judge Fuentes respected the office, but saw himself as very human. About the second week of Jim's tenure, when Jim was still feeling pretty important, Judge Reuben asked one of the women in the clerk's office to come in early with her portable sewing machine. He thought it was about time Big Jim's feet touch the ground. On Judge Reuben's direction she sewed the sleeves of Big Jim's robe closed, reinforced them with several rows of stitching, and then carefully re-hung the robe on the rack in Big Jim's chambers.

Big Jim, enthusiastic in his new position, came to work whistling every morning. He always arrived early. His court convened at 9:00 a.m., usually with arraignments, but he was in his chamber reading the day's files by 7:30 a.m.

Judge Fuentes always made it a habit to stop by his young protégés chambers every morning. On this particular day all six foot four inches of Big Jim Richards stood struggling to get his arms into the sleeves of his judicial robe. Judge Reuben maintained his poker face as Big Jim's struggles became increasingly vigorous and in vain. Try as he might, the big man could not robe himself for court. Judge Reuben continued talking about some arcane aspect of the law, calm, casual, and nonchalantly. He even called in the court staff on some pretext and the three women all watched Big Jim try to dress himself unsuccessfully for court and then throw the robe down across the back of a chair with a resounding "Damn!" The whole staff started laughing. "Jim why don't you try this one," Judge Reuben said as one of the women brought in another unaltered robe. And the Big Fellow realized he'd been had and laughed too.

Naturally Big Jim had to even up the score. Thus began a series of practical jokes that stretched over Big Jim's and Judge Reuben's tenure together—colleagues, mentor and student, and friends.

Judge Reuben was unofficial head of the Hispanic community in Curry County. On many occasions Hispanic constituents would come to the magistrate court to seek Judge Reuben's counsel about business matters, family problems, or trouble with their children. If there was a feud between Spanish families Judge Reuben would sit down with both sides and try to resolve the matter with uncommon good sense and wisdom, always honoring each side and allowing both families to save face. Resorting to the courts became a rare last remedy that was to be avoided because it opened an even deeper breach between the families and a rife in the Spanish community. Big Jim heard those cases.

Over many years Judge Reuben's generosity, wisdom, and experience helped the members of the Hispanic community. Whenever Father Moises Lopez, the Catholic priest, needed help—financial or otherwise—he came to see Judge Reuben. If the church roof needed repairs, or the food pantry needed to be re-stocked Judge Reuben was instrumental and always liberal in seeing that these things happened. He was considered a wise and valued member of the Clovis community by both Spanish and Anglo citizens. He lived well within his means, and only two miles from where he was born in Spanish Town. County Commissioners always sought him out about plans and projects in the Spanish community and Judge Reuben always made sure his Spanish constituents received a distribution of community funds and projects. He also made certain the Spanish members of the community voted: it was an indispensable part of governing the workings of their small section of town.

With the Spanish population of Clovis growing faster than the Anglo population, the future belonged to them, and in the coming generation or two there would be an inevitable power shift away from the once Anglo dominated town.

Reuben's wife, Ida, was a quiet, dignified woman, a wife who took pride in her husband's achievements and his many important friends. She was an ideal companion, a dynamo in her faith, and a continuing support for her husband. On Sundays they would walk to ten o'clock mass together arm in arm wearing their Sunday best and greeting neighbors, their custom since their marriage forty-four years before, back to a twosome now that their children were grown and had their own families.

Judge Reuben was always a "soft touch." There was not a charity, honest cause, or local person he would not contribute to. "Juan, here is a hundred dollars for your son Pablo to go with his class to Washington, DC. I hear good things about him from the school. I know he is a good boy. Let him come to see me with his report card at the end of the term. If his grades are good I'll find work for him down at the courthouse for the summer." In this way Judge Reuben helped a poor, simple Mexican woodcarver, who had a promising son. Reuben was always available and always generous.

All this changed when Judge Fuentes took the bench. His demeanor, his bearing, his intent were transformed when he dispensed justice—and justice it was—swift, decisive, and firm. In criminal cases Judge Reuben had little tolerance for criminal behavior. He, himself, had been poor; he knew poverty, but crime he would not tolerate. It didn't matter if the defendant were Spanish or Anglo: if there was probable cause that a defendant was alleged to have sold drugs or harmed another person Judge Fuentes listened to the evidence and set high bonds. He didn't want the defendant out on the street, or in the community recommitting crimes while waiting for the criminal justice system to do its work.

Among the people who came before Judge Fuentes there were the "regulars"—troubled young men and street toughs, who each thought he was the "baddest" *hombre* ever to walk the earth, took pride in his criminal reputation, and had no fear of the law. Judge Fuentes knew the type from his years of experience and knew that the stern application of the criminal justice system was the only solution to the problem. He felt strongly about his obligation to keep the law abiding citizens of Clovis safe.

Occasionally, Judge Fuentes had to deal with local farm kids who had gotten into trouble. Here the justice was the same. If an offender spent a few days in the Detention Center it might be the best way to bring him back to the straight and narrow. In these cases Judge Fuentes would intentionally take the bail request under consideration for 24 to 48 hours and in the interim send the farm boy back to the jail to have a taste of incarceration. Often this delay solved the problem in a flash. These farm boys longed to return to the free, unfettered life they had grown to know on the plains surrounding Clovis, and that little taste of confinement was the dose of medicine they needed. They didn't like being locked up with kids from the other side of the tracks who glorified jail as a mark of manhood and saw these farm boys as easy prey.

Judge Reuben still lived in the house where he had raised his family. His children were now grown and gone. They had all completed college; he and Ida had seen to that. His son had gone on to law school and practiced in a major law firm in Santa Fe. His two daughters had married, one to a doctor, the other to an Air Force officer she met while they were both students at U.N.M. and he was enrolled in the R.O.T.C. program. She taught school in Tucson, where her husband was stationed as a major at Davis-Monthan Air Force Base.

Reuben liked to walk briskly to work; it had been his habit for years. Promptly at twenty minutes to eight he left his home and walked at a pleasant pace through the cottonwood lined streets to arrive at the magistrate courthouse, just a little down the block from the district court, at 8:00 a.m.

4

he district court was a large four story tall stone building that dominated the downtown area and overlooked the nearby smaller, simple magistrate courthouse that had been erected by the county with state funds, a single story red brick building that had a large anteroom for the public. The other half of the area was kept from the public by a desk-high partition and served as the clerk's office, where the court staff worked, keeping the flow of cases going, accounting for the payment of fines and bail bonds, and establishing the daily court docket.

In the middle of the building were Judge Fuentes' and Judge Richards' sparsely furnished courtrooms. Each courtroom was divided in two by the bar of justice—a wooden gate and fence-like, thigh-high affair that separated those admitted to the bar and the court participants from the public. Directly in front of the bar and the central feature of the courtroom was the dark wooden judge's bench. The judge occupied the highest seat in the courtroom, symbolizing his authority and neutrality. He sat above the dispute. Behind the judge's bench left and right stood full sized American and New Mexico state flags, the only trappings of the court's authority on display. Just below the judge's bench was the elevated witness stand and on the side wall facing the witness stand was the jurors' box, a single step-up platform with twelve plain wooden chairs. The platform was surrounded by a 24" high slatted wood fencing separating the jurors from the rest of the courtroom, but where they could be plainly observed.

In front of the judge's bench were two counsel tables and chairs for the opposing lawyers and their clients in the case to sit and confer with during the trial. In front of the witness stand was a lectern where the lawyers stood when questioning a witness.

On the other side of the bar of justice sat the public in four rows of benches. In the back behind the courtroom were a series of holding cells for incarcerated defendants who had hearings that day and waited for their turn in the courtroom. In front of the holding cells was a staging area for sheriff's deputies to shackle and unshackle a defendant before and after his or her court appearance. Armed deputies were all over the courthouse and in the courtroom providing security, studying their arrest reports before testifying, or guarding prisoners. Assistant DAs, public defenders, and law enforcement personnel all mixed in the hallways before hearings trying to nail down bits of evidence, come to a plea agreement, or "horse trade" information for leniency or a lighter sentence.

Some defendants let it all roll with the demand for a jury trial and their insistence of innocence; others pled guilty and faced the music now rather than risk an elaborate trial, a harsher district court judge, and more severe penalties later. Everybody knew one another and their appointed task in the script of the day.

The lawyers—both DAs and public defenders—knew the score with Judge Fuentes: strict, hard, and fair. The courthouse was like an oriental bazaar of law enforcement—uniformed and plain clothed—court staff, criminal defendants, lawyers, and judges all thrown into the confines of the small building. Here was a cross section of Clovis, some high born and educated, some law abiding and hard working, some taking the low road and the fast life at the expense of others. In the halls of the magistrate court all these parties met the destinies determined by their deeds and roles.

Deals were often made in these crowded corridors. One drug detective, with the approval of the DA, would offer a public defender a sweet deal if his client would "turn" the dealer who sold him the crack; otherwise the defendant was looking at 18 months in the "Big House" (the state pen) up north outside of Santa Fe, for possession with no early release, or time off for good behavior.

Other plea proposals came from the assistant district attorneys: "I'll ask for pre-prosecution diversion if your client will attend drunk driving school and go to AA for six months without missing a meeting." The wheels of justice would grind in the corridors of the magistrate court. The state got convictions and jail time for defendants, saving the tax payers money by allowing defendants to plea bargain for simple victimless crimes without the cost of jury trials.

This was the atmosphere that Big Jim came to love: the give and take of the lower court, the chance to see life up close and real. Jim had a close relationship with his court staff, and over the years Judge Reuben had become more than a mentor: a stately, respected father figure. He was a solid steel stanchion in the chaos of arraignments and hearings and simple jury trials.

Though the corridors and hallways were filled with the give and take of plea bargaining, once a defendant was in court before Judge Reuben Fuentes a new feeling permeated the scene. The gravity and firmness of the man and the respect he garnered from all parties conveyed itself to the defendant. The law took over, the majesty of Justice reigned, and no one would be tolerated who dared to disrespect it.

Jim remembered how smoothly he had fit into the life and routine of the magistrate court. As the "new kid on the block," he was often the recipient of one of Judge Reuben's practical jokes, but Jim learned fast.

One beautiful, blue sky spring day, the first of April, when the crops were just breaking through the soil and the fields were everywhere green, Jim struck.

He knew Judge Reuben's routine for Thursday Kiwanis lunches. And on this Thursday, as Judge Reuben walked out of the back door of the courthouse, he found his car up on four cement blocks, with all its tires missing. He looked around, befuddled. No one was about.

"Gosh darn!" was all he could muster. He was in a quandary. How would he make it to his meeting? He was stuck. Where were his tires?

Reuben looked around and from the windows of the district court overlooking the magistrate courthouse he saw the entire staff watching his reactions. From the roof of the district court two janitors unfurled a sheet with these words in large letters:

HAPPY APRIL FOOL'S DAY JUDGE FUENTES
FROM JUDGE RICHARDS

Just then, by design, a big convertible with its top down full of Kiwanis Club buddies pulled up to the parking lot.

"Reuben, we heard you needed a ride to lunch."

"I sure do!" He said, amused now, as he looked back over his shoulder at his stranded car. He shook his head and laughed to himself, and waved smiling at his friends in the district court.

When Judge Reuben returned from lunch his tires had been remounted as if nothing had happened. Big Jim greeted him with a large, lovable smile: "Did you have a good lunch Reuben?" Big Jim learned from the master and was fitting in perfectly in his new job.

That was not all the Big Jim learned. Long years on the bench had given Reuben much experience in studying and applying the criminal code. Self taught, he had read and studied the law diligently over many years. He had asked questions of the district court judges and the best lawyers who had come before him. By a process of discipline and osmosis and day by day arduous study Reuben had become a formidable criminal law judge over the course of thirty years.

For civil court matters Judge Fuentes had observed that greed or hurt pride lay at the core of most of the civil cases and that the parties, if given a chance to be heard by a judge who was impartial, strong, and willing to render a fair decision or encourage the parties to a just settlement, most matters could be resolved.

Over time Judge Reuben had become a keen student of human nature. He had learned the signs and behaviors of liars and the false contrived tears of women trying to win sympathy. He had also seen the real tears of men realizing that the next stop was many years' confinement in the state penitentiary. What Reuben had seen sharpened his understanding of the human condition. By the time of Jim Richards' elevation Judge Fuentes had this wealth of information and he shared it freely with the younger man, when asked.

Richards represented the new breed of magistrate judge. The state had adopted statutes that required magistrate judges to be graduates of law school who had passed the bar exam and were members of the state bar. The older, currently sitting magistrate judges were "grandfathered into" their positions and held them until their retirement, death, or defeat at the polls. Judge Richards brought with him the energy of youth and an eagerness to learn.

Judge Fuentes had become prescient over the years. "Margaret," he called from his chambers one morning to the clerk of the court, "could you come in for a moment please? Call the iron works shop out on Pile Street and have them come out and give us an estimate for installing a sheet of steel on the inside of the judges' courtroom benches to make them bullet proof."

Two weeks later, into the magistrate courthouse came a defendant who had been put out of his house after his wife had filed a temporary restraining order for domestic violence. A hearing had been set before Judge Fuentes, but in the interim the defendant was out of the house.

He was a surly, tall, angry man. He wore jeans, boots, and a jean jacket over a plaid shirt. He smelled of alcohol. He was over six feet tall and about 40 years old. The women in the clerk's office found him threatening and were afraid of him. Margaret went into Judge Fuentes' chambers to alert him.

"Judge, there's a defendant outside and we're afraid of him. He's been drinking. He told Linda, 'No one's going to tell me how to treat my wife and force me to leave my home, especially some little Mexican judge. I'll see to that.'"

Judge Fuentes had heard this before. He wasn't particularly alarmed.

"Are the deputies here yet?"

"No Judge, they're getting together this morning's prisoners from the jail and it will be another half hour before they walk them over from the jail."

"Okay Margaret. Call the sheriff's office, and tell them to send over a deputy now."

Suddenly there was a commotion outside the door. "You can't go in there."

And there in Judge Fuentes's office stood the tall, angry, drunken man.

"You the Mexican going to tell me I have to leave my own home and how to treat my wife?"

"I'm Judge Fuentes and I'm going to hear your case this morning.

"Why don't you wait outside, or if you like, in the courtroom until it's time for your hearing?" Judge Fuentes said courteously.

"You're not going to judge me, little man. I am an American. No Mexican is going to run my house."

"Have you been drinking today?" Judge Fuentes could smell the stench of alcohol coming from the man.

"What if I have? What's it your business? This is still a free country. A man can do what he wants to do. I don't have to answer to any Mexican!"

"My friend," Judge Fuentes said firmly but kindly, "why don't you go back to where you're staying and sleep it off. We'll adjourn your case for today and you can come back next week."

"Like hell! I want my day in court! I'll show that bitch who runs this family. She can't toss me out of my own home. I want my hearing today."

"Then you're going to have to wait quietly outside until court starts at nine. Can you do that?"

One of the clerk's women had gone to Judge Richards' chambers to get him.

"Come quick! Judge Fuentes needs you."

No deputy had arrived yet, but Judge Fuentes was not afraid. He had seen this type before, all bluster, hatred, and alcohol—not much else.

Judge Richards hurried through the clerk's office and was coming up behind the man.

"I'll show you!" The man said to Judge Fuentes, and then reached into his jacket and pulled out a pistol.

Judge Richards propelled himself through the doorway and tackled the man. The gun discharged. Big Jim smothered the man and grabbed for the gun. They both wrestled for it, but the man held tight. Judge Reuben immediately came over and tried to pry the gun loose—it was no use; so he just stomped his boot heel hard on the drunken man's hand. The man yelped, the gun fell free, and Reuben scooped it up.

"Okay Jim. I've got it."

With the sound of gunfire, sheriff's deputies flooded the courthouse with guns drawn. They found Judge Fuentes holding a pistol and Judge Richards holding the suspect. The man was immediately cuffed and arrested.

Now he had more to worry about than a temporary restraining order and being drunk. He was looking at hard time.

Reuben turned to Jim, "Are you sure you played only second string at Tech? You move pretty fast for a big guy. Glad you're on my team." And Big Jim returned the appreciation with a big smile.

The adventures of Judge Fuentes and Judge Richards went on daily for six years. Their antics enlivened daily routine in the courthouse.

Then one day Suzanne, the district court clerk, called Reuben to report that Judge Harris had just turned in his resignation.

"How old is Bill now," Reuben asked.

"He's seventy. He says he's tired and would like to spend time with the grandkids and just relax. He says twenty five years is enough."

"He's been a good judge for you over there—he'll be hard to replace."

"Judge Reuben, you would be his natural replacement," she said.

"Thank you, Suzanne, for the confidence, but I don't have a law degree and I'm nearing my own retirement. But Judge Richards is ready. Jim has learned a lot in the years he's been over here. He's a good young man, easy to work with, and the staff here loves him. He's knowledgeable and young with many years of service ahead of him. He'd make a good addition to the district court. When is Bill leaving?"

"In two months. He's got a few trials and some cases on his docket he'd like to dispose of. He sent his letter of resignation to the governor today, and he called Santa Fe and spoke with the chief justice to let them know his plans."

"Has anyone expressed interest?"

"It's still a little early, but Bob Fallows and Stuart Campbell have had their eyes on the bench for a while. They're both interested."

"Both of them are good lawyers. The governor can't go wrong naming either one of them. Suzanne, thanks for calling me. I'll see you soon."

The contest for the district court judgeship was intense. Jim went to Reuben and asked his advice about seeking the office. Reuben sat back, put his hands with his finger interlaced behind his head and leaned back in his big comfortable judicial desk chair.

"Jim, this is your chance. You've learned a lot here these past six years. You'll need to drum up local support, but you're ready for bigger things, bigger challenges."

Jim was 40 years old. He was younger than Fallows or Campbell, but had more hours of courtroom and practical judicial experience than either. He had not been an office lawyer putting together commercial transactions, writing wills, and doing divorces. He had been a hands-on judge, well trained and disciplined in the law by Judge Reuben Fuentes. He was a rising star in Curry County.

Following the Code of Judicial Conduct scrupulously, Jim quietly lobbied the important decision makers of Curry and Roosevelt counties who made up the judicial district as did Fallows and Campbell.

One of the most important meetings was with Hank Taylor, the managing editor of the *Clovis News Journal*, the town's daily newspaper, a man with penetrating eyes and a sharp intelligence. They sat together in Hank's office one summer's eve, after the paper had gone to press. They talked the talk of small towns: rains and crops, wives and kids. When Hank shifted in his chair, Jim recognized this change of posture as signifying that the interview was beginning in earnest.

"Okay Jim, so you want the *Journal's* endorsement for the district court position. Bob Fallows and Stu Campbell have also been over to see me about it. What makes you the best choice?" This was the question he asked all three men.

"Fallows and Campbell are good lawyers" Jim said. "They've both worked hard these last few years building their practices, but I have real judicial experience. I've been down at the magistrate courthouse day after day for the last six years hearing cases, rendering decisions, and fashioning legal remedies for the county. More importantly, I've been enforcing the criminal laws. Neither Campbell or Fallows has any experience in criminal cases, which make up at least half the caseload of a district court judge. Neither man has sat behind the bench, or sentenced a defendant to jail time. I do that on a daily basis and have been doing it for the last six years. When a man is elevated to the district court he is expected to know the law. There is no time for schooling. The docket is heavy and growing every month. I have that experience.

"In addition, I was selected by Chief Justice Chavez of the supreme court to serve on the statewide computer management system committee for the courts, to establish greater use of computers in our court system. The computer is the way of the future in the courts and will help bring uniformity throughout the state as well as help the public here in Curry County. It's been a great experience to come together with judges, court administrators, and lawyers from around the state to work out modernization and improvement of our court system.

"My membership on this committee led to Curry County's selection as one of the pilot counties in computerizing the courthouse and brought two hundred thousand dollars into our local economy, money that would have been spent somewhere else if I had not been on that committee. For these reasons, Hank, I think I am the most qualified for the district court judgeship."

The *Journal's* endorsement was essential for any candidate who wanted the appointment. It showed the governor which candidate had support in the local community. Judge Harris was to retire mid-term as was the time honored tradition in New Mexico, thus giving the governor the opportunity to freely appoint a successor and give that appointee a foot up in the next general election, when the new judge would stand for election.

Hank Taylor listened carefully, his eyes fixed on the man before him; he knew his decision would be pivotal in determining the next district court judge. Quietly, he took the measure of the man before him, as he had also done with his rivals. Hank sat contemplating with his finger steepled. Friendship did not count in this. Hank had an important job to do, a responsibility to his community.

Hank thought, *"Jim is younger than the other two, but he is right, he has more judicial experience and that's the telling point. He knows criminal law. He's learned from the master, Reuben*

Fuentes, and it has shown over the past few years. And he is well positioned to bring in state funds and expertise to Clovis."

Hank and Jim talked for over an hour about everything from building a new courthouse complex in the future, to the local drug problem among the town's young people. When the conversation came to a natural ending, Hank separated his hands and sat forward. "Okay, Jim. I'm going to sleep on it."

Hank rose from his chair and Jim stood also. "By next week I'll make a decision and let you know before we go to press."

Big Jim rose from his chair, all six foot four inches of him. "*He is a big man, impressive in size and bearing,*" Hank thought. "*And he has acquired the deliberateness and balance of speech that reminds me of Judge Fuentes. Good traits for a judge. Big Jim has been an apt student.*

The other two men were good lawyers, pleasant and straight. They knew the town and her people. They would be adequate for the position. Their children had finished college and they needed less income and wanted the prestige of being a judge—a kind of semi-retirement, but Big Jim had been groomed for the future. He would not retire to the district court; for him it was just the beginning."

Jim went home after the interview, and found that Karen, who had taught all day, had made a special dinner: brisket, mashed potatoes, and slaw.

"Well how did it go with Hank Taylor?" she asked, eager to hear about the interview.

"It went well, I think. I told him I'm the only one with judicial experience and criminal law background, even though I'm younger than the other two."

While Jim was talking, the kids had finished dinner and left the table, and he started clearing the dinner dishes, his nightly routine. Karen cooked; Jim cleared the table, rinsed the dishes and placed them in the dishwasher. The pots and pans he scoured by hand.

Theirs was a durable, strong marriage, a comfortable working relationship. It had been solid and mutually supportive. Even if the excitement had waned, what was left in its place was something strong, sturdy, and adaptable. Karen and Big Jim had had their rough spots—no different from others. Four years ago, Jim was targeted by a beautiful paralegal from a local firm. She was a striking blonde with large blue eyes in her late twenties, unmarried and without children. She often came to the magistrate courthouse to file papers and flirt with Jim. While Jim was drawn to her, he loved Karen. He loved his children. He had seen the ravages that divorce inflicts upon the children.

He was drawn to the other woman, he admitted that to himself. Passion, infatuation, her beauty, lust were all there, but on the other side of the equation was his family. No, it was a non-starter and when Jim stopped responding to her flirting, the woman moved on to other fields.

Karen was a good wife and friend, perhaps not as attractive as the other, but intelligent and fun and always a good advisor. She called Judge Fuentes one year, just before Jim's birthday. She got right to the point, "Next week is Jim's birthday and I'd like to surprise him. Something funny and I know how good you are with these things, do you have any ideas?"

"Karen, give me a couple of days to think about it and I'll get back to you."

"Thanks Judge Reuben, I knew I could count on you."

Reuben was as pleased as a school boy with a frog in his pocket at school. Now the tables were turned.

It took a week before Judge Reuben cooked up a "fitting tribute" for Big Jim's birthday.

A magistrate judge has to be a good actor; he must play stern when he is imposing a sentence. If he is convincing he puts fear into the heart of the defendant and this serves as a valuable deterrent to any future crime. He also has to be a little bit of a soothsayer, a diviner of truth, and a social worker. Jim was honing all these skills and learning every day when Judge Reuben got the call from Karen Richards.

Clovis had its local drunk, and as winter approached the graveyard shift of sheriff's deputies would arrest Old Biff Glover to keep him from freezing to death in the cold January nights when the temperature dropped below freezing on the high plains.

The deputies would let him sleep it off in the jail house and bring him before the magistrate judges for sentencing on public drunkenness charges. He was harmless. In the winter months the deputies would arrest the old timer, put him in the back seat of a cruiser, and drive him to the jail where he'd be placed in a cell to sleep it off.

Judge Fuentes and Richards felt kindly to Old Biff and always tried to sentence him to the maximum during Clovis's cold winter snap. It was their way of doing social work from the bench. No one talked about it; everyone went along with it, for no one wanted to see the old man freeze to death in the streets.

After Judge Reuben got the call from Karen he set his mind to working mischief. Jim had got him good when he dismounted his tires on that April Fools' Day. Now it was time for payback.

Late one afternoon as court was closing for the day, Judge Reuben sat in Jim's chambers discussing the events of the day as was their habit. Secretively, Reuben had sent one of the women from the clerk's office into Big Jim's courtroom to snatch his gavel off his bench.

The courthouse closed for the night and Reuben walked home in the cold January air with Jim's gavel in his coat pocket.

Before dinner, Judge Reuben went to see his friend Tony Trujillo, a master carpenter, at his home. "Tony, you're sure you can fix it like I asked and it won't show? I need it back by tomorrow morning."

"Judge Reuben, I'll bring it back to you after my dinner. I can do it."

The next morning Reuben placed the gavel on Big Jim's bench at 8:55. He also place a rag soaked in rubbing alcohol in his waste paper basket under Big Jim's bench. He then put a slow burning cigarette a little distance from the rag on some water-dampened paper so it would not immediately ignite the remaining paper in the basket. All this he did while the staff kept Judge Richards occupied. Court started at 9:00 a.m.

The first case on the docket was State versus Biff Glover. Old Biff had been found dead drunk on the street last night as usual in violation of the Criminal Code.

"How do you plead to the charge of public drunkenness?" Judge Richards asked.

"I'm guilty, Judge."

"I'm sentencing you to the maximum sixty days in jail." And with that Big Jim brought down the gavel. The gavel broke in two, the head flying off into space like Sputnik, and Jim just sat there looking in disbelief at the handle still in his grasp.

Old Biff, still feeling the lingering effects from his last drink that morning and having the clarity of mind and keenness of observation often given to those under the influence chirped in, "I may drink strong liquor to fortify myself, but I've never been as strong as that. Are you a drinking man, Judge? You know if you'd only given me thirty days, instead of sixty, it might have gone easier on your hammer."

Judge Reuben had come into the courtroom at the start of the case to see how things would evolve; he just sat back and watched the commotion in glee, while Jim kept looking around for his gavel's head and Biff Glover philosophized. The waste paper basket just then exploded into flames two feet high and visible to all in the courtroom. Judge Reuben's eyes danced as Big Jim swirled in his bench chair, jumped, and ran for the fire extinguisher mounted on the courtroom wall panic across his face. He scurried into action and blasted the blaze with retardant until the fire was out.

Jim sat down exhausted. He was beleaguered: first the gavel; then the fire. He turned and said aloud to all those assembled in the courtroom, "Maybe I should have stayed in bed today."

To which the philosopher drunk made his wry/rye observation—or perhaps it was vodka or gin that had sharpened his powers of discernment. "Judge there's an empty bed next to mine in the jail house for the next sixty days. The way things are going for you over here today you'd be a lot safer down there with me this winter." Thus the ancients were proved right once again: 'There's truth in wine.'

Old Biff was led out to start serving his "warm time" stay in the "County Hotel." Jim sat recovering his wits from the flying gavel and the fire when Judge Reuben came up to his young colleague as he sat behind his bench gathering his nerves and asked, "You okay Jim? I was worried about you. By the way, I'm looking for a new set of tires for my car. Any ideas where I can get a good deal? Touché Jim?"

And Jim just shook his head in disbelief, pointed his finger, and smiled at Judge Reuben and just said "You!"

"Happy Birthday, Jim, from Karen and me." The originality of it brought laughter to Karen and Jim for years afterwards.

Thus were their lives made up of ordinary comings and goings: school plays, and Christmas pageants, the orthodontist, and Friday night high school football games, the endless driving of the kids to friends' houses and the nightly dishwashing, intimate talks and after-the-kids-were-asleep-embraces, these were the details that filled Big Jim and Karen Richards' lives back in the days when Jim was just a magistrate judge.

5

As Jim sat in there in his chambers in the supreme court he remembered receiving two of the career making phone calls of his life. A week after the interview, Hank Taylor called him. After exchanging pleasantries Hank said, "Jim, *The Journal* is coming out with an endorsement for you in tomorrow's edition. The staff and I agree that your judicial experience and current work in criminal cases make you the best qualified. Good luck and I hope you'll get the call from the governor."

"Thanks, Hank. I appreciate it."

Jim put down the phone. A large private smile creased the corners of his mouth, followed by a feeling of humility.

After the endorsement, Jim heard through the local grapevine that the governor's office had been calling around to local Curry County movers and shakers to see if Big Jim met with their approval and if his closet held any skeletons that might be an embarrassment to the governor.

Jim was also busy quietly marshalling support, asking friends and supporters to call or write to the governor's office on his behalf. This was standard New Mexico politics, how things were done in the state.

Two week later the phone rang in Jim's chambers. "Judge Richards, please hold for the governor." Jim took a big breath.

"Big Jim, this is Fred," this was the warm and friendly way the governor referred to himself. "I'm appointing you to the judgeship for the District Court of Curry County for the unexpired term of Judge Harris. We wish you the best of luck down there. I'm sure you'll do a great job."

"Thank you Governor. I really appreciate it. I'm going to try."

"I'll come and see you when I'm down your way. Good luck again," and with that the governor hung up.

Jim was filled with excitement and immediately called Karen at school, hoping to catch her in during a recess, but she was busy in her classroom. He left a message with the school secretary. Just a terse phrase: "I got the call." He knew she'd understand.

Jim walked from his chambers into Judge Reuben's courtroom where Judge Fuentes was presiding and finishing up a hearing. Jim took a seat in the back. In a few minutes there was natural break in the proceedings after one witness finished testifying, and Judge Reuben took a recess.

Jim walked forward to the bench and approached his mentor. "Judge Reuben, I just got off the phone with the governor. He's appointed me to the district court."

Judge Fuentes face lit up in a broad smile. "Congratulations Jim! You'll be a great district court judge! You're the best man for that position."

Two weeks later, Jim stood before family, friends, colleagues, court personnel, and local media in the packed district court courtroom. District court judges from neighboring judicial districts stood in their black robes in front of the jury box lending an austere air to the ceremony. Jim stood in front of what was to be his new bench, wearing a dark blue suit, white shirt, and tie. Karen stood beside him holding the family Bible. Judge Reuben Fuentes, robed, stood directly in front of him.

With his right hand raised, Jim looked directly into Judge Reuben's eyes, determined and unshakable with just the barest hint of a smile.

"Please repeat after me," Judge Fuentes said. "I, James Canfield Richards, without any mental reservations, pledge to uphold the Constitution and laws of the state of New Mexico and the Constitution and laws of the United States of America impartially to all who come before me, regardless of race, religion, or political belief and will apply that law with justice equally to all, so help me God."

Jim's three children stood behind Karen. Catherine, their youngest, stood between her two older brothers Bing and Bobby. Together they were holding their father's new black judicial robe across their outstretched arms. Catherine fidgeted and smiled freely, showing her braces, her bright red hair even redder today, and her freckles seeming to dance as she proudly watched her daddy. After the oath, they came forward and all three helped their father into his judicial robe.

Jim's new chambers would be in the district courthouse that sat in the center of town, the four stories constructed of large blocks of stone and cement, and seeming rooted in the ground, part of the land, and part of the people of Curry County. Its interior had been refurbished and modernized in recent years. The building stood as a symbol of the new prosperity of New Mexico and Curry

County since the hard days of the Depression. It was a stately, beautiful building.

In Jim's chambers sunlight cascaded all day from the bank of windows behind his desk. He always knew the time of day by the sun's progress across the wall facing his desk. It added to the even, steady pace of Jim's days.

His office was not dissimilar from the other judges' chambers with its array of family photos and mementos. The picture he kept on his desk was of Karen and the kids with Judge Reuben at his swearing in ceremony. A large part of his office was taken up by bookcases filled with law books that had scraps of yellow legal pad marking important decisions of the New Mexico's appellate courts.

On a small table to the right of his desk sat a computer that Jim was still mastering; he preferred the old law books to the new computer, but he knew times were changing, the computer was the future, and he made an effort to become fully competent.

The day's files sat in a pile on the left side of Jim's desk. He would start at the top, choose one file at a time, bring it to the center of the desk, concentrate all his attention on it, look up a case or statute, and then make a note on some point or write a question to ask the lawyers. In criminal cases, before the time of sentencing, he'd read the pre-sentencing report, then write the sentence he'd plan to impose on a small sheet of yellow paper and paper clip it to the court file. When a criminal defendant appeared before him later in the day for sentencing Jim was fully prepared, having given the file full consideration earlier that morning.

After he finished reviewing a file in the center of his desk and made his notes, he would move it to the right side of his desk and continue the process with the next file, whittling down the two foot stack stroke by stroke as a lumberjack fells a large tree.

Leading from his inner office was a private hallway to the courtroom and the bench where Jim presided. Just outside Jim's inner chambers was the anteroom of the office where his secretary sat.

The most important decision Jim made after his elevation was the selection of his secretary, the linchpin of chambers. She more than anyone else set the tone of the office that Jim wanted to project to the lawyers, the litigants, and the public. For this job Jim selected Jeanine Lundee.

Jeanine had a spitfire sense of humor, intelligence, and a Johnny Carson wit. Jim had hired her from the clerk's office in the magistrate court. She had been a fixture in that court for over a decade, knew all the lawyers in town and how to make them laugh, and she worked well with the public. She also knew the inner workings of the Curry County court "family" and could skillfully navigate any rough waters that might arise.

Jeanine's shining brown eyes were always filled with mischief and fun. She presided in her own "court" in the judge's antechamber. In her presence nothing was sacrosanct; everything was up for grabs and subject to her savage wit. She efficiently managed the substantial flow of daily paperwork and pleadings, keeping the lawyers happy as they waited for their hearings with the judge, and helped members of the public who might come into chamber with various inquiries. She was loyal in safeguarding Big Jim. The Code of Judicial Conduct did not allow Judge Richards to see unrepresented litigants who came to see him about their particular case without the other party present. Sometimes they would receive a legal document in the mail and immediately drive down to the courthouse to explain to the judge the circumstances in their case.

"I just want to explain one thing to the judge, then he'll understand," they'd say as they came into chambers with a sense of urgency, "I just need to see him."

Jeanine was a respectful, polite, and firm gatekeeper. No such party got to see the judge without a scheduled appointment, a lawyer, and the other party to the case present.

A thoroughly effervescent, delicious personality, Jeanine was a kind, friendly woman, who could tell a dirty joke better than a sailor to the older seasoned attorneys; she'd fix up the young, uninitiated, unmarried lawyers with the single young women who worked in the courthouse. She had the knack of making everyone around her laugh, feeling comfortable and at ease, breaking the routine of daily work. She was sunshine and had a big fan club in the courthouse. Staff and lawyers would stop in to hear her latest joke or the newest courthouse news.

With Jim's quiet assent, she frequently entertained the *Clovis News Journal* reporters in chambers and was a good "unidentified source" in the courthouse for news stories—someone who knew both the inner poop and local politics.

Jeanine was also a star graduate of the Reuben Fuentes school of mischief and was always into something. Her anteroom had five comfortable chairs surrounding the walls for the lawyers and parties as they waited for the judge. Two framed Georgia O'Keeffe posters, one a sun-bleached cow skull, the other a flower blossom, faced Jeanine's desk and computer hutch. Jim had made a wise choice for his secretary when he brought Jeanine with him from the magistrate court.

Off to the right of Jeanine's office in a tiny room was Mike Gomez's office. As bailiff, Mike stood as sentry to the jury deliberation room, and no one messed with Mike while he shepherded a jury during a trial. He was the jury's protector and guardian while they were impaneled to hear and decide a case.

Before coming out of retirement to join Big Jim's staff, Mike had served thirty years as a United States marshal. He was strong, purposeful, and very clever. No manifestation of the criminal mind was new to him.

The doorway to the jury deliberation room abutted Mike's office, and he made certain that no one except jurors entered the jury room during deliberation. Mike was armed with a concealed weapon in a shoulder holster beneath his natty sport coats. He provided protection for the judge and staff if needed; he also carried and picked up files and pleadings from the clerk's office and carried confidential information among the judges' chambers in the courthouse.

Mike also opened court, announcing, "All rise. The district court of the state of New Mexico for the Ninth Judicial District, Curry County is now in session, the Honorable James C. Richards presiding." And Big Jim would enter the courtroom in his judicial robe and take his seat behind the bench to start a day in court.

Off Jeanine's office to the left and opposite Mike's was the office of Raquel Lopez, Judge Richards' young court reporter. She had luminous long black hair and sparkling dark eyes, and was quiet and slender. Jeanine took her in hand and made certain that only the best single lawyers courted her, treating her as a naïve younger sister and daughter. This was Big Jim's staff.

It was in the courtroom where Big Jim's real work took place. The district court courtroom was much like the magistrate courtroom, but much more elaborate, modern, and substantial. The finely crafted judge's bench sat elevated above the rest of the courtroom. The judge alone sat above all others in his moral and legal authority. The witness box sat next to the elevated jury box, so the jurors could observe the demeanor of the witnesses during direct and cross examination. In front and below the judge's bench was the court reporter's work area, where ever-present Raquel sat transcribing all that went on in the courtroom: the lawyer's questions, the testimony of the witnesses, the rulings of the judge on evidentiary issues, and the judge's instructions to the jury at the conclusion of trial.

On the right side of the judge's dais stood the American flag and to the left the flag of New Mexico. Mounted on the wall behind and above Big Jim's seat hung the Great Seal of the state of New Mexico.

In front of the judge's bench to the left and right were the counsel tables where the lawyers and their clients sat. A lectern stood some feet back from the witness stand from which the lawyers questioned the witnesses. Facing the judge's bench behind the rows of benches for the public was a full bank of windows with curtains pulled back allowing in the ever present sun of New Mexico.

The staff was selected, they moved into their new courtroom, and Jim wanted to set the ground rules for how he wanted his chambers to run. Soon after his appointment he took his staff out to lunch at Dolly's Mexican Restaurant, the best in town and the most successful.

In the private back dining room Jim sat at the head of the table, Jeanine to his right, Raquel next to her, and Mike on the left. As they ate, they chatted about small doings and families. When the meal was over, Jim started talking about the matters of importance.

"It's nice to be out with you. I hope this is the first of many such occasions.

"We are family now—work family—and I want to talk to you about a few things as we get started in our new jobs. We'll have fun, but first comes work. I come to work early and stay late, but you don't have to do this. If you'll be in chambers at eight a.m. and leave at five p.m. that's all I ask. If you need time off for doctors' appointments or family matters just let Jeanine know. She's going to be my right hand person in chambers. I'm going to rely upon her heavily."

Jim continued, "When we're in trial, you're going to have to stay in chambers and be available; that's when you're needed most. Mike may need help with the jury. You may even have to stay late if we are waiting on a verdict.

"Most of the lawyers we'll see are going to be from Curry and Roosevelt counties. We've known them for years. Just about all of them are men and women who can be trusted to do what we tell them to do. Extend courtesy to them and a helping hand. There are a couple of bad apples, but don't worry about them now. Jeanine or I will handle them.

"I'd like you to treat all the lawyers whether from here or other parts of the state in a friendly, respectful way. They're our customers and I want them to come away from our chambers feeling that they had a fair and honest chance to prevail in court before a courteous staff.

"If problems come up in chambers or at home in your personal lives, my door is always open and you can always come in and talk with me about anything.

"When we have criminal hearings, be alert. Mike has heavy responsibilities on those days. Keep your eyes opened. The alleged criminals, who are in custody, will sit in the jury box with their shackles on until their cases are called. Then they'll be released and come to the defense lawyer's table under guard. There will be three or four armed sheriff's deputies in the courtroom at all times.

"Mike is also there for our protection. He's been a United States marshal for over thirty years. He is armed and a skilled marksman, but we hope we never need his expertise.

"We will definitely celebrate birthdays and have our own chambers Christmas lunch on me, in addition to the big courthouse Christmas party.

"We will look out for one another. Being the newest and youngest judge in the courthouse, I will be closely watched to see if I measure up to the standards of the other judges and their staffs. I have no doubt that together we will pass the test.

"Be careful what you say to reporters, even if you like them and have known them for a long time. Don't talk to them about pending cases, and don't quote me.

"You're going to see and hear a lot of things about our Clovis neighbors. Remember that in lawsuits people make lots of allegations, especially in divorce and custody cases, or where children or large sums of money are concerned. Listen, listen carefully and with discernment. Some of what you hear will be true, some false, but when you leave here at night let it stay here. It's not for community gossip. That's all I've got to say. Thank you. Let's go back to work." So ended Big Jim's instructions to his staff, they were taken to heart, and helped forge a cohesive chambers team.

The days passed, punctuated with activity: hearings and trials, lawyers and litigants; parties appearing before Judge Richards seeking justice, wisdom, revenge, or cash, all in the passage of time and the life of the law.

The clerk's office assigned cases by random selection so that each judge had an equal number of cases assigned on a monthly basis. Based on the laws of probability Big Jim would get his share of high profile cases equally with the other judges. Each judge had a civil and a criminal docket. Big Jim's first high profile case was a homicide.

6

*T*he homicide defendant, 26 year old Carl Anthony, was alleged to have killed his wife and a young couple engaged to be married. His wife's body was found at their home on the outskirts of town with three bullet wounds: one to the head, two others to the torso.

The couples' bodies were found in their apartment in town: the woman naked in the bedroom, the fiancé dead on the living room rug. Cocaine was found on the living room coffee table.

The defendant had been arrested right off. During interrogation he had made a full video tape confession. The sheriff's office and the district attorney each made several copies of the confession.

Jim's job was to make certain the defendant got a fair trial, with an impartial jury, and that no error be committed that would allow for reversal on appeal. Jim had to rule on the admissibility of the video taped confession. This took place at a suppression hearing before the trial.

The state had to show that the defendant's confession met the legal standard of being voluntarily and knowingly made; that he had been given his Miranda warnings incident to a legal arrest. Furthermore, the burden was upon the state to show that the deputy sheriff informed the defendant that such statements could be used against him in a court of law, and that no coercion or promises were used to obtain his confession. Big Jim ruled that the confession met the legal standards and would be admissible at trial.

The trial started. The jury had been selected and the state was presenting its case against Carl Anthony, attempting to build a conviction one witness at a time. The prosecution called to the stand Deputy Sheriff Saunders, to be questioned by Mr. Willis, the assistant district attorney.

"Okay, Deputy Saunders, what happened next?"

"I arrived at the home of Carl and Sarah Anthony at about two o'clock on the afternoon of April twenty-fourth. There had been a report of gunshots fired in the area earlier that day, so I was dispatched. Outside city limits it's not unusual for kids to bird hunt or shoot squirrels so I thought nothing would come of it."

"Then what happened?"

"While I was out there, I noticed a late model dark gray Chevy pickup parked at the Anthony residence."

"And why was that significant?"

"A truck like this was seen parked at the apartment of Mark Hart and Carol Shaw the previous night—the night of their homicides."

"What happened next?"

"I pulled up to the home where the truck was parked."

"Would you describe the home and surroundings for the jury?"

"The house is on about ten acres set back from the road with a dirt drive. There's a corral for horses just east of the house. The area is fenced, and there is a small barn. The house itself sits in the center of the property. The dark gray truck was pulled up in the drive to the front of the house."

"What did you do next?"

"I called for backup. I had the feeling that something wasn't right. The house seemed too quiet for that time of day.

"When Deputy Sheriff Valdez arrived on the scene, we noticed the horses hadn't been fed. We approached the house and knocked on the door."

"Then what happened?"

"Mr. Anthony came to the door."

"Is he here in court today?"

"Yes. That's him sitting over there in the white shirt next to Mr. Newkirk ." The deputy said, extending his hand in the direction of the defendant.

Mr. Willis said, "Let the record reflect the witness has identified the defendant Carl Anthony."

Judge Richards responded, "It is so noted."

"Then what happened?"

"Mr. Anthony came to the door."

"How did he appear to you?"

"It looked like we woke him. He came to the door bare-chested and wearing jeans."

"Okay. Then what happened?"

"We asked him if he had heard shots fired earlier in the day. And he said no, he'd been asleep."

"Did you notice anything unusual at that time?"

"Yes, behind him and balled up to the side of the door was what looked like a white tee shirt. It was covered with what appeared to be blood.

"I asked him, 'what's that?'

"He said 'It's a tee shirt. One of my dogs got cut on some barbed wire this morning and I stitched her up.'"

"How did Mr. Anthony appear to you as he told you this?"

"He appeared very tense."

"Then what happened?"

"I asked him who else lives here."

"He said his wife, Sarah."

"I asked, is she here now?"

"He said, no, she's in town marketing."

"At that time did you notice anything unusual about his behavior?"

"Yes. When I started asking him about his wife his lips drew back and tightened slightly and he became even more tense."

"Then what happened?"

"I asked, 'How many vehicles do you own?'"

"Three. A Chevy truck, a blue Mustang, and a tan Buick."

"Which car does your wife drive?"

"The Buick."

"All three cars are here now. How did she get to town?"

"She went with her friend Pam from down the road."

"What's Pam's last name?"

"Fuller."

"Where does she live?"

"Her place is one and a half miles down the road. The white house with the tin roof barn on the other side of the highway."

"Do you know when your wife will be back?"

"She's usually here by five o'clock getting dinner ready."

"Will you have her call me when she gets home? Here's my card."

"Oh, where's the dog you stitched up?"

"She's running around the place."

"Okay, have your wife call me when she gets in."

"Sure."

"Then what happened, Deputy Saunders?"

"Officer Valdez and I backed off and we walked to our cars. I told Deputy Valdez I thought the defendant was lying, but what about? Did you see how stiff he became when I started asking about his wife?"

"What happened next?"

"To check out Mr. Anthony's story, Deputy Valdez went to the Fuller residence, and I waited down the road from the Anthony house so it was visible to me, but where I couldn't be observed."

"I have no further questions of this witness at this time, but I will be recalling him after Deputy Valdez testifies about what occurred at the Fuller residence," Assistant District Attorney Willis said to the court.

Defense Attorney Sam Newkirk's cross examination yielded little. He was waiting for the dynamite to come. He was just marking time until the jury heard the explosion. The question was who would let it out first.

The state's next witness was Deputy Sheriff Henry Valdez, a stocky man, compact and strong. He was in uniform, but without his weapon. He took the oath and Willis began his examination.

"Will you state your name?"

"Henry Valdez."

"And your profession?"

"Deputy sheriff, Curry County sheriff's office."

Then the assistant district attorney brought the questioning around to the time when Valdez and Deputy Saunders separated.

"So after speaking with Mr. Anthony what did you do next?"

"I proceeded to the home of Pamela Fuller a mile and a half further south on the road on the west side of the highway, for the purpose of checking his story."

"What happened when you arrived?"

"I drove up to the house and rang the doorbell, and a woman came to the door who identified herself as Pamela Fuller."

"Then what happened?"

"I asked her if she had heard from Sarah Anthony today?"

"No, but I'm expecting to. We drive into town together and do our grocery shopping on Wednesdays."

"I asked her to give me a call at the sheriff's office if she heard from Mrs. Anthony."

"Do you know her husband?"

"She grimaced and asked, startled, 'Has Carl done anything to Sarah? She told me that some day Carl was going to kill her. Is Sarah okay?'"

"Objection! Your Honor." Sam Newkirk said as he sprang from his chair. "This is hearsay and does not fit the state of mind exception to the rule! I move for an immediate mistrial, that the response be struck, and that the jury be instructed to disregard the answer."

Willis responded, "Your Honor, this is a state of mind exception to the hearsay rule and should be permitted."

Jim had to rule. "Your objection is sustained Mr. Newkirk. The victim's state of mind is hearsay only when offered to prove the defendant's state of mind. Strike the answer from the record. The jury will disregard that answer of the witness. Your motion for a mistrial is denied. Proceed Mr. Willis."

"Let me ask you Deputy Valdez, what else did Mrs. Fuller tell you as you were trying to locate Sarah Anthony that day and check out the defendant's story?"

"She said, 'Sarah should've called me already this morning. She's always home. Where is Sarah? Is something wrong?'"

"We don't know that anything's wrong with Mrs. Anthony, we're just trying to contact her.

"We'd appreciate it if you wouldn't call the Anthonys at this time. Do you know what kind of work Mr. Anthony does?"

"Sarah told me in confidence that Carl works for the D.E.A. undercover.

"You mean the Drug Enforcement Administration? I was startled."

The courtroom became still. The jury's attention was seized.

"Are you sure?"

"Yes, that's what Sarah told me."

"As I left I asked her to give me a call if she heard from Sarah, gave her my card, and thanked her for her help."

"I have no further questions of this witness."

Judge Richards turned the witness over to opposing counsel Sam Newkirk.

His cross examination gleaned little other than to re-emphasize to the jury that Carl worked for the D.E.A.

"Mr. Willis, call your next witness."

"The state calls Pamela Fuller."

A petite blonde woman in her early thirties followed the bailiff into the courtroom, all eyes followed her up to the witness stand. As she took the witness stand and was sworn her face seemed set and resolute, determined to do justice for her dead friend.

Judge Richards said, "Mr. Willis your witness."

"Will you state your name?"

"Pamela Fuller."

"Where do you reside, Ms. Fuller?"

"About five miles south of town not far off the Portales Highway."

"Is that in Curry County?"

"Yes."

"How old are you?"

"I'm thirty-two."

"Do you work, Ms. Fuller?"

"I'm a farmer's wife. I do whatever I can to help my husband around the place: from feeding the chickens to riding the tractor when my husband is off doing other chores. I also raise my girls—three of them."

"How long have you lived in Curry County?"

"All my life. I was born here. My parents moved here from Sweetwater, Texas during the Depression and we've been here ever since."

"Did you know a woman named Sarah Anthony?"

"Yes, she was my best friend. She lived up the road from us."

"I want to draw your attention to March and April of this past year. Did you see Sarah Anthony during that time?"

"Yes, we talked just about every day on the phone. She was younger than me and wanted children. She was always curious about my girls and how we got along. We also had a standing date to go into town together on Wednesdays and do our shopping. I'd pick her up in my truck and we'd drive into town. If the weather was bad, she'd drive her car to keep the groceries dry."

"Was Sarah Anthony married?"

"Yes," she answered tersely.

"To whom?"

"Carl Anthony."

"Is he here in the courtroom today?" Up to this point she had avoided looking at the defense table.

"Yes."

"And will you point him out."

"That's him sitting over at that table wearing the white shirt," extending her finger at the defendant, but stridently avoided making eye contact with him.

"Let the record reflect that the witness has identified the defendant Carl Anthony."

"During the period of March and April of last year did Sarah ever talk to you about her husband?"

"Yes, many times."

"Did she tell you what kind of work Mr. Anthony did?"

"Yes. One day, after we had known each other for several years, we were driving to town and I asked Sarah if Carl was independently wealthy. I wondered how he made a living because they had a small place, less than twenty acres, and he was always home daytimes. And Sarah swore me to secrecy. She made me promise not to tell even Jack, my husband, and I never did."

"And what did she tell you?"

"She told me that Carl worked undercover for the D.E.A."

"Did Sarah Anthony tell you what the D.E.A. was?"

"Yes, she said it was the Drug Enforcement Administration, and that Carl worked the southern part of the state and wherever else he was needed."

"What else did Sarah Anthony tell you about the defendant's work?"

"She said his work put him constantly on edge. He was always afraid someone would recognize him, that he'd get shot. He always carried two pistols: one in his waist or in a shoulder holster and another strapped to his ankle."

"Did Sarah Anthony say anything else about Carl Anthony's work?"

"She said he had guns in his car, in their bedroom, by the front door. He had guns everywhere in the house and not just pistols."

"No further questions of this witness," Willis said as he took his seat, knowing the jury was not likely to forget what Sarah Anthony had told her friend.

"Mr. Newkirk, your witness," Judge Richards said.

Sam Newkirk, the "Red Fox" needed Pam Fuller's cooperation about what she saw and knew. He didn't want to alienate her with a rigorous cross examination if he was going to save Carl Anthony's life. That was what the whole trial was about: saving Carl Anthony's life.

He walked to the lectern purposefully, without notes. This interchange would be important. He wanted to be fully focused on her and not on some papers with questions.

"Ms. Fuller, is it fair to say that Sarah Anthony talked a good deal with you about her husband?"

"Yes."

"Is it also true that she talked with you about her husband's mental state? How he behaved towards her. The pressure of his job. His fears. All of those things?"

"Yes."

"Did she ever say to you that Carl Anthony was paranoid?"

"Objection! Calls for an opinion beyond the expertise of this witness," Mr. Willis interjected.

"Your Honor, I'm only using the term as it is used by laymen every day, not as a technical term of psychiatry."

"Okay Mr. Newkirk, but perhaps you can rephrase the question."

"Is it true Mrs. Fuller that Sarah Anthony told you Carl Anthony was suspicious of other people?"

"Yes, she said he was always suspicious, always afraid he would be killed, or recognized."

"Many times?"

"Yes, many times."

"Is it true that Sarah Anthony told you that Carl had to sample the illegal drugs when he made drug buys for the D.E.A.?"

"Yes, she said he couldn't sleep in the morning when he got home because he was high from cocaine or speed."

"Did she describe to you how Carl worked? Did he work in a team or alone?"

"Yes, she said that Carl often worked alone without back up or protection; that if something went wrong he was on his own; that he lived by his wits, on the edge."

"Is it true that Sarah Anthony told you that at any instant Carl could be killed if his identity were discovered?"

"Yes."

"Did you know Carl Anthony during your friendship with Sarah Anthony?"

"Yes."

"How did he appear to you?" Sam Newkirk knew it was a risk, asking a key state witness an open ended question, but he felt safe in her response. He knew some of how she felt about Carl Anthony, and so took the chance.

"He looked and acted to me like a pressure cooker about to explode. He was suspicious of everyone. He was always very nervous, never comfortable in public. If Jack and I went with them to dinner, Carl's eyes would dart around the room. He was always checking out all the people at the other tables. He shifted constantly in his seat, and he kept his hand inside his coat like he was going to grab something out. He always wore a coat or sports jacket. He was very tense. We stopped going out with them because of that."

As she spoke she became more and more agitated. She saw Carl Anthony sitting at counsel table glaring at her. Her hands clenched and unclenched in her lap as she spoke with more and more intensity and determination.

"Ms. Fuller, did you ever give Sarah Anthony advice about Carl?"

"Yes. At first I told her she and Carl should get counseling, but Carl wouldn't go. Then I told Sarah that Carl was crazy and paranoid and she should separate or get a divorce. I told her that someday Carl would come home and hurt her. But she wouldn't leave him. She said she loved him. And now she's gone." And with that Pam Fuller lowered her head and several tears ran quietly down her cheeks which she wiped away with her finger tips.

"I have no further questions of this witness, your Honor."

"You may step down Ms. Fuller. You are excused," Judge Richards said, and Pam Fuller left the witness stand and sadly walked from the courtroom.

7

"Mr. Willis?" Big Jim asked waiting for the state to produce its next witness.

"The state would like to recall Deputy Saunders."

As the deputy took his place in the witness stand Judge Richards said, "Mr. Saunders, I want to remind you that you are still under oath. Mr. Willis you may resume questioning."

"Deputy, when you left the stand earlier you told us you and Deputy Valdez split up. He went to Pamela Fuller's residence. What did you do?"

"I stayed in sight of the Anthony residence on a high curve in the road in a stand of cottonwoods overlooking the residence, but out of sight of anyone in the house."

"Then what happened?"

"Deputy Valdez had rejoined me. He said that he had finished speaking with Pam Fuller, that she had been home all day and had not heard from Sarah Anthony, but that it was their usual routine to go into town together to grocery shop on Wednesdays. He also told me that she said Carl Anthony worked undercover for The D.E.A., that he always carried two pistols, that there was trouble in their marriage, and that Sarah Anthony was afraid of him."

"What happened next?"

"Later that afternoon around four o'clock Mr. Anthony came out of the house. He went behind the barn and started a backhoe and pulled it into the barn."

"Then what happened?"

"He started using the backhoe in the barn in one of the horse stalls."

"How do you know this?"

"I could see him, because he left the front and back barn doors pulled back and open. He dug for about twenty minutes—a trench about six feet long and three feet wide. I couldn't tell exactly how deep it was from where I was situated, but he kept piling up the dirt."

"Then what happened?"

"He pulled the backhoe outside the barn and parked it."

"Then what happened?"

"Deputy Valdez and I staked out the Anthony residence. Around ten o'clock that night Mr. Anthony came out of the residence and backed up the tan Buick so that the trunk of the car faced the front door of the house. He opened the trunk and went back into the house."

"Then what happened?"

"He came out of the house carrying something big and heavy across both arms stretched in front of him. Whatever it was, it was wrapped in what appear to be a white sheet and he put it in the trunk. Then he closed the trunk and drove to the barn with the car lights off, backed into the barn, and opened the trunk."

"Then what did you do?"

"Deputy Valdez and I left our vehicles and headed down to the barn."

"What did you observe?"

"The defendant had removed the object wrapped in the sheet from the trunk of the car and placed it in the trench in the stall, then he began shoveling the dirt into the hole."

"Then what happened?"

"Officer Valdez went to the rear barn doors and I stayed at the front. When Deputy Valdez was in position we both entered the barn with our weapons drawn and told Mr. Anthony to freeze."

"What did you observe?"

"In the hole there appeared to be a body wrapped in a white sheet and duct taped. I jumped into the hole—it was about five feet deep—cut some of the tape, pulled down the sheet, and saw the face of a young woman.

"Deputy Valdez placed the defendant under arrest and immediately read him his Miranda Rights. He was handcuffed and searched for weapons. We found a 9mm pistol on his waist and a thirty-two caliber pistol strapped to his ankle. We walked him up the drive to the road and placed him in the back of my cruiser. We immediately radioed into dispatch to report a homicide and waited for the crime lab people and the homicide detectives to arrive on the scene. Deputy Valdez and I remained with the defendant. We considered him extremely dangerous."

"Then what happened?"

"Once the crime lab people arrived Valdez and I transported the defendant to the jail in town. We hoped to get some information from him, so we started a conversation. The defendant could hear us from the back seat of my cruiser through the grating in the car, and we carried on our conversation with the intent to draw him out."

"Was that his wife, Val?"

"I don't know, but she deserved better than to be buried among horse shit in a barn stall. She deserved a Christian burial."

"Was that Sarah, Carl?"

Silence.

"What happened back there?"

Silence again.

"She was at least entitled to a decent grave. No matter what happened between you.

"Carl was quiet, but we could feel that he was nervous, his neck was twitching, his shoulders hunched over, and his hands cuffed behind his back."

"Then what happened?"

"The Anthony place was about five miles from town. We drove with our emergency lights on, but no siren. It was past midnight when we arrived at the jail. He wouldn't bite. Carl Anthony didn't say a word all the way into town.

"The defendant was booked and taken to an interrogation room where Sergeant Mowers was to interrogate him."

"I have no further questions of this witness Your Honor."

"Mr. Newkirk, your witness."

Newkirk's cross was routine and short. His client's defense did not lie in his identity as the perpetrator, no he had a different theory of the case on which to defend Carl Anthony. "I have no further questions for this witness, Your Honor," he concluded.

"Okay Mr. Newkirk.

"Mr. Willis, your next witness," Big Jim said from behind the bench.

"The state calls Gary Anderson."

A slight man who looked like a librarian came into the courtroom and up to the witness stand.

"State your name for the record please."

"Gary Anderson."

"And what is your profession?"

"I'm a deputy sheriff in the Curry County sheriff's office."

"Do you have any special duty as deputy sheriff?"

"I'm the evidence room supervisor."

"What are your duties?"

"I preserve and protect all the evidence that officers secure in the course of their investigations and arrests. For example, if there's a murder, I hold the suspected murder weapon in the evidence room. I log it in, give it a number, seal it in an envelope, and keep it locked until the item is needed for testing or when it is entered into evidence at trial."

"Do you have a sealed envelope with you today containing a video cassette recording from the evidence room in a case captioned State versus Carl Anthony?"

"Yes, I have."

"Has the seal been broken or tampered with since you initially logged it in?"

"No."

"Do you have the log book with you indicating the date this tape was logged into evidence?"

"Yes, I do."

"And what date was that?"

"It was logged into the evidence room by Sergeant Dennis Mowers on April twenty-fifth of this year at o-nine-hundred hours the day after the homicide, and it has been locked in the vault inside the evidence room since that date."

"Who has access to the vault?"

"Only the sheriff and I know the combination to the vault."

"Has this envelope with the cassette been in your custody in the evidence room vault since the date Sergeant Mowers logged it in?"

"Yes, it has."

"Will you open the sealed envelope?"

"What is inside the envelope?"

"A video cassette."

"Is there any writing on the cassette to identify it deputy?"

"Yes, it is labeled State versus Carl Anthony."

"Thank you Deputy Anderson." Willis handed the tape and envelope to Sam

Newkirk for inspection. Then Willis walked the cassette to the court reporter and said, "Your Honor I'd like to have this cassette marked as exhibit number one for the state and have it played for the jury."

Big Jim turned to Sam Newkirk, "Mr. Newkirk?"

"The defense objects, Your Honor, the taped confession was obtained without the defendant knowingly and voluntarily giving it, because the defendant was suffering from a mental disease inflicted as a result of his work as an undercover agent for the D.E.A., and therefore, the confession is improper and should not be admitted into evidence. In addition, the defendant was without assistance of counsel at the time of the interview and was not properly given his Miranda Warnings."

"Your objections are noted for the record, Mr. Newkirk. The videotaped confession will be admitted into evidence and allowed to be played."

"Okay, Mr. Willis."

"I'd like to move into evidence state exhibit number one at this time, Your Honor."

"It is so moved, Mr. Willis."

There had been a suppression hearing before the trial brought by Sam Newkirk to try to keep the taped confession out of the case and from the jury's hearing based on the same objections Newkirk had just made at trial, but Big Jim ruled at the hearing that the defendant had voluntarily and knowingly given the confession after properly being given his Miranda warnings by the arresting officers. Jim knew that if the tape were admitted and played to the jury the defendant was looking squarely at the death penalty. The confession was the crux of the whole trial: whether Carl Anthony would be convicted or not and ultimately be executed depended upon the jury's reaction to the taped confession. High stakes indeed.

"Proceed, Mr. Willis."

"I have no further questions of Deputy Anderson at this time."

"Mr. Newkirk, your witness."

Sam Newkirk's cross examination of the evidence room deputy was sparse. His defense did not rest here and after a few cursory questions he excused him.

"Mr. Willis, call your next witness," Big Jim said from the bench.

"The state calls Sergeant Dennis Mowers."

Bailiff Mike again went into the hallway and called, "Dennis Mowers."

An ordinary man, with intelligent brown eyes, walked confidently, purposefully behind the bailiff up to the witness stand.

Though he dressed the part, Dennis Mowers was no cowboy. He had been an Air Force interrogator for twenty years before retiring and joining the Curry County sheriff's office in his home state. He had been trained in the psycho-dynamics of interrogation and steeped in psychology. He was born to the trade.

Assistant District Attorney Willis commenced the questioning.

"Will you state you name for the record?"

"Dennis Mowers."

"And your occupation?"

"I'm a sergeant in the Curry County sheriff's office."

"Do you have any special duties?"

"Yes, I'm the chief interrogator for all serious felony cases in Curry County."

"Have you received special education and training to be an interrogator?"

"Yes, I have a bachelor's and master's degree in psychology from the University of New Mexico in Albuquerque. I served for twenty years as a military interrogator in the Air Force. During that time I received special training from the F.B.I. and the Central Intelligence Agency. I also took courses at the War College on interrogation and psychological tactics in warfare as part of my training."

"What was your rank in the Air Force?"

"I was a captain."

"About how many interrogations have you participated in?"

"Many thousands during my service in Viet Nam, the first Iraq war, and in other conflict zones."

"Did you also do criminal interrogations for the Air Force?"

"Yes, during part of my career I was assigned to criminal investigations, and performed interrogations of criminal suspects."

"Approximately how many criminal interrogations did you do?"

"Many thousands."

"How long have you been with the Curry County sheriff's office?"

"Eight years. After I retired from the Air Force I returned home to New Mexico and applied to various agencies around the state. Curry County offered me a position."

"And in the course of your eight years in Curry County how many interrogations have you taken part in?"

"Approximately one thousand."

"Now Sergeant Mowers," Mr. Willis continues, "I'd like to call your attention to the night of April twenty-fourth of this year around eleven-thirty p.m. Where were you that evening?"

"I was at home with my wife asleep when the phone rang. It was dispatch telling me there had been a homicide and asking me to come down to the jail and interrogate the suspect."

"I dressed and met with Deputy Saunders at the sheriff's office at twelve-thirty a.m. outside the interrogation room."

"Did you have a conversation with Deputy Saunders?"

"Yes."

"What did he tell you?"

"He told me that he and Deputy Valdez had arrested the suspect as he was burying the body of a female they believed to be his wife in a horse stall in his barn outside of town. And that the suspect may be employed as a D.E.A. undercover agent, but he wouldn't talk."

"Then what happened?"

"I observed the suspect for several minutes through a one way window before entering the interrogation room. Deputy Valdez had remained with the suspect while Saunders briefed me. We don't leave suspects alone, especially homicide suspects."

"Okay, now what did you observe before going into the interrogation room?"

"The suspect sat at a table facing the one way mirror. Deputy Valdez sat opposite him."

"Do you see the suspect in court today?"

"Yes, he's sitting at counsel table beside Mr. Newkirk wearing a white shirt."

"Let the record reflect that the witness has identified the defendant Carl Anthony."

"Then what happened?"

"I entered the room, and Deputy Saunders introduced me to the defendant as Sergeant Mowers of the sheriff's office. I was in plain clothes and had checked my weapon before entering the room."

"Then what happened?"

"Deputy Valdez and Saunders stayed in the room and talked with me about fishing and going to the lake, but the defendant said nothing. He just sat there rigidly. He seemed like a volcano that had exploded and could explode again. After fifteen minutes Deputy Valdez left the room and then after thirty minutes Deputy

Saunders left the room, both by pre-arrangement. They waited and watched outside through the one way mirror. The defendant was still considered dangerous, but he had been uncuffed when he was brought into the interrogation room."

"Then what happened?"

"I was alone with the defendant. He seemed more relaxed with the uniformed officers out of the room. Some of the tension eased, but not all. I started talking to him about small things, nothing to do with the allegations against him or his actions in the last forty-eight hours.

"I wanted to have some exchange with the defendant. This is called engagement—without it there can be no movement forward in an interrogation.

"I called him Carl. I said, 'Carl, would you like a cup of coffee? It'll warm you up. What do you say?'

"He nodded his head and said 'Yes'.

"I opened the door and called Flo, our nighttime administrative assistant, dressed in street clothes, to bring in two cups of coffee.

"Carl how do you like your coffee?"

"Milk and sugar."

"He had spoken.

"At that point I didn't want the defendant to have any contact with uniformed personnel. Flo came into the room with the coffee. 'Here Dennis,' she said giving me mine, 'this one's for Mr. Anthony, with milk and sugar.'

"He drank the coffee. 'Warms you, must feel good.' I said."

"How was the interrogation going?" District Attorney Willis asked.

"The defendant was gauging the situation silently, trying to figure out the environment he was in. Every action, every movement, every word spoken—and those not spoken—tells you something about a suspect. His behavior and state of mind talk to you, and you have to be able to listen. He thanked me for the coffee. He was very tight and had a lot of self control, but beneath that, where I wanted to go, he was smoldering.

"Then he played a card. He said, 'I work for the D.E.A. I want them notified I am here.'"

"Okay. Who do I call at The D.E.A.?"

"Agent Rick Gaspar in Santa Fe."

"Carl what do you do for The D.E.A.?"

"I work undercover."

"How long have you been working for them?"

"About six years."

"I hope that will help you get out of this fix Carl. I'll have Flo call. Do you have the number?

"While we're waiting for Agent Gaspar's call, could you tell me what's been happening with you the last couple of days?

"This request was made in a non-threatening way, more as a friend talking to a friend."

"'I don't know,' he said almost in a whisper, as if he were talking to himself—alone—as if I weren't there at all. And then he just bowed his head and put the heel of his palms over his eyes, his fingers pressed on his forehead and scalp, his elbows on his thighs carrying the weight of his head, as if the events of the last 48 hours were too heavy for him to carry or think about. He needed to unload."

At this point the courtroom was darkened and the video was started for the jurors and all in the courtroom to see. There on the large video screen was Sergeant Mowers and Carl Anthony was speaking.

"I don't know," and bowed his head nodding "no."

"What happened between you and Sarah?"

"I got home yesterday morning around eleven after a drug buy. I had some cocaine in my system. You've got to taste the goods—judge the quality—before you make a buy. It's the way it's done out there. So I was a little high and paranoid; cocaine always makes me paranoid. I'd been out all night. I usually get home around five or six in the morning. Sarah was upset. She wanted to know where I had been all night and morning. I told her I was at a drug buy."

"Did Sarah know you worked for the D.E.A.?"

"Yes. She wanted to know when I would start living my life like other people, having a home life and a family and working day times. She wanted all the guns and drugs out of the house.

"She just started yelling over and over at me: 'You need to end this drug career! This is insane! We can't go on like this! You're paranoid all the time—it's dangerous for you and you've pulled me into it. I want out! Either you end it or I'm leaving! I'm scared all the time. I want a normal life.'

"And I told her, look what I've bought you: this house, the horses—all the things you've ever wanted.

"'I don't care about things anymore! I want out! I don't want to turn up dead shot in the head because my husband's a D.E.A. informer.' And then she pleaded with me. 'Carl please, we can have a good life. We can get away from Clovis. We can sell the house and start over where no one knows us. We can get a fresh start.'

"I knew she was telling the truth. It had been exciting at first, but now it was hell. Sarah was right.

"'Carl you don't even make love to me anymore, you're so tense or strung out all the time. We have no life.' She was begging me. And then she started yelling again. I think she surprised even herself. 'I want out! Either you get out or I'm getting a divorce!'

"You're not leaving me. I've worked hard for everything we have.

"'Get your drugs and guns out of this house or I'm out! I'm leaving!'

"And in my head over and over all I could hear was Sarah saying 'I'm leaving, I'm leaving.' Just ricocheting over and over in my head.

"'You're not leaving me.' I had never thought she'd leave me, never thought she'd go through with it, but now I could tell by her voice she meant it.

"We were in the kitchen. I pulled my pistol from my shoulder holster pointed at her, and squeezed off a round to the left of her head. It hit the cupboard to her left. Then I aimed the gun to the right of her head and squeezed off another round which hit the cupboard to her right.

"'You're not leaving me!' I said.

"Instead of scaring her, this made her angry. She snarled at me, 'You're not man enough. You can't even get it up!'

"I took slow, deliberate aim. Everything seemed to stop around me. I can remember everything, every detail: the glare in her eyes—her defiance—the rise of her chest as she took in and let out a breath—every movement. That moment seemed frozen and more real than anything before and every second seemed like an hour. I didn't mean to; I didn't want to. I just felt pulled like by a magnet. She was yelling at me. I didn't even hear her. It was like watching a silent movie in slow motion. I pulled the gun level with her head and I just eased a little pressure—just so slight—and Sarah's head exploded. I squeezed twice more before she hit the floor.

"Then something inside me snapped. It wasn't silent or slow motion anymore, there was sound. What had I done? I immediately regretted it; I wanted her back; I loved her; I had killed her."

Talking in a very soft voice Sergeant Mowers said, "Okay. Carl, you need some rest. We've taped our talk together, I told you that earlier. Is that okay with you?"

"Yes, that's okay."

Everyone in the courtroom was transfixed.

8

ig Jim sat nailed to the video. It was chilling and ruthless. He looked over at the jury who were sullen-faced. The defendant was agitated and nervous. He held his head down and met no one's eyes. Then Newkirk, his lawyer, conferred with him, quietly whispering to try to settle him down like a frightened horse who has been in a fire that needs calming by his master. Big Jim kept a poker face. In no way did he want his inner feelings expressed on his face for the jury to see.

Jim reasoned that the taped confession would seal the defendant's guilt. Now the real battle would begin: would Sam Newkirk be able to save Carl Anthony's life, or would the jury seek the ultimate penalty and impose it? Newkirk's avenue of escape lay in an insanity defense and the mitigating factor that Carl Anthony worked for the D.E.A., keeping drugs off the streets. Those, and only those elements might save his client's life.

The state continued its case, anticipating the defense's strategy of insanity. The state called its expert Dr. Burton Pedersen, a psychiatrist on the faculty of Texas Tech Medical School in Lubbock. He was an expert in forensic psychiatry. He had an air of dignity and an understanding of the average man, but did not consider himself one.

District Attorney Willis started the questioning. Sitting at his counsel table and assisting him in trial was his paralegal Ashley Lewis. She made notes about the witnesses, and kept her eyes on the jury, gauging their reactions to the testimony and particular lines of questions being asked. She was astute and efficient and had the ability to read people with clarity. She observed while Willis questioned.

"Will you state your name?"

"Burton Pederson."

"Where do you reside?"

"At two-two-three Reid Avenue in Lubbock, Texas."

"What is your profession?"

"I'm a medical doctor."

"Where do you practice medicine?"

"I practice and teach at the Texas Tech Medical School in Lubbock where I am a full professor."

"Do you have a specialty, doctor?"

"Yes. I'm a psychiatrist."

Opposing counsel Newkirk stood up. "Your Honor, the defense will stipulate that Dr. Pedersen is an expert in psychiatry." It was a standard stipulation used in order to prevent the state from parading before the jury the qualifications of their expert.

Willis responded, "The state would like the jury to know the extensive education, qualifications, and background that Dr. Pedersen has and the expertise he brings to this matter when he gives his opinion."

"Proceed Mr. Willis," Big Jim ruled correctly. And for the next ten minutes Willis advised the jury of Dr. Pedersen's extensive curriculum vitae.

"Doctor, what is a psychiatrist?"

"A physician who diagnoses, treats, and prevents mental illness."

"Where did you attend medical school?"

"At Tulane University, in New Orleans, Louisiana."

"How many years did you attend medical school?"

"Four."

"And after medical school did you have any additional training?"

"Yes, I did an internship and then a residency in psychiatry at Baylor University Medical Center in Houston, Texas."

"How long were your internship and residency?"

"One year for my internship and three years of psychiatric residency."

Finally, Willis said, " Based upon Dr. Pedersen's education, training, and experience we would ask that he be qualified as an expert in psychiatry and be permitted to give his expert opinion in this matter, Your Honor."

"Mr. Newkirk?" Big Jim asked.

"No objection."

"Then Dr. Pedersen will be qualified as an expert witness and can render his opinion in this matter. Proceed, Mr. Willis."

Then Willis walked the witness through every step of the crime, asking the doctor his opinion about Carl Anthony's mental state at the time of the death of Sarah Anthony. Then came the ultimate questions.

"Doctor, do you have an opinion about whether the defendant was laboring under a mental defect at the time of the homicide of Sarah Anthony so that he could not distinguish between right and wrong and did he know the nature and quality of his act when he shot Sarah Anthony?"

"I do."

"And what is that opinion Dr. Pedersen?"

"Carl Anthony, while he may have been under enormous stress and intoxicated from cocaine on the morning of the homicide of Sarah Anthony, could distinguish right from wrong and knew the nature and quality of his act when he pulled the trigger."

"I have no further questions, Your Honor."

"Mr. Newkirk," Judge Richards called. The Red Fox rose from his chair at the defense table. He knew Carl Anthony's life now rested in his hands. The jury sensed this also. The next hour would be the test. The Red Fox came from people who were hard scrabble dirt farmers, around Clovis and Portales, eking out a living, never prosperous, but teaching their son the value of sweat and hard work. He, himself, had been a roustabout on the oil rigs around Hobbs, New Mexico during the summers and holidays to earn enough money to work his way through law school. His parents never gave up and neither did he. He got his nickname from his once bright red hair and his uncanny cunning in the courtroom.

Newkirk, the country lawyer raised and schooled in New Mexico public schools faced the polished, patrician, formally trained psychiatrist: thirty years of law practice and reading people were now on the line against an expert psychiatrist. The duel began.

"Good morning Dr. Pedersen, I'm Sam Newkirk, the lawyer for Carl Anthony. I have some questions for you. If you don't understand me or hear me just let me know, okay? I'm getting to be an old man so I speak softly now," he said with a tone of cordiality.

"Dr. Pedersen, how much time did you spend examining Carl Anthony?"

"I met with him for about an hour and a half."

"And when was that meeting?"

"About two months ago. He was driven to Lubbock for an examination in my office by your sheriff's office."

"That was how far in time from the death of Sarah Anthony?"

"Let me see here," looking through his notes.

Sam patiently let him look so the jury could see some uncertainty, some lack of assuredness on the part of the unflappable doctor.

"The homicide occurred on the morning of April twenty-fourth of this year."

"And today's date is the twenty-third of September, is that correct doctor?"

"Yes."

"And what was the date of your examination, doctor?"

"August second."

"And isn't it true doctor, from your experience as a psychiatrist, that a lot can happen to a personality in the course of three months?"

"Sometimes there can be some changes, yes, depending on the environment and stress and other life events."

"Do you know whether or not Mr. Anthony was receiving medication while he was incarcerated and awaiting trial?"

"Yes, he was placed on medication by Dr. Roberts right after his arrest. I reviewed Dr. Roberts' notes. He saw Mr. Anthony on April twenty-fifth, and put him on medication."

"What medications were these, doctor?"

"I'll have to refer to my notes again."

"That's fine doctor." Sam knew every reference to his notes made the doctor appear less self-assured in the eyes of the jury.

"Yes, here it is. Dr. Roberts started Mr. Anthony on a low dose of Haldol, then increased it to ten milligrams twice a day. He was also taking five hundred milligrams of Lithium three times a day, two milligrams of Lorazepam three times a day, and five milligrams of Cogentin twice a day."

"Now isn't it true, doctor, that Haldol is used to treat psychotic disorders— or what we layman call breaks with reality?"

"Yes, that's one of the uses."

"Was that the use in this case doctor?"

"Yes, it appears so, and also to treat his methamphetamine addiction."

"So the two reasons that Carl Anthony was placed on Haldol in this case were because he had a break with reality and was addicted to meth. Is that correct doctor?"

"Yes."

"Now doctor, Carl Anthony was also placed on fifteen hundred milligrams of Lithium a day, isn't that correct?"

"Yes."

"Is it true, doctor, that Lithium is a mood stabilizer?"

"Yes."

"Isn't it true, doctor, that fifteen hundred milligrams of Lithium administered in three five hundred milligram doses is a high dose?"

"Yes, that's a high dose."

"And isn't it true, doctor, that a patient would have to have a very severe mood disorder to be placed on fifteen hundred milligrams of Lithium daily?"

"Yes."

"By the way, doctor, do you know Dr. Roberts?"

"Yes. He's a very well thought of psychiatrist here in New Mexico. I've met him on several occasions. I believe he has an office in Albuquerque."

"So you don't doubt that if Dr. Roberts prescribed these medications the patient needed them?"

"I have no doubts about Dr. Roberts' decisions concerning these medications."

"What about Lorazepam doctor? What is it prescribed for?"

"It is used in the treatment of anxiety and in high doses helps a patient sleep."

"So Carl Anthony had anxiety and sleep disturbances, isn't that correct?"

"It would appear so."

"And isn't it true, doctor, that sleep deprivation increases a person's stress level?"

"Yes."

"Now doctor, what is Cogentin used for?"

"Congentin is used to counteract muscular rigidity which is a side effect of the Haldol."

"Would you consider this regime of medications substantial and very heavy doses doctor? Isn't that true?"

"Yes."

"Now doctor, isn't it true that Mr. Anthony was taking all these medications when you saw him in your office in Lubbock on August second?"

"Yes."

"And isn't it true that these medications had been in Mr. Anthony's system since Dr. Roberts prescribed them for him the day after his arrest more than three months earlier?"

"Yes."

"Isn't it also true, doctor, that the entire jail record of Mr. Anthony has been made available to you by Mr. Willis office?"

"Yes, that's right."

"And isn't it true, doctor, that those jail records report that Mr. Anthony was given these medications several times daily starting right after his arrest?"

"Yes."

"So you don't have any doubt doctor that Mr. Anthony received these medications?"

"No, I've seen the dispensing nurse's notes and I don't have any doubts that Mr. Anthony received these prescribed medications."

The Red Fox could taste it. He was close. He had to be careful now. Dr. Pedersen was very smart. If he could sense some of his undoing, he could wiggle out.

"So doctor, when you examined Carl Anthony in your office he had been on substantial doses of psychiatric medication for some period of time, enough time for those medications to work effectively. Isn't that correct?"

"Yes."

"And doctor, these psychiatric medications alter a person's moods, thoughts, and personality? Isn't that correct?"

"Yes."

"So the Carl Anthony you examined in your office in Lubbock for ninety minutes on August second, who had been on heavy doses of psychiatric medications several times a day since April was not the same man—psychiatrically speaking— who was arrested on April twenty-fourth. Isn't that correct doctor?"

The Red Fox had asked his question. The jury heard it. The answer seemed almost irrelevant. But Dr. Pedersen tried to salvage the situation.

"That's not quite accurate. He was medicated, true, but the essential architecture, the components of his personality were the same."

Then Sam Newkirk raised the tenor of his voice: "And you were certain doctor, beyond a reasonable doubt, that the Carl Anthony who had been taking twenty milligrams of Haldol, fifteen hundred milligrams of Lithium, six milligrams of Lorazepam, and ten milligrams of Cogentin daily from late April to August second was the same personality who allegedly shot Sarah Anthony and not some medically drugged up zombie of a personality?"

"I could not be certain."

"You could not be certain? Is that your opinion doctor?"

"Yes."

"Okay doctor. So you weren't certain whether or not the Carl Anthony you saw on August second was the same man psychiatrically speaking as the Carl Anthony who was alleged to have shot his wife on April twenty-fourth, isn't that correct?"

"Objection! Your Honor, that question has been asked and answered. It is repetitive." Willis said trying to break the Red Fox's momentum.

"Sustained," ruled Big Jim from the bench, "move on Mr. Newkirk."

"Doctor, were you aware that Carl Anthony worked undercover as an informant for the Drug Enforcement Administration?"

"Yes, I learned that."

"Now doctor, would you agree that an undercover informant would be subjected to intense psychological pressure in the day to day commission of his duties?"

"Yes, I would agree that such a person would be living under intense psychological pressures."

"Now doctor, assuming that Carl Anthony was under this intense psychological pressure where at any moment his cover could be blown, and his life placed in imminent danger, isn't it possible that a person subjected to pressure of this kind on a day to day basis over the course of several years could lose touch with reality?"

"Yes, it's possible."

"Now doctor, add to the pressure of having his cover blown, that he was compelled daily to sample quantities of cocaine or methamphetamines. Wouldn't that add to the pressures he was under psychologically? Isn't that true?"

"Yes."

"Isn't it also possible that as a result of sampling the illegal drugs over a period of years Carl Anthony became addicted to them?"

"Yes, that's certainly a possibility."

"And isn't it also true, doctor, that long term use of cocaine and meth can cause what psychiatrists call cocaine or methamphetamine induced psychotic disorder?"

"Yes, that's true."

"Even if the usage of those drugs was done for purposes of law enforcement, isn't that true doctor?"

"Yes, use of drugs is use of drugs. The role of the user does not alter their effect."

"And isn't it true, doctor, that the symptoms of cocaine and methamphetamine induced psychotic disorder are hallucinations, delusions, and especially paranoia that resembles paranoid schizophrenia?"

"Yes, that's true."

"Isn't it true that these hallucinations, delusions, and paranoia are mental defects doctor?"

"Yes."

"Isn't it also true that a person who suffers from these defects and who believes the content of the paranoid delusions is likely to commit violent or even homicidal acts because such a person has lost touch with reality?"

"Yes, that is true."

"Isn't it also true, doctor, that such a person, in losing touch with reality, might not be able to distinguish the difference between right and wrong and know the quality of his acts? Isn't that possible doctor?"

"It would take enormous pressures for that to occur."

"But it's possible doctor, isn't that right?"

"Yes."

"And isn't it true, doctor, that Carl Anthony suffered enormous pressure in his work?"

"Yes, I would have to agree that he suffered from enormous pressure in his job and as a result of long term drug use."

"Isn't it also true, doctor, that the long term use of both cocaine and methamphetamines can lead to impotence, and as a result, put greater pressure on a marriage relationship?"

"Yes, long term use of these drugs does lead to impotence."

"Doctor, have you ever treated patients who were addicted to cocaine and methamphetamines."

"Yes, I have."

"And these patients, doctor, suffer from hallucinations, delusions, and paranoia and other serious psychological problems because of the nature of the drugs' effects upon them. Isn't that true?"

"Yes."

"Now assume, doctor, that in order to be believed in his role as a buyer, undercover agent Carl Anthony had to ingest quantities of cocaine and methamphetamines on an almost daily basis as part of his undercover role. Isn't it true, doctor, that he too would become addicted to cocaine and methamphetamines, even though his job was to keep these drugs off the streets?"

"Yes, that's true."

"And isn't it correct to assume that he would experience the symptoms of cocaine and meth addiction: the paranoia and distrust, the hallucinations and delusions, the hyper vigilance, the inability to sleep, loss of appetite, impotence, and all the other symptoms, pressures, fears, and cravings of cocaine and meth addiction?"

"Yes, that's a correct assumption."

"And cocaine and meth are highly addictive drugs, isn't that true doctor?"

"Yes."

"Isn't it also true, doctor, that intense cocaine and meth addiction can cause a person to lose touch with reality? To suffer psychosis?"

"Yes, that is true with heavy use of both drugs."

"And, doctor, the inability to distinguish between fantasy and reality is considered to be a mental defect. Isn't that correct?"

"Yes."

"Even if that defect arose from pursuing criminals, isn't that correct?"

"Yes, that's right. A mental defect can arise from a lawful activity, or law enforcement work."

"In fact, doctor, isn't true that Carl Anthony was suffering from a severe mental defect or disease on the morning of April twenty-fourth of this year?"

Softly Dr. Pedersen responded, "Yes."

"So assuming all that has been told you about Carl Anthony: his dangerous and intensely stressful profession, his cocaine and meth addiction as a result of his law enforcement activities, and the pressures in his marriage, isn't it possible, doctor, that Carl Anthony lost touch with reality, and suffered a mental defect or disease that would not allow him to be able to distinguish between right and wrong on the morning of April twenty-fourth? Isn't that possible, doctor?"

Grudgingly, Dr. Pedersen tersely replied, "Yes."

"No further questions for this witness."

The Red Fox had done what he set out to do: he got the state's expert to concede that Carl Anthony had turned into a welder's torch flame of emotional rage and turmoil, ready to ignite at the slightest suspicion, provocation or delusion.

The jury had become restless during the testimony. What had seemed so simple before had become complicated and they were squirming with that possibility.

"Mr. Willis?"

"I have one question, Your Honor."

Willis knew he had been undone, but he wanted to salvage what he could and so went for the home run.

"Dr. Pedersen, not taking into account an imaginary person, or a person like the defendant, or assuming possibilities, but the actual Carl Anthony, do you have an opinion about whether the defendant could distinguish between right and wrong on the morning of Sarah Anthony's homicide?"

"Yes I do."

"And what is that opinion doctor?"

"He could distinguish between right and wrong on that morning."

"No further questions, Your Honor."

The Red Fox rose. "One question on re-cross, Your Honor. Dr. Pedersen, was Carl Anthony suffering from a mental defect on the morning of April twenty-fourth?"

The doctor paused; the jury waited and sat forward. Dr. Pedersen did not answer. The Red Fox asked again with emphasis, "Was Carl Anthony suffering from a mental defect—a psychosis—on the morning of April the twenty-fourth doctor?"

"Yes."

"No further questions."

"The state would like a recess."

"Ladies and gentlemen of the jury," Big Jim announced, "you've had a busy morning and it's nearing lunch hour. We'll take a break for lunch now. Please remember you are not to discuss the testimony among yourselves until all the evidence is in, and I give you your instructions how to deliberate in this case. Go with Bailiff Gomez. He'll take you to lunch and I'll see you back here at two o'clock. Court is in recess. Mr. Willis, Mr. Newkirk, may I see you in chambers?"

9

The three men walked down the private hallway directly into Big Jim's chamber. "Judge, the state will rest when we reconvene," Mr. Willis said.

"Sam, what do you have scheduled for this afternoon?" Big Jim asked.

"I have the D.E.A. agent in charge."

"Okay. I'll see you a few minutes before two p.m. here in chambers. Have a good lunch."

After reconvening, the state rested. The Red Fox stood: "The defense would like to call Agent Rick Gaspar."

A tall witness with dark eyes and a mustache entered the courtroom. His eyes were steady, conveying confidence and certainty, seemingly ready to respond quickly and resolutely to situations, very much a man's man, in command of himself. He was at ease in court, having been in these surroundings many times before. After he stepped up to the witness stand and was sworn in, Sam Newkirk started questioning him.

"Will you state your name for the record?"

"Rick Gaspar."

"And what is your profession, Mr. Gaspar?"

"I'm an agent for the Drug Enforcement Administration."

"Where do you work?"

"My assigned jurisdiction is the entire state of New Mexico."

"Where are you based most of the time?"

"My chief office is in Albuquerque when I'm not in the field."

"And how often are you in the field?"

"About three weeks a month."

"Now Agent Gaspar, will you look at counsel table over there." Sam Newkirk asked extending his arm to his defense table. "Do you recognize the man at the table?"

"Yes, I do."

"And who is he?"

"He is Carl Anthony."

"And how do you know Carl Anthony?"

"He was one of my undercover informants."

"How long have you known Carl Anthony?"

"Approximately six years."

"Has he worked for you all that time?"

"No, not exactly."

"Well, how did you first meet Carl Anthony?"

"I arrested him for possession of a very small amount of cocaine approximately seven years ago."

"Then how was it he came to work for the Drug Enforcement Administration?"

"It was apparent, at the time of his arrest, that he was very intelligent and resourceful.

"He would have served around six months in the county jail if convicted. He was a minor player, and the cost and resources involved to bring the prosecution under federal law didn't justify proceeding. We intended to turn the case over to the state, but first we gave him the option to cross over, to supply the D.E.A. with critical information: names and locations of dealers, and after ten convictions he could walk away from his charges."

"Did Carl Anthony help you in drug prosecutions?"

"Yes, he did."

"And how long did it take him to help in ten convictions."

"About six months."

"Is that a reasonable amount of time in these situations?"

"Oh, yes. That's very fast. After the tenth successful conviction all his charges were dropped and his record sealed. He was a free man."

"Did anything unusual happen with Carl Anthony at that time?"

"Yes, he spoke to me about continuing to work for the agency. I told him I would have to take it up with my supervisors and get back to him."

"And did you take it up with your supervisors?"

"Yes, we reviewed his work and his potential help to the agency versus his previous drug involvement and felt the potential benefit was greater. We wanted to have a reliable source in the southern part of the state."

"Did Carl Anthony become a full-time undercover informant for the D.E.A. in Curry and the surrounding counties?"

"Yes he did, but not right away. He was tested for honesty and loyalty. He was sent on assignments where, unknown to him, agents posed as dealers to see if he would report back accurately and not pilfer the drugs or money and he did a good job."

"What was your role with Carl Anthony?"

"I was assigned to manage him and set up his assignments."

"How did he perform?"

"He was exceptional. He did excellent work for the agency."

"How many arrests and prosecutions was he involved in?"

"Over three hundred convictions."

"How much narcotics was seized based upon the information that Carl Anthony supplied the D.E.A.?"

"Nearly one ton of marijuana, several hundred pounds of cocaine, and the closure of one methamphetamine lab and distribution network."

"How did that compare to other undercover informants the agency had in the state?"

"Carl was the top performer in the state."

"What kind of work relationship did you have with Carl Anthony?"

"It was very good. It took us a little time to trust each other and develop a working relationship, but after a short while we worked well together. Carl was an excellent source. He has a remarkable memory and the ability to place himself into the minds of the drug dealers and anticipate their moves – and this significantly helped the agency."

"Agent Gaspar, was Carl Anthony paid a salary for his work?"

"Yes he was."

"How much was that salary."

"Fifty-two thousand dollars a year."

"Was that a reasonable figure?"

"Yes, considering the on-going risks involved and the chance of having his cover blown at any moment, it was a fair salary and on par with the others in the field and in line with Washington's guidelines."

"Was Carl Anthony's cover ever blown?"

"No. He was very cautious and a survivor. He knew how to protect himself. The only things standing between him and a bullet to the head were his intelligence and wits. Carl was very smart and cool."

"Did Carl Anthony have to make drug buys?"

"Yes."

"And in order to make these drug buys was he given large sums of money?"

"Yes he was."

"Did any of that money ever go missing?"

"No, Carl never stole or siphoned off any funds from the agency."

"To make these drug buys did Carl Anthony have to sample the drugs?"

"Yes, it's part of the drug transaction. No one is going to pay a hundred thousand dollars cash for a shipment and not sample the goods. It would be ridiculous to believe otherwise. "

"Did Carl Anthony become addicted to cocaine in his capacity as an undercover informant?"

"Yes he did. It couldn't be helped. It's one of the hazards of the work."

"What do you do in the agency when that happens?"

"We wait for the right moment, after arrests or prosecutions, to pull the informant out of the situation and get him into a D.E.A. rehab program."

"Now will you think back to earlier this year and the end of last year; were you working with Carl then?"

"Yes"

"And what kind of case were you and Carl involved in?"

"We were working on locating a methamphetamine lab in Lea County."

"What was Carl Anthony's role in that case?"

"He claimed that he wanted to make a large purchase of approximately a hundred fifty thousand dollars to deal the meth through his distribution network in West Texas.

Carl wanted to know how much meth they could supply on a monthly basis, and he wanted to see the lab. They were reluctant to take Carl to the lab."

"What was Carl's mental state at this time?"

He was under a lot of pressure, and he was impaired."

"What do you mean by impaired?"

"He was addicted to cocaine and developing a dependency for meth. The group he was dealing with was very smart and ruthless. They had successfully operated their lab, or series of labs—we didn't know which—for nearly a decade, and were supplying dealers in New Mexico and Texas. They were shrewd, cunning, and vicious, and had avoided the law up until now."

"And what happened next?"

"One night the lab dealers set up a rendezvous with Carl for a drug buy out in the country. We thought it was just an introduction—a tease—to show the quality of their goods. Carl had twenty thousand dollars in a money belt. Instead, four of them showed up and pulled their guns; Carl was frisked; his money and pistols taken, even the one on his ankle, and he was cuffed, and a hood put over his head. They drove away with Carl on the floor in the back seat with two men in back, two in front."

"How do you know this?"

"Another agent and I were in the pasture of a local sheep herder nearby. We saw the whole thing. We observed Carl being frisked, cuffed, hooded, and placed in the car."

"If it was night how were you able to see?"

"We had night vision glasses from the Department of Defense. Luckily, that night Carl didn't have a wire on him; that saved his life."

"Okay, so then what happened?"

"Carl was on his own. All contact was lost. The pursuit vehicles that were waiting were called off. They would only have placed Carl in additional danger. We just waited, that's all we could do."

"Then what happened?"

"We learned from later investigation and from what Carl told us that they drove for about two hours up into the mountains. Carl could tell this by the drop in temperature, the scent of the pines, and the climbing and winding of the road.

"Then they turned onto a gravel road and drove another half hour until they reached a dirt road. Carl could tell this because there was gravel hitting the undercarriage of the car and tires as they drove, and then the road noise stopped and the traction was very slippery from mountain run off when they drove onto the dirt road."

"Then what happened?"

"The car stopped, and he was taken from the back seat and led up a path. The hood was taken off, and he found himself inside a mountain cave that had been turned into a meth lab. It was very ingenious; no wonder we couldn't find it.

"After showing Carl the lab and letting him see its large capacity for turning out meth he was again hooded and driven back to the original rendezvous point.

"We observed him, but did not make contact with him in case there was counter-surveillance by the meth gang. It was still very dangerous for Carl.

"He had been given twenty thousand dollars worth of meth when they dropped him off. It was near dawn. It had been a long, long night."

"What happened in this case?"

"Carl purchased approximately one hundred thousand dollars a month of meth for six months. We found the location of the lab; we tracked the money; we followed the money trail and had the whole operation in the net. It even included a banker."

"How did this investigation end?"

"After six months we arrested everyone. The lab was closed. Even Carl was arrested to eliminate any suspicion that he was working for us. He was placed in jail with the others where they were all separated. He pled guilty to trafficking and was placed in federal prison for two weeks, then transferred to Danbury Minimum Security Prison in Connecticut and quietly released after two months."

"What happened to the others?"

"The meth gang received long prison sentences. They are all still serving time in a federal maximum security prison."

"How would you rate Carl's role in this case?"

"He was outstanding. His work and the risks he took led to the location of the lab and the ultimate arrests of the entire network. He kept his head in very dangerous situations. We were indebted to him. He kept a lot of meth off the streets and out of schools."

"Did you ever have a problem with Carl and the sums of money he was given for drug buys and operations costs?"

"No, Carl was given substantial amounts of money, and as he gained our confidence he was given greater and greater amounts, and it was always accounted for at the end of each operation."

"Now returning to Carl's drug dependency—in February, March, April of this year what can you tell us about that?"

"It was apparent that Carl was impaired. We knew he needed help. He was becoming increasingly paranoid as a result of the cocaine and meth he had been forced to use in the course of the work and that endangered operations and everybody's life that was involved."

"What did you do?"

"I arranged to see Carl in early April. We met in Albuquerque in a small restaurant I know there where no one would know us."

"How long did you meet?"

"For over two hours."

"How did Carl Anthony appear to you at that meeting?"

"He was played out and very paranoid. He was gaunt."

"What did you talk about?"

"I told Carl I was worried about him; that he had done good work for us, and we owed him. I told Carl he was at risk and we wanted to get him help, and give him some time off. I told him he needed help, and that the agency would stand by him. We have a special program in the agency for agents who become drug dependent. I told him he was not to blame, that it was just a dirty part of the job. 'The agency will help you get clean and take care of your financial obligations while you're in the program. You can even take your wife with you. There is an adjunct program for spouses.'"

"What did Carl tell you in response?"

"He told me, 'Rick, I'm scared. Whenever I leave the house I think this may be the last time I'll see my wife. I walk down the street and a guy looks at me and I think does he know me from a drug buy? Did I bust him? Is he a dealer? I'm afraid wherever I am. I pull up at a red light and see young guys playing loud music and think they're going to shoot me. I reach into my holster just in case.'"

"I asked him, Carl are you armed now?"

"I'm always armed."

"When we walk out of this place I want you to come to my car and give me your weapons."

"I can't do that Rick. I'm a marked man. I need them. Anyway, I have more weapons at home."

"Carl, if you come into this program we'll provide protection—you'll be safe."

"What if there's a dirty agent? He can finger me."

"Carl, I'm putting you on leave with pay starting Wednesday, April thirtieth as soon as I can get someone to replace you in the southern region. That Wednesday morning I'm coming out to your place and driving you and your wife to the airport. Pack for a couple of months. The agency will cover your house payments and expenses, and see that your horses are fed. You'll be on full salary. This is an order Carl. You can't opt out.

"You'll be going to Maryland, outside Washington, DC. I'll accompany you on the flight and see that you get settled in okay.

"Wednesday the thirtieth of April I'll be at your place at eight a.m. You and your wife be ready."

"Then what happened?"

"Carl made the long drive back to Clovis. He was alone. I was worried about him. I learned he'd arrived back in Clovis. And then in the early morning of April twenty-fifth, I got a call from the Curry County sheriff's office that Carl Anthony had been arrested for the murder of his wife."

Sam Newkirk gave Agent Gaspar plenty of room. Every sentence, every word gave Carl Anthony the chance to have his life spared.

The cross examination by District Attorney Willis did not lessen the impact of Agent Rick Gaspar's testimony. The agent answered the questions truthfully, telling the facts from his perspective: Carl Anthony had been an outstanding, resourceful undercover informant. He got addicted to cocaine and methamphetamines through his work and allegedly shot his wife in a paranoid psychotic state days before he was to fly out and begin a rehab program. Through his work Carl Anthony had kept a substantial amount of drugs off the streets of New Mexico.

At the conclusion of the cross examination, Sam Newkirk, who had already examined his own psychiatrist, rose and addressed the judge: "Your Honor, the defense would like to move into evidence Exhibits A through S that were introduced at trial."

"Does the state have any objections to any of the exhibits?" Jim asked.

"No objections, Your Honor."

"The defense exhibits will be so moved and so accepted," Big Jim ruled.

"The defense rests, Your Honor."

Big Jim turned to the jury. "Ladies and Gentlemen, we're going to take a recess at this time. Please go with Bailiff Gomez. When we reconvene you will hear final arguments from the state and defense. Then I will charge you with your instructions on the law, and you'll begin your deliberations. Thank you for your attention and patience to this point. Your hard work is about to begin. We are in recess." And Big Jim brought down his gavel.

10

im had kept his thoughts to himself during the trial. He believed after Newkirk's cross of Dr. Pedersen and the testimony of Agent Gaspar that the death penalty would not be imposed, that Sam Newkirk had saved the defendant from lethal injection.

Big Jim had been cautious during the trial not to commit error. He didn't want to be reversed upon appeal. He had been careful in his rulings. He thought he had presided over a clean trial without error.

There were two phases of the trial for the jury to decide. One was the guilt or innocence of the defendant. Big Jim, Sam Newkirk, and District Attorney Willis all thought it was a foregone conclusion that Carl Anthony would be found guilty of the homicide of his wife. The second phase and what the trial was really all about was the penalty phase and if the death penalty would be imposed.

It took the jury one day to decide Carl Anthony's guilt. Officers Saunders and Valdez's testimony and the taped confession to Sergeant Mowers convinced the jury that the defendant was not insane and was guilty of the murder of Sarah Anthony.

Big Jim reconvened court when he learned the jury had reached a verdict.

"Ms. Foreperson," Big Jim asked, "has the jury reached a verdict?"

In a firm and strong voice, as if bolstered by the other eleven, she responded, "Yes we have, Your Honor."

"Will you give your verdict sheet to the bailiff."

Mike took the folded verdict sheet from the foreperson and handed it to the judge. Jim opened it, studied it for a second. He showed no expression on his face. There was silence in the courtroom, all eyes were upon him.

Big Jim turned to the foreperson and asked, "What is your verdict?"

"We find the defendant, Carl Anthony, guilty of the murder of Sarah Anthony in the first degree."

Big Jim gave a few seconds for gasps and tears in the courtroom. Sarah's father, mother, sister, and brother all embraced and tears flowed. Carl Anthony and Sam

Newkirk were huddled together quietly conferring. Big Jim waited for the emotion accompanying the verdict to subside.

Then he looked squarely at the jury and addresses them. "You have reached a verdict in this case. You have found the defendant Carl Anthony guilty of murder in the first degree. Now you are required by law to decide upon a penalty. Testimony will be presented to you starting tomorrow morning. The state and defense will both present testimony and argument about what they believe to be the appropriate penalty in this case. When they conclude you will again deliberate. This time you will determine the penalty the defendant will face. We are in recess until nine tomorrow morning."

Clovis is a conservative community, a Christian farming town. The rains fall, crops grew; cattle were raised up, then they were slaughtered; there was a murder, now there must be a punishment. That was how life was lived on the rugged High Plains; it was the way things were done—had always been done. It was the law of God and nature.

After the lawyers had presented their cases for aggravating and mitigating circumstances, the fate of Carl Anthony was left to the jury.

Bailiff Mike sat outside the jury room for three days, barring anyone's entrance into the area while the jury was deliberating in their room. He heard the voices raised in heated debate. Inside the room two middle aged women on the jury wanted the death penalty. Privately, each had fears of their own husbands—they had both been struck—but they never would have admitted a thing like that, in a town like Clovis, even privately.

One juror, a minister, sought mercy for Carl Anthony. He had one supporter among his fellow jurors.

"What about Agent Gaspar's testimony that he kept drugs off the streets."

"He was a user, and a dealer who got caught and this was how he survived," several jurors retorted.

Between the two poles, those seeking the death penalty and those who favored life in prison, sat the other members of the jury. They would be the ones to decide the fate of Carl Anthony, the ones to reach a decision, to be persuaded one way or the other. But they would not be easily moved or swayed. They were men and women strong and resilient and practical like the cottonwoods planted round farm and ranch houses on the *Llano Estacado*—The High Plains—to provide shade and coolness in the blistering summers and to serve as a wind break from the northern winds of winter.

"Let's vote," one voice said over the melee of the others.

"Okay, that's a good idea," said the foreperson, "at least we'll know where we stand. Here, take a piece of paper and a pencil." The pencils were the three inch short yellow kind with no erasers, that Mike had sharpened that morning, the paper was just small rectangular scrap paper from Jeanine's work mistakes that had been cut into two inch by three inch ballots.

"Write your penalty, fold it, and place it in the middle of the table."

The foreperson pulled all the ballots before her and started reading out the votes.

"One for death.

One for life imprisonment.

Another for prison.

Undecided.

Another for death.

Another for death.

Prison.

Not sure.

Prison.

Injection.

Undecided.

On the fence.

Okay, that's four votes for the death penalty; four votes for life in prison; and four votes undecided. Let's talk about it."

A rancher spoke up, and everyone paid attention. "I listened real careful. He killed his wife; he wasn't insane—the tape showed that—I agree he bought himself the death penalty. Closed book. But then I considered that he spent five years working for the D.E.A. He could've gotten out after busting the first ten dealers, but he stayed and worked full bore for them. That makes me think there's something in his favor. Like a rattlesnake that eats mice—you know he's dangerous—but he does you some good so the mice don't eat your grain. You best be careful and step high if he's around."

"A middle aged woman jumped in: "He's a killer! He took his wife's life! There's no forgiveness, that's that. He deserves the death penalty."

Then a more thoughtful woman said, "But what did the judge say, 'Mitigating circumstances'. He helped keep drugs off the street and out of the schools. Maybe that's reason enough to spare his life. I don't know. I'm not certain. I can't make up my mind."

"He worked for the D.E.A. because he was a drug dealer and got caught," another juror said. "He was trying to keep himself out of jail; that's how he got started in all of this. It allowed him to use drugs without facing the music, and he got paid for it on top of it all. He was hooking our kids before he got caught. He deserves the death penalty."

"Yeah but he stayed at it for five years," another man interjected. "He had an easy way out after the first arrests. He stayed with them. Is that enough to save his life? Frankly, I don't know."

Then an older woman spoke up her voice, taut with emotion. "What about his wife's life? The life he took? You heard her family; she stayed with him; stayed loyal to him through all his moods and evil. And for this he kills her. He's unforgivable. He deserves the death penalty. He's a cold, calculating murderer and drug dealer, that's all."

Hour after hour it went on—argument, reason, and emotion—weighing the testimony, deciding on a penalty. None of it came easily. Mike Gomez sat sphinx-like at his desk guarding the door. The three voting blocks held firm: death, life imprisonment, and undecided.

About six o'clock the first evening there was a shift in the ballots. One of the undecided voted for the death penalty. The blocks now stood at five for death, four for life in prison, and three undecided.

The jury broke for dinner. Mike took his charges to a restaurant across the street from the courthouse with the help of two sheriff's deputies. They had called ahead to get the back room. All twelve of them wore juror badges and were isolated from the general public.

The patrons of the restaurant knew what they were about. The deliberation had been the news of the day in *The News Journal* and everyone was talking about it in the way of small towns. The customers stopped talking momentarily when the jurors came in, and then started the hum and speculation on the possible results and when they would decide.

The jurors, under Mike's watchful eyes, remained aloof as they marched into the back room. They took seriously the awesome duty imposed on them: whether to take a man's life or to spare it.

While the deliberations were going on, Big Jim reviewed his role and his notes on the trial. He had his court reporter, Raquel, transcribing parts of the transcript so he could review his rulings during the trial. He found that all the exhibits had been properly moved and admitted into evidence. The rulings were proper and within his discretion, and the flow of the trial, testimony, objections, and argument had moved smoothly. The record appeared clean: the defendant had had a fair, impartial, speedy, and orderly trial. Jim had committed no errors. He would not be reversed on the appeals to follow.

That first night, the jury was sequestered at the Holiday Inn. They were not allowed the newspaper, radio, computers, cell phones, or TV. All media devices were removed from their rooms.

On the second day of deliberation, the jury met again in their room. All they had to rely upon was the testimony they had heard from the witness stand, the exhibits properly admitted into evidence and taken with them into the deliberation room, and the written instructions on the law given to them by the judge. All else was excluded; all else was irrelevant in reaching their decision: whether or not to execute Carl Anthony.

During the second day, the jurors deliberated from 8:00 a.m. until 6:00 p.m. They were given an hour and a half for lunch, trudging across the street again to the back room of the local café and then back to the deliberation room. They were feeling the strains of their ordeal. They were weary.

Another juror had come over from the undecided block to join the five settled upon the death penalty. And the deliberations continued into the third day.

On the evening of the third day long after sunset, the door of the jury room opened. The foreperson said quietly to Mike, "We've reached a decision."

Mike looked into her face, he knew the signs—he had been around courthouses for over thirty years.

"Judge," Mike said as he knocked and opened Big Jim's door. "They've reached a decision."

"Okay Mike, tell Jeanine to call Mr. Newkirk and Willis, tell them that the jury has reached a decision, and to be over here in fifteen minutes."

Ten minutes later, Sam Newkirk and DA Willis came into chambers to see if Jeanine knew the result. She didn't, so they drifted into the courtroom anxious and impatient.

Big Jim put on his robe and headed down the private hallway to the courtroom. It was a long walk tonight. As he entered the courtroom, Bailiff Mike trumpeted. "All rise. The District Court of Curry County, state of New Mexico is now in session, Judge James C. Richards, presiding."

"Please be seated," Big Jim said after he had taken his seat. He paused for a moment. Before him sat the attorneys and Carl Anthony, who had been brought across the street from the jail where he had been held since being arrested. The room was crowded with Sarah Anthony's family, the newspaper reporters, and curious townspeople all eager to hear the outcome. "Mr. Newkirk, Mr. Willis we have a decision. When the jury announces their decision there are to be no outbursts in the courtroom."

"Okay, Mr. Gomez, bring in the jury."

The jury filed in, taking the same seats they held during the trial. They looked worn and tired. They had taken their oath seriously; the decision lay heavily upon them; they did not look at the defendant.

"Madame Foreperson, have you and the members of the jury reached a decision as to the penalty stage of this trial?"

"Yes, we have, Your Honor."

"Is it the unanimous decision of each and every member of the jury?"

"Yes, Your Honor."

"Will you give your decision form to the bailiff."

Mike walked to the foreperson, took from her the single folded piece of paper, walked it to the judge's bench and handed it to him.

Big Jim, moving slowly and deliberately, unfolded the piece of paper. He was conscious of all eyes in the courtroom upon him. He looked down.

"Will the defendant rise." Carl Anthony and Sam Newkirk rose at defense table. "Mr. Anthony, it is the decision of this jury that you be sentenced to death for the murder of Sarah Anthony. You shall be delivered over to the custody of the Department of Corrections and your sentence shall be carried out by lethal injection in accordance with the statutes of New Mexico on the twenty-ninth day of October of this year."

Sobs and gasps arose from all parts of the courtroom. The newspaper reporters charged out the door to write their stories. The family of Sarah Anthony sat crying and hugging one another. There were outbursts everywhere.

Big Jim struck his gavel upon the bench three times. "Order. Order in the court." The noise died down.

"Your Honor," Sam Newkirk spoke loudly over the crowd and everyone was silent. "I'd like the jury polled, and my client would like to have sufficient time to review the record and file an appeal."

"That's fine Mr. Newkirk." The jury was polled to determine if each member had voted for the death penalty. They had.

"You have thirty days to file your appeal, Mr. Newkirk. Is there anything else?"

"No, Your Honor."

"Mr. Willis, do you have anything?" Big Jim asked.

"No, Your Honor."

"Ladies and Gentlemen of the jury, I want to thank you for the time and effort you have put into the deliberations in this difficult case as well as the serious manner with which you approached your responsibilities. It is because of you that our justice system works. You are discharged and free to return to your homes."

Taking his gavel in hand again, Jim said, "This court stands adjourned."

11

As soon as the decision was announced, four sheriff's deputies converged on Carl Anthony at the defense table where he was taken into custody, told to stand to be cuffed. Sam Newkirk told him, "I'll see you early in the morning before you leave." The defendant would spend the night in the Curry County jail in solitary confinement, and then be transported to the state penitentiary the next morning where there would be a cell waiting for him on death row.

After everyone else had left the courthouse, Jim was still finishing up in chambers when he noticed the lights still on in his courtroom. The courthouse was empty—the janitors gone home. Walking into the courtroom, Jim looked around at the ordinary space where so much had taken place in the last month.

He thought: *"This is just four walls and some simple pieces of furniture—pieces of wood held together by nails and glue. How many major decisions had been made by the twelve people who sat in those chairs in that jury box? How many tears were shed and lives ripped apart or restored by the judges who sit on that bench. How many witnesses on the stand had lied or held to their sworn oath and duty. How many lawyers and litigants have sat at those counsel tables after having argued vehemently or with cool reason—sometimes successfully, sometimes not? These pieces of furniture were where the stories of New Mexico's crimes and conflicts unfolded: this jury box, this judges' bench, this witness stand, these counsel tables, were where justice was sought and punishment meted out like judgment day. How many more men will I have to sentence to death before I, myself, pass away and another will sit where I sit now?"*

Jim stood alone in his courtroom the night he sentenced Carl Anthony to death.

12

J im drifted back to the present, back to his chambers in the Supreme Court Building in Santa Fe, to his life as it now was, back from the past, knowing that Carl Anthony's night of reckoning was here, knowing that the price would be paid tonight. *That's why I'm thinking about that case today, and my role in it, and the after effects it had on my career.*

Jim knew that the reason the governor appointed him to the supreme court was his handling of the Anthony case and his imposition of the death penalty. When a vacancy occurred on the supreme court some years later, the governor wanted to appoint a supreme court justice who would be tough on crime and Big Jim's handling of the Anthony case gave that impression around the state and led to his appointment.

Big Jim sat poised between the past and the present and at midnight the two would intersect and enter the veins of Carl Anthony in the death chamber at the prison on the outskirts of Santa Fe over a decade after he had killed his wife.

A lot had happened in the years since that trial. Judge Reuben Fuentes, Jim's mentor and friend, had died recently. Karen and Big Jim had attended the funeral in Clovis; it seemed the whole town was there at the Catholic Church in Spanish Town giving the grand old man of the courts a final salute of respect. Karen and Jim had moved to Santa Fe after Jim's appointment to take up duties at the supreme court. The house was empty now, the kids were gone. Jim was mapping out his plans for the primary election campaign for United States senate. So many memories, so many happenings, but tonight his thoughts turned to the impending execution.

Sam Newkirk and the state appellate defenders' office had learned earlier that afternoon that Anthony had been denied a stay of execution by the United States Supreme Court in Washington, DC. Carl Anthony would eat his last meal, walk his last walk to the death chamber at midnight, and be strapped down to the execution table, unable to move arms, legs, and torso. And then the warden would release the drugs into his open veins. Jim avoided the media that day, and left the Supreme Court Building at 4:00 p.m. by a side door.

Big Jim went to bed the same time as usual on the night of the execution, but he didn't watch the late news as was his custom. He just retired. Karen knew. Jim thought for a moment about the young woman, Sarah Anthony, murdered senselessly. He also thought what a good and durable system of justice we have. "*A jury of twelve people imposed a sentence. I just presided over the trial and dispensed the law. The division of power between judge and jury safeguarded all who participated in reaching a verdict.*"

He told Karen at dinner, "My role ended years ago. At midnight Carl Anthony will surrender his life. That is the price he'll pay for killing his young wife."

Big Jim slept easily through the night. At dawn he went out into the driveway, as he always did, picked up the rolled up *Santa Fe New Mexican*, took off the blue rubber band, and unrolled the newspaper. The headline screamed: **CARL ANTHONY EXECUTED!** in big bold letters. Jim went to work that day and made sure he performed his duties as usual, calling no attention to himself.

Since his appointment and subsequent successful election to a full term in a statewide election, Big Jim had become well known throughout the state. He now sought higher political office.

As an associate justice of the New Mexico Supreme Court he had become known in the state as "Judge Big Jim Richards," and he made it a part of his job to speak frequently around the state, talking at local Bar Association luncheons, as well as meeting privately with lawyers and members of citizen groups of all political complexions. No citizen of New Mexico was ever turned away from seeing Judge Big Jim when he was traveling the state and alternatively sowing seeds for his future.

He was a friendly, gregarious man by nature. He would listen to anyone except litigants in cases pending or likely to be heard in the courts of New Mexico.

"Big Jim Richards" spoke at high school commencements, Kiwanis Clubs, and Garden Clubs across his beloved and beautiful state. He never missed a chance to share with others what a great place New Mexico is and the success that awaited any young person who would work hard and plan wisely "in our great state." He extolled the virtues of her warm and friendly people and the beauty of her boundless plains, high mountains, and ever-changing desert all beneath the wide blue and ceaseless skies. Big Jim Richards was making a name for himself in New Mexico as a dynamic leader, a friendly judge, and a man with a future to play in the state.

13

teve Light sat dejectedly in his Clovis office of the Legal Aid Building. He had just learned from the main office of Legal Aid that he would not be given a one-time bonus of $1,000 that was to be disbursed to all lawyers and support staff because his start date was two months after the arbitrary cut-off date selected by the executive director, Ramon Cruz.

Steve knew the real reason. His family had been prominent in New Mexico for two generations and Cruz awarded himself the extra thousand dollar bonus because he felt that Steve didn't need the money, and he resented Steve's family, connections, and education.

It was a slap in the face. Steve hadn't taken a penny from his family since law school and never sought a favor. He wanted to be his own man. He savored his independence and had been carrying himself on the meager salary of a Legal Aid lawyer. He knew that this was Ramon's payback for Steve's privileged background.

In his dejection Steve opened up the weekly Bar Bulletin which contained the latest decisions of The Court of Appeals and The Supreme Court of New Mexico. In the closing pages of the bulletin was a classified section for lawyers' jobs in the state. As Steve read over the ads one caught his eye:

ADMINISTRATIVE LAW JUDGE CHILD SUPPORT HEARINGS

Steve read the qualifications below the caption. He met them. At that moment he determined to send in his letter of interest. He received a letter in response and a date for an interview for the position.

The interviews were held at the Supreme Court Building. Each of the five candidates met individually with two district court judges who reviewed the candidates' experience and qualifications. The administrative law judge would sit in lieu of the district court judges in all child support cases. The selected candidate would have the authority to hold those who didn't pay their child support in contempt of court and with authority to sentence offenders to the county jail.

Four judicial districts were involved in the project, covering one quarter of the state. All the candidates were well qualified. Some of the judges involved in the final decision were supporting a lawyer from their own district. Steve did not feel overly confident that he would get the position.

Three weeks had passed since the interviews, and Steve had heard nothing. But behind the scenes, in the quiet way of New Mexico, matters were being worked out. "Horse trading," it used to be called. At Harvard Business School they called it "building consensus." Old favors would be called in; support would be sought for additional employees in the court clerk's office at the next legislative session in return for support of a particular candidate now. All this was done very quietly, in a friendly way: seeking the best candidate with the least commotion. It was the way things were done in New Mexico, and had been since statehood, and even in territorial days.

Several days later the phone rang in Steve's office. It was Alexis Zachery, Judge Thomas's secretary. "Hello Steve, the judge would like to talk with you. Please hold."

"Hello Steve, how are you?"

"Just fine, Judge."

"I'd like to offer you the child support position if you're interested?"

"Yes Judge, I'm interested."

"Good. Why don't you come over at nine tomorrow morning and we'll get you started."

"Thank you Judge, I'll see you then!"

Steve was elated. He had done his yeoman's work well at Legal Aid these past years and now he would move up.

Judge Ben Thomas was a fair man. His moral compass had been fixed steady and firm long ago. He was unwaveringly honest and demonstrated his integrity both on and off the bench to litigants, neighbors, and friends. He was also kind. He didn't hold himself aloof or distant from the townspeople of Clovis, whom he loved and had known all his life.

When Judge Thomas sat on the bench he dispensed justice with a firm hand to keep his town safe and criminals off the street. He also sent that message to the *desperadoes* in Clovis that justice would be strict and severe. But Ben Thomas was also merciful.

An 18 year old boy, a high school senior, had been arrested with four ounces of marijuana. He hadn't sold it, there was no evidence of that, but he smoked some every day after school. He had average grades, and never been in trouble before. He was a skinny, pimply kid, who hadn't taken on the physical features of a man yet, and needed a strong hand now that his father, a local farmer, had died suddenly of a heart attack two months earlier. The boy's mother was now left alone with the farm and four children to raise—this son being the eldest. A small life insurance policy covered the cost of the funeral and a few outstanding bills, but not much else. What remained were the farm, some old irrigation equipment, and a tractor. This year's crop was still in the field.

The boy had pled guilty to possession of a controlled substance with intent to distribute, a more serious crime than just simple possession, because the amount in question exceeded two ounces. His mother had come with him to every court appearance. She was a slim and sad woman, who wore no makeup, had her hair pulled back and tied, her hands clean, but worn and callused from the years of constant work around the farm and house. It was clear her heart ached for her husband; she was adrift without him, and now for her son. It had been a hard life helping her husband feed a family from the hard earth he worked to make a living. She always sat in the first row separated from her son by the bar of justice.

Today was sentencing, and for the first time she sat beside her son and his public defender. Before imposing sentence, which Judge Thomas felt should be middling and involve jail time, he asked the woman if she had anything to say.

"Your Honor, Seth is a good boy mostly. I forget he's eighteen and not a boy anymore; he's a man, especially now that his father is gone. He's all I have to work the fields and lay down the irrigation lines. If I can't bring in this year's crop we'll likely lose the farm and house. If you put Seth in prison, I have no one to rely on. He finishes high school in May and then I need him full time in the fields. His brother and sisters can help, but they're still young and in grade school. I've got no one to lean on. My husband's gone just two months now."

She looked older than her years, haggard and bereft by her husband's death and her son's inevitable incarceration. She was a good woman, as good as ever walked the land.

Ben Thomas sat back in the big judges' chair on the bench and thought, "How can I help her and not lose the boy? He has done wrong and needs punishment now, or it will get worse." He announced aloud, "Let's take a recess." It was 10:30, a natural time for a break. "We'll reconvene in twenty minutes."

With that Ben left the bench and walked back into his chambers through the private door behind the bench. He went alone into his office and closed the door. His staff knew to leave him alone when he closed the door. Out loud he said to himself: "Save the family. Save the farm. Save the boy with firmness." Then Ben did what he had done all his life. He closed his eyes, bowed his head and said softly under his breath, "Dear Lord, give me the wisdom to make a just and wise decision for the people of Clovis, for the boy, and for his family in accordance with the law. In the name of Jesus."

Twenty minutes later Judge Ben Thomas reconvened court. "Mr. Shancer, please rise," the judge said to the boy. His mother and the public defender also rose at the defense table.

"It is the judgment and sentence of this court that you be incarcerated for a period of two years in the state penitentiary. Then Ben took a deliberate pause. The mother grasped her son out of reflex, realizing he was gone. Then Ben continued, "All of that sentence to be suspended except for three hundred sixty-four days in the county jail, and that after serving said sentence you will be placed on probation for a period of three years. Said sentence will be imposed from Friday five p.m. until Sunday five p.m. until you harvest or should have harvested this year's crop. After harvest time you will serve consecutive days in the county jail until planting time next year, when you will be permitted to plant your crops and return nightly to the jail. After your crop is in you will again serve full consecutive days in the county jail until your full sentence is served. If you ever fail to report to the jail as ordered today, the full sentence will be imposed upon you at the state penitentiary.

"You are to successfully graduate from high school with your class this May doing your school work in the jail. In addition, after your release you are to attend the county's drug rehab program for the next two years at your own expense. You are to submit to random drug testing when ordered by the sheriff's office in the county jail and while you are on probation thereafter. If you test positive for any drugs you will find yourself on your way to the state penitentiary.

"Mr. Shancer, you are a very lucky young man to have such a fine mother. Don't disappoint her, and don't disappoint me or come before me in any other matter. Do you understand?" Judge Thomas said in his sternest tone.

"Yes, Your Honor."

"Mrs. Shancer, I have shown your son some leniency today because of you and your circumstances. I realize this is a difficult time for you and your family having to adjust without a husband and father for your children. Keep your son on the straight and narrow. I have taken him off the streets on weekends to help keep him out of trouble. Keep him on the farm and be sure he helps you bring in this year's crop."

Tears of gratitude frankly flowed down her cheeks. She looked up and said, "Thank you Judge; I'll keep Seth on the straight and working the place. We won't disappoint you."

True to her word, she succeeded. Seth Shancer graduated from the high school, and took over the working of his family's farm, supporting his mother and younger brother and sisters.

Older, successful farmers from the community would drive out to the Shancer place now and again just to give some encouragement, or help the boy with some difficult chores around the place, or answer the boy's questions about some agricultural decision he'd have to make for the first time. All this happened because Ben Thomas made some quiet phone calls to farmer friends of his in the county.

This was the kind of man Ben Thomas was. Seth Shancer, with the help of his mother, walked the straight and narrow thereafter and throughout his life. He became a credit to Clovis, all because Judge Ben Thomas took a chance.

Steve Light visited Judge Thomas's chambers the next morning at nine as requested.

Judge Thomas came out from his office from the back of chambers stretched out his hand and smiled.

"Good morning Steve, come on in. They walked back into his office. "Have a seat."

"Well congratulations, Steve, You're going to be our child support man."

"Thank you, Judge."

"You know your way around here by now. How many years have you been in Clovis now?"

"Three years, Judge."

"You've always been respectful to me and the other judges. Now you'll be working for all the judges on this side of the state from Clovis right up north to Taos and over to Raton three hundred miles north of here."

"You're going to have to develop rapport with all of them. Call and set up an appointment to introduce yourself and drive north to meet them all. They're good judges. I'm sure they'd all like to meet you.

"Listen to their concerns and problems with child support cases in the individual districts. Get a feel for how they'd like you to handle cases in their counties. We have a big backlog of cases here in Clovis and I suspect the other judges do also. We'd like to move the docket on these cases and we're counting on you to do that.

"You'll have a staff of two: a secretary/paralegal and a court reporter. It will be your responsibility to hire and train them. Your chambers will be here in the courthouse. You can use the auxiliary courtroom on the first floor for hearings. Contact the sheriff's office in this building, and let them know who you are. I'll also be sending them a letter to let them know you're on board.

"In some cases you'll want security in the courtroom. These are domestic cases, so there is a chance of some problems arising, especially when ex-spouses have to meet one another in a courtroom over money or about children. Stay alert. There is a silent alarm button under the right side of every bench in the courthouse. If you need a deputy, they'll respond immediately to that alarm.

"After the shooting incident in San Miguel County several years ago, all the judges' benches statewide have a panel of steel to make them bullet proof. Judge Torey of Carlsbad even took to wearing a pistol under his robe. I don't think you need to go that far.

"We know you'll do a good job for us, Steve. Get around and meet the other judges, and if you need anything call, I'll handle it. Good luck."

Standing, Judge Thomas reached across his desk extending a hand and smiling as Steve rose, grasped Judge Thomas's hand, and knew he had the support of a good man.

Steve's next stop was to Judge Paul Mann's chambers. Judge Mann was a thinker and scholar, a quiet, soft-spoken and deliberate man, who loved the law and the hours he spent studying the statutes and reading the decisions of the appellate courts.

In appearance, Paul Mann's stature was unremarkable, but his expectations for lawyers appearing before him were tall. He expected them to conduct themselves as gentlemen and to know their cases and the applicable law. He was a careful, thorough listener and quickly grasped the essential facts and their relevance to the law. He never ruled in haste, but when he ruled, in contrast to his quiet voice and low key manner, he showed a strong hand to convicted criminal defendants at sentencing, a vestige of his ten years as district attorney in Curry and Roosevelt counties before rising to his judgeship.

When Steve went in to see him, he was greeted by a quiet, modulated voice. "I'm glad you got the job, Steve. Ben got you squared away with the courtroom downstairs?"

Judge Mann calling Judge Thomas by his first name to Steve signaled that was his official entry into the judicial family.

"Yes, he took care of me."

"Good."

"Steve, the Children's Department has not moved cases on my docket in months. I've gone to setting hearings myself. They have a woman attorney, but she's not very ambitious. She comes down from San Miguel County and uses my jury room to settle only three or four cases in an entire day, when I have hundreds of cases on my docket, and then she's gone for a month or two—she doesn't do much." And then he imparted his directive: "Push them. Push them, Steve."

Steve left Judge Mann's chambers believing the Curry County District Court judges wanted the cases brought to hearings and the current docket reduced, and that if he did so he would have the support of the judges.

Over the next three weeks Steve drove northward, from the plains of Clovis into the rising brown foothills, and then into the high blue and purple mountains of New Mexico. His jurisdiction covered an area equal in size to all of Ireland—eleven counties.

As Steve drove he saw the newly green irrigated pastures and native wild flowers by the roadside: the colorful orange Indian paintbrush and red globe mallows, the tall wild grasses and the yucca flowers that had all been brought on by the winter snows and spring rains. Everything reached upward for the sun like infants reaching for the warmth and nurturing of their mothers. In the mountains, brooks were running fresh and clear from the winter's melting snow pack, brim full with brown and German trout, mountain aspens, their uniforms of new green leaves fluttering in the wind made the music of the forest, as they stood in tall stands trim and taut and straight: the soldier sentries of the mountain uplands.

But it was the sun that Steve noticed most; the sun was the unifying feature of all of New Mexico's vast and spreading land. The four seasons came at their appointed times, even the yearly late spring snow fall. By April the sun-warmed soil, picked up in a handful, was moist and rich and separated easily, not clumping together or running muddy as it had in winter. The spring soil was ripe again for growing. The land had the smell of new life. It was the sun that gave the earth new life: life to the summer crops, to the high mountain flowering meadows, to the broad plains of grazing land.

New Mexico's brilliant sun lit the high desert's thinner atmosphere with shades and brightness of colors that were to be seen nowhere else. Fortress-like cloud formations gave movement to the panoramas: shapes to the sky, and ever changing shadows upon the land. The crystalline light made the state a mecca for painters, giving them great possibilities with light, and color, and shape. The land played like a symphony: majestic, ever changing, and always in motion.

The blue, blue sky was New Mexico's ocean, stretching unbroken except for the chiseled silhouette of a high mesa or mountain range that stood fixed timeless and without motion on the horizon. In contrast, the dynamic sky was alive. Its clouds ambled above the land, usually white, but sometimes black with thunderheads full of rain and lightning, hurling bolts of swirling untamed energy on the land below, making clear to the men and women of New Mexico how temporary, how transient, their place was in nature's scheme. Nature's forces were everywhere evident, and they humbled all who lived beneath her skies. After every storm that kinetic blue sky returned, revealing again the boundless, unperturbed vistas.

When the sun set and night came, the land cooled rapidly and took on a mysterious foreboding. Shadowy ghostlike shapes prowled the wild. Wolves and coyotes loped easily across moonlit mountain canyons and down desert arroyos in search of sustenance from the land. Occasionally, the unsettling howls or yelpings of these creatures pierced the night when they talked to one another or had made a fresh kill. The night lacked the truth and frankness of the day's ferocious roaring sun. All this Steve knew and took for granted as he headed north. They were the truths of New Mexico, and he accepted them without question for he was born of this land.

Steve stopped off at each courthouse along the way, introducing himself to the district court judges he would work for. In every courthouse the message was the same: "There's a large backlog of child support cases, and every month that number grows. We need your help. Let's deal with the backlog, let's get the docket under control. That's your job now." At last they thought somebody will help us deal with this problem.

14

The year before Steve took his position the Children's Department was penalized $500,000 for failure to meet federal regulations to dispose of 90% of the cases filed within three months of their filing.

The feds were involved because every father who paid his rightfully obligated child support meant that his children would stop receiving AFDC (Aid to Families with Dependent Children) and thus reduce the welfare rolls and the taxpayers' burden.

In some counties cases were years old. They lay dormant in the file rooms of the court clerk's office with neither a hearing set, nor a dismissal order entered for failure to pursue the case. Word of Steve's trip reached the Santa Fe headquarters of the Children's Department before his return, and he was invited to meet with the top officials of the department, so they could get to know each other, he was told. It was a four hour drive, and gave Steve a lot of time to think.

As he again traveled north from Clovis to Santa Fe he drove from plains to mesas, then into the mountains that ringed the city on two sides. Spring always comes late to Santa Fe. Despite the strong sun, the mountaintops were still encrusted with snow that glowed brightly during the days and were radiant in the full moon. Skiers from the flatlands of Texas and Oklahoma still flooded the city, intent on a few last runs before the end of the season. Tourism, the outdoor sporting life, and state government provided Santa Fe with its solid financial base.

Less than half a mile from the downtown tourist hotels and restaurants, the art galleries, and Native American jewelry stores was the cluster of state government buildings, the capitol, called the Roundhouse where the legislature sat and the governor's office was located, and the Supreme Court Building. All were an easy saunter from downtown watering holes and eating establishments, where many negotiations were carried on during the legislative session.

The Children's Department was tucked away in one of a series of modern state office buildings added some distance away as state government had expanded.

The building's exterior was nondescript. It had the honeycombed tinted windows of modern buildings. For security reasons there was no sign indicating what services were provided in the building.

Steve observed all this as he walked into the building to meet with the head of the Children's Department. He told the receptionist that he had an appointment with Mr. Arnold.

"Please have a seat, and I'll let him know you are here."

"Thank you," and before he turned to sit down Steve asked, "is Bill Losum in?"

Losum was staff attorney for the department. He coordinated the interviews with the judges and oversaw the selection process for the candidates for Steve's position.

In a moment, Losum appeared was congratulating Steve on his appointment. "I'm sure you'll do a great job for us. Why don't you come to my office we can talk before the meeting begins."

On one wall hung a Georgia O'Keeffe matted and framed print of a sun-bleached cow skull backed by the endless blue sky of the southwest. Bill's radio played classical music. Both sight and sound were at odds with his desk which was a massive disarray of papers and yellow legal pads with an occasional file mixed in.

"We're very eager to get you started. You're going to have to assemble a staff and start an office in Clovis."

"I'm already looking for a secretary. I thought I might hire a part-time court reporter for each judicial district when I sit, rather than having a court reporter traveling around the state with me. That way the chief judge of each district would have some largesse to distribute and this might help promote stronger ties to the program."

"That's a good idea. It's just about time for the meeting." Bill led the way past the receptionist's desk and then down the hall into a large office where Bill introduced Steve to three men whom he had never met before.

"Steve, I'd like you to meet Vance Arnold, the Director of the Children's Department, George Cody, Chief Deputy Director, and Len Coffee, our Chief Financial Officer and procurement specialist."

Vance spoke first: "It's good to have you on board Steve. We look forward to working with you." Then he jumped right in: "The area you'll cover will be the northeastern quadrant of the state. Currently, we have a large number of cases backlogged in this area with many new filings a month. This area is underserved and has never had a child support judge before. We're anxious to make headway in these cases and will support you all we can."

As Vance talked, Steve looked around at the men in the room and took his measure of them. He knew very little about them, as they did of him. He had learned only recently that Vance Arnold had served in state government for the past twenty five years. Vance started his career as a police officer in Clovis and then served as police chief of Clovis, where he formed a lifelong friendship with Chief Justice Big Jim Richards. Vance Arnold helped in Big Jim's elections, lining up support from various law enforcement agencies for Justice Richards' election to the district court in Clovis and then to the state supreme court.

Steve didn't know the entire history of the friendship between Vance Arnold and Big Jim, but Losum filled him in later. He did know that Big Jim Richards came from Clovis.

Big Jim had quietly engineered Vance Arnold's appointment to the directorship of the Children's Department with a series of private calls to the governor and other New Mexico grandees. So Vance followed Justice Richards to Santa Fe and both men climbed and prospered.

Steve refocused on Vance, who was still speaking. He was a man who knew his way around state government and the legislature. He had been on top a long time; he was a survivor and could scrap like the wildest wolf if cornered. His face had a colder, harsher look than one might expect in a state bureaucrat; his eyes did not sparkle, but had in them the cunning to rule. His grip on the others in the room could be felt. He was shrewd. But there were limitations to his raw intelligence, and he knew that if he were going to hold power, he needed to hire men who were capable where he was deficient. The men he hired rarely challenged him. They knew his capacity for wrath. Steve sensed all this.

Steve could feel George Cody's eyes upon him: observing, gauging, inquiring. It became obvious to Steve that between George and Vance there was an ongoing continual series of non-verbal signals and cues being exchanged. They were connected, and Steve felt George's intelligence and soon learned that he was both articulate and dutiful. During the course of the conversation Vance would defer to George's suggestions with no resistance.

George was a handsome young man about Steve's age, with longer brown hair and intelligent, inquisitive dark eyes. He held no rancor for some of the unpleasant tasks or people he faced. It was all a challenge to him, a mental game. He was a good listener, studying situations and people well before seeking solutions that were pragmatic, and could be implemented—not dreamed about—but he was not a politician. That he left to Vance. George was a technocrat, a new breed of younger educated managers in state government: the next generation of leaders.

Later Steve learned from Losum that George had been with the Children's Department since he graduated from college fifteen years before, as an entry level case worker in Aztec, the county seat in the northwest corner of the state. George worked hard, learned his trade, and became knowledgeable about the operation from the ground up. Then he began to move up: after five years in the department he was head of the Aztec regional office. His office continually exceeded goals in completing cases within the time periods allowed. The revenues from his office increased every year and the morale of his staff was high, an unusual occurrence in child support work.

It took Vance two years to realize that it was George's talents in Aztec that made the office effective and he then brought George to Santa Fe to be chief deputy director of the department and oversee all four regional offices.

From the beginning of George's tenure, moves were taken to increase revenues and build a dedicated staff. George supervised the regional offices, one in each quadrant of the state. His efforts were greatly resisted by the inertia that had characterized the regional offices with their local bureaucracies.

In New Mexico things moved slowly. Slowly, slowly went the state workers of New Mexico waiting for that day thirty years down the road when they could retire with a pension. No hurry, no need to worry, just another day closer to retirement. And the local office workers would think: "This new, young chief deputy in Santa Fe will be gone with the next governor. He will visit only one day a month—we can put up with that; we can wait. He will be gone and we will go on." And then they would resume the snail-like pace of their work, remembering that New Mexico had a 500 year old history. But George fooled them. He had lasted through several governors' terms. But the inertia too remained.

Steve sensed from the back and forth in the room between Vance and George that George was the brains of the operation. If things worked well George could collect between eighteen to twenty million dollars a year for the department in past due child support, and there were also tens of millions of dollars in additional monies that also filtered through the department. But as of now past due child support revenues ran at only twelve to fourteen million. George spent his days thinking how to bring in the projected revenues, how to move the inert regional offices and local regional administrators. George thought, but the ability to act lay with the local regional offices.

George had privately and quietly explained to Vance previously that a child support judge could help increase revenues in the northeast quadrant of the state from a regional office that ranked close to the bottom in performance by merely moving the schedule.

Len Coffee sat across the conference table from Steve. He was hail-fellow-well-met, friendly and affable, a *coyote*, the New Mexico term for someone who is half Anglo and half Spanish. He looked like he could lift a heavy filing cabinet or hold his own in any brawl. He did as Vance and George instructed, never causing a ripple or advancing an objection. He procured supplies for the department: computers, furniture, and office equipment were his specialties. He was the department's man about town; he had grown up in Santa Fe and had a coterie of friends in state government and private business who always were willing to do a favor and conduct business with one another on short notice.

Steve had quickly picked up from the seating pattern and unspoken cues the relationship of the men in the room.

Bill Losum sat quietly off to the side during the meeting. It was clear he was the odd man out. He was never called upon and his advice was not solicited. He was present at the meeting, but silently excluded. He was originally from Pennsylvania and was regarded as an outsider: a non-player.

"Steve, when we're done here go with Len and he'll get your office set up in Clovis with furniture and computers, whatever you need," Vance said.

At the end of the meeting George told Steve candidly, "We'll help you if you can get that backlog moving, and get that guy up there in San Miguel County working. Let him have a few of the gray hairs I'm getting down here. When you come through town stop in and let me know how things are going."

Len waited for Steve to finish with George then said, "Okay let's go to my office and see if we can't get you set up."

Len led the way, but when they reached the staircase instead of going up, as

Steve had expected, they took the flight going down. Steve thought this was curious. *"Here's one of the most important members of this agency and instead of a window view he has his office socked away in the bowels of the basement, in the least accessible and most remote part of the building. Why?"*

Four women were seated at their desks at work.

Steve asked out of curiosity, "What goes on in here?"

"These are my girls," Len said with a smile and loud enough for them to hear. They giggled. "Lois, Tiffany, Sylvia, and Rose I'd like you to meet Steve Light. He's the new judge for the department from Clovis."

Len explained, "They count all the money that comes into the department for child support from the fathers, although a few mothers pay child support too. Anyway, the girls count the child support checks that come in. They're all made out to the department. We accept only money orders or certified checks, and then we credit the account and issue our check to the mothers for that month's child support. In the afternoons I deposit the incoming money orders and checks at banks here in town."

Len then ushered Steve into his private office. Len left the door open. He had few secrets from "his girls." "Steve, I can get you a good deal on office furniture here in Santa Fe through Prison Industries. They make good, sturdy, and attractive furniture and the cost is one half what you'd pay in a store. Your budget allows for the complete furnishings of your office, your secretary's and court reporter's."

"Sounds good, when can they deliver?"

"I'll call over and find out."

"This is Len Coffee. Is Juan in?"

"Juan, como estáis?" Len moved freely in and out of Spanish. "Listen, I have the new judge from Clovis in my office. He'd like you to furnish his office in the courthouse down there. How long would it take you to make a delivery?"

Then turning to Steve, Len asked, "What do you need?" Steve responded and Len repeated into the phone. "He needs three desks: one executive, one secretarial, one court reporter's, two couches, six office chairs, one executive chair."

"He wants to know what color you want," Len said to Steve, "Gray, tan, or maroon?"

"Tan."

"He wants tan."

Then more back and forth. "He can have delivery on Thursday." Len looked across at Steve who shook his head yes in agreement.

"Good, Juan! Thursday delivery after one p.m. at the Curry County courthouse, Judge Light's chambers. My love to Loretta and the kids. I'll see you soon. *Luego amigo.*"

Business had always been done in New Mexico informally through a close network of friends and family relations. In fifteen minutes Steve's whole office was furnished at a savings of 50% without ever walking into a store.

At Len's door George appeared, and nodded his head to Len, who took the cue and left the room.

"I wanted a word with you. Your family's from here, you understand the state, and how things are done. Politics being politics and all that, Bill is in the process of leaving the department. We've given him some time to find a new job; we've had a parting of the ways, but we want him to have a chance somewhere else. If you have a problem anywhere come and see me or Len. We'd appreciate it if you wouldn't go to Bill with department problems, especially now that he's on the way out."

"Okay," Steve responded, "but he's got the ears of the judges."

"That will change when he's replaced."

"Okay then, I'll come to you or Len."

"That's all I came down to tell you."

On the drive back to Clovis Steve tried to sort things out. As he drove south through the snow covered mountains, down through the mesas and into the high plains the land mesmerized him, put his mind at peace. He thought back upon his meeting and the players. Then the present claimed his attention as the red and purple sunset broke across the land from horizon to horizon; he felt his insignificance among living things.

The sky soon turned black. He was out in the barren land; yet, off in the distance he could see the halo of light from Clovis across the plains thirty miles away, a beacon welcoming him home to safety. Clovis—home—Steve always looked forward to coming back to the warm and friendly people of his town.

As Steve drove he thought back on his meeting and the personalities he had met today: "There are fissures in the Children's Department and the politics look messy, but that's none of my business. I'll steer clear of that. My job is to serve the judges, move the docket, and work down the backlog. That's the one thing everybody agrees upon."

On Tuesday afternoon Steve would hear his first case in Judge Aaron White's district courthouse in Tucumcari, Quay County. Steve arrived early in the morning, even though the hearing was set for 1:30 p.m., to count the open cases in the Quay County district courthouse and to see how long they have been opened in the court clerk's office. The feds mandated that 90% of all cases be concluded within three months of filing.

Steve started going through files, noting the date each case was filed, whether it had gone to hearing or not, and if any action had been taken in the matter.

Quay County had 112 Children Department cases. Some of these cases were as old as three years and had seen no further action since the initial filing of the complaint. Steve had the inclination to dismiss these old cases for failure to move forward, thus pruning the caseload to current cases, but before taking any action he wanted to talk to Judge White. It was Judge White's district, and Steve felt compelled to discuss with him any action he wanted to take within it.

Judge White was one of the most respected trial judges in New Mexico. Working alone and isolated from his colleagues across the state, he had built a stellar reputation for himself as a judge's judge. He knew the law and how to apply it evenly, and from the weekly Bar Bulletin, judges and lawyers alike learned of his judicious rulings in reported cases where he was rarely, if ever, reversed. He was a burly former athlete. His hair was salt and pepper and receding. Yet, there was something timeless in his face, perhaps the knowledge that he expected the law to carry on long after he was gone and the precedents he had set to last beyond him. He was a fair man who spent his free time studying the law; he allowed no shenanigans in the courtroom. Litigants before him could always expect a fair and even handed trial with strict application of the law.

When Steve finished his census in the clerk's office he walked down the hall to Judge White's chambers. He was waiting in the anteroom when Judge White saw him and waved him into his inner office.

"Steve, come in. How are you today?"

"Fine, Judge White."

"What brings you to Tucumcari?"

"I have three hearings scheduled for this afternoon so I thought I'd come up early today to see what the caseload looked like in Tucumcari."

"How are we doing?"

"You have a hundred and twelve cases on your Children's Department docket. Sixty are over two years old with no action taken by the department except the initial filing. The remaining cases are current. I'd like to dismiss the cases that are two years or older with no action, but this is your district. What do you want done?"

"Steve, go ahead and dismiss the older cases. They've failed to move forward."

"Judge, I'm afraid the department won't like this."

"Dismiss those cases, that's fine," Judge White reassured him.

Steve could tell by Judge White's tone that he had been accepted as a junior colleague: taken into confidence and trusted. "If you draft the order Steve, I'll sign it."

"Thank you, Judge."

"If you need anything this afternoon, I'll be in my courtroom."

At 1:30 p.m. a delinquent father sat at counsel table in the courtroom ready to proceed. The department's lawyer had not yet arrived. She was driving south and east from Las Vegas, New Mexico the county seat of San Miguel County, where she was stationed at the regional office of the department. The trip was no longer than an hour and twenty five minutes on the clear, mostly empty, state road.

At 1:30 the appointed time there was no lawyer present from the Children's Department. Then 1:40, 1:45, 1:55 p.m. no lawyer. But then at two minutes after two a woman pushed through the double swinging doors with a burst of energy, out of breath and loaded down with statute books and papers stuffed into law books stacked and cradled in her arms to mid-chest and her pocketbook open and falling off her shoulder—a cyclone of disorganization.

"Judge, I'm Cindy Dolant. I misjudged the time it would take me to drive down from Las Vegas."

"Come in, Ms. Dolant. Catch your breath and we'll start in ten minutes."

Judge Light and his court reporter looked at each other in a telling way. Lawyers are not supposed to be late for official court appearances. Ms. Dolant's blouse was half tucked in. One stocking had a run in it. She was disheveled and thoroughly disorganized. Steve wondered what the hearing would be like.

15

Steve convened court and went on the record at ten after two. "We are convened in the district court of Quay County in the matter of The Children's Department of the state of New Mexico versus Ronald Ness case number CD-two hundred seventy-one. The Children's Department is represented by attorney Cindy Dolant and Mr. Ness, the defendant, represents himself.

"Mr. Ness, do you realize that you have the right to have an attorney present to represent you today, and that as a result of this hearing you could be held in contempt of court and confined to the county jail if you fail to take an appeal?"

"No, I didn't know that."

"Do you still want to proceed without counsel today?"

"Yes, I do."

"Okay, Ms. Dolant, please proceed."

"Judge, if I could meet with the defendant in the hall there's a chance that we could settle this case."

"Ms. Dolant, why haven't you done that before now?" Judge Light asked with some irritation in his voice.

"We couldn't reach Mr. Ness by phone, Judge."

"Okay Ms. Dolant, take some time to speak with Mr. Ness. Mr. Ness, do you understand that Ms. Dolant is interested in trying to settle this case before you come to hearing and therefore wants to meet with you?"

"Yes, Sir."

Fifteen minutes later, Ms. Dolant and Mr. Ness, a young man in his late twenties in a work shirt and jeans, returned to the courtroom. "Judge we've reached an agreement. Mr. Ness owes twelve thousand eight hundred and twenty dollars in back child support, and has agreed to pay three hundred and twenty dollars a month on the past due balance and an additional three hundred and twenty for his current month's payment."

"Ms. Dolant, I have some questions for Mr. Ness before approving this agreement. Mr. Ness do you currently have a job?"

"Yes, I do."

"What do you do?"

"I work in heavy construction. I'm in the apprentice program as a heavy equipment operator."

"How much do you make weekly?"

"I clear four hundred and eighty dollars every week after taxes until I complete the program."

"When will you complete the program?"

"April of next year."

"When you complete the program, Mr. Ness, how much will you make a week?"

"Over fifteen hundred a week take home."

"Okay Ms. Dolant, your agreement with Mr. Ness falls within the established child support guidelines. I'm going to approve it for now with the provision that he complete his apprenticeship program, and at that time, the department will bring another hearing to increase his payments in accordance with his increase in income. Mr. Ness, when you complete your program you will be ordered to produce proof of your income. Do you understand what we've agreed upon today? Do you have any questions?

"You understand that in the future when you are making more money your children are entitled to more support."

"Yes, I understand."

"Okay then Ms. Dolant, your agreement with Mr. Ness is accepted. You are free to go, sir. Ms. Dolant, you'll draft and forward the order to my chambers in Clovis for signature."

"Yes, Judge."

"Okay. The next case on the docket today is Children's Department versus Charles Sebring. Is Mr. Sebring here, Ms. Dolant?"

"Yes, Judge."

"Are you Mr.Charles Sebring?" Judge Light asked the man sitting in the front row of the courtroom, also in jeans and a plaid shirt, with a cowboy hat in his lap.

"Yes, Sir."

"Mr. Sebring, have you had a chance to meet with Ms. Dolant of the Children's Department?"

"No, Sir."

"Why don't you take ten minutes to meet with her and see if you can work this out? We'll reconvene in ten minutes."

Ten minutes later, Ms. Dolant and Mr. Sebring re-entered the courtroom.

"Ms. Dolant, have you and Mr. Sebring reached an agreement?"

"No, Your Honor."

"Then we'll proceed."

Going on the record, Judge Light opened court and explained to the defendant his rights. Then he turned to Ms. Dolant, asking about the status of the case.

"Your Honor, Mr. Sebring owes fourteen thousand and four hundred dollars in back child support. He states his ex-wife refuses to let him see his kids, so he doesn't make payments."

"How long has it been since he has made a child support payment?"

"Three years, Judge. He has a previous contempt order in the court file and I would ask that the court hold him in contempt again."

"Okay Ms. Dolant."

"Mr. Sebring, do you realize that Ms. Dolant is asking me to find you in contempt and you could be jailed as a result."

"Are you for real? I can't see my kids and you're sending me to jail. What about my ex? Why don't you jail her!"

"Mr. Sebring, this is a serious matter. You haven't supported your children in three years. And you have been held in contempt by Judge White's previous order that you pay four hundred dollars a month to support your children. Why haven't you made any support payments, sir?"

"My ex hasn't let me see my kids in three years. I'll be damned if I'm gonna pay her money and can't see my kids. Put me in jail, I don't care. I'm not gonna pay that bitch any money. You're a judge. Make her let me see my kids! That's all I've gotta say." And he sat down angry and defiant, hands crossed over his belly.

Judge Light had to step aside from the angry language and defiance. He took a deep breath. He could not respond to every parent's wrongs inflicted by an ex-spouse. His focus was upon child support, not visitation and divorce court.

He addressed the angry defendant. "Mr. Sebring, my authority extends only to the issue of child support. I have no jurisdiction, that is, no power to order your wife to give you visitation. I am not permitted to change your divorce decree or give you legal advice. Did you have an attorney represent you when you got divorced?"

"Yes," came back the terse answer, "And he charged me five thousand dollars. He didn't do a damn thing! I lost everything, except my truck and tools, and had to pay child support of four hundred per month."

"I told you earlier, you can have an attorney represent you today. Do you want one?"

"I don't want one! My ex told me as long as I don't pay support she wasn't going to let me see my kids."

Steve again tried to reason with the man, "Have you spoken to your lawyer about having visitation with your children?"

"No, I wouldn't let that sorry assed excuse for a lawyer help me again."

"Okay Mr. Sebring, I'm sorry that you're unable to see your children, but we're here today on the issue of child support. According to the Children's Department you have not paid any child support in the last three years. You are currently in the arrears. Do you have anything you want to tell me about that before I make a decision?"

"I've told you all I've gotta say. She won't let me see my kids, I'm not paying."

"Mr. Sebring, it is the recommendation of this court that you commence payment of four hundred dollars a month on the arrears amount and that you maintain your current monthly child support obligation of four hundred per month bringing your total monthly payment to eight hundred dollars per month. If you fail to make a payment this month you will be in contempt of court and will be incarcerated until you start to make payments. Thereafter, if you fail to make a payment in any month you will again be held in contempt for that month, and will be sentenced to the county jail until you make your payment for that month. You have thirty days to appeal this order to the district court.

"Ms. Dolant, will you give Mr. Sebring the address where he is to send his payments. If you have any questions sir, you can contact Ms. Dolant at the Children's Department regional office in Las Vegas or see an attorney. We'll be in recess."

After the recess, there was one more case on the docket for the afternoon. It was fairly straight forward: Ms. Dolant and the father agreed to a repayment schedule of a delinquency of fifteen hundred dollars.

"Ms. Dolant, will you please draft the orders in these cases and forward them to my office in Clovis for signature."

Court concluded around 4:45 p.m. Steve stopped in to say goodbye to Judge White, but he was still on the bench, so Steve started the drive back to Clovis.

He thought about the tardiness and slovenliness of Ms. Dolant and how unprepared she was: not speaking to litigants before hearings, when she could have met the opposing parties before the scheduled hearing at 1:30 p.m. Now she had three orders to prepare. He would see her work in drafting.

Considering the substantial backlog, Steve intended to streamline the system. He held hearings; he made rulings; now he had to wait for Ms. Dolant to draft the orders, mail them to his office for signature, and then file them in the various county courthouses where the hearings were held. That would take time and mean money lost. He put his mind to thinking about addressing the delays in the system and reducing the backlog.

As he drove, Steve looked out on the massive sweep of the brown and green plains before him. Sunset was coming and the few nimbus clouds in the sky would soon display the deep reds and rich purples in the west; the sky would blaze with splashes of violet and orange and then turn black as the earth rolled around the sun and the early stars welcomed their mother—the night.

In spite of his concerns about the challenges of his new job, his mind was elsewhere, captured by the powerful beauty of the sunset and early night stars. He thought of the immense beauty of New Mexico: from the snow peaks, to the fast running rivers, and the solitary, mysterious Chihuahuan Desert teeming with life.

16

When Steve reached Clovis it was after nightfall. When he arrived at his home, a single family brick house on a quiet residential street with a fenced yard, he unlocked the front door and there to greet him with boundless joy and energy were Luke and Blaze, Steve's golden retrievers—awakened from their late afternoon slumber. Lucas, a large male, was fearless, a swift muscular runner, and loyal to his master. His coat was a tawny deep bronze. When Steve took him into the wild, Lucas relied on his strength and swiftness to meet any challenge. He was devoted to Steve and their bond was impregnable. Blaze, the female, was smarter. What she didn't have in size she made up in intelligence. Her coat was golden. She was more particular than Lucas, with an air of femininity and disdain for Lucas' reliance on strength alone. She knew how to make her point to Lucas with a threatened or actual nip to his scruffy neck. She rationed her affections to both Steve and Lucas, and thus she held sway in the household. She guarded her prerogatives: sitting in the front seat of Steve's small pickup, while Lucas rode in the back under the camper shell, his head stuck out one of the small camper windows scenting all of Clovis' aromas as Steve drove around town. Blaze always insisted that her coat be brushed first when Steve cleaned their coats daily. She was fastidious. The two guys in the house just accepted Blaze as the queen of the roost. Steve and his dogs were a fixture in town. Whether off to the supermarket, or on their way out of town to Ute Lake in Quay County, Luke and Blaze accompanied their master.

Clovis being a peaceful and friendly town, Steve left the back door of his house always open so Luke and Blaze could come in from the backyard if it rained or thundered. They guarded the house and all Steve owned, which wasn't much, but included books, a stereo, a TV, and a DVD player.

When Steve came home in the evening he made it a ritual to take his dogs out and run them. He'd lower the tailgate on his camper and call them, they'd scamper in, and off they'd go to the outskirts of town. When they arrived at a fallow field or some vacant farmland, Steve, would pull off the road and lower the tailgate. Luke and Blaze would explode out the back of that camper and give chase to a jack rabbit or flush a bevy of quail, Lucas striving mightily to snare a bird in mid-flight or run down a jack rabbit by superior stamina.

Lucas ran like sheer poetry, every sinew stretched for speed in full taut stride as he strained at and beyond his limits, swift and true in magnificent exertion. He was peerless—a champion. Reaching forward, his forepaws touching the earth for just an instant as he propelled himself into his next stride, chasing his prey with magnificent speed and agility. He almost never succeeded: the quail flew just two feet higher than he could jump and the jack rabbits were even more indomitable runners than Lucas. But he gave his all in the chase, trying valiantly.

When he returned to Steve's side, striding just a few paces ahead, he smelled out animal burrows in the grassy margins of the fields in an easy saunter. Blaze followed Luke or stayed close by Steve's side as he walked.

Returning home after their roving, the dogs would lap at their water bowls cooled down with ice cubes, and they'd lie peaceful and content on the cool tile of the kitchen floor while Steve prepared his own dinner. For some reason which Steve never understood the dogs always waited until Steve started to eat before they would begin to eat.

Lucas had other endearing qualities. He and Blaze would sleep in Steve's bedroom on the carpeted floor—or at least that's how they started out. During the night Blaze would climb onto the bed and curl up in a ball at Steve's feet. Lucas remained on the floor.

When the alarm rang in the morning, Lucas would stir awake as Steve struggled for five more minutes of sleep. Starting from the floor at the bottom of the bed, Lucas would inch his nose, then the rest of his body under the sheets and blankets and crawl his way up to the head of the bed. When he was even with Steve's face, he'd nuzzle Steve's cheek and forehead with his cold, wet nose and start to give him lavish, wet, unrestrained kisses. This had the desired effect. Steve was now awake, and thus began a new day of adventure in Clovis.

On some evenings after dinner, Steve would call Jaylynn, his girlfriend. They would visit by phone the nights they weren't together, sharing the details of their day's doings and talk about what the next day would bring.

They spent weekends together, mostly at her place. Steve kept house like a true bachelor: the clean wash was always unfolded and adorning the living room couch. Jaylynn's feminine sensibilities found it hard to impose domestic order in Steve's life, try as she might.

She was one of the most beautiful women in New Mexico. Her exquisite auburn hair hung to her shoulders and her green eyes were alive with humor and sensitivity. Little missed her perceptive attention. Her face was beautiful: a perfectly sculptured nose, and lips soft, even, and pliant.

She was intelligent, well traveled, and discrete, a good conversationalist, who gave solid advice and could be trusted. She had lived for two years in England and traveled throughout Europe, so her frame of reference ran well beyond the confines of Clovis or even New Mexico. She read and was inquisitive and had refined and elegant tastes that were reflected in her antique-filled home. The years in England gave a sense of restraint and understatement to her style.

Her grandmother had been an early dowager settler of Curry County and Jaylynn as her only grandchild and sole heir had some private income and the independence it brought. She was pleased about Steve's new work, knowing it benefited women across New Mexico.

Their weekends together were fun and loving. Jaylynn would prepare European gourmet dinners, or they would go to the movies and later just lounge around her home and walk his dogs. On many a Saturday night after a candlelit dinner they would sit in the living room and talk. They loved to talk tenderly and listen to each other. Steve would kiss her, deceitfully shy at first, for he longed to taste her red lips, but knew to prolong and draw out their pleasure with teasing small caresses. Steve would bring his lips to Jaylynn's sensuous neck and lavish it with discrete and tender kisses and soft love bites. He'd trace the line of her neck with his tongue and close his eyes to intensify the taste of her skin; the luxurious scent of her body was mixed with the slightest hint of expensive perfume. Steve was enticed by her aroma. He would force his eyes open to behold her beauty and teasingly unbutton her blouse, slowly, one button at a time. Then they would walk to the bedroom hand in hand. He would undress her and behold her beauty by the candles she lit. The light cascading over her body formed beautiful shadows on her full breast and ample nipples, her tapered waist, and her round and soft hips. She had long and shapely legs. Her body was a beautiful contrast of rounded shapes and lines rippling into one another.

Her breasts were full and indulgent and he lavished attention long and lovingly over them, kissing and tendering them. Often he would place some scented oil on her nipples and gently massage them until they hardened and replaced his gentle fingers with his warm and voluptuous lips and his playfully adventurous tongue and teeth.

Her stomach was soft and flat, hinting at the pleasures awaiting them. Steve would kiss her tummy, nibble and swirl his tongue in her bellybutton, all in anticipation of her treasures. She was an orchid of beauty, fresh with rare delicacy and exquisite color, and she lay beneath him.

She was his: she gave herself to him fully and he marveled at the height of her passion. And in the throes at the apex of their ultimate pleasure he would call her name over and over like a magical spell, never wanting the sensation to subside, never wanting their pleasure to cease. Giving Jaylynn pleasure only intensified Steve's pleasure: to give and behold her beauty was an intoxicant to him. She, with her alabaster skin, high and full breasts, and the intensity of their pleasure would build and build to a resounding crescendo for both of them. In their after pleasure they were filled with contentment and love. Then they would separate again with an ache of being two not one inseparable being.

On those nights when Steve and Jaylynn stayed apart, Steve worked at his sculpture bench in a room off the kitchen. He enjoyed sculpting, using his hands. It was a relief from his daily mental work. His home displayed much of his work. While he sculpted Luke and Blaze lay at his feet watching their master and resting. After two hours of sculpting and one last walk for the dogs, Steve was ready for bed.

17

ig Jim now sat as Chief Justice of the state of New Mexico. The selection of chief justice or C.J. was an internal judicial matter that the members of the court decided among themselves. The post would rotate every two years and another member of the court would assume the position with all the attendant administrative duties of supervising the administrative office of the courts and the supreme court clerk's office, as well as exercising superintending powers over all other state courts and judges.

Big Jim had the respect of his colleagues. He was a moderate, a legal thinker, at the center of the court on most issues. He slightly favored the rights of the injured over the interests of the insurance industry, but not by much. He was very conservative in criminal cases, often confirming the actions of the trial court in meting out strict justice and lengthy prison terms for convicted criminal defendants.

The hum and monotony of the daily routine, the atmosphere of deliberate detachment, and the rarefied internal conditions of the work environment made the court a place for quiet deliberation and reflection for researching and writing decisions with clarity, tranquility, and an unemotional point of view: a smooth lake without a ripple.

In this atmosphere of reflection, Jim remembered back to the events that led to his first step down the slippery slope that had become his course. It was brought on by a family emergency. He had been on the bench hearing oral argument one snowy winter morning when he received a handwritten message from his secretary that something urgent had happened and he needed to call his sister immediately.

At the first opportunity for a break Jim took a recess and went upstairs to his chambers. There Theresa, his supreme court secretary, poured out the news.

"Judge, your niece has been in a serious accident. The snow storm's been bad on the eastside of the state and her car was hit by a semi on the Interstate. Your sister called. She is headed by car to Amarillo the Interstate is still open. They've Air-Vac'd your niece to the Trauma Center there. Here's your sister's cell number. She asked that you call her immediately."

Big Jim went into his chambers and called the number.

"Jenny."

"Jimmy," she started sobbing into the phone, "Annie been badly hurt, that's all I know. She's been Air-Vac'd to Amarillo. I'm headed there now. I'm about a hundred and forty miles away."

"Are you near Tucumcari? I'll call the state Police and have them drive you to Amarillo."

"I'm twenty miles south of Tucumcari."

"Let me call Major Townsend to arrange it. I'll call you right back.

"Theresa, get Major Townsend on the phone. It's urgent."

Within minutes Major Art Townsend, head of the state Police, was on the phone.

"Judge, your secretary said it was urgent. How can I help?"

"Art, my niece has been injured in a car accident on Interstate Forty. She's been Air-Vac'd to the Trauma Center in Amarillo. My sister is twenty miles south of Tucumcari and the interstate junction. She is frantic. Can one of your men meet her and drive her to the hospital in Amarillo?"

"Find out where she is and what kind of car she's driving and I'll have one of my men meet her and drive her to Amarillo."

"Hold on, I'll call her cell phone.

"Jenny, Major Townsend is on my other line. Where are you exactly and what kind of car are you driving?"

"I'm about fifteen miles south of the junction of Interstate Forty and Tucumcari."

"What kind of car are you driving?"

"My silver Toyota Corolla."

"Hold on." Big Jim switched to the other phone line.

"Art, she's about fifteen miles south of Tucumcari and Interstate Forty and driving a silver Toyota Corolla. Her name is Jenny Reilly."

"Okay, one of my men will meet her at the Dairy Queen parking lot in Tucumcari in ten to fifteen minutes and take her to the Trauma Center in Amarillo, pronto."

"Thank you Art."

"Judge, I hope your niece will be okay."

After the recess, court re-convened, Jim heard the remaining arguments of the case before the court. There were several other matters to be heard that morning, and Jim quietly, deliberately went through the business of being the Chief Justice of New Mexico. After all the arguments, Jim returned to chambers. That afternoon had been set aside for writing and researching decisions, but Chief Justice Richards had other plans.

"Theresa," he called to his secretary from his office, "call Chad Holloway out at the airport and tell him I need to charter a flight to Amarillo, that I'm leaving the court now and will meet him at the airport in twenty minutes. Tell him it's an emergency."

"Yes, Judge."

An hour and forty minutes later, Chief Justice Richards was walking through the double doors of the Trauma Center in the Amarillo Medical Center.

Sitting alone on a hospital bench outside the Trauma Center operating room was his baby sister Jenny.

She caught sight of him. "Jimmy!" She stood up and ran to him: "Jimmy." When she felt his strong arms encircle her, she started weeping again.

"Annie's being operated on in there. Her legs are broken, her pelvis is shattered, and her back is broken too. She had on her seatbelt and the airbag kept her from going through the windshield, but from the neck down everything is broken. I don't know about her insides."

"Jenny, we'll wait. We'll wait together. Where's Nate?"

"He's on his way. He dropped the kids off at his mom's house, and is driving here now."

"This is bad weather to be driving in. What happened?" Jim asked.

"Annie was driving home from U.N.M.—to visit. This late winter storm came down from the mountains by surprise; you know how we have them. The roads turned icy and slick, visibility was very poor, and the snow just kept coming and coming. A trucker came up fast behind her, punched his brakes, skidded, and overturned, pinning Annie's car beneath his rig. They had to cut her free from the wreck. When they had a break in the storm, they Air-Vac'd her here. That's all I know.

"She's in a bad way, Jimmy. I don't want to lose her—she's only nineteen." Jenny started crying. "They were operating on her when I arrived. They're not worried about her legs or arm, but her internal injuries, her pelvis, and her back."

"How long have you been here?"

"I don't know. It seemed like forever. Maybe two hours. Major Townsend's man got me here fast, roaring down the Interstate through the storm with sirens on and lights flashing. When the storm broke a little near the Texas line, he flew."

Jim and Jenny had taken a seat on the wooden bench against the pastel colored hospital wall. The smell of the hospital—a mixture of Clorox and Pinesol—came to Jim's senses. He hadn't noticed it until now. Nurses and hospital visitors walked by, but Jim and Jenny took no notice.

Then a man in surgical blues came out of the operating room.

"Mrs. Reilly, I'm Dr. Greenman." Jenny and Big Jim stood up, eager for the news. "We've finished operating on your daughter. That helicopter pilot got her here just in time. She has no head injuries. The airbag saved her life. But we had to operate to stop internal hemorrhaging. She's suffered severe trauma to her liver and lungs, and she's had substantial blood loss. Her pelvis is badly shattered, her back, and her legs and right arm are broken. The next forty-eight hours are critical; if she makes it through them her chances are much better. She's young and strong and she wants to live. All these are strong factors in her favor. Now we have to wait."

Jenny's knees weakened at the news. Jim steadied her. "When can I see her?" Jenny asked with insistent concern.

"You can visit with her a short while at seven tonight, and then again tomorrow morning."

"Do you have a chapel?" Jenny asked.

"Yes, go down this hall and make a left. You'll find it easily."

"Thank you, doctor, for all you've done."

Jenny and Jim walked hand in hand down the hall to a simple, austere room. Several candles were lit and three rows of straight backed chairs faced a small lectern with a Bible open on it. A simple vase of gladiolas stood on a table nearby.

Jenny and Jim sat down. Then she got on her knees and prayed in just a whisper with tears running down her cheeks. "Dear Lord, please don't take my baby. She's so young. She has so much before her. So much to live for: her wedding, her children. Please spare her. Take me Lord, but let Annie live. I'll try to be a better person. I'll raise my children up right, but please let my baby live, Dear Jesus."

Jim let Jenny kneel a little longer and then reached down and put an arm across his sister's shoulder and brought her back up to the chair beside him.

He was sad. He loved his niece and sister. Now it was in God's hands. He closed his eyes and said a simple prayer quietly in his heart: "Lord, please give your grace and healing to Annie. Let her survive and go on to a full life. Let her know your love for her and ours. Please keep Annie with us for Jenny's sake. In Jesus' name, Amen."

They sat there quietly—brother and sister—surrendering to the grief of the moment, but praying for healing and the grace of God. Time was lost to them as they waited, waited for eternity.

Jim interlaced his finger with his sister's and they sat without speaking for long moments. Time seemed suspended to them; yet, time was all they wanted: time for their daughter and niece to run and jump and play with her yet unborn children upon the earth.

They sat in silence and waited—the horrific wait—for a young woman with a slender attachment to life to hang on.

When Nate Reilly entered the chapel he found Jenny and Jim sitting sad and quiet side by side. He sat down next to his wife, worry and anxiety in his face. He was a working man, with large, worn, strong hands, wearing jeans and comfortable old cowboy boots. He had a small engine repair shop in Clovis and eked out a living for his family. He had not gone beyond high school. He ran his business squarely and dealt honestly with his customers, but Japanese lawn mowers and small engines rarely needed repairing or maintenance. Big Jim often helped carry their family. It was an unspoken conflict in their marriage.

He broke the sad silence, bringing Jenny and Jim back to the present. "How is she?" he asked with an anxious voice.

Jenny gave him the details: "They've finished operating. The doctor came out and said the next forty-eight hours are critical. She had internal bleeding and a broken pelvis and back. Both her legs are broken and so is her right arm. Now it's up to her. The doctor said she's young and strong and wants to live. We wait."

Then Nate said, "Thanks, Jim, for getting here so fast. We really need you today."

The three of them sat quietly in the chapel sharing memories of Annie's growing up: the daily doings of a family in a small town, her first date, learning to drive, high school graduation, and going off to college.

When Jenny got up to go down the hall, Nate turned to Jim with dread in his eyes. He had something to tell his brother-in-law: "I cancelled Annie's health insurance in September when she started at the University. The business isn't doing all that well and the rates jumped sixty percent. I knew she'd have health coverage at the Student Health Center at U.N.M. if she got sick. I didn't think she needed anything else. How are we going to pay for all this?"

Jim said what he had said to Nate many times over the course of Nate's marriage to his sister. "I'll help you take care of it. Right now let's get past the next forty-eight hours."

Jenny returned, and again they all sat quietly talking in the chapel. No one else had come to pray.

Outside, the winter storm continued. Its full force had now reached Amarillo. The relentless snow lashed by the fierce winds drove everyone inside and made travel impossible. The murderous winds changed delicate snowflakes into treacherous killers on the roads and interstates.

They sat quietly reminiscing: laughing a little and then crying, marking the oppressive 48 hours, and time kept moving forward, gaining for them a momentum of hope.

Jenny spoke, "Do you remember Annie's first date? It was with Al Whistle's son, Bobby. Nate and I left them alone in the den watching TV on the couch one Saturday night. They were kissing and got their braces locked and couldn't separate, and Annie began frantically calling me and I found them joined together, their wires entangled. It took all my self-control to keep from laughing, but I didn't.

"Nate and I called Dr. Burchett and met him at his office at nine thirty on a Saturday night to get them separated. Annie was so embarrassed and humiliated and Bobby Whistle blushed like a ripe red chile pepper. Stu Burchett tried not to laugh as he worked on disengaging them. Bobby didn't call much after that, and Annie didn't go out on another date for two months, her confidence was so shaken."

Between stories Jenny would withdraw, considering the possibilities. She didn't want to lose all her memories; all her dreams and hopes for the future. Jenny clung tightly to seeing her daughter's wedding day and the joy of having grandchildren. She tenaciously prayed and kept pictures in her mind of her daughter recovering.

In the urgency of the crisis, Jim had forgotten his own family, and his duties at the supreme court, but now these responsibilities nudged him. He walked out of the chapel, found a quiet corner and called his Karen.

Karen was at home in Santa Fe. School had been let out early because of the storm.

"Jim, how is she?"

"She's bad. She may not make it. They operated on her and she's in intensive care now. The next two days will tell. Her pelvis and back are broken. Both legs and her right arm are also broken. She had internal bleeding. The doctor said if she can come through the next two days her chances improve considerably."

"How's Jenny?"

"She's trying to hold together. One moment she recalls Annie as a baby, the next she's crying and inconsolable, and then she becomes withdrawn. She's holding on, barely.

"Nate's here—he drove over from Clovis when he heard. They're together."

"Do you want me to come over?"

"No. Stay with the kids. Another storm may come through and the roads are very bad. Don't risk it. I'm going to stay here for the next two days. Jenny's going to see Annie this evening for a few minutes. It's important she know the family is here. It will raise her spirits, they say.

"This is hell, Karen, waiting and waiting, not knowing minute to minute if Annie is going to make it. The uncertainty of it all. I've always loved Annie; she's my baby sister's baby daughter." Then, overcome by the emotion of it all, Jim started to cry. "Karen, I never imagined what it would be like to go through this."

"Jim, we love you. Nothing is going to happen to us. Get Jenny and Nate to eat something. Can you get a room for the night in Amarillo?" Karen asked.

"I think we're going to keep vigil outside the intensive care unit tonight. Jenny and Nate won't sleep. In the morning we may get a room to wash up."

"I love you Jim. Hug Jenny and Nate for me."

Next Jim called his chambers to report that his niece was in critical condition and that he would stay at the hospital. He was told that he had no oral arguments until the next Monday and Tuesday, a juvenile court rules committee meeting on Thursday, and on Friday an interview with *The Santa Fe New Mexican*, and a speaking engagement before the Downtown Kiwanis Club at noon. The rest of the time he was scheduled for writing in chambers. On Saturday the full court was scheduled to meet with the members of the state district attorneys association to discuss some changes they are seeking in the rules of evidence. He decided to ask that most of these obligations be re-scheduled or go on without him with one of the other justices presiding.

"Okay Theresa, call Judge Blair and Armijo let them know my situation. What's the weather like there?"

"The storm blew through. We've had about a foot of snow, the wind has died down and everybody's digging out. It's supposed to be in the teens tonight."

"Okay. Ask Judge Blair to let everyone go home at three-thirty p.m. Theresa thanks for holding down the fort. I appreciate your hard work; all of you drive safely on the way home."

"You're welcome Judge. I'll pray for your niece."

"Thanks, Theresa."

Outside the intensive care unit the minutes were interminable. Each second passed like an hour; each hour weighed a ton. Patients were allowed one visitor for ten minutes at 7:00 p.m., 9:00 a.m., and 1:00 p.m. It was ten to seven. Jenny was anxious to see Annie. A nurse came out from the unit. "Are you Mrs. Reilly?"

"Yes."

"Your daughter's on pain medication post-op. She's been through a lot and I just want to prepare you for what you'll see so you don't get frightened or frighten her. She has a series of lines running into her arm and is receiving a transfusion because of blood loss. She's breathing oxygen through tubes to her nostrils. There are a several monitors above her bed with lines attached to her body. She is very weak. Try to raise her spirits. Let her know you are here for her. It's so important. You'll only be able to stay with her only a few minutes. Are you ready?"

"Yes."

"Okay let's go in."

Despite the warning, Jenny was not prepared. Annie lay sleeping; her face was translucent, pale and fading. She appeared to have only a thinest thread holding her to life.

She opened her eyes. They took a moment to focus.

"Mom," she whispered.

"Annie," Jenny nearly whimpered, but checked herself.

"I'm sorry, Mom."

"No, baby, don't be sorry. Daddy and I and Uncle Jimmy are here. Everything is going to be okay. You rest. We love you, Mackintosh," using Annie's childhood pet nickname.

Annie smiled weakly, "I love you, Mom."

"And we love you baby. Stay with us."

"I will, Mom."

The nurse came to say, "It's time to go."

"I'm right outside, Annie. I'll see you in the morning." And Jenny bent over the hospital bed, over the tubes and wires and kissed Annie on the cheek.

Jenny left the unit and walked out into the hall shaken and scared and started wailing. "I don't want to lose my baby!"

Nate and Jimmy enveloped her in a hug.

"She looks so frail."

Jenny, Nate, and Jim kept communion through the night, outside the intensive care unit, in the hospital cafeteria drinking coffee, or in the chapel where they sat in silence or prayed.

Two, three, four o'clock into the dead of night they waited, weary and worn through the unendurable hours, with the hope of people that dawn would bring deliverance.

At five there was a streak of red in the east; the black night was ebbing into the purples and violets of dawn, giving birth to the day in the eastern sky. The storm of the day before had passed, leaving its snowy crust. The sky grew lighter. The few clouds started to radiate the colors of the rising sun. They had made it through the night, three tiny people on a vigil with the single prayer of keeping one of their own alive. Next to the majesty of dawn, their prayers seemed of little consequence.

"Mr. and Mrs. Reilly," the night nurse called to them.

"Yes," Jenny responded immediately. They approached her hopefully.

"Your daughter slept most of the night peacefully. Dr. Greenman will be here shortly. You can visit your daughter again at nine o'clock."

"We made it through the first day," Jenny said, "one more to go. Let's give thanks in the chapel and then get something to eat." There was a new verve in her voice and stride.

Dr. Greenman came in at 7:00 a.m. and greeted them and then went into the unit. After fifteen minutes he came out and met with Jenny, Nate, and Jim. "She's doing much better. She's young and strong and loved. But we still have another twenty-four hours before she's out of the woods. I'm here at the hospital all day if she needs me. I'll look in on her again this afternoon and then again before I go home this evening."

The second day went by faster. Annie slept and ate and got stronger by the hour. Her youthful vitality started asserting itself—she was stabilizing and rebounding like a tennis ball off a racquet—sure and fast. Dr. Greenman looked in on her twice more that day and was pleased.

On the morning of the third day Dr. Greenman came out of the unit after seeing Annie. "She's out of immediate danger. If she stays on track for the next few days we'll move her from I.C.U. She's still got her pelvis, back, legs, and arm to deal with. She's going to need physical therapy and rehab. She'll have to learn to walk again. It will take a little time, but she's a fighter. She'll be okay.

"I'm here all day again. I'll look in on her often. She's going to be fine now."

Dr. Greenman's predictions proved true. Within seven days Annie was moved from I.C.U. to a hospital room. The crisis had passed. Before returning to Santa Fe and the yoke of his responsibilities, Jim once again visited Annie. She smiled when she saw him and he kissed her telling her, "You're a fighter Annie. You stay with it."

After she was moved and gaining some strength, her pelvis was reconstructed and pinned, her legs, back, and arm dealt with. She was on the mend.

Annie was in physical rehabilitation when the first bills arrived two months later. The outstanding balance was over $250,000. Jenny was relieved that there was medical insurance.

Nate and Jenny were sitting at dinner in the kitchen talking about Annie and the day's doings when he told her, "Annie doesn't have medical insurance. I cancelled her coverage when she went off to college. I knew she would have medical coverage at the Student Health Center at U.N.M. so I paid for that and took her off my policy at work. They wanted an extra thousand dollars per month to cover her. I couldn't afford it, so I cancelled her coverage."

Jenny didn't respond. She was too tired and drained from the last two months to get angry. She just looked at her husband, comprehending his words, but dazed by his stupidity. She turned her gaze out the window, too disgusted and too tired to fight, "What good would it do?" she thought.

Then she spoke softly: "How are we going to pay these bills? Annie needs the rehab program. She has to learn to walk again. What are we going to do?"

"I'll call Southeastern New Mexico Insurance Company tomorrow. Maybe we can enroll her retroactively, or get her reinstated on my policy."

"No one's going to want to take on bills of over two hundred thousand dollars."

"I don't know what to do," he said.

"I'll call Jimmy tomorrow. He'll have some ideas."

They sat in silence the rest of the meal, barely eating. Jenny's only concern was for her baby and when she would walk again. All else paled in comparison.

Next morning, Jenny called Jimmy in his chambers. "Nate told me last night that he had cancelled Jenny's medical insurance policy when she started U.N.M. He thought that the Student Health Center policy would cover her if she got sick."

Jim had become accustomed to this: he had bailed Nate out on a regular basis since he married Jenny. But $250,000 was not a sum he could loan or forgive, and Karen would be justifiably angry if she learned that Jim had borrowed that amount of money because her irresponsible brother-in-law could not meet his family obligations.

"Jenny," he told her, "I need a little time to think this over. Karen is not too likely to want me to borrow this kind of money. I'll get back with you in a few days."

"I'm sorry Jimmy. I didn't mean to bother you with our problems."

"Don't worry, Annie is my favorite. I'll get back to you."

18

*L*ater that week, Big Jim had his standing lunch date with Vance Arnold, his long time friend from Clovis days and now the head of the Children's Department thanks to Big Jim's maneuvering behind the scenes. Tens of millions of dollars flowed through Vance's main office every year.

Feeling like a man in need of a friend, Jim couldn't help pouring out his dilemma: "Remember I told you about my niece Annie's accident. Well she's in rehab now. We're lucky she's alive. But my brother-in-law cancelled her medical insurance when she got to U.N.M. last fall. He got her the Student Health Center policy for a hundred and twenty dollars a year and cancelled her comprehensive medical insurance. She has no coverage for any of her medical bills.

"After her accident, the bills have been coming in and now total a quarter of a million dollars, with more owing each month for her rehab and physical therapy. She's a great kid and I love her, but I don't have that kind of money lying around and my sister's husband can't afford to pay for it. I feel like that trapped defenseless mouse in a cage with a snake that hasn't eaten for a month. Something bad is going to happen; I just don't know when, and there's nothing I can do about it. I don't have many options.

"I called my insurance agent this morning and he said no one is going to offer her retroactive coverage, especially since she's had these catastrophic bills.

"My brother-in-law has borrowed on his house to pay some of the bills, but he's borrowed the maximum against his equity and the bank won't loan him anymore. His small engine repair shop has been struggling for years, and I've often helped to keep it going.

"Karen flat out refuses to let me pledge our house as collateral for a loan, and I don't blame her. She's worked hard to make our life easier and she's right: it shouldn't be our place to continually bail him out. But she's my niece and no one's to blame. It was just an accident. It's only by the grace of God that Annie's alive. I'm stuck. Any suggestions?"

"Let me think about it. You should be able to purchase some health insurance for her that would exclude anything resulting from the accident, but would give her future coverage." Then Vance asked, "Did they charge anyone with the accident?"

"No. The state Police said it was an accident caused by the weather and no one was cited. There're no liability issues."

Two days later Jim got a call from Vance. "Can you meet me in the parking lot of Furr's Cafeteria on Cordova Road at five thirty?"

"Sure, I'll see you there."

The afternoon had started to turn gray. Storm clouds were coming in from the west and the sunset would be dramatic, but now the sky threatened another late spring storm working its way across the state.

Vance sat in his car and Jim got in on the passenger side. They were unnoticed in the lot. Vance reached under his seat and pulled out a black laptop computer carrying bag with a shoulder strap and handed it to Jim.

"This is a quarter of a million dollars. It's a loan. You're going to have to pay it back."

"I can't take this money. I can't pay it back."

"It's a loan from my department to you. Let your family get out of this hole and then they can start paying me back. There's no interest."

Jim didn't ask how Vance got access to the money, but he knew Vance didn't have authority to lend department money intended for the support of poor children. He also knew Vance bent the rules as he pleased. He had learned that long ago in Clovis when Vance sought convictions rather than justice. Jim had never before gone against his conscience. He had lived on the straight and narrow—he was Chief Justice of the state of New Mexico.

"I can't take it. I appreciate it, but I can't take it."

"We've known each other going back twenty-five years. This is a personal loan. There are no strings attached. You've been there for me, now it's my turn. When your niece is walking again you can start paying me back. Take the bag. It won't be missed, no one will know, and you're going to pay it back. It's just a loan."

Jim knew his sister and her husband could never qualify or pay back a bank loan of this amount. He weighed the cost like a solo mountain climber, his arm gripped and wrenched tight in the deadly teeth of a mountain crevice with sub-freezing ice black night coming on. The only thing that stood between him and death was his razor sharp knife. He had to choose: cut off his own arm or freeze to death. Jim was so clenched between family loyalty, personal ambition, and what he held inviolate, impregnable: the law.

He hesitated, then reaching over Jim took the bag. He thought it might be okay. He, Jenny, and Nate could cover the loan and pay it back before the money was missed. And Jenny and Nate wouldn't have to go bankrupt or cheat the doctors and hospital out of their fees. They could pay Vance money each month.

He would have to put the money in his safe deposit box at the bank tomorrow. He couldn't account for it on his taxes. Perhaps the hospital would work out a monthly payment plan for Jenny and Nate to pay for the services Annie received so he could surface the money a little at a time.

His mind was racing—*"Too much to think about now. I can always return it,"* he thought. "Okay. When Annie starts walking again we'll start to pay it back." Jim slung the black bag over his shoulder and walked to his car.

He felt agitated and his mind swirled with fear. He was sinking in quicksand and trying not to be smothered by frantically thrashing an arm here a leg there, all to no avail. The more he thought the faster and deeper he sank.

Now he had to decide whether to tell Karen. Their marriage had not been one of many secrets. They shared nearly all their private and intimate thoughts. When Jim sat on the district court Karen knew the length of his sentencing decisions before the defendants did, and Jim for his part knew Karen's likes and dislikes among his relatives and friends and her pupils' parents and her colleagues.

Karen had been home from school since 4:30 and was preparing dinner. He walked into the kitchen, gave her his customary kiss. She paid no attention to the computer bag, assuming it was just some work from his office. He drifted into the bedroom to take off his tie and shirt and get into his knock-around-the-house-clothes.

Their children had grown now, and although they visited frequently, mostly it was just the two of them. There was little to hide or be hidden.

At dinner they shared their doings of the day. Most of the stories were small happenings: a child broke a tooth during recess; an old political acquaintance stopped by to say hello and catch up on the latest doings in the capital.

Tonight was different. Karen saw Jim shuffle his food from one side of the plate to the other. He hadn't gotten the name "Big Jim" because he was a poor eater.

"Okay, what's going on?" she asked sensing his disquietude.

"I saw Vance today. A few days ago I told him that Jenny and Nate were having trouble paying the hospital bills. He knows I've helped them in the past. Anyway, he gave me a quarter of a million dollars from department funds to pay off Annie's medical bills."

"A quarter of a million dollars from department funds! Jim! What are you getting into!" She was incredulous and angry. She knew about the unsavory side of Vance's personality from way back.

He avoided looking at her. "He said it was a loan, and we are to begin paying it back once Annie starts walking again. That he can cover us for a little while."

Karen was screaming inside and tried to restrain herself.

"I can return it. It's been gnawing at me ever since I took it. I've never done this before."

Karen kept trying to grab hold of her emotions, but they were wringing tighter than clothes in an old time washing machine: "Just give it back!"

"I thought that as soon as I took it. I can just give it back, but where would that leave Jenny and Annie?"

"Nate's a big boy now. It's his job to support and protect his family! You've come to their rescue every time there's trouble."

"She's my baby sister, Karen, and Annie is my niece. I love them. They're in trouble. I have to help. We've been lucky; we have everything we've ever wanted. I just want them to be okay. If they lose their house how am I going to feel, knowing I could've helped and didn't? That I just stood by and let events pull my sister and her family under, that I let them drown. I can't do that, Karen! They're my blood. And Nate, Jenny, and Annie are going to have to work and contribute monthly to pay back this money."

"Jim, where did this money come from?"

"It was money under Vance's control."

"It came from his department. It belongs to poor children out there," she said with the swept of her arm. "Do you realize what you're getting yourself into? You've never done anything like this. Jim, you need to give this money back. You're the Chief Justice of New Mexico. You can't take this money!" she said, her voice strident, full of insistence and anger.

"Let's sleep on it," he said, "and we'll talk about it in the morning."

"A night's sleep isn't going to change where this money came from. You're in deep water, Jim, and I doubt you'll sleep well tonight."

He knew she was right.

"Okay Karen, what suggestions do you have? I'm listening."

"First give back the money! If you want to loan Jenny the money you can put a mortgage on our house. I don't like it, but you can do it, so long as THEY pay it off every month."

"You'll go along with that?"

"I don't think I've got a choice."

"Okay. I'll give the money back and arrange for a mortgage. I'll go to the bank in the morning. You know, I was going to borrow on the house for my senate campaign. Now what do I do?"

"You can't do both. Give it back. We'll be poorer; you'll still be a judge, instead of a senator, but you'll sleep easier," she said.

Before going to the supreme court the next morning Jim went to his bank. He had the computer bag with him and went to his safety deposit box. In the secure private room next to the vault, he put the cash that Vance had given him into his large safety deposit box and then had it locked in the vault. He would arrange for a mortgage loan later in the week.

19

im had been quietly but actively running for Republican Joe Templeton's United States senate seat. Joe would step down in 18 months. Karen knew Jim's mind, but had taken a wait and see attitude about it. It was going to take money—and lots of it—if he wanted the position. He had hoped to secure several hundred thousand dollars of seed money by borrowing against their home. Now that intended money would be gone, because of Nate's bad decision.

If Jim ran, he realized the real race was going to be in his own party—the Democratic primary, and in that there would be considerable competition. If he could secure the Democratic nomination, he would win in the general election. He would be a United States senator. But first came the primary and the need to finance and run a well organized campaign. Where was the money going to come from if he borrowed against the house for medical bills? He still intended to return the money to Vance.

But here was a snag. Jim had ambitions: *"To be a United States senator—one of a hundred,"* he thought. *"Me, a poor boy from Clovis, in the United States senate. I need to get to the court. I can come back to the bank later when I won't be so rushed."* So it went. By the end of the second week the money was still in the vault and the loan had not been made.

For some lingering ineffable reason every time Jim went to retrieve the money from the safe deposit box and return it to Vance a meeting came up, a decision had to be circulated to the other judges, or a speech had to be given. He just never found time to give the money back. Then by the third week he thought, *"I'll pay it back when I get elected. It won't be so hard to raise money once I'm a senator. It's just a loan."* And so the money stayed in the vault and he used it for the campaign, he borrowed against the house to pay Annie's medical bills, and he lied to Karen. He sat in chambers remembering these events that were his first steps down the slippery slope: the path he was now on.

20

teve Light wanted to start driving a circuit in the northeast quadrant of the state as the old time district court judges and lawyers had. He thought he would begin each week heading north out of Clovis and pick up the Interstate, then drive way north to Taos up in the green and lush mountains near the northern state line with Colorado; then to Raton on Tuesdays; Wednesdays in Las Vegas; Tucumcari on Thursdays; and back to Clovis and home base on Fridays. In this way he could address the backlog evenly in all the judicial districts and spend time weekly in every district. It was a grueling schedule, but he was young and could handle it, he reasoned, if the department would set a full docket of cases daily.

One of the early tasks that Steve had set for himself was to read the federal statutes that created the child support program. He already knew the program was established by the states and federal government working together to get child support payments from delinquent fathers and to get children and their mothers off the welfare rolls. These measures would ease the tax payers' burden, ensuring that fathers rightfully pay child support, and further reimburse the federal government for any support it had paid out to the family when the fathers failed to pay child support.

The federal government, Steve read, issued grants to the states and set guidelines for the enforcement program. To speed the process, Hearing Officer Judgeships, like Steve's, were established to hear delinquent child support matters. This was the crux of the program that he was to work within.

In addition to his child support duties, the district court judges also used Steve to hear emergency temporary restraining orders for domestic violence (TROs) against men who had threatened domestic violence against their wives or domestic partners.

Judge Mann told Steve in their first confidential discussion after his appointment that, "Issuing domestic violence TROs is the most dangerous part of your job. The husbands and boyfriends are angry that they're being thrown out of their homes, and they're often denied visitation with their children. At the same time, the courts are ordering the men to pay child support. It's like pouring gasoline on dry kindling: one small spark and it will ignite.

"You know about the silent alarm beneath the bench. If you ever have even the slightest feeling something violent might happen, play it safe. Press the alarm. An armed deputy or two in the courtroom is a real deterrent when violence is a possibility." Steve listened to Judge Mann's words and remembered.

It happened in Taos. A sad eyed Hispanic woman had come before Judge Bass for an emergency temporary restraining order to be put in place to force her boyfriend to move out. The couple had never married, but had three young children. She considered him very violent. He had an array of rifles and pistols. She told Judge Bass that in the past, he had beaten her and threatened her with the weapons. Judge Bass heard her petition and granted the temporary restraining order, that allowed the boyfriend to come to the house in the presence of a sheriff's deputy and remove all his personal affects. He was also ordered to stay away from the woman and the couple's home, located outside of town. He would be allowed supervised visitation with his children once a week for three hours at the sheriff's office in the courthouse complex.

Judge Bass signed the order and returned to his chambers. Suddenly there was shouting from the main atrium of the courthouse. "You bitch! You're not taking my kids! I'm not leaving my house!" Then a scream and two shots thundered in the courthouse.

The woman lay dead, deep red blood pouring from her head and mouth. The shooter ran from the courthouse, jumped in his truck, and drove off headed north towards his home and the mountains.

He had a three minute head start before pursuit began. All attention was focused upon the woman. Everyone was initially stunned and immobilized by the killing. The main effort had been to try to resuscitate the woman. Sheriff's deputies then started the pursuit.

The dispatcher got the location of the home out in the country and radioed the location to the pursuit vehicles: "Six miles north of town on highway three." Everyone feared for the children. School was about to let out.

The first deputy arrived on the scene. The perpetrator's truck was pulled up in the yard. There were several other vehicles in the yard near the house. No one could be seen. The lone deputy radioed for back up. He opened his door and stepped out of the car.

The report of the rifle was immediate. The round struck the officer through the front of his forehead, and he died before he hit the ground.

Springing from inside the front door carrying two rifles and a backpack, the shooter ran from the house to his truck, threw the guns across the front seat on the passenger side and sped away up into the mountains and the Kit Carson National Forest.

Not two minutes later two other deputies pulled up to the residence and saw Deputy Tibault dead beside his car.

They radioed dispatch. "This is Raymond. Tibault's been killed. The suspect may still be in the residence. We need back up."

The two deputies backed off and waited. Six deputies and state Police vehicles converged on the house within five minutes. All law enforcement personnel were heavily armed and vested. They cautiously moved toward the house calling for the suspect to come out. The front door had been left open and swung back and forth, eerily into the frame with every burst of breeze. Tibault's body still lying where he had been shot, the thirsty earth soaking up his blood.

The children were still on the school bus making their way home from school. A relative was contacted and brought to intercept the children before they arrived at the house.

The standoff continued. Law enforcement waited. They used loudspeakers to talk into the house. No response. A full half hour passed with everyone in place. The circle tightened around the residence. Tear gas was fired into the house before the deputies charged in and learned it was empty. The children's school bus had been stopped a mile from the residence and they were taken off by their grandmother.

The search now expanded and intensified. It was a foregone conclusion that the suspect had made his way to the mountains. The National Forest with its boundless mountain range lay only two miles east of the house. The suspect had killed a law enforcement officer: all resources would be used to capture or kill him. The pursuit would be relentless. But it could take weeks to flush him out if he had any savvy about the mountains.

The National Forest Service management office in Taos was the makeshift center for coordinating the manhunt. There law enforcement and National Forest staff met to coordinate the search. The forest had to be closed and campers, hunters, and backpackers had to be cleared out while the manhunt went on. There were hundreds of square miles of mountains and forest to search. A man who knew the wild, and could keep on the move, might hold out for months. A state Police helicopter was dispatched from Santa Fe to start a scan of the area. Sunset was approaching. The search would begin in earnest at daybreak. For now the killer had a twelve hour head start.

21

Steve was driving from Tucumcari returning to Clovis when he heard the news over his car radio. Judge Mann's prediction had come true. The news flash did not mention the killing of the deputy, only the shooting of the woman in the courthouse. Deputy Tibault's family, Steve learned later, had not been notified yet. The details had been sketchy: it was a "developing story."

When Steve reached the courthouse in Clovis, he heard the full story from the deputy on duty at the courthouse: the murder of the woman and Deputy Tibault, and the impending search about to begin in the Carson National Forest.

The killings were the biggest news story in the state over the weekend. Volunteer law enforcement personnel from around the state had come to Taos to help track and search for the killer, who had not been sighted since his escape.

Steve headed north again on Monday to Taos. He met with Judge Bass who was grim about the killings in "his" courthouse. New security measures were already in place. Everyone entering the courthouse was to be searched for weapons or anything that could be used as a weapon. A metal detector wand was passed over every person who entered the courthouse and an X-ray scanner was on order. All packages were searched. No sealed packages were allowed into the courthouse. All lawyers' attaches and women's pocketbooks were also subject to search.

When Judge Bass invited Steve into his office, on his desk were several of the leading newspapers from around the state featuring stories about the killings. In an editorial, *The Santa Fe New Mexican* called for heightened security at all courthouses across the state. It read: "Violence has no place in our courthouses. New Mexico now has experienced the violence that is present in other parts of the country."

Steve continued to hear cases argued by Cindy Dolant. True to her original appearance, she remained tardy, unprepared, careless in her preparation and presentation of cases, and always slovenly dressed and disorganized. She used court time to meet the delinquent parent, rather than arriving early at the courthouse and meeting with the opposing parties before the designated time for the court hearing.

Steve had reservations about her abilities and made it his standard practice to question the delinquent parents as to the amount of the settlements only after placing them under oath and examining them himself about their assets, sources of income, and ability to pay.

"Mr. Ortega, you and Ms. Dolant have reached a settlement in your case—is that correct?"

"Yes sir."

"And the amount of that agreement is four hundred dollars per month to be paid to the Children's Department for support of your children, is that right?"

"Yes."

"Do you understand that I have to approve that settlement agreement?"

"Yes, she told me that."

"Okay Mr. Ortega, what do you do to earn a living?"

"I'm a welder."

"Where do you work?"

"A&E Welding Services of Taos."

"And how much do you earn working at A&E?"

"Five fifty a week."

"How often do you get paid?"

"Every other Friday."

"Do you ever do side jobs?"

"Sometimes I do small jobs on the weekend or at night for relatives or friends."

"Are these cash jobs?"

"Yes."

"And how much do you make a month doing these side jobs?"

"About two hundred dollars a month."

"Did Ms. Dolant ask you about side jobs?"

"No, she only wanted my payroll stubs."

"Do you own any land?"

"Yes."

"Does it have a house on it?"

"Yes."

"Where is this land located?"

"South of town along the river on the road to Espanola."

"How many acres do you own there?"

"About forty acres."

"Do you raise crops on that land?"

"Yes, it's an apple orchard. My father planted it, and when he died it came to me and my brother."

"You harvest the orchard every year? How many bushels of apples do you harvest yearly?"

"We harvest around two hundred twenty bushels per acre. We yield about eight thousand eight hundred bushels of apples every year from my forty acres."

"How much do you earn from the orchard every year?"

It was clear to Steve that Cindy Dolant didn't even know the orchard existed before Steve started questioning the witness. She merely took the weekly pay stubs as the sole source of income not digging any deeper, or working a little bit harder to find out the full picture. She just did the minimum, just enough to get by. Steve knew that in New Mexico everyone had second or third income streams; it was the only way to get by and raise a family in a poor state that had a large agricultural base.

"My brother and I together make ten thousand from the orchard every year, just about; it depends on the price of apples and the yield and expenses."

"And you split fifty-fifty?"

"Yes."

"Now, Mr. Ortega, let's go back to the property for a second. Earlier you told me there is a house on the property, on the forty acres. Is there more than one house?"

"Yes. There are two houses on the property. One is on my brother's side of the property the other is on mine."

"Who lives in these houses?"

"I want to remind you, Mr. Ortega, that you are under oath. Do you understand that?"

"Yes."

"And all Ms. Dolant has to do is go downstairs to the Property Appraiser's office and check out the property roll and if you have answered my questions falsely you have committed perjury which is a felony punishable by a possible sentence in the state prison. Do you understand that?"

"Yes, Judge."

"Okay. Now let's return to the houses on the property. Who lives in the houses?"

"My brother and his family live in their house."

"And what about your house?" Steve set his eyes on the witness.

"I rent my house out to my cousin and his family for five hundred per month."

"They pay you rent?"

"Yes."

"How much cash do they pay you each month?"

"Three hundred fifty a month and they work the orchard for the rest. They've lived there for years."

"How big is the house on the orchard?"

"Three bedrooms, two baths. My brother, my cousin and I built it."

"Returning to the land for a moment. How much land was in your father's original parcel?"

"My father owned eighty acres. When he died forty acres went to me and forty acres went to my brother."

"Do you have a fruit stand on the road selling apples in season?" Steve knew this was typical in this part of the state.

"Yes."

"What is your financial interest in the fruit stand?"

"My brother, cousin, and me each get a third apiece."

"My cousin and his wife run it for us while my brother and I are at the shop."

"How much income does the fruit stand earn in a year?"

"About eighteen thousand."

"Have you ever had the orchard appraised and do you know the value of the land? You said it was on the river, right?"

"We think the land is worth about twenty-two thousand an acre right now."

"Mr. Ortega, how much is the house worth that you built on your land?"

"We built it for sixty-five thousand, but we put in all the labor, the three of us."

"Do you have any livestock on the land?"

"Just two horses, a pony for the kids to ride, a few head of cattle, and some chickens."

"Mr. Ortega, who owns A and E Welding Services?"

"Me and my brother."

"Is A&E a partnership or corporation?"

"A corporation."

Steve was surprised by this answer. "Do you own shares in A and E Welding?"

"Yes."

"My father and his brother incorporated the business when my father bought the land."

"So you receive a salary and dividends from the welding business?"

"Yes."

"How many years has A and E been in business?"

"Since nineteen forty-six, right after the war. My father learned welding in the Navy and when he came home he taught my uncle; that's when they opened the shop. They were the original A and E: Arturo and Eduardo Ortega." Mr. Ortega was very proud of this, his family history, and almost forgot the purpose of the hearing as he became more open with Judge Light.

"What per cent of the shares do you hold in A and E?"

"I own forty-five percent of the shares, my brother owns forty-five and my cousin owns ten. He didn't want to do welding so my brother and me we bought out most of his shares."

"So you receive a salary and dividends from the business, if you have a profitable year?"

"Yes."

"How much do you receive in dividends a year?"

"About twenty-five hundred."

"Who keeps the books?"

"My cousin's wife. She's our bookkeeper."

"What's her name?"

"Nancy Ortega. She works at the business in the morning and she's at home with her kids after school."

"What is the address at A and E?"

"Six twenty-four Albright Street."

"And the phone number?"

After noting the number, He said, "Mr. Ortega, I want to thank you for your honesty today. I'm not going to accept your agreement with Ms. Dolant of the

Children's Department, but based on your testimony today, I'm going to raise the amount of your monthly payment to support your children so that your children get some additional money. Your testimony reveals that you have additional income from your side jobs, the orchard, the fruit stand, the rental home on your property, and your dividends from your business. Adding up your additional monthly income and your yearly dividends that amounts to approximately four thousand fifty-eight dollars per month over a twelve month period. I am going to recommend that your monthly child support payments be two thousand dollars for your three children, instead of the four hundred dollar figure that you and Ms. Dolant reached earlier.

"You have thirty days to appeal my decision to the district court. If you do not appeal, you are bound by this decision. We are in recess." And down came the gavel.

And thus it went, Ms. Dolant unprepared and never exerting any extra effort to look beneath the surface of the non-supporting parent's answers to questions in order to do a thorough examination of the defendant's assets. Steve did the work; Ms. Dolant did the barest minimum and did that poorly.

Steve was concerned with the flim-flam way Cindy Dolant went about reaching settlements with the non-supporting parents, arriving at figures without exploring other obvious sources of income that should have been included in their income. That's why he always questioned the delinquent fathers himself.

22

The Children's' Department regional office in Las Vegas, San Miguel County set the hearing schedule for all eleven counties in Steve's quadrant, but the calendar was always meager despite the backlog. Usually one or two hearings were scheduled on each day of the week. Steve was puzzled by this. Now that he was committed to hear the cases full time and the regional office had twelve thousand cases backlogged with over 400 hundred new filings a month how come they could muster only 24 cases a month for hearing? It didn't make sense.

He kept pondering it, and let the situation simmer in his mind. The state had been fined $500,000 the year before Steve came on board for failure to meet the time lines and performance levels set for the Child Support Enforcement Act of the federal government. Nowhere in the regional office of the department was there a sense of urgency or importance in trying to get the cases on the docket and moved to court hearings.

The district court judges had let the problem linger for years. This was a portion of their caseload that got overlooked. These were "stepchild" cases quite literally. The judges had local lawsuits and criminal trials to move and oversee. The time lines set in Washington, DC had little impact on sleepy, poor, New Mexico (the 48th in per capita income).

As a consequence, the San Miguel County regional office in Las Vegas ran on its own initiative, or lack thereof, in the backwaters of the state. It was a feudal fiefdom in state government, far enough from Santa Fe to be forgotten and left alone.

The manager of the San Miguel office, Raul Guzman, was like an old Chinese warlord unanswerable to anyone and free from interference far away in the hinterlands. He was unprepared for Steve Light, a young man who sought action, wanted results, and had a mandate from the judges to move the cases in the region.

After the killings in Taos, Ms. Dolant started traveling to hearings with a male member from the office in Las Vegas. Jaime Powell had been a state Police officer for twenty years, and was reaching retirement when Raul Guzman recruited him to be his assistant manager in the San Miguel regional office.

Jaime was a responsible assistant. He knew there were problems in his office. He recognized the magnitude of the backlog, even if Santa Fe, the headquarters office for the state, didn't. But he couldn't get the autocratic Raul to address the problem despite their long time friendship.

Raul's chief concern was keeping his beautiful young wife in clothing and faithful, the second being his paramount concern; the fear that some younger man would seduce her with finery or jewelry or vigorous sex was always lingering in his middle aged performance plagued mind. He devoted himself tirelessly to opening up charge accounts with local merchants, applying for new credit cards when old ones were maxed out, and extending himself beyond any reasonable limits in an effort to quiet the unquellable fear and ultimate humiliation of a Hispanic male: being cuckolded.

The first thing on Monday mornings' Raul would say to Jaime, "Let's go get some coffee." And Raul and Jaime would drive to the local café and have donuts and coffee, leaving the office staff unattended, unsupervised, and feeling unimportant. There Raul would unburden himself about his wife's latest spending spree and their quarrels over the weekend.

"She spends like I'm a Texan. All she does is buy, buy, buy. I can't keep up with her, and it never stops. And the truth is," he lowered his voice so no one could hear, "I can't keep up with her. Know what I mean? She's thirty-five this year, I'm fifty. She wants more. I don't have it, either money or the other."

Jaime remained a true and trusted friend no matter how tyrannical Raul became in the office. Jaime never betrayed these confidences, never revealed the details of Raul's private life. The length and volume of Raul tirades in the office were in direct proportion to the amount of money his wife had spent the day before and that he had learned about in the evening. When she'd spend he took out his anger in the office. But what bothered Jaime even more was that Raul would discuss the intimate details of his life. Jaime was concerned about the slack work in the office, the ever increasing backlog, and the poor morale of the office staff caused by Raul's frequent, extended trips to the cafe. Jaime felt relieved to accompany Cindy Dolant on her hearings carrying his own attaché case of files in the aftermath of the shootings.

One day in the San Miguel County courthouse, after concluding the morning docket, Steve turned to Ms. Dolant and asked, "Are you a little unsettled around our defendants since the shootings in Taos last week?"

"I was at first, but I'm not nervous now."

"Why's that?"

"Because Jaime has a gun."

Steve was startled by her answer and dumbfounded. He turned to Jaime who was in the courtroom to deal with this revelation.

Jaime turned to Cindy and asked, "Why did you tell him?"

Steve again asked with a little more authority in his voice, "Do you have a gun with you in this courtroom?"

"I had it earlier Judge, but I put it in my car."

"Jaime, I know you were with the state Police for a long time and personally I'm not opposed to guns, but this is a courtroom."

And breaking in, Jaime explained, "We're afraid of what happened in Taos last week; I was only providing her with protection."

"Is the gun out of the courthouse now?"

"Yes."

"Then we'll leave it at that. No guns in the courtroom."

Steve drove through Santa Fe on his return to Clovis and stopped by the headquarters office of the Children's Department. Len Coffee saw him and quickly pulled him aside. "Cindy Dolant called and said you allowed a pistol in the courtroom this morning."

"Listen to me! Jaime Powell brought that pistol into the courtroom without my knowledge, and she let it slip that he had a gun in the courtroom. When I questioned him about it he said he had taken it out of the courtroom and put it back in his car. I told the two of them, that this is a courtroom and there are to be no guns in it. And he assured me the pistol was out of the courthouse and in his car and that's the way we left it."

"Well she's saying you said it was okay to have a gun in the courtroom. You'd better write a letter to cover your ass."

On the way back to Clovis, Steve realized that not only was Cindy Dolant incompetent, but she was also a liar—a strong word in New Mexico. A hundred years ago its use would have gotten a man shot.

When Steve reached Clovis he sat down and wrote Ms. Dolant the following letter with a blind copy to George Cody as Len suggested:

Dear Ms. Dolant:

Now that we are beyond the hysteria of last week's shooting in Taos, I would appreciate it if you would again instruct Mr. ————— (Steve left out the name intentionally) no longer to bring a weapon into my hearings in the courtroom, as I mentioned to you earlier today after our hearing in San Miguel County.

Of course, I would not have known that Mr. ————— had a gun in the courtroom without your first telling me. Despite Mr.—————'s career in law enforcement and in light of the events of the last week, I think this is the best policy and has been the law and custom in New Mexico since statehood that guns remain out of the courtroom. Therefore, in the future we will have no guns in the courtroom.

Thank you for your attention to this matter.

Very Truly Yours,

Steven Light

Signing and mailing, Steve was as angry as a cornered alley cat. He had learned an important lesson: that despite being a member of the bar, Cindy Dolant was unscrupulous. He would have to watch her more cautiously and protect himself in the future.

23

The killer was still at large in the Carson National Forest. In the nearly two weeks since the shootings no one had spotted him. He was thought to be in some remote recess of the forest, at least that's what scores of law enforcement and Forest Service staff believed. In fact, he had circled back out of the forest on a cold, wet, moonless night, and made his way to his lawyer's home in Taos. In a small town there are no mysteries about where anyone lives.

Joe Towers stood unarmed on the back stoop of Richard Fowler's home and knocked on the door. A light came on in the kitchen and then on the back stoop. Richard had known Joe for years, and as native *Taoseños* they knew each other well. Joe had been one of Richard's clients in Joe's purchase of the house and his minor scrapes with the law.

Richard invited him in. "Elsie, make Joe here some hot coffee and food. He's been out in those cold mountains for nearly two weeks and he looks like he could use a hot meal." She went scurrying off to do as her husband asked. Richard Fowler was a lawyer's lawyer who was respected and held in high esteem for many quiet kindnesses he had done over the years, and for his integrity. Now he would be tested again.

"Mr. Fowler, I killed Marne and that deputy. I don't know why. I was just so angry. I just" . . . and he broke off the thought—incomplete—as if the saying of the thought gave life to the deed all over again and if he didn't say it; it hadn't happened.

"Now I have to pay the price. I didn't want to be shot like a wild animal in the forest—tracked and hunted down and killed on sight. I need your help. I don't have a lot of money."

"Joe, the best service I can do for you right now is to get you to turn yourself in safely so you won't be shot on sight. That's my counsel. I'd like to try to get you safely to the jail. Are you with me?"

He hung his head, nodded, and quietly said, "Okay."

"I'll accompany you to the sheriff's office and jail and make sure nothing happens to you on the way. Joe, you may have some legal defenses, but we won't talk about that right now. Let's get you some hot food and then safely into town.

"There's only one bit of legal advice I'm going to give you—don't give a statement. Tell them that you are my client and that I advised you not to talk without your lawyer present. Can you remember that?"

"Yes. Mr. Fowler will you represent me?"

"Yes, Joe.

"Elsie, how's the food coming?"

"I'll be right there."

Elsie Fowler came into the dining room, where Joe Towers and her husband were talking, with a tray of hot food and coffee. Elsie and Richard watched as Joe surrounded the plate with his hands and enveloped the contents. He apologized to Mrs. Fowler for eating so fast.

"That was good. Thank you.

"I did a lot of thinking out there in the mountains at night. I'm sorry I killed Marne. She got me so angry taking the kids away. And then the deputy. There's no place to run.

"Mr. Fowler, I don't know how I'll pay you."

"We'll cross that bridge later. But turning yourself in may help at sentencing. Are you ready to go into town Joe? I'll take your Wagoneer, Elsie. No one will recognize me in it and Joe will be safer. Joe I'll come see you tomorrow in the jailhouse. Don't worry and remember: no statements.

"Elsie give me Sheriff Baca's home number. We'll call him from the car just to make certain there's going to be no problems or circus at the jail."

So Joe Towers and his lawyer started the drive to the sheriff's office and the jail complex. Richard cell phoned Sheriff Gene Baca's home number. Gene answered.

"Sheriff, this is Richard Fowler. I'd like to meet you at the jail. I'm bringing in Joe Towers. He wants to surrender. He's unarmed and we don't want him shot between here and the jail and we don't need the newspapers or TV. We'll be at the jail in about five minutes."

"Mr. Fowler, I'll call ahead, they'll be no problem from my people. I'll meet you in town in about 10 minutes. Pull around to the side door of the jail complex. He can enter from there."

As Mrs. Fowler's jeep pulled beside the side door of the jail, Richard and Joe got out and walked to the door and knocked. Three deputies came out. They read Joe his rights and cuffed him. The media was still out in front of the jail: TV trucks with their antennas extended and reporters with cameras were all waiting. Fowler had bypassed all that, when Joe ducked down in the Wagoneer.

Then Gene Baca came upon the scene.

"Joe, I'll see you in the morning," and for the benefit of the sheriff and his staff who were standing next to him. "You are not to give a statement or be questioned without my presence. That is the advice of your counsel."

Fowler and Baca waited for the deputies to walk Joe to booking. When they were alone Gene turned to Fowler and said, "Joe's looking at the death penalty this time."

"I know."

"Thanks for your help tonight, Gene."

"That's the way it's supposed to be."

"I'll see you in the morning. Good night."

"Good night Mr. Fowler. You can tell me tomorrow how you got him off those mountains."

"Client privilege, Gene."

And each man went his way—different men on different paths.

The sheriff's office radioed all those out in the mountains looking for the perpetrator telling them that the alleged killer was now in custody. The manhunt was over. He had eluded them for two weeks; it was unlikely he would have come off the mountains alive other than the way he did.

Next morning the news across the New Mexico was about the surrender and arrest of Joe Towers, alleged killer.

24

Judge Light continued to hear cases; Cindy Dolant continued in her incompetence and ineptitude. The Children's Department still calendared not even 24 cases a month. Steve was beside himself that he couldn't get the department to move with any more speed in bringing cases before him. At the current pace, Steve would hear only 288 cases per year. That didn't address the backlog of 12,000 or take into account the 400 plus new filings every month. The caseload would never be significantly reduced. There had to be a better way to reduce it. Steve pondered the problem.

Unbeknownst to Steve, George Cody, the brains of the department, was pondering the same question: how to increase the productivity in the San Miguel County regional office. George, Len Coffee and Bill Losum had come up with a plan to by-pass the hearings. They had Raul drive down to Santa Fe to explain their plan.

"Raul," George said, "we want your case workers to start calling these fathers and offer to settle all the old cases at fifty percent of the amounts of the arrears before they go to court. Explain to them we have a very strict judge now, who will not hesitate to jail them for failure to pay child support and we are offering this one last chance at settlement.

"If they accept, arrange a payment plan and mail them the papers. Have them sign, and direct them to send their payments to Len's office here at headquarters. This way we avoid Judge Light. There'll never be a court record of the case, he'll never know, and we can deal with the backlog. Do you understand?"

"Yes, I think so, settle and have the money sent to the main office."

"If they don't accept, set them for hearing before Judge Light. After he starts jailing them, then the word will get out how strict he is and others will want to settle."

Steve Light too was thinking of ways to decrease the backlog, but he also had his day to day responsibilities to hear cases. He could not easily pull back from the day's activities and foster solutions. It was only when he drove that he set his mind in neutral and was eased into a meditative state by the rugged and vast spreading terrains of New Mexico.

Then his mind would bubble up with fresh insights and ideas to solve a problem, he was then convinced, the department also wanted solved.

He came up with two ideas during his drive time séances on the back roads of New Mexico. One was to take over the calendaring and scheduling process himself. He and his staff could send out notices of hearings with a summons to appear at court. The second idea was to use private process servers who would be driven to perform by financial incentive to serve summonses to delinquent parents who were difficult to locate.

Still thinking the problem lay in just the regional office, Steve went to George Cody and Bill Losum with his idea of using full time private process servers to serve summonses on dead beat fathers to mandate court appearances. He explained that they would have a higher percent of successful returns of service and therefore more hearings, with a resulting increase of revenue collected by the department.

"We'll try it," George said.

Two months later, Bill Losum called Steve. "Your idea about using private process servers has really worked. Raul said he is getting eighty percent successful returns of service on delinquent fathers now. He told George you have some really good ideas."

Cindy Dolant continued her incompetence. A high profile case came up for hearing at this time in Raton.

Ms. Dolant went into the hall and called out for the delinquent father who had been summoned to appear in court: "Tom Pierce."

A man in khaki pants and green down jacket followed her into the courtroom and sat at one of the counsel tables before the bench.

"Mr. Pierce?" Steve asked.

"Yes," came the reply.

"Mr. Pierce, you have been summoned to the court today from a contempt order for failure to pay your child support. Do you understand?"

"Yes."

"Do you realize that, if you are found in contempt today, I could recommend that you serve time in jail here in Raton?"

"Yes."

"Because of the possibility of incarceration do you want to get a lawyer? If you do, I will reschedule this hearing and allow you the chance to secure counsel."

"No Judge, I just want to get on with it."

"Okay Mr. Pierce.

"Ms. Dolant is the lawyer for the Children's' Department. She will present the case against you. When she is finished, you will be permitted to present your case. You also have the right to cross-examine witnesses that Ms. Dolant calls and to put your own witnesses on the stand. Do you understand?"

"Yes."

Sitting with Ms. Dolant at her counsel table was a woman whom Steve took to be the mother of the children. "Okay Ms. Dolant. Please proceed."

"I call Ms. Debbie Pierce."

The woman beside Ms. Dolant rose and walked to the witness box. Her face was set with lines of determination and firm independence, and she walked with confidence. When she took her seat in the witness box she looked directly at her former husband, her shoulders tensed and her jaw tightened in anticipation of the unpleasant hearing before her, but she had the self-confidence to know she would manage successfully during the next hour. Her self-confidence was the reward of her independence that had been hard won over the years. She was sworn. Steve said, "Please proceed Ms. Dolant."

"Will you state your name for the record?"

"Debbie Pierce."

"And where do you live Ms. Pierce?"

"In Santa Fe."

"How long have you lived there?"

"I moved there after I divorced, thirteen years ago"

"And who were you married to?"

"Thomas Pierce."

"Is he present in the courtroom today?"

"Yes."

"Will you point him out."

With a look of disdain, Debbie Pierce pointed at Thomas Pierce.

Since Ms. Dolant didn't do so, Judge Light interjected, "The record will reflect that the witness has pointed out the defendant. Proceed Ms. Dolant."

"How many years were you married to Thomas Pierce?"

"Seven years."

"Did you have any children during the course of that marriage?"

"Yes, one."

"What is the name of that child?"

"Christina Pierce."

"How old is Christina?"

"She is twenty."

"And what does Christina do?"

"She's a junior at the University of New Mexico in Albuquerque."

"Okay, returning to your marriage. When did it terminate?"

"I filed for divorce thirteen years ago."

"And was that divorce granted?"

"Yes."

"Were you awarded custody of Christina?"

"Yes."

"Was your ex-husband ordered to pay child support?"

"Yes.

"Did he?"

"No. To this day I never received one dollar of child support from him."

"What kind of work do you do, Ms. Pierce?"

"I'm a nurse in the hospital in Santa Fe."

"Have you ever asked your husband for child support?"

"Many times."

"So over the course of the past thirteen years you haven't received any child support from your husband?"

"That's correct."

"And the court awarded you child support until your daughter turned eighteen?"

"Yes."

"I have no further questions, Your Honor."

As usual, Ms. Dolant left out some salient facts. New Mexico law allows the judge to ask questions of the witness, so Steve started to fill in the holes left by Ms. Dolant's examination.

"Ms. Pierce, do you have an official copy of your original divorce decree with the child support provision with you today?"

"Yes."

"May I see it?" She reached into a file she had carried to the witness stand and passed it over to the judge. "Mr. Pierce, would you come forward? The defendant walked to the bench. "Is this a true copy of your divorce decree?"

He perused it, and answered, "Yes."

"Okay Mr. Pierce. You may be seated."

In addition to not entering the decree into evidence, Ms. Dolant left out an essential fact: the amount of the monthly child support. "Ms. Pierce, it says that you are to receive a sum of five hundred fifty dollars a month in child support. Is it your testimony today that the father of your child never paid you any money on a regular monthly basis as ordered, or has the amount been modified since you were divorced?"

"Judge, he has never paid child support and there have been no modifications. We have been back and forth to court for thirteen years. The judges sign orders, but I never receive child support. He and his family have lots of connections and he has never paid a single dollar to help raise Christina—his own daughter—or to pay any of her college bills and I mean never! He doesn't even know his own daughter, and that hurts me because she's hurt. She wants a dad just like her friends and I'm powerless to help her. Her father abandoned her and forgot her thirteen years ago."

Bringing her back to the issue of child support, Judge Light asked, "You were awarded five hundred fifty dollars per month in your divorce, until she turned eighteen. Is that correct?"

"Yes."

"Have either you or your husband ever sought to modify this divorce decree?"

"No."

"Mr. Pierce, you have the right to cross examine this witness. You may ask her questions that would help your case and that contradict the testimony that she has given earlier today. Do you understand?"

"Yes, Your Honor."

"Didn't I give you money when Christina needed her appendix out?"

"That was an emergency when she was seven years old and you gave us five hundred dollars. She's now twenty, and that's the only time you ever gave us any money."

Tom Pierce stood silent before this accusation. He had neither questions nor answers for his ex-wife. He stood silent and immobilized, and then turned to the judge. "Your Honor, I can explain. I'm a recovering alcoholic, and I've been in treatment centers for some of the time Christina was growing up."

Steve took control of the courtroom. "Mr. Pierce, do you want to excuse this witness? Do you have any more questions for her before you testify in your own behalf?"

"No, Your Honor," he responded, looking relieved that he would get to tell his story.

"Okay Ms. Pierce, you may step down and resume your seat.

"Mr. Pierce, I'm going to place you under oath. Take a seat in the witness box, and then you may tell me what you want the court to know in your behalf." Steve knew this was very formal, but it served to keep order and form in the courtroom, and allowed the litigants the feeling of having their day in court. It also gave Ms. Dolant the opportunity to cross examine the witness after he concluded his statement.

"Your Honor, when Debbie and I married we were twenty-two. We graduated together from U.N.M. and got married that June.

"In college we would go to frat parties after football and basketball games and I started drinking—mostly beer. It was fun and felt good, and Debbie didn't seem to mind if I got drunk on Saturday nights back then.

"After graduation, I would get drunk without any reason. I just needed to drink, to have alcohol in my system. It felt good. It was fun.

"After I graduated, I got a job in Senator Sanchez's office."

Steve interrupted: "United States Senator Michael Sanchez?" Steve now knew Pierce was well connected politically. The United States senators didn't hire just anyone right out of college.

"Yes, he was a family friend going back thirty years. My father was an early supporter of his.

"At first I worked in his Albuquerque office and then got promoted and moved to Washington, DC. Every night after work in DC the staffers would meet at bars near the capitol. I was always closing up the places.

"Debbie would wait up for me. Life was good. I was twenty-four years old and an aide to a powerful United States senator with a baby on the way.

"I always showed up on time for work, no matter what time I got home, but Debbie was losing patience, being left alone all day and night and pregnant besides.

"We had quarrels about my drinking. I told her it was my job to socialize with the staff and to meet with other congressional staffers. It made things easier at work. I told her we were the next generation of leaders, that it was our future I was building. It was essential. She listened and even took to meeting me after work, for a while, but she was pretty uncomfortable, pregnant and all, and the doctor had told her not to drink. It was hard for her.

"She spent the last three months of her pregnancy alone. I would come home loaded at one or two in the morning and collapse on the couch—I didn't even take my clothes off or make it to the bed.

"After Christina was born, Debbie wanted me to help with the baby, to come home early and have dinner together like a family. To have a home life. But I still continued to drink and hang out at the bars after work.

"My performance at work suffered, and by the time Christina was a year old, the senator's chief of staff asked me to return to New Mexico.

"When we got back to New Mexico, Debbie thought we'd have a new start. We could have a family—live the family life—like everyone else in New Mexico, like my father and mother and my brothers and sisters. But I couldn't stop drinking. The only change was that now I was drinking at home instead of at the bars. People started to talk. I was asked for my resignation.

"I went to work for my family here in Raton, helping my father with the parcels of land that he owned. My father knew I had a problem; he knew that my drinking was the reason I was sent home from Washington, DC and then forced to resign. He tried talking to me, but at first I didn't listen. Finally, I admitted to myself that he was right. He got me going to A.A. meetings in the basement of our church at five-thirty every day after work, and then he asked me to go to a hospital in Amarillo for alcoholics for thirty days.

"Debbie was supportive, and I knew that I had obligations to my father and to Debbie and our little daughter. I went to the program in Amarillo—where things started to make sense. I realized I was an alcoholic and could not drink at all without getting rip-roaring drunk and passing out.

"I stopped drinking; I went home to my family and things were better between Debbie and me. I worked during the day with my father, and at night I was home with Debbie and Christina. Everything was good.

"Then one afternoon I met some old high school buddies. They asked me to join them for a drink. One turned into several, several turned into midnight, and I passed out on the bar. My "friends" left me there without a care. The bartender took me home after he closed the place.

"I was off the wagon; I couldn't stop drinking again. Every day I drank after work. I spent less and less time with Debbie and Christina. I stopped going to A.A.

"My father convinced me to go back into rehab. I went through the program again. I was away in Amarillo for another thirty days. I came home again determined to try. Debbie was at the end of her rope. This time I had to succeed, she said, or she would leave me.

"I failed, and she left, taking Christina. She walked out of my life and other than a few phone calls I made to try to get her back I haven't seen her or Christina in years.

"I was alone. In the past I knew I couldn't drink; now I couldn't stop. I had lost my wife and daughter. I was alone, really alone, and only drinking made me feel less abandoned.

"My father died soon after that and there went my financial security and his good and wise counsel. My brothers left me on the payroll at a small salary, and I dug up mountain aspen from my father's properties and sold them to nurseries in Santa Fe and Albuquerque to earn money.

"My rehab bills kept coming in, but this time my brothers refused to pay them. The bills went to a collection agency and they sued me and garnished my salary. My brothers, fearing lawsuits and legal entanglements, formed a new corporation and voted me out as a member, but continued to pay me a small salary, whether I came to work or not.

"I still drank and have been drinking since then to now. I know I owe Debbie money. I just don't have it, not even for Christina. That's all I have to say, Judge."

There was silence in the courtroom. The evil of alcohol uncontrolled had been made apparent to all in the courtroom. Tom Pierce had brought his life to the courtroom. Now Judge Light, despite any sympathy he felt, must rule.

During the testimony the Judge Light had listened to the witnesses. He now wiped his mind clear of all sympathies and influence of the parties and had to deal solely with the law as he was sworn to do—as an impartial judge. Now he had to apply legal analysis and reasoning to the testimony presented at trial and reach a just solution.

The complainant, Ms. Pierce, testified that the father of their child had never made any child support payments in nearly thirteen years.

Mr. Pierce also testified to the fact that except for a contribution he made when the child had her appendix out, he had never made a payment. So, both parties testified that the only payment Mr. Pierce ever made was when the child had her appendix out.

Okay, Steve thought, *did Mr. Pierce the defendant/ respondent present any defenses that would have relieved him of his obligation of child support? Mr. Pierce had testified that his alcoholism kept him from paying.*

Next question in the legal analysis, Steve reasoned to himself, *is whether alcoholism and habitual intoxication are a defense against the obligation of paying child support?*

No way, they are not.

Nowhere in the statutes is there any language abrogating a parent's duty to pay child support because of alcoholism. Even if taking that into consideration, saying that alcoholism is a disease, and not something someone chooses to do is no defense for failure to pay child support.

Is the defendant in contempt of the previous court orders by the failure to make monthly payments, as the district court judge ruled two years ago when he heard this case?

Yes.

Steve checked the court file for the judge's signed order requiring monthly child support payments of five hundred fifty dollars. It was in the court file.

The defendant was, therefore, held in contempt of the previous court order issued by the judge.

Steve had answered all the questions required of the legal analysis without regard to the party's station or status in the community.

Now Steve had to focus on the hardest question: *what should the punishment be?*

Over thirteen years the defendant had made only one partial payment when the child was sick. This is a flagrant violation of all previous court orders and outrageous behavior. The defendant should be incarcerated.

How can I structure the punishment so he can begin to make his child support payments and not be a burden on the tax payers of this county?

These were the legal analyses that were going on silently in Steve's mind. While Steve had listened to the testimony and now while the parties waited for his decision. The parties and the spectators in the courtroom knew none of this—the thinking, the analysis, and the reasoning that was the backbone of judging—they only awaited a decision. They were not interested in the unbiased thought process that went into an individually crafted legal decision in the interest of both parties, the child, and the state.

Steve also had this thought: *putting the defendant in jail would have the effect of keeping him out of bars and sober so he could begin to make child support payments.* Judge Light was ready to announce his decision.

"Mr. Pierce, yours is a sad story; I hope you can find some way out of your problem. But my concern today is about the support of your daughter, Christina, who you have failed to support all these years. You come from a family, Mr. Pierce that has prospered in New Mexico, and you, sir, should have been contributing to the state; but instead, you are taking away from her by not even contributing to your own daughter's support and becoming a burden to the tax payers of the state.

"Mr. Pierce, it is my recommendation that you immediately commence child support payments of five hundred fifty dollars a month on your past due child support. This will be applied to your arrears of the last thirteen years and reimburse the state for the support provided your child over the last thirteen years. Since your daughter is now twenty, your obligation ceased at her eighteenth birthday. You will be given credit for the payment you made to help with your daughter's emergency appendectomy when she was seven. Beyond that, there are no further credits. Your total delinquent child support payment totals seventy-two thousand four hundred dollars less the five hundred you gave when your daughter was sick.

"Finally, your failure to make even the slightest effort to comply with the previous court orders is a flagrant and total disregard of the law, and as a result, I recommend that you be sentenced to a full six months in the county jail here in Raton with work release Monday through Friday between the hours of seven-thirty and five-thirty p.m.. Every evening you are to return to the jail. You are to obtain full time employment and make weekly payments of one hundred thirty-seven dollars and fifty cents to the office of the Children's Department. Ms. Dolant will provide you with the address to send your payments. If you fail to make even one weekly payment you will be in contempt and required to spend the entire six months incarcerated. In addition, for every night that you spend in the jail you will be assessed a charge of ten dollars to be paid to the county for the cost of your confinement so you are not a burden to the tax payers of this county.

"You are to spend every weekend in the county jail from Friday at five-thirty p.m. until Monday morning at seven-thirty when you will report to your job.

"In addition, you are to attend all the A.A. classes that are held in the jail and to receive the counseling offered while you are incarcerated. A copy of your attendance sheet for these services will be forwarded weekly to my office in Clovis.

"If you fail to attend your job or classes as instructed today you will suffer the severest consequences. Do you understand?"

Hanging his head, Thomas Pierce replied, "Yes, Judge."

"Mr. Pierce, you have thirty days to appeal my decision to the district court or to begin serving your sentence and making payments. You must surrender yourself to the county jail thirty-one days from now, unless an appeal is on file. That's all. We are in recess."

The spectators mulled over the decision. This new judge meant business: the Pierces were prominent people, but he put Tom in jail. Both parties and sets of family members who had come to the hearing purposely gauged their departures from the courtroom so they wouldn't encounter one another in the courthouse halls.

25

Steve sat alone on the bench. Judging, he thought, was more difficult than he imagined before he took the bench. It looked easier then. Now he made decisions that ruled peoples' lives. He had obligations to children he had never seen nor ever would. He had sworn duties to protect them and get them support even from fathers who were delinquent, alcoholic, or flat out bums. He was forced to fashion remedies from nothing, but he was resourceful.

Ms. Dolant continued her sloppy lawyering. Steve tolerated it because she was the only Children's' Department lawyer in any of his cases.

A case came before Judge Light's court that showed his resourcefulness. Ms. Dolant presented her case in her usual half prepared, ill thought out fashion. It was her hallmark. When she finished questioning the defendant, Steve was always left with unanswered, pertinent questions that he proceeded to ask.

"Mr. Jemez, where do you work?"

"I'm disabled. I don't work. I hurt my back real bad a year ago. I collect Social Security."

"How do you pay the rent?"

"I own my own house. I built it myself with my cousins some years ago."

"How many vehicles do you own?"

"I own my old Chevy truck and I have a Honda."

"How old are your vehicles?"

"My truck is sixteen years old. I got it from a junk yard and rebuilt it. It still needs a paint job—it's rusted in spots—but it runs real good. The Honda is eight years old and has a hundred fifty thousand miles on it."

"Do you own these cars?"

"Yes, I own them."

He spoke English with the New Mexico Spanish intonation—the rising and elongation of syllables and vowels in a sing song fashion at the end of a phrase or question. The sound was particular to New Mexico where many people spoke both

English and Spanish fluently, using the languages every day and interchangeably. New Mexicans called it "Spanglish."

"Well, you can sell one of your vehicles to satisfy part of the past due child support payments."

"Yes, I'd do that. I love my kids."

"You owe ten thousand five hundred eighty-two dollars, Mr. Jemez. How can you satisfy that balance?"

"I can give fifty dollars a month from my disability check."

"And sell the Honda," Judge Light reiterated.

"Yes, I'll sell it, and when I go back to work I'll pay another four hundred a month. Okay?"

Cindy Dolant shot to her feet. "Judge, we'd like to formalize this testimony that the witness has just given on the record and draft an order to that effect for your signature."

"Thank you Ms. Dolant, but I have a few more questions," She resumed her seat angry and antagonized that her "good" lawyering was not acknowledged.

"Mr. Jemez, how far did you go in school?"

"Eighth. The eighth grade."

"And where did you attend school?"

"In Truchas."

"What do you do for work?"

"Construction, remodeling. I fix up houses, or work new construction, whatever comes along."

"Are you a contractor?"

"No, I'm a laborer."

"Do you have a contractor's license?"

"No."

Judge Light was looking for money and sources of income. He was trying to get him to talk.

"You stated before you were disabled, is that correct?"

"Yes. I got hurt at work."

Bells went off in Steve's head. He felt a nibble, but had to be patient. "Who were you working for when you got hurt?"

"Johnson Brothers' Construction out of Santa Fe."

"What kind of job was it?"

"We were building a public school, and I fell through the roof. I hurt my back real bad."

Now Steve knew that there was Workers' Compensation Insurance. Since it was a public school built with state funds, the law required that contractors for state jobs carry this kind of insurance. He set the hook: "Are you currently receiving Workers' Compensation for that injury?"

"Yes, I meant Workers' Comp, Workers' Comp, Social Security. I get them confused. They both come from the government."

"How much is your Workers' Comp check?"

"I get four hundred thirty-six dollars every two weeks."

"Do you also get a Social Security Disability check?"

"Yes."

"So you get two checks?"

"Yes."

"And how much is the second check?"

"I get six hundred twenty-three dollars a month."

"Do you have a doctor?"

"Yes."

"What does he tell you about returning to work?"

"He says I may have to find a new line of work, that I need back surgery."

"What other work can you perform?"

"I think I could learn computer bench work with one of those new computer companies that are opening in Albuquerque. I could sit most of the day and get up when I needed to stretch my back."

"That sounds like a good plan, Mr. Jemez. Now let me ask you: do you have a Workers' Comp case filed?"

"Yes."

"And a lawyer?"

"Yes."

"What does your lawyer tell you about your case?"

"He says that after back surgery I'm going to need re-training and support while I'm in school learning a new trade."

"Has your lawyer told you how much your case is worth?"

"Yes, he says between sixty and seventy thousand dollars."

Steve had gotten what he wanted and gotten it civilly, something Ms. Dolant couldn't fathom. "Mr. Jemez, would you be willing to let Ms. Dolant file a lien against any recovery from your Workers' Comp case for the entire ten thousand five hundred eighty-two dollars of your past due child support?"

"It sounds okay. Yes, I would do that."

"Okay Ms. Dolant go ahead and file a lien against Mr. Jemez's Workers' Compensation recovery for the full amount of the arrears."

"I'm a very busy person. I don't have time to file a lien!"

Steve heard it, couldn't believe it, but controlled his anger. She had crossed the line. Now he thought, "What should I do? She's incompetent, disorganized, a liar, and now she's insolent, disregarding a reasonable request from the bench."

Steve was bulldog raw with anger, but he controlled his response. Here was one of the poorest practitioners he had ever seen, refusing in open court to follow a reasonable directive from the bench which would have resolved the case and settled all outstanding child support issues in the matter.

Steve guessed correctly that Ms. Dolant's insolence was based upon the fact that she did not know how to file a lien, and this golden opportunity would now be lost.

She was clearly disrespectful in refusing to follow a request from the bench. He could hold her in contempt or bring her before the disciplinary counsel of the state bar. But Steve knew that with the problems he was having with the Children's Department in just setting cases it might be wiser to just let the matter go. Steve swallowed hard, and let go.

That night Steve thought over the entire landscape of the Children's Department. Something was wrong with the caseload and the department had scheduling snags which resulted in not addressing the cases. He didn't know what it was exactly; he could just feel it, like the very slight tugging sensation: "Is it a fish tentatively hitting the bait—or is it the wake of a passing boat?" It kept gnawing at him. He couldn't pinpoint it—the sensation—just a shadow of a suspicion: but something was wrong.

Nightly, he continued to read the U.S.C. (The United States Code) and the C.F.R. (The Code of Federal Regulations) that governed the child support program in the country and New Mexico's Children's Department. In The Code he found a provision that he had not been aware of: the Children's Department must file a yearly report with the secretary of The United States Department of Health and Human Services on state program performance including such information as may be necessary to measure the state's compliance with federal requirements for expedited procedures in collecting child support. Using the data filed by the states, the Secretary of Health and Human Services files an annual report on child support enforcement with the Congress of the United States.

Now Steve knew there were federal records and documents he could examine that would give him performance numbers of the Children's Department. In further reading he came across provision 45 of the C.F.R. Chapter III, Part 305, Section 305.60 "Entitled: Types and scope of Federal Audits. (a) OCSE (The Office of Child Support Enforcement) will conduct audits, [of state programs] at least once every three years. . . [to determine that]the funds are fully accounted for." Steve thought a lot could happen in the three years between audits.

After reading The Code, Steve had an idea. During the weekend when he was in Clovis he would read and re-read the federal regulations governing the child support program. The Regs. required that all cases be heard within 90 days of filing; yet cases in New Mexico were backlogged for years. That was the basis of the $500,000 penalty the feds levied against the state the previous year.

On Monday morning, Steve went to Judge Thomas' chambers in the Curry County courthouse. The judge's staff was always friendly towards Steve. He enjoyed their friendship: the charming secretary and the humorous court reporter that made up Judge Thomas' staff made all who came into chambers welcomed and at ease with their kindness and big Clovis smiles.

Steve watched while Judge Thomas finished some matters in the courtroom; then Steve was called into chambers. "Good morning Steve, come in. How are you today? What can I do to help you?"

"Good morning, Judge. I'm sorry to trouble you with this. I know you're busy."

"It's all right."

"I'm having a very difficult time with the Children's Department. They're setting about twenty-four cases per month, that's about one a day, but they're years backlogged with thousands of cases in the regional office, and hundreds of cases that have been filed and are sitting in the court clerk's offices with no action taken on them. I am available to hear cases. I'll work twelve hours a day to bring down the backlog. But they do nothing. They take no action.

"I'd like to send them a wakeup call and dismiss (for failure to prosecute) those cases that have been lingering in the court clerk's office for years. Then I can move forward once they know that we're serious about the backlog. I'm also thinking about scheduling the cases myself using my staff to send out summonses and notices of hearings.

"I've drafted a short letter asking them to report on how many cases have been heard month by month for the first quarter of this year and how much revenue has been raised compared to last year when they didn't have a judge hearing cases. That way we would know if I'm being effective. Would you send it out under your signature? I have the letter here." And Steve passed the letter to the kindly Judge Thomas.

"It looks okay to me. I'll have Alexis send it out on my letterhead."

"Thank you, Judge."

"Stick with it. You're doing a good job."

26

On Thursday the letter arrived in Santa Fe. That evening after the state employees had gone home there was another meeting in Vance Arnold's private office. Present were Vance, George Cody, and Len Coffee.

"What do you make of it?" Vance asked the other two.

Len spoke first: "It's that kid!"

"But it's a judge writing. We have to answer it," George said.

Vance sat listening, thinking. Then he asked, "Does he know?"

"No," George answered, "but we need to be prompt and careful in answering. The kid is still thinking about case load and performance over the years, he's not thinking about money yet."

"Maybe we should give him the full case load and let him smother in it—that way we'll keep him busy and out of our hair," said George.

"What if he's successful?" asked Vance.

"That's a big risk to take. If he is successful everything will be apparent. They'll be no hiding behind the case load." George said.

"What about her—what's her name?" Vance asked.

"Cindy Dolant," Len replied.

"What's she like?" Vance asked.

"Slow, sloppy, and lazy, but loyal to the department," Len said.

"What if we dumped her, or transferred her somewhere else, and said she was the cause of the backlog?" Vance asked.

"We'd still have him to deal with, and he'd be more efficient without her, putting us at greater risk of his questions," George replied.

"But maybe if we could get someone who knows the work and could move faster and reduce the caseload the kid would settle down and be happy, and so would we," Vance said.

"She's the only attorney who applied for the job. How are we going to get someone to take her place?" said Len.

"Incentives," said George.

They talked for another twenty minutes, then Vance said, "Let's think about it and meet again tomorrow at five. George, you draft a reply."

It took twelve days for the reply to be finally drafted and mailed to Judge Thomas' chambers. They met three more times before a reply was finally fashioned.

The letter read:

Dear Judge Thomas:

Enclosed are the statistics you requested for your quadrant, the area that includes: Clovis, Tucumcari, Las Vegas, Taos, and Raton.

The numbers show a comparison of the first quarter of last year's revenues and cases heard and this year's statistics since the addition of the new child support judge who started in December.

I apologize for taking so long in getting back to you with this information.

Yours truly,
Len Coffee
Chief Financial Officer

Judge Thomas called Steve when he had received the letter. "Here it is Steve," said the judge as he pushed it across his desk to the young man he trusted.

Steve had what he wanted: figures committed to black and white of the Children's Department collections before and after adding a judge for his region.

The state had been divided into four quadrants of approximately the same population, and assuming the divorce rate was pretty much equal throughout the state—in fact, the rate of divorce was increasing yearly throughout the state.

Steve did the math from the figures supplied: $883,000 multiplied by four for all four quarters of the year, equaled $3,532,000 for the northeast quadrant of the state alone for the year. Multiplied by four again for all four quadrants of the state, that were divided equally in population and assuming the divorce and rates of birth were uniform throughout the state, would yield $14,128,000 this year in collected child support from the state. Steve could now show that the introduction of a child support judge had increased collections in his quadrant by $152,000 a year over the previous year at the present trajectory of collections, and he wanted to do more.

Steve knew he could double check his figures against the number of divorces printed locally in the newspapers, or against the local court clerk's daily filings.

He also factored in that there were non-marital domestic unions with children, and finally he also subtracted out a factor for dissolved marriages without children.

In addition, Steve took into account a slow December collection of revenue because of Christmas, and an increase in child support collected in April and May when the federal government withheld income tax refund checks from delinquent dads for past due child support obligations.

Steve now had a ballpark figure of the projected revenue of the department for a year just for filed cases. In addition, approximately another $30,000,000 a year passed through the coffers of the Children's Department in collections, salaries, etc.

27

*S*ome time later, there was another after hours meeting in Santa Fe at the Children's' Department main building. Vance talked for a while and then got to the crux of the meeting: "Maybe we can dump that kid?" Vance asked.

George pointed out a fact that Vance did not understand: that Steve Light worked for the judges: "We can't fire him, and if we tried, it would call attention to us. Better to let things settle down. Just sit and wait," he advised.

"Let's see if he's got any dirt in his closet," Len suggested. "I can call some friends at the Public Safety Department and they can check him out."

"Good," said Vance. "At least we'll do something instead of just waiting. What about having Losum call or visit the judges to tell them about the way the kid handles hearings. Increase the pressure on him. Do we have any friends among the judges?"

They all knew the unspoken answer to that question: Vance and Chief Justice Big Jim Richards went back near thirty years.

"I'll speak to Losum tomorrow and see what he can do," said George.

"Let's see if there's any way to dump this kid. You guys think about that and we'll get together later in the week," Vance said.

28

S teve continued to read the Code of Federal Regulations. He wanted to see the Report to Congress based upon the figures that New Mexico's Children's Department supplied the federal government, since the money came from the feds and federal law had implemented the program and granted to the states the necessary funds.

As he sat in his office in the courthouse in Clovis, he pulled out his Albuquerque city phone directory, looked under federal government for a number and dialed.

"Good morning, Senator Templeton's office. Can I help you?"

"Good morning, my name is Steven Light and I'm the child support judge for the northeast quadrant of the state. I wonder if Senator Templeton's staff could send me some information. I'm interested in getting a copy of the Annual Report to Congress of Child Support collected in New Mexico for the past two years."

"Let me connect you to our Washington office. They'll be better able to help you."

He spoke to the Constituent Representative in the Washington office and explained what he needed.

"We'll try to get that information to you within the next two weeks. Give me the address where you want me to send it."

Steve was doodling on an always present yellow legal pad while he gave his address and for a moment kept the receiver to his ear while he scribbled away when he heard it—just a click—after the senator's office hung up. He paused for a second, and then dismissed it as just some static on the line. It wasn't.

Another element of the job was that all the district court judges had secure telephone lines that could not be tapped into or conversations intercepted in any fashion. Thus confidential conversations took place between judges without any fear of intrusion, but Steve wasn't a district judge and his phone didn't have this feature.

Steve continued his circuit riding, heading north out of Clovis on Monday at dawn or on Sunday nights. He had bought a motor home that he used as a night time office and as well as hotel room and kitchen. He even decided to take Luke and Blaze with him most of the time. The dogs slept in the motor home while Steve conducted court. They went with him all over the N.E. quadrant of the state, and after hearings he ran them in parks or around the various courthouse squares. Sometimes the dogs stayed home and Jaylynn looked in on them.

Cindy Dolant continued her slipshod lawyering, forcing Steve to actively question the delinquent fathers about their financial resources and possible hidden assets or other income streams. Steve was polite in questioning. He believed Churchill's words: "You can always be civil to a man, even if you're going to hang him." But while Steve was civil, he was always probing for assets and resources that could be used for child support.

Steve got a call one day while he was hearing cases in Raton. Between hearings he returned the call.

"Judy! How are you? It's good to hear your voice. How did you find me?"

Judy Goodman and Steve had become friends during their judicial clerkship days. After they had worked together at the state supreme court as law clerks for different justices, she had taken the job of deputy counsel for the Public Safety Department. Calling Steve jeopardized her, but friendship prevailed.

"What are you doing these days, Steve?"

"I'm the child support judge from Clovis to Raton."

"Big territory."

"I just bought a motor home as my mobile hotel room, kitchen, and night time study."

"I want to give you a heads up. Someone is unofficially asking a lot of questions about you. I thought you'd like to know. Gotta go!"

Steve made it a habit to go into the Curry County courthouse on weekends when he returned from his circuit. Two weeks had passed when a large envelope arrived from Senator Joe Templeton's office in Washington, DC. Upon seeing it he tore into it excitedly, expecting to find answers to his questions about the Children's Department.

He opened his locked desk drawer and took out the letter the department had sent Judge Thomas with the figures they had committed to paper and laid it beside the report filed with the feds. There were huge variances between the two sets of figures the department said it collected. The difference was $65,000 per quarter for the northeast quadrant alone. Steve felt sure that the same was true for the rest of the state. He knew that all the funds were paid directly into Len Coffee's office in the headquarters building. If the variances were the same in all the quadrants that would make $260,000 per quarter, times four quarters in a year totaling $1,040,000 per year, that he suspected was being skimmed from the child support fund statewide on an annual basis.

Suddenly Steve felt a quiver of fear in his stomach. He thought: "Is this true? Are they really skimming? How long has this been going on? How much money has really been taken over the years?" He had to go to the district court judges. They would know what to do.

Someone else was up early that weekend morning. Vance Arnold drove to his long time friend Big Jim Richards's home in Santa Fe. "This new kid from Clovis has gotten everyone nervous. He's into the numbers, he's pressing our lawyer, he wants to move more cases every month, and has now come up with the idea of taking the certified checks and money orders at the time of hearing. He's really pressuring us. He will force us to change our system. He's already having us use private process servers to speed things up. We've started settling cases with our case workers so we can make use of these funds. Can you stop him and keep this kid from hearing too many cases and rendering faster decisions?"

"Does he suspect anything?"

"I don't think so yet, but he's capable of breaking the whole system. Can you do something?" Vance asked.

"Let me think about it."

"How's the campaign going?"

"I'm going to announce on May first. Can you help again?"

"Yes, I was planning on it, but this kid has got everyone shaken. We need to stop him."

"I'll do something. We have the judges' convocation in Santa Fe in two weeks. All the state's district court judges will be here, that will be a perfect time to quietly speak to some of them. Do you have anything on this kid? What's his name?" Big Jim asked.

"Steve Light. He worked at the supreme court as a law clerk some years ago. Here's a copy of his resume," Vance said.

"I may know him from the court."

"As a personal favor some of my friends at the Public Safety Department checked him out."

"Any dirt?"

"No, he's clean. His girlfriend is the most eligible single women in Clovis."

"Drugs or alcohol?"

"No, he lifts weights at five in the morning. A straight arrow mostly."

"Okay. I'll see what I can do," Big Jim said as he stood and Vance followed suit.

29

Monday morning first thing Steve went to Judge Mann's chambers. There he carefully laid out in detail all that he had learned and the facts that he had acquired and finally showed him the letter Len Coffee had sent on behalf of the department to Judge Thomas and the report filed with Congress in Washington, DC.

"There are major financial discrepancies between what the Children's Department claims it's collecting in its annual report filed with the Department of Health and Human Services in Washington, DC and what they wrote Judge Thomas earlier this year.

"Considering the gravity of the allegations, I'm coming to you. I believe they're into the funds and that that is one of the reasons we have the backlog. They're milking the files by keeping the cases in limbo for long periods of time without bringing them up for hearings. The department's case workers pressure the delinquent parent before there is any hearing and collect fifty or a hundred dollars of the previous court ordered two fifty dollars a month from thousands of files from all around the state. They never file a court case so there's no hearing or record, and all the money comes in as certified checks or money orders making it difficult to trace."

"Steve, I want you to come to our judges' meeting Wednesday after lunch and bring all your facts and documents. Keep pushing. You're doing a great job for us."

On Wednesday, Steve presented his material to the three judges of Curry County. They listened, sober and stern faced. Then came the questions.

"Steve, these are serious allegations. Are you sure," Judge Thomas asked while Judge Mann and Judge Flynn listened hard.

"I don't know for certain. I only know that there are irregularities in financial reporting. All this indicates malfeasance on the part of the Children's Department that leads me to the conclusion that they're skimming the funds."

"Okay Steve, don't do anything," Judge Thomas said emphatically. No letters, no meetings, no allegations, and especially no newspaper stories. Give us some time alone to discuss this and I'll get back to you."

Steve left the chambers and headed for his office in the courthouse. The three remained. "Did you notice his face? He's got a tick. He's nervous," Judge Flynn said.

"Wouldn't you be?" Judge Mann said.

"He's scared," Judge Thomas said, throwing it open to the other two, "but he's never lied to me in any matter. He's always been polite, respectful, and restrained. What do you think?"

"He's been doing a good job for us. We've had problems with the department not moving cases for years," said Judge Mann. "But Bill Losum, the counsel of the Children's Department, called me and said they'd like to meet with us in Santa Fe. They're dissatisfied with his work and would like to replace him. He's called all the judges in the region and asked to meet with us jointly in Santa Fe during a break in the convocation," Judge Mann said.

"Have you listened to the tapes of his hearings?" Judge Flynn asked.

"Yes, I listened to a few. He's thorough and polite. Their lawyer is a mess: sloppy and lazy. He has to advocate for her," said Judge Mann.

"Okay, what are we going to do?" asked Judge Flynn.

"I'd like to call Aaron and Franklin and speak to them about this, see what they think and how Steve's been in their courthouses and their impressions of the department," said Judge Thomas.

"This could get ugly," said Judge Flynn.

"But what if it's true, what if they're skimming the funds? Then we need to take action; to inform the district attorney in Santa Fe where the Children's Department main office is. That's what the statute requires," said Judge Mann.

"What do you think about the Children's Department?" asked Judge Thomas.

"They're notorious for not moving cases. Steve's right. They have cases sitting in our clerk's office for years, never getting them heard; never moving them forward. He's been diligent from the beginning. He's wanted to move the docket; to get matters heard, and to bring his caseload into compliance with the federal statutes and regulations.

"He's done a great job for us. I told him from the beginning to push, and he keeps pushing to move the docket. He's done that and he may be right," said Judge Paul Mann.

"I agree with Paul. Steve's been before me and he's always polite and prepared. He represents his clients well. He may be right that they're siphoning off funds," said Judge Flynn.

Steve walked down the polished black stone stairs of the Curry County courthouse to his office. He knew he had a tic in his face. It had started the day he compared the figures. He was frightened. He thought, *What if some politico or judge is involved in this?* He felt very alone and vulnerable. *"Judge Thomas, Judge Mann, and Judge Flynn are good men and Judge Aaron White is honest as the day is long. I can count on them. But nobody wants to uncover this kind of dirt; nobody wants to be in the vortex of a scandal, especially judges."*

Back in Judge Thomas's chamber the three Curry County judges agreed. "I'll call Aaron tomorrow. We'll see what he has to say, and take it from there. The Children's Department has been trouble for years. Maybe now we know why," said Judge Thomas.

The next morning, Judge Thomas called Judge Aaron White in Tucumcari.

"Steve's been doing a very good job up here," said Aaron. "He comes up here and works well with my clerk's staff. He's prepared to hear cases. I support him in wanting to dismiss the dead wood. Let them re-file or move the cases forward. Some of them have had no action taken for years. About the funds, I don't know. You've seen the numbers, what do you think?"

"Aaron, I'm going to fax you the numbers they sent me and the numbers they filed with the feds. Based on these figures we may have a real problem. There's a discrepancy of sixty-five thousand dollars from our region in just the last quarter. If it's going on across the state, then the question is for how long?" said Judge Thomas.

"Ben, I think we need to meet. What about Santa Fe?"

"That's where the Children's Department wants to meet with us."

"I think Steve should come to Santa Fe too." Aaron said. "He's been trying to rein in the department by himself and now they're kicking and screaming because he wants them to work. He needs our support. In the past five years they've done nothing to move the cases. They file them and they don't move them forward. I bet it's the same thing in Franklin's court too. Steve is right, he should dismiss these cases."

"It's true for us here in Clovis too. They don't move the docket, but what about the money?" said Judge Thomas.

"That's more troubling Ben. If they're into the funds, we need to turn the whole thing over to the district attorney in Santa Fe or the United States attorney. I hope like hell they're not into the funds. We'll get a better picture in Santa Fe."

"Okay Aaron. I've got a case to hear, then I'll fax you the figures. See you in Santa Fe. Regards to your family."

Steve continued his circuit riding; Cindy Dolant continued her excruciating lawyering: it reminded Steve of when he was in grade school and the teacher scratched the chalk across the board so it screeched. She made little improvement and had no imagination or inkling about how to grow as a lawyer or improve her courtroom skills.

In Santa Fe, Vance called George and Len into his office for a private meeting. "That kid's got the numbers. He's only a step away from putting this whole thing together and bringing us all down. We need to act. George, call him here for a meeting with you and Len after work; make him an offer, subtly. See if he bites and joins us. If he does we can set him up for a fall or let him in at our option. Either way our problem will be over. If he doesn't bite we need to get rid of him. I don't want to spend twenty years in a federal penitentiary."

Opening his bottom desk drawer, Vance pulled out a sealed large brown envelope. "Len take this; stay close to George; if you need it, use it. The clean one is in the plastic bag."

Len pulled the envelope across the desk; he opened it; there were two pistols inside, one in a plastic zip lock bag. He showed George.

"I don't like this, Vance," George said, "we don't have to go down this road."

"It's just for protection. Maybe he'll take our 'generous' offer. Then we'll have nothing to worry about. After that we can throw him to the DA, and say we were running our own investigation of him."

The call came into the Raton courthouse clerk's office where Steve was conducting court. "Can you have Judge Light call me in Santa Fe? My name is George Cody I'm with the Children's Department."

Steve returned the call after finishing the day's hearings at 4:45 p.m. "George, it's Steve Light. How can I help you?"

"Can we get together in Santa Fe this week after you finish your cases for the day?"

"I'll be in San Miguel County on Wednesday. I can drive down when I finish. How about Wednesday evening?"

"That's fine. Six o'clock, my office."

"I'll be there."

As both men hung up the phones each wondered what the other had in mind.

Steve thought, *"Why a meeting now?"* and his face started twitching again. His tic had become more pronounced in the week since his meeting with the judges in Clovis. No one commented on it, but it was observed and noted. Cindy Dolant called Bill Losum about it. Steve had also become more tense, and he startled easily. *"Anything,"* he thought, *"can happen on these dark stretches of mountain roads at night. Me and the dogs, thank God for the dogs, we're alone at night in the vast spaces between New Mexico cities."*

Now they wanted a meeting. They knew he had the numbers from Judge Thomas's request. Just the thought and his cheek started twitching again, his stomach knotted.

Steve had an uneasy feeling about this meeting: alone after work on their turf, knowing that he had been assembling the information that could send them all to prison. He sought for a solution. First he told himself: "Don't meet with them alone." Working with Steve at this time was a college senior who was thinking about a career in either law or political science. He had become Steve's law clerk and sounding board. His name was Barnett Leigh called Bart.

Bart was smart and as able as they came. He was good with his pen and a forceful debater. He understood the political game, and had an eye for detail and what motivated people. Steve considered Bart a real asset, and he welcomed his intelligence and hard work.

Steve would have Bart meet him in Santa Fe and accompany him to the six o'clock meeting with George Cody. He'd be a good witness if it came to that and put a damper on the meeting. Steve knew better than to meet alone with Vance Arnold's crew.

George Cody was afraid of Steve Light; afraid of what he knew and was capable of learning. The Children's Department had to rid themselves of Steve or make him complicit in their nefarious plan.

"Len," George said, "I'm not going to meet with Steve Light alone. You can help, and if we need a witness or the meeting takes a wrong turn you'll be there.

You'd better bring Vance's envelope with the two persuaders with you just in case. We're all set for Wednesday at six o'clock."

At 5:30 p.m. Steve met Bart in Santa Fe, a mile or so away from the Children's Department, in a WalMart parking lot that was busy with shoppers. In the motor home, Steve filled in the backdrop of the meeting for Bart.

"George Cody, the guy we're going to meet tonight, is the brains of the Children's Department. He makes all the big decisions that impact thousands of families and children across the state. He's bright, articulate, and forward thinking— he's the future of New Mexico.

"I hope he's not involved in what seems like a big problem, but he's too high up not to know what's going on. He directs the department in every part of the state. If things were different I would've liked working with him—he could have taught me a lot.

"Bart, step back and really listen. Focus on George—one way or another he'll tell us all we need to know—either in words or behavior. Study him.

"I'll be pitching, you see how he hits. Okay, let's head over."

30

It was near six o'clock when Steve and Bart walked through the main doors of the chrome and glass modern building. No one was around. Steve was not concerned: state employees were notorious for leaving work promptly at 4:59:30 seconds p.m. He pointed out to Bart that for security reasons there were no signs or any indication of what went on in the building. Fathers could be irrational when it came to their children, and large sums of money passed through the building, so there were no signs. The building remained anonymous.

From the main hall behind the reception area came a voice. "Steve, is that you?"

"Len?"

"Yes.

"We're back in Vance's office," Len's voice advanced before him as he came to greet Steve and seemed surprised to see Bart. He stuck out his hand and greeted Steve.

"Len, this is my law clerk, Bart Leigh."

"Nice to meet you Bart. I'm Len Coffee."

They shook hands. "George is waiting for us. Let's walk back."

They walked down the deserted, darkened hallway of the headquarters building passing rows of empty desks and computers. No one was in the building but Len and George.

George was waiting in Vance's suite of offices. He got up from behind the desk and introduced himself to Bart, who he seemed surprised to see.

"Why don't we sit over here," indicating the two overstuffed chairs. Len and George sat on the couch facing Steve and Bart in the corner.

George spoke first. "How are things going out there?"

"The situation is about the same. Cases are being opened much faster than they're being disposed of. I hear twenty-two to twenty-four cases a month, about one case per working day, but filings for divorce in the region are much greater than the number of cases I am hearing, even considering that not all couples have children. Many couples who have children have never married, so the divorce rate figure is not an accurate indicator of the number of unsupported children in the quadrant. In fact, the figure is too low. The unmarried couple with children is the profile of a great many of our cases in the region: parents who have never married have children, and then separate with no provisions for child support. So I'm hearing only a small percentage of the cases out there," Steve said.

"What're the impediments? How can you hear more cases a month?" George asked.

"As I've told you before, I'd like to take over the docket and the scheduling of cases. My secretary can send out notices of hearings and prepare summonses for the parties so I can hear six to ten cases a day, thirty minutes each. That would save the department work and build more efficiency into the system."

George glanced over at Len in a telling way. Steve caught this; so did Bart.

"At that pace we could hear between a hundred thirty-two and two hundred twenty cases per month, start to address the back log, and be free of the fine that the state had to forfeit to the feds last year for failure to meet timelines. My office could also prepare the final orders via fax machine and present them to the parties right in court. Then Ms. Dolant could collect the certified checks and money orders right at the hearing. These men come to the hearings with cash on them, they're afraid of being jailed. Let Ms. Dolant take cashier's checks or money orders from them after I rule, at that time. We'd dispose of hundreds of cases faster and efficiently and increase the revenues of the department." At the mention of collecting money at the hearings another telling glance was exchanged between George and Len. "Why is it so impossible to increase the rate at which cases are heard?" Steve asked.

Handing over a piece of paper to George he continued, "Here are the statistics of cases heard in the last six months: one hundred and thirty two cases. I might as well take a cruise! That's about one case per every working day. At this rate the backlog will never be addressed and the state will continue to be cited by the feds."

"Len, go make a copy of Steve's stats for me and Vance," George said.

"Bart, why don't you come with me?" Len said.

"Bart, here are all my statistics on cases heard and the backlog that's not being addressed. Take them with you and make copies for George and Len." Steve was making a last ditch effort for compliance and efficiency in the hearings. He was hoping he was wrong about the money and that George, forward thinking George, would understand and see reason.

When George and Steve were alone, George leaned forward in a more confidential, earnest posture. His tone and manner of speech changed.

"Steve, you've been making it very difficult for us here in the department. You've painted a picture of us to the judges that shows us in a very unflattering light; you've demanded levels of work that we simply cannot achieve. You've become an adversary to the department and are leaving us with fewer and fewer options. We have made mistakes in the past, we acknowledge that, but we are trying to address them. We'd like you on board with us Steve.

"The truth is that in a short time you've tightened our performance and made the entire district for the first time accountable for their cases; so for this we'd like to show our appreciation and initiate a new spirit of cooperation between you and the department. What would it take to have you work with us? What do you want from us, Steve?

"Is there anything we can do to make your life easier? We'd like to keep the cases moving through the system at the same pace they are moving now. There are certain advantages that accrue to us in doing that. How can we cement your cooperation and show you our gratitude? We'd like you on board with us. We can make your life much simpler, much easier, more pleasant. Think about it."

Steve was startled. He wasn't certain what he was hearing. What was George asking him, he asked himself. What was George offering?

Up to now Steve had hoped he had been wrong, that the problems were caused by ineptitude and slovenliness. But now George was making him an offer to become entangled in their web. He could not know for sure, but he got queasy, uncomfortable, and scared all at once, like being in an elevator at the top floor of a tall building when the cable breaks: no salvation seems possible.

The Boy Scout in Steve was indignant and repulsed at the offer, but he knew he could not show his repugnance to George alone face to face. He knew he had to get Bart and himself safely out of this meeting. George's words could be construed many ways, but the tone could not, and of course, there were no witnesses.

Steve responded, "I'm not sure what you're asking of me George, but I probably need to think about it carefully. I need some time." Steve's instinct said

"Get out of this meeting." He was responsible for Bart, and this was a last ditch ultimatum by the department. No telling what would come next.

"Sure, Steve, take some time, think about it and get back to me. Why don't you stop by next time you drive through town on your way north and we can get together again privately, just you and me."

They heard voices coming from the outer office. Len and Bart were returning from the Xerox machine. George sat up straighter. His tone and manner resumed the more formal attitude of the group discussion. "How is Cindy Dolant doing?"

"She needs work in the courtroom; she's slow and leaves a lot of stones uncovered."

The four of them continued talking for another forty minutes. Steve made no accusations. He just wanted to get himself and Bart safely out of the meeting, away from the building, and out of the parking lot.

31

As they drove away he turned to Bart. The first words he uttered to him were, "I think he just offered me money. He was skillful and crafted his offer carefully, so he could deny it, and there were no witnesses. That's why Len took you out of the office. He didn't need a hand copying four pages of documents. No, he offered me money. What happened when you were with Len?"

"He talked about you, and wonders why you're so intent on wanting to hear so many cases faster," Bart said.

"Federal law and a five hundred thousand dollar fine should motivate anyone to move and hear two year old cases." Strengthening his conviction, Steve said, "I have no doubt that these boys are into the money. Now, how do I wake up the judges?

"The judges' convocation is here in Santa Fe next week. They've asked me to come and talk to them about the problems I'm having with the department, and the department also wants to talk to the judges. The showdown will be at the convocation."

Bart looked over at his mentor, whom he admired and respected. He noticed Steve's cheek was twitching again, and now the whole side of his neck and his temples twitched every few seconds.

"Damn nerves!" Steve said.

It was obvious to Bart that Steve had changed in the last two months. Bart thought, *"He used to be so easy going. Now he's a jangle of nerves without his hallmark wit and humor. He's become so intense about these guys and their corruption. He needs a rest. I'm going to stay with him. He's my friend. Maybe he can get some rest before going to Santa Fe."*

Back in the headquarters building, Len asked, "George, does he know?"

"He knows now. I made him the offer. Now we'll see what he does."

"He's strung tighter than a guitar string," Len said. "Well we won't need these now," reaching into his pockets and taking out the pistols.

"Give them back to Vance," George said. "I'm no murderer."

"They were just for our protection if he came unglued," Len said.

"We've got to stop him. He's so close to unraveling this whole thing. We've got to stop him. He's been thinking numbers of cases; if and when he shifts his focus to number of dollars, we're cooked."

"I made him a subtle offer tonight, but he's on a crusade; I don't think he'll take it. We've got to get him off these cases or we're going to take a very long vacation at the 'Big House.'"

"He's just crazy George; but he'll take the offer; give him a little time."

"What did you say?" George asked.

"He's just crazy."

"That's it! If we can ratchet up the pressure on him maybe he'll crack. He's already close. Did you see him twitching?

"If we get him off the cases, we'll have time to cover our tracks, and the judges will take back the cases and fit them into their schedules as a low priority. They won't appoint anyone soon after this because of the dust blown up over everyone, and that will buy us even more time.

"Are any of the judges on our side?" George asked.

"I don't know. Losum has been keeping in touch with them," said Len.

"When he comes in tomorrow tell him I need to see him. We're going to put our own plan in play. The meeting is next Wednesday here in Santa Fe. We've got to derail him. We've got to act first," said George.

Bart and Steve went back to the WalMart parking lot where they sat and talked. Bart began, "We've been through a lot together since I started working for you at Legal Aid. We've become friends. I want you to know I'm concerned about you. I've never seen you like this. You're bristling with tension and fear and anger all the time. This department is consuming you. You are not going to last if you continue like this. Why don't you take a few days off before going to Santa Fe, maybe see a doctor and get some pills. You're in no shape for a meeting with all the judges and the department. You have only till next Wednesday to get it together. How can I help you?"

"I haven't told anyone this, but a friend of mine from my supreme court days who works at the Public Safety Department called me and gave me a heads up. She said some parties have been making inquiries about me, checking my background.

"When I'm on my phone in the courthouse I deliberately wait to hang up after the other party concludes the call, and I hear one and then a second click on my phone line, like someone is in on my phone conversations. I know it sounds crazy, but it's true.

"I'm scared, Bart. I'm in well over my head. If they're into the money they'll stop at nothing. My office is funded by federal dollars. That means they're looking at federal charges not some rinky-dink state charge they could possibly beat or get probation for because of political connections. This is serious, and I'm the one who uncovered it.

"Bart, I know I need help. New Mexico is a big state. A lot can happen on those lone empty mountain roads at night or on the deserted high plains and no one would be the wiser.

"I'm just so enraged at how they have taken advantage of these kids and poor women diverting the money to themselves without any accountability to the law. They've got their dukedom across the state and no one has looked at them because everyone assumes that someone else is doing it, and this has gone on for years. They've been milking the cases. Even now the judges can't accept the idea that they're into the money.

"So I'm scared, and I know my rope is badly frayed. I just don't know what to do about it right now. I'm incensed with their blatant corruption. I thought if the judges knew they'd take action, but I forgot that the term 'with all deliberate speed' means tomorrow or thirty days or the month after that. The judiciary is constitutionally made to be a slow responder.

"If I had to do it again, I wouldn't have taken this job on a bet. It's been hell."

"You need some rest before the judges' convocation."

"Okay, I'll listen to you."

The next morning, a clear, hot New Mexico Thursday in August, Bill Losum, the department's lawyer was asked into George Cody's office. "Bill, Steve Light was here last night. He's on the verge of making a lot of trouble for us. We have the judges' convocation next Wednesday, here in town. I'd like to increase the pressure on him so he'd be forced to take time off—a rest. Can you do it? If he'd miss the meeting with the judges that would be a big plus for us, and there's the chance that without him the whole thing would blow over. Are any of the judges in our corner?"

"One, maybe another with some persuasion, these two don't see what the big deal is all about. Their attitude is 'so the department is slow, it's always been slow, this is New Mexico, what do you expect?' I can tighten the screws on Light. I can visit all the judges, except the ones in Clovis, who are solidly behind him. I'll leave in the next hour. I just need to pack."

Bill Losum had his suspicions about Vance, George, and company, but he was a "short termer" and not in the inner circle. His time as the department's lawyer was coming to an end, but he was not all together an innocent. It was Losum who had advised Raul to schedule Steve only one hearing in Taos and then just one in Raton, forcing Steve to drive the three hundred grueling miles one way from Clovis, just to show Steve who was boss, and as a way of toying with him and punishing him with the schedule for all the trouble he was making. Losum moved easily with the snakes of the department, and was more than willing to drive around to see the judges, bad mouthing Steve and intensifying the pressure on him, as George had asked. He knew it could only raise his stock with Vance and George and would buy him more time to get out of the department 'gracefully.'

After putting Losum on his assignment, George next went to see Vance. He closed the door of the office. "I saw Steve Light last night. He's very close to knowing what's going on."

"What about the offer?"

"I made it; but I don't think he'll take it. Losum is going to speak to some of the judges. He's leaving soon. Maybe we can increase the pressure on Light."

"Good. Keep me posted."

Vance waited for George to leave his office, then he took out his personal cell phone and a scrap of paper from his pocket and dialed. He wanted to send a message to Steve Light, a message he would not forget. "Hello, is Ed there? This is Vance Arnold in Santa Fe." They hadn't spoken in some time, but Vance had once been Ed's guardian angel when Vance was with the Police force in Clovis. He turned a blind eye to Ed's illegal activities in exchange for information about certain criminal characters in Clovis. A relationship sprung up between them born, not of friendship, but of necessity and survival.

A man's gravelly voice came on, "Hello."

"Ed, this is Vance Arnold, I'd like to meet you tonight, Interstate 25 this side of Las Vegas road mile marker twenty-three coming north from Santa Fe at seven p.m.."

As arranged, two cars pulled off the side of the Interstate. A big man wearing a white tee shirt and blue work pants got out of his car and into the passenger side of Vance's car.

"It's been a while, Ed. How are you?"

"Pretty good, Mr. Arnold."

"You still work at the sanitation department?"

"Yep, it was the only job I could get after getting out. I'm still at the dump."

"We've both come a long way since the streets of Clovis. How many years are you out now, Ed?"

"It will be ten years this November around Thanksgiving."

"You been straight all that time?"

"Yes sir."

"Well, I was glad I could help you at your trial and after you got out. Not everybody gets a police officer to testify for him on a manslaughter charge. I always thought it was justified, but the jury didn't see it that way."

"I'm past that all now, Mr. Arnold. I appreciate your help in getting me my job. I'm grateful."

"You're probably wondering why I called you after all this time. I've got a problem: his name is Steve Light. He's making my life very difficult. I want to send him a message, to teach him some manners and respect for his elders. Here's a little something for your time and troubles." Vance pushed over an envelope containing $500 in cash. "I'm sure you can handle it," he said to the big man. Ed looked into Vance's eyes when they finished talking ten minutes later to make certain he understood what he was supposed to do. Vance's eyes were stone cold hard and insistent.

Steve finished his week's cases and headed back to Clovis, there to see Jaylynn and try to bring some normalcy back into his life. They would be together, and he could talk, and she would listen attentively to Steve with concern and caring and love.

When Steve returned to Clovis he was tired, but called Jaylynn and set a date for Saturday morning to wash their cars. On Saturday a bright, blue near cloudless day greeted Steve. He loaded the dogs in his pickup and headed to Jaylynn's house just a couple of miles away.

She was happy to see him after a week's absence, but she saw he was tired and his face showed the tensions and pressure of the week. He was gaunt from the week's combat. Jaylynn could see he needed a break.

Steve let the dogs scamper free as he connected the hose and doused Jaylynn's Honda. He was dressed in jeans and sneakers and a white tee shirt, she in cutoffs and a tee.

Jaylynn had the pails, rags, and liquid dish soap ready outside. "We'll do your Honda first. I'll hose it down, then we can wash it. Then we'll do my pickup," Steve said.

Luke and Blaze loved water, they were crazy for it, they were water dogs—golden retrievers—and were clamoring around the cars barking at the hose once Steve had turned it on. The dogs ran about Steve as he sprayed down Jaylynn's car catching the water that splashed off her car on their faces.

Steve may have been tired, but he was still full of mischief and seeing the joy of the dogs for the water he turned the hose on Luke, and Luke instead of being driven back by the water jet ran directly into the stream getting his tawny coat and Steve drenched. Blaze, tagging behind the more adventurous Luke, did the same thing. Now both dogs started jumping on Steve leaving their muddy paw prints on his white shirt.

Luke and Blaze jumped and ran through the water jet and the puddles forming in the driveway happy and gleeful. Steve was transported watching his dogs' joy in the water. They were like school boys at their favorite water hole on a hot spring day who had just skipped out of class to escape the boredom and burdens of school to swim and romp at their swimming hole on a hot afternoon free from all the cares and burdens of life, just frolicking and relaxing and lulling in the sun and water. The dogs were like those school boys, giddy with excitement at having cut out of school and at the illicit pleasure they were having at the water hole: the sight of the water and its feel against their faces and bodies. To Luke and Blaze there was nothing finer in the world than the warmth of the sun and feel of a cool jet of water against their bodies.

"Mister," Jaylynn said mockingly, "is this a dog wash or a car wash?"

Steve in a burst of impish I—can't—resist— this—temptation swiveled the hose on Jaylynn as she soaped the roof of her car, aiming the high pressure stream of water to bounce off the roof of her car and hit her squarely in the face.

Mad as a wasp, she threw the sponge at Steve, striking him on his forehead. He retaliated and fully drenched her. She ducked behind her car. The dogs were loving it, chasing the water jet wherever it was turned. In triumph, Steve turned the hose on the dogs once again. But when his back was turned, Jaylynn came from around her car and dumped her bucket of soapy water and rags over Steve's head. There are some advantages in being a tall woman.

Now all pandemonium broke out. Steve was chasing Jaylynn with the hose until she was fully soaked and defeated; the dogs were barking and jumping through the water stream; they were all drenched like ducks swimming in the rain. Thinking he had vanquished his enemy, Steve thought now was as good a time as any to wash the dogs. He put down the hose and called Luke over and squirted some dish soap into his coat, lathering him. Steve's strong hands and fingers worked over Luke's back, shoulders, and ribs, his finger on Luke's tawny bronze coat turned the dish soap into a full lather. Luke's rugged, strong muscles rippled beneath Steve's motion up and down his body. Steve even washed Luke's head and paws.

Blaze, seeing all the attention Luke was getting, barked for her own coat to be washed. Steve rinsed Luke then answered Blaze's summons; repeating the process with her, paying special attention to the top of her head, her ears, her underbelly and tail. Her golden blonde coat was alive and covered in suds.

Surreptitiously, while Steve's attention was fixed on the dogs, Jaylynn seized the hose. Paybacks are hell, and Jaylynn in full retaliation turned the pressure full force with the narrowest stinging stream on Steve, revenging her earlier dousings. Steve was wet to the core. Even his sneakers squished and sloshed as he chased her, but he was driven back by the vigor of her attack as she continued to blast away like "Machine gun Ma Barker."

Steve tried to wrestle the hose from Jaylynn's grip, but at two feet she was deadly. Then in desperation, Steve just encircled Jaylynn in his grip, but she still fired away, the dogs jumped on. They became a melee' of water and suds and dog coats, a consortium of confusion, a carnival of chaos, fun, and fur. The dogs jumping now on Steve, now on Jaylynn: it didn't matter. The dogs were jubilant, rollicking, and barking. Steve started laughing so did Jaylynn. He felt utterly happy, exhilarated for the first time in months, and Jaylynn cherishing the moment—her man was himself again—untroubled by the demands of work. She relished her victory despite being soaked and paw printed.

"I surrender," Steve said. "Truce. We're even now."

"Give me your word it's over and we'll wash the cars if I let you off," she said.

"I promise. Truce. I surrender."

"No fingers crossed or any of that stuff," she said knowing his ways and raising the hose directly at his face. "Give me your word."

"I promise no funny stuff. I surrender."

"Good. Let's finish the cars then go in and change."

The cars were washed; the dogs were rinsed and dried, but they took to rolling on their backs in Jaylynn's front lawn to finish the job in the scent of the grass. All had thoroughly enjoyed themselves. Luke and Blaze stayed obediently on the front stoop, waiting for their master, true goldens.

Jaylynn and Steve went inside to dry off change and have lunch. She made grilled cheese and tomato sandwiches and they drank milk, and after eating they continued to sit at the table talking.

Steve talked about the matters that were consuming him: the department's ineptitude, Cindy Dolant's poor preparation, disrespect, and deceit. He did not tell Jaylynn about the suspected corruption, he didn't want to draw her into this mess. He was circumspect about that aspect. She didn't need to be a witness and the fewer people who knew, the easier to deal with the poison.

As he continued venting, she tenderly took his hand and placed his palm against her smooth cheek. Then she brought his hand to her lips and kissed his hand, as if each kiss took the weight of another incident with the department or Cindy Dolant from memory, as if each kiss was a healing salve that told him his work was important, that poor women and children around the state mattered, that his days in the courtroom and the longer nights studying the statutes was for an important purpose, that it was worth it all. These healing salve-like kisses eased Steve's mind and had a soothing effect.

"You shouldn't chuck it all, but fight back against the inertia, the laziness, the disrespect," she told him. "You count in the lives of children and women who have no voice, no one to listen to their needs." And her kisses upon his hand were a sign of her love, her caring, her support for what he was giving, each kiss a gift of tenderness and affection.

When they finished talking, Steve took the dogs home. They had waited patiently, true to their master. He would return Saturday evening and take Jaylynn out for dinner at one of Clovis's better restaurants.

As he left Jaylynn thought, *"This morning Steve was like he used to be before the department and their miserable lawyer."*

There were no cases scheduled for Steve the week of the convocation to allow everyone time to prepare and travel to Santa Fe. Steve met with Bart at the Curry County courthouse Monday and Tuesday. They had a lot of material to review before Steve left for Santa Fe. "I've been to the doctor and got some pills. I also promised him I'd take some time off after my meeting. Between you and me, I'm ready to chuck the whole thing. I just want to get through this meeting then we'll see where we are and if the judges are going to do anything."

Together they worked until Tuesday into the evening. Steve practiced his oral presentation several times. He had audio tapes of cases which supported his contentions of Cindy Dolant's insolence and poor lawyering. Bart listened carefully and objectively, without taking his friendship or loyalty to Steve into consideration, and he found that the evidence was strong and convincing. Bart felt the facts supported the conclusion that there was corruption in the Children's Department.

Vance Arnold was up late too in Santa Fe, thinking, culling the facts. He knew the figures he supplied to the judges were at variance with the Annual Report. *"How do I explain that if that kid brings it up?"* he thought over and over. Tomorrow he, George, and Len would meet with the judges.

"If that kid presents the set of numbers in the Annual Report to Congress and the variant set of numbers we sent Judge Thomas earlier as evidence against us and the judges believe it, they'd turn the whole matter over to the district attorney here, a grand jury would be impaneled, and the feds would be notified.

"That kid, that kid. How do I keep him from meeting the judges?" Vance thought, as he sat up in the quiet of his home past midnight. He went into his study and from his bottom desk drawer he pulled out his small private phone book and placed a call. He didn't hear the faint click on his line, since the headset was on his desk when he dialed and held the book open. Downtown, in a small auxiliary office building, two men listened as Vance dialed the number. The office they sat in, in the federal building annex read: Federal Bureau of Investigation.

Vance had made monthly "loans" to Big Jim's campaign. Big Jim had already declared himself a candidate for the Democratic Party's nomination for Joe Templeton's United States senate seat. Jim had been testing the waters for months. He was present at all Democratic fund raisers in the state, increasing his visibility at party functions among the faithful whom he would have to sway if he were to win the primary. Attending party functions, he was always introduced as the current chief justice of our supreme court and candidate for the United States senate. The state law in New Mexico was quirky, allowing a sitting judge to be a candidate for another office until 30 days after the general election. If Jim won the primary and the general election he would resign his judgeship, and if he lost, he would retain his current office. It all worked perfectly into his carefully thought out plans.

Jim had friends in the media around the state write stories on his rise from magistrate court to the state supreme court. His family was always featured in the articles in pictures and text. He bought advertising time on TV, radio, and in the newspapers. 'Big Jim Richards: The common man's common man' was his campaign slogan, and the theme he emphasized again and again in the news articles, advertisements, and in his personal appearances around the state.

Jim was always trying to gauge the reception of these articles and advertising, his name recognition, and his viability as a candidate for United States senate.

But there were changes in Big Jim, and Karen was the first to notice them. At first she attributed the changes to his candidacy and excused his sometimes short and snappy answers to her questions as just part of the stress he was under. All the tension of campaigning was upon him, his non-stop schedule of personal appearances around the state. The interviews for TV and radio, the advertisements' taping, and distribution: he was involved in all aspects of his campaign and it consumed 24 hours a day seven days a week. So she made excuses for him.

At a rare dinner at home one night, Karen had made Jim's favorite: beef brisket. She sat across from him at their small intimate kitchen table. The children were gone now—off to college or married.

"How is the campaign going?"

"Oh, the usual," he said in a clipped voice that said 'leave me alone.'

"I was just trying to make conversation," she answered, hurt, and then fell silent as they continued eating.

"I'm sorry, Karen, I'm under a lot of pressure with the campaign and work. I didn't mean to be short." He explained the quirk in the law that allowed him to remain on the supreme court and run for the senate. They called it "Beecham's shuffle."

"Back in the nineteen thirties," Jim explained, "Governor Beecham could not succeed himself as governor because of term limits, so he ran for United States senate and got the legislature to pass a law that said any sitting office holder could run for another office without resigning his current post until 30 days after the general election. Back then the governor wagged the stick and the legislature jumped. The legislators thought that sending Beecham to Washington for six years was a good way to get rid of him, so the law's been on the book all these years and has become a time honored custom here in the state. So one way or another, I'll be in office come November seventh, but if I could just win that primary."

But Karen saw beneath his reassuring explanation. In the last few months several nights a week when he was home Jim would toss and turn and then wake up in the middle of the night, turn on the lights, and go sit in his study alone with his thoughts, just staring vacantly at a favorite New Mexico landscape painting. Sometimes he would search the bookcase for a book to distract him enough so that he could return to bed and sleep. She found him in the study several times at 3:30 a.m. doing that. But sleep was elusive. He sought it, but it would not come, so there was no peace or ease of mind as there once was. One night she found him thumbing through the Bible looking, looking, she didn't know for what, she didn't know about the series of "loans" from Vance's department to the campaign. She only knew that he was lost.

It had become a New Mexico folkway that her politicians had always come up with schemes and plans to pilfer the public coffers. Now Jim was into it and it was eating his conscience.

He would sit alone during these long night vigils and think, *"I've come a long, long way from Curry County magistrate court to chief justice of the Supreme Court of New Mexico. Taking the money is wrong. I know that, but without the money there is no campaign, no United States senate seat. I can pay it back when I'm elected. I can do a lot of good for the people of New Mexico in the senate. The President needs another vote to push through his programs. I could be that vote. I can't return the money to Vance now; I'm in too deep. I need the money now, before the primary, to buy ads on TV, and radio and in the papers. But all I've stood for these past years is gone. I can make up for it,"* he thought quickly so as not to let the previous thought take hold.

"*I can be honest again and deal straight with people. It's just for a little while. Just this once."*

Over and over again he would ruminate in the study. He looked for comfort in the Bible, but he could not renounce the thing he'd done and he would not return the money.

Vance, he thought, had been hardened years ago by the police work. He always thought everyone he arrested was guilty. Sometimes they weren't, but that never stopped him. He operated in the realm of gray, skirting the line of truth, coloring his testimony to get a conviction, for Vance, the result was justified and he had little trouble or recriminations with his conscience. Jim had been different, clean, at least, up until now.

Jim, who was trained in the law, thought differently than Vance. Judge Reuben Fuentes had honed that difference. Even before that, as an assistant district attorney he looked at both sides of a case; he looked hard at the defendant; he studied the law and listened to the testimony, and only then crafted his case or plea offer justly. He had always maintained his objectivity, his honesty, while still being an advocate. That's what made him such an outstanding judge: he could simultaneously gauge both sides of a case judiciously.

But Vance would not take the money back. Jim was on an immoral path and he didn't know how to turn back. Disgrace and jail were on one side, and the United States senate on the other. Either was a possible outcome. He closed the Bible. He did nothing. He languished in his own indecision, and maintained his present course. With the same objectivity that had characterized his career Jim admitted to himself, "I've become poisoned by my own ambition."

That's as far as he got in his soulful late night battles with his conscience. He'd turned the lights off as he made his way back through the house. It was a long walk back to the bedroom. His integrity was gone, lost. So was his self-respect. And he would do anything to retrieve them, anything except give the money back and end his campaign. He was no longer an innocent. He wandered back to his bedroom and beside Karen began his intermittent angst-filled attempt to sleep.

"Are you okay?" Karen asked, stirred awake by his return to the marital bed.

"I'm fine, I just couldn't sleep."

"Do you want me to make you some herbal tea or hot chocolate? It will help you sleep."

"No, I'm fine now. I'll be okay."

"Sure?"

"Yes, go back to sleep. I didn't mean to wake you."

"I'm worried about you."

"I'll be okay. Go back to sleep."

Jim slipped beneath the covers next to his wife, and she turned to him, molding her body next to his. She stroked his face and kissed him. Then her hand slide down his thigh, but he rolled over and silently rebuffed her, and she, rejected, rolled over to her side of the bed and resumed her sleep. Jim lay still, alone, and awake. Neither his conscience nor his body slept.

32

He arrived late at chambers the next morning. He always arrived before 7:30, but it was now after 9:30. Everyone was in chambers: the law clerks and Theresa Lucero, his secretary.

"Good morning Judge," Theresa said, curious to know why he was coming in late. She thought it had something to do with his campaign. And then she thought, *"Being chief justice allows him the luxury of not having to explain his actions to anyone—except the voters, of course."*

"Good morning, Theresa."

"Judge, I have your speech ready for the convocation. Do you want to go over it? I have plenty of time today to make changes."

"That's fine Theresa," came Big Jim's answer from inside his office. That's the way they worked, communicating to each other from their separate desks; neither of them going to the other's room unless they had a draft opinion that needed some specific changes. Their intra-office communication skills was an ongoing long distance conversation back and forth across the rooms all day long.

Theresa's office was the ante-chamber that sat between the judge's large office on the right and the law clerk's office on the other side of her office to the left.

Theresa also served as the relay system between the judge and the law clerks. She was the lynch pin for all communications in chambers. She was "Queen" of the courthouse, as secretary to the chief justice, and had been his secretary ever since he moved to Santa Fe to sit on the high court. Like his wife, she carefully studied her boss, anticipated his actions, his needs, his moods. She was also clairvoyant.

"Theresa, have you seen this or that file or brief? Where is that draft opinion Seth is working on?" he would ask. With her magical powers she could find anything—divine where it was—almost like witching for a water well. From a stacked pile of papers she could pull a single page with a needed phone number, or an important document out on the first try. Lately, using her powers of divination, she sensed something was wrong with her judge.

"*Maybe he's sick? Maybe it's the stress of the campaign? I don't think it's his wife—she's a gem. But there's something. He's got those rings under his eyes and he's not fun like he used to be. He hasn't joined in the jokes in chambers or with the other judges and their staff. He's just not himself anymore. He doesn't smile. He's lost his zest,*" Theresa thought.

"Judge, when will you be leaving for the convocation?"

"Sometime tomorrow afternoon, that's when the judges from around the state will start arriving. We have a cocktail hour at La Fonda Hotel tomorrow before dinner."

He came out of his office sometime later. "Theresa can you get this draft to me quickly? I've made some changes and I'd like to circulate it today."

"Here you go Theresa," Judge Richards said as he handed her the draft opinion. She noticed that the papers were slightly fluttering, and looked at his hands: they were shaking, ever so slightly. Jim caught her eyes looking at his hands, and then their eyes met, but no words were exchanged; yet the knowledge was there on both sides.

"*Yes, he's sick,*" she thought.

And he thought, "*She knows something's up, and so does Karen.*"

Karen and Theresa weren't the only ones to notice changes in Big Jim. He had always had warm relations with the other members of the court. There was during his tenure mutual respect and strong bonds among the justices.

In the not so distant past the court was divided with petty jealousies and rivalries, but during Big Jim's tenure these seemed to have receded into the background. Jim fostered mutual respect and strong bonds among the justices. He emphasized that each member had a pivotal role to play. Under his leadership a sense of duty and purpose emerged in guiding the state they all loved, in resolving problems, and in advancing the rule of law in New Mexico. All the justices had reached the apex of their careers, and here, where Jim had worked so hard to craft consensus and respect among the members, the justices noticed changes in their chief.

During oral argument one day Big Jim dove into the argument of one young defense attorney, peppering her with question upon question, talons bared, never giving her a chance to answer his queries. The case before the court was an appeal of a first degree murder conviction. The defendant had been convicted of killing a state Police officer who had made a routine traffic stop on Interstate 40. The state trooper approached the defendant's car and asked him to produce his license, registration, and proof of insurance. The defendant stepped out of the car and when he couldn't produce the registration or proof of insurance, he pulled a gun, and shot the trooper three times in the chest at point blank range, immediately knocking the trooper to the ground. The trooper had on a bullet proof vest and was still alive, but stunned. The defendant straddled the trooper's body and deliberately put a bullet through his head. The trooper died instantly.

The defendant then walked briskly to his car and sped away. Passing motorists called 911; others stopped to render aid. The blue and white emergency lights of the trooper's car were still flashing. It was nearly noon. The young trooper lay dead in the emergency lane of the Interstate, his life extinguished, but his emergency lights still flashed brightly.

Screaming down the Interstate came several state Police cruisers. The whole incident was videoed and audio recorded by the troopers' relay system that allowed dispatch to see and hear all the troopers' actions in the field.

The killing had been senseless. Several roadblocks were immediately established in both directions of Interstate 40. Witnesses said the defendant's car headed west. Fourteen miles down the road at a road block, state troopers, with shotguns and assault rifles at the ready, stopped drivers and asked them to step from their vehicles, produce licenses, registration, proof of insurance, and open their trunks. There were approximately twelve troopers at each road block, east and west. Six officers did the immediate stop and searches, the other six provided coverage and support with weapons, their safeties off, their fingers on the triggers.

Police cruisers were splayed out across the highway in a "V" formation, funneling all traffic into a single lane and allowing only one car at a time to pass through the security net. Passersby had given a description of the shooter and his car. He was a tall blonde male in a white tee shirt driving a large older sedan, maybe a Buick or some other American car.

A dark older model Buick was approaching the road block when the driver suddenly accelerated, made a U turn across the wide grass median, and started down the Interstate in the other direction. Six troopers started after him. The big Buick and the state cruisers rocketed down the highway at over 100 miles an hour. The shooter did not realize there was another road block ahead 12 miles down the road to the east.

The pursuing troopers radioed ahead. At the road block they were ready. As the Buick approached the driver accelerated. He aimed the Buick for the thinnest part of the barricade of Police cruisers lined up across the highway in double file broadside except at the extreme right side of the barrier where there was only one cruiser, and that's where the suspect piloted his Buick. The state troopers opened fire on the vehicle, aiming for the tires and radiator. The car kept coming. The big Buick was a speeding fortress on wheels at 100 m.p.h. It punched through the last cruiser on the right, hitting it between the front and rear doors, and thrust it out of the way. The troopers kept firing, now aiming at the driver, no longer at the vulnerable parts of the car. The Buick flipped and somersaulted sideways three times, then came to rest. The wheels were still spinning; the initial impact and the gunfire caused steam to come from the radiator.

The troopers held their fire, but had their weapons poised for a final assault. They did not come too close to the vehicle, fearing a fire and explosion from the gas tank. The car's engine was still running and fluids spilled from under the hood onto the macadam. There was no movement in the vehicle.

They waited five minutes. Several troopers approached the vehicle, and shut off the engine while others stood at the ready, tense and set to fire. They pulled the suspect from the car. He had been shot and had several bleeding wounds and said only, "I wished I killed more of you." He then passed into unconsciousness. An ambulance was called; the medical team saved his life.

After recovering, he was tried for the murder of the young trooper and convicted. The jury voted him the death penalty and the judge imposed it.

Now, three years later, the New Mexico Supreme Court was hearing an appeal brought by the public defender's office. The state was represented by the attorney general's office.

The appellate public defender, Carol Ames, a determined young woman and able attorney of about 35, who had appeared before the court on several previous occasions, was prepared, articulate, and skilled. Although she found the defendant's actions morally reprehensible, she believed that he had a constitutional right to competent representation and she sought to provide it. Her job and her belief was that the law demanded no less of her.

In the courtroom Big Jim took her on: "Ms. Ames, you mean to tell me that this conviction should be overturned because the defendant was not properly

Mirandized at the roadblock, when he was wounded, bleeding, made the incriminating statement, and then fell into unconsciousness?"

"Your Honor, the..."

And Big Jim sharply cut her off, "Ms. Ames, how can you tell me that the officers should have Mirandized him at the scene while he was bleeding and before he made the statement, 'I wish I killed more of you?' Do you expect this court to agree?"

Ms. Ames knew she was on thin ground. The case against her client was substantial, but she had a job to do and she intended to do it. Whether she liked or didn't like her client or his behavior was not the point: her duty was to represent him ably even though he had been convicted as a cold blooded killer. The rest of the justices knew this; knew she was just doing her job, and it was pretty apparent, barring some gross injustice, that someday the defendant would be executed for his crime. But Jim kept chewing on her.

"Do you really believe, Ms. Ames, that this case turns on that confession? What about the relay video, the eye witnesses, the matching ballistics tests of the weapon found on the defendant at the time of his apprehension?

"You come before us today with this scant issue. Is that what you're appealing—this issue?" Big Jim asked irascibly, cutting her off again.

"Isn't this a premeditated murder, Ms. Ames? Didn't the trial judge proceed cautiously in this case because of the grave possible outcome that the defendant faced? Frankly, I've seen no evidence that would mitigate the punishment. Nor have you presented any argument that would give me reason to overturn this conviction: none, Ms. Ames none: whatsoever. This defendant callously ended a state trooper's life and as a consequence he has been given the severest penalty from a jury of this state. Can you show us anything in the record at trial or within the factual context of his arrest and apprehension that will impede the wheels of justice in meting out the penalty when all this defendant's appeals are exhausted?"

Up and down the bench the other justices looked at Jim and then at each other. They had never seen this testiness in him before—it was out of character. They all agreed in principle that the appeal was going nowhere, that it had no grounds for success, and that Ms. Ames was only doing her job—trying to save her client from the lethal injection. This was her duty. There was no need to humiliate her. *"What,"* his colleagues wondered, *"is going on with Big Jim? Where was his usual civility and kindness to young lawyers?"* It was Big Jim's behavior, rather than the appeal, that occupied the other justices' attention.

There were still other changes in Big Jim. Karen noticed that on those nights when he wasn't flying around the state campaigning, he played with his food at dinner. Using his fork and knife, he moved the position of the food on his plate from one side to another without taking a taste; sculpting the potatoes; sliding the vegetables; barely eating. She gently would ask, not wishing to stir the lion, "You're not hungry?"

And he'd answer, "No, not really."

So they would sit quietly at dinner without talking one or the other, a coolness and quiet distance coming between them. Karen felt less and less able to reach him. Jim, she thought, had lost interest in her as a woman. The change started about six months ago. At first she thought he was just getting older, but she came to believe it was something deeper and more isolating. Something was strangely amiss with her husband.

At breakfast Wednesday morning he said, "I'll be at the judges' convocation this afternoon."

"I wish I didn't have to be at school."

" If you need me, call my cell. I'll be at La Fonda."

"Okay. Do you have your credit cards in case you need them for anything?" she asked in a tender, almost motherly way.

"I'm okay." He got up from the breakfast table, bent over her as she sat finishing up her coffee and toast, and kissed her on the top of her head, and saying, "I love you," as was his habit.

She listened as he drove his car from the garage and backed out of the driveway. She waited just a moment, then called her school. "Mary, this is Karen. I won't be in today through Friday. Something came up in the family and I have to take care of it. I'll be back on Monday."

Karen showered. And she thought to herself, *"There'll be a cocktail party tonight and a formal reception dinner Saturday night. I'll need a new dress, and I'll have to get my hair done today and buy a few things. I need to look attractive as the wife of the chief justice and perhaps the next United States senator."*

Big Jim headed for the supreme court. He wanted to practice the speech he was to make to the judges of the state before his law clerks again and then take care of a few details in some opinions before walking over to La Fonda on the plaza.

33

Vance Arnold, George Cody, and Len Coffee were in Vance's office going over the numbers with orders not to be disturbed. Len sat and kept quiet.

"Okay, let's go over this again," Vance said as he sat at his desk. George sat at the table in front of Vance's desk with his private, personal laptop open examining spreadsheets as Vance peppered him with nervous questions.

Vance asked George, "How much have we 'borrowed' from the fund this year?"

"A little over one million."

"How much have we contributed to the judge's campaign so far?"

"Two hundred eighty-five thousand. We're prepared to lend him half a million for his campaign."

"Can we deliver?" Vance asked.

"That shouldn't be a problem, except for Steve Light," George said.

"What are we going to do with that damn kid?" Vance asked.

"This meeting will take care of him," George said.

"What if Light has figured it all out by now?"

"We'll have to scramble," George admitted. "We can resurface nearly a million dollars back into the fund and show the rest of the money making its way through the system from the various regional offices in files that the regional case workers have settled," said George.

"That should satisfy the federal auditors, and anyhow the feds are more interested in making the five p.m. flight back to Dallas than really inspecting our records. We can snow them. Remember they only audit once every three years. That gives us lots of time."

But Vance persisted: "What happens if Light convinces the judges we're into the funds?"

"We could be screwed. But he doesn't have all the numbers, and without them it might be hard to do. The numbers we sent Judge Thomas are the proof, but they were only for one quarter, and we can always say we made a clerical error. And even if Light is able to prove anything, the judges will be slow to act. They'll want to discuss it, debate it, agree among themselves, and then go over it all again to make sure that they're on solid ground before they do anything. That will give us the time we need to resurface funds. But if they do act, they'll turn it over to the district attorney in Santa Fe and he'll investigate. That's our cue to head for Venezuela. They won't honor their extradition treaty with the United States."

George paused, then said, "That's how the cards look face up on the table. We've got to get through this meeting and then we're in the clear."

Vance leaned back in his chair looking comfortable and at ease. He failed to tell George or Len about his own plans for Steve Light: for the "Big Man" to deliver a message to Light that he wouldn't forget: that he was playing with the big boys now and there was a price to pay for meddling.

Vance was different than George and the judges. He acted fast, and acted ruthlessly, when threatened. He struck whether provoked or not; he was not cunning or subtle; he just acted, not like George who used his analytical skills to weigh risks and outcomes and plan for eventualities. Vance was one-dimensional; if he had a problem he crushed it.

Steve Light left Clovis early Wednesday morning soon after sunrise, a bank of clouds growing violet, red, then orange to the west as the new day's sun rose higher in the eastern sky, the vast horizon of the plains stretched out before him, the plains met the sky out in the distance, a place that he could see but never seemed to reach, the horizon was ever elusive, just out of grasp, always only a few more miles ahead. Driving past large ranches near Fort Sumner and Santa Rosa that were thousands of acres in size he saw herds of cattle welcoming the new day, making their way to water and morning forage. These sights greeted Steve as he drove to the judge's convocation.

Steve planned to drive into Albuquerque and then head north on Interstate 25. It was a straight shot into Albuquerque once he hit the Interstate at the truck stop near Santa Rosa, and from there it was just west on Interstate 40.

Steve loved New Mexico; he took pride in and was humbled by her encompassing natural beauty and historic past. He loved to drive around the state, often stopping to read at state historic markers. He took back roads and explored new villages and vistas, and his job gave him the freedom to search out the half-known treasures of his state: sites of historic interest, new streams to fish, or places to let Luke and Blaze run and scamper free, small quiet town cafes and restaurants of Mexican or western American foods where he could sample a new style enchilada, or chicken fried steak with biscuits and gravy. He even found secluded swimming spots where he'd skinny dip alone in the moonlight, the dogs either jumping in or wading near the bank. Yes, Steve loved New Mexico.

His job took him from the mountains and lakes in the north to the mesas and high plains in the central region and from there it was not too far a drive to the edges of the Chihuahuan Desert in the south. As he drove, Steve looked at the ever changing New Mexico landscape: the mountains were concertos in stone; the mysterious desert's burnt reds and oranges, were as foreboding as a black squalled sea; and the rivers pouring forth from upland mountain snowfields flowing broad and sweet and true, bringing life to all in their path. His state had been the frontier just ninety years ago, when men rode horses and carried guns. Some of the old timers' stories told of women wearing shawls and long dresses and 45 colts strapped around their waists. It was the way of the West. New Mexico had its wild and varied history; she cast her magic upon all who rode beneath her sky. Nowhere else was there land so open, majestic, and free.

Steve could picture the once enormous herds of buffalo moving across the plains from Kansas westward to the high plains of New Mexico. He had found arrowheads in streams in the south and wondered what the Native Americans who had fashioned them thought of the vast beauty of the land. At night when he was out with the dogs he would look into the deep black night and see the 'pathway of the stars' across the heaven. Occasionally, a single shooting star would spark a streak for just a luminescent second across the vastness of eternity, and Steve felt his insignificance beside the night sky with her dazzling jewels. As hard as it was to believe, the nights, the sleek, naked nights of New Mexico were even more compelling, more beautiful than her brazen, sunlit days.

Steve drove into Albuquerque on Interstate 40 through the Tijeras Canyon, the rock and mountain gateway to the city on the east. The young city spread out before him as he emerged from the canyon heights. Down from the foothills of the Sandia Mountains he headed west into the city's heart. Miles below a ribbon of green lay in the valley: the Rio Grande, and her surrounding woods and fertile agricultural land. Across the horizon at the opposite edge of the city, nearly 50 miles away, lay the three dormant volcanoes marking the western boundary of the city.

Steve left the highway at San Mateo Boulevard and headed south. He hadn't noticed the white Ford that had been behind him a mile or so since he entered the Interstate near Santa Rosa. Nor was he aware that the two men in the white Ford were contacting others. Two other cars pulled onto the street, following at an unnoticeable distance behind. One car was an earth colored Honda, the other a Chevy truck, and each had a single passenger, staying back a comfortable distance from Steve Light's gray pickup with the camper shell. He had left the motor home and the dogs at home for this trip.

Steve headed south towards Kirtland Air Force Base. He knew there was a Lota Burger hamburger stand there that made the best green chili cheeseburgers around and he had a yen for this New Mexico delicacy.

Traffic was always heavy down by the base entrance and Steve was eager to get lunch and head up to Santa Fe. He ran a yellow light. An Albuquerque Police car turned on his lights and pulled Steve over.

"Your license, registration, and proof of insurance," the officer said, coming to the car window, taking the documents, and walking back to the patrol car. Steve knew he was in the wrong; knew he'd have to wait. Several minutes later the officer approached Steve's pickup again.

"Your registration doesn't match. This vehicle was reported stolen. "Please step out of the truck," the cop said authoritatively.

Steve opened the door and stepped out, attempting to talk to the officer. The cop told him to turn around. He was patted down, then the cop cuffed him, Mirandized him, walked Steve over to the Police cruiser, and put him in the back seat.

Steve was scared. He had never been arrested before. He knew the vehicle wasn't stolen. It had been his for the last three years, but how was he going to prove it before the meeting at the judge's convocation.

The cop opened the back door of the cruiser; pressed on Steve's head to get him to bend and Steve crunched into the back seat.

Steve hadn't noticed, but another person sitting in the front seat of the cruiser in plain clothes, a woman. She turned around and smiled at him.

Steve's eyes opening wide in astonishment. It was Crystal Deland, the accountant specialist at the Curry County courthouse. They were friends; she had always helped him out; helped him navigate the finances and courthouse personalities safely.

"Don't worry," she said, "you're not under arrest." He was separated from her by the steel mesh wiring between the officers' front seat and the back seat for the criminals. "Although you did run that light," she continued. "We've been worried about you lately, Judge Thomas, I, and some others. We didn't want you to go to the meeting with the judges. We're not ready yet. You've stumbled into something much bigger than you realize and you're right to be frightened. We need your help. But you've got to agree."

"Who's we?" Steve asked.

"That will become clear later. What do you say? Haven't I always looked out for you?"

"Yes, you have."

"I know it's hard to trust right now, but give me a chance."

"Okay," was all Steve said.

Just then a tow truck had come on the scene. The cop put his head in the front door, "Where do you want the pickup towed?"

"Ask the guy in the white Ford," Crystal said.

The cop came back in the car. "Where to?"

"We're going to the inn on base."

"You need some help, you know that?"

"Yes," Steve said, admitting to Crystal what he already knew with tears streaming down his face.

"Those bastards are into the money aren't they? They ran me ragged, sending me to Taos and Raton, scheduling just two fifteen minute hearing, over six hundred miles of driving round trip just to break me. Just to punish me, because I was looking at their level of performance and suspected worse. I'll never give in."

"Okay, that's the attitude that got you this far. Now you're going to relax for a while and get strong again and let us do the work. But we need your cooperation; we want to know all that you know and how you figured this out. Agreed?"

"Agreed. I want those bastards."

"Let's get you to a place where you'll be safe. We've taken a room for you at Kirtland Air Force Base Inn. No one will be looking for you there."

Steve was uncuffed. "Steve, are your truck keys in the ignition?"

"Yes."

"Gerry," Crystal called to the Albuquerque Police officer, "Let's get him on base. Don't run your lights—we don't need to draw any more attention to ourselves." It became obvious to Steve that Crystal was acting as more than just an accountant specialist at the courthouse in Clovis.

The officer headed for the San Mateo gate of the base. The Honda preceded them, and two other vehicles followed: a standard sized Chevy pickup and a white Ford.

The military policeman at the guardhouse waved them all through after the Honda's driver showed his I.D. The cars proceeded to the inn.

Crystal approached the reception desk. "We have a reservation in the name of Crystal Deland, Department of Justice." Steve just listened.

An Air Force sergeant manned the inn's reception desk.

"Yes, here are your room keys. The rooms are adjoining each other on the second floor around the back of the building as requested: rooms two sixteen and two seventeen."

The party now consisted of Crystal and Steve, the two men in the Ford, and the drivers of the Honda and white Chevy pickup.

"Let's go." When they settled in their rooms Crystal came to him.

They sat on beds facing each other. The four men were in the adjoining room talking. She saw that Steve was weary and exhausted. *"He had fought the good fight,"* she thought.

"We want you to rest and get strong again so you can testify against them. We think they've been stealing money from children and mothers for the past five years. With your help we can put them away.

"It's going to take us take ninety days to trace some of these money orders and certified checks that have been paid for child support. You're going to have to stay here for the next ninety days. I'll be updating you, and I'm certain we'll have a lot of questions for you on an ongoing basis.

"You'll have security here; you'll be protected. We're going to circulate a story that you were killed in a car crash on Interstate Forty today and put it out in the New Mexico newspapers, radio, and TV stations. An agent will inform your family that you are under the bureau's protection, but you're not to call anyone, especially in Clovis or in the state. Understand? Why don't you relax and get some rest before dinner? I'll be right next door, then I'll be heading back to Clovis after you settle in. You've got friends, Steve, and people are looking out for you. You've done an amazing amount of work for us.

"Tomorrow morning we want you to get some counseling while you're here so you'll be strong and healthy. Everything will be taken care of for you. We need your help with the investigation and later at trial."

"What about my dogs?"

"Barbara from the clerk's office in Clovis is going to take care of them. She'll feed them every day. Is that okay? They'll be well cared for and you'll see them again soon."

Steve didn't like being separated from his dogs, but he didn't have much choice.

"Get some rest," Crystal advised. "The guys will walk you over to the officers club later to get some dinner."

34

eantime in Santa Fe, Vance, George, and Len were meeting in Vance's office on and off throughout the day. Big Jim was preparing to walk over to La Fonda from the supreme court.

The bureau was busy planning the "death" of Steve Light out east of Albuquerque some 45 miles. A simulated accident took place on the Interstate involving a gray pickup with a camper shell that looked a lot like Steve Light's and a second vehicle. There was smoke and fire and blood. The New Mexico State Police were called, an ambulance was summoned with sirens and lights blaring, and a body was put on a gurney and covered with a sheet from head to foot, and then taken by a slow moving ambulance to the medical examiner's office in Albuquerque.

In the back of the ambulance were two F.B.I. agents. "Okay Harry, you can come back to life now." And the man under the sheet sat up and pulled off the sheet.

"Now that I've had my near death experience, does anyone have a sandwich or a cup of coffee? Dying made me hungry."

"You're going to die again when we roll you into the M.E.'s office," said one of the agents.

Towards the end of the day Vance, and Len were in Vance's office when George burst into with *The Santa Fe New Mexican* newspaper: "Look at this! Steve Light's been killed!"

"What?" said Vance.

"Steve Light's been killed in a car accident on Interstate Forty," George repeated.

"That sonofabitch is dead?"

"Yes."

"How'd it happen," Len asked.

"He was killed in an accident on Interstate Forty forty-five miles east of Albuquerque and died at the scene. He was en route to the New Mexico's judges' convocation being held in Santa Fe. A memorial service will be announced by the family. That's all it says," said George.

"We're rid of that kid," said Vance, "let's go get a drink."

"Well, now at least part of our troubles are over," said Vance.

"We just have to hope he hadn't already shared his information with the judges," continued George.

"No, he was coming here to do that. He was going to spell it out to them when he got here," said Len.

"I think we're in the clear," said Vance. "We just have to keep our cool with the judges and let them appoint a new judge to replace Light when they're good and ready. I don't think they'll want another mess like they had with Light. What time is it?"

"Just after six," said Len.

"Let's have that drink," said Vance.

They walked out into the waning sunlight and looked for a place to buy a drink and celebrate.

That evening all the New Mexico papers announced the death of Steve Light.

After they left Vance's office and the building, two janitors, a woman and a man in their work uniforms entered the rooms, leaving their cleaning cart just outside Vance's office door. The state had contracted a janitorial company to do the cleaning of state buildings so the janitors were always changing.

"Where do you want to put it?" she asked.

"Inside the smoke alarm detector. Just take off the facing." In thirty seconds they had completed their task. They emptied the trash, dusted, and swept the floor, then left, rolling their cart out of the office in the empty building.

A mile away Big Jim was walking into the La Fonda lobby for the cocktail reception at the start of the judge's convocation, greeting colleagues and their wives in the lobby near the registration table, when walking into the lobby he saw Karen looking beautiful in a new dress and some silver and turquoise pieces of Indian jewelry. He hadn't expected her. He smiled, his big warm smile, the smile that she hadn't seen for six months. The prospect of another evening away from home didn't warm the cockles of his heart. "What are you doing here?"

"I didn't want you to be alone. I missed you."

"What about school?"

"I took a few days off."

Jim was relieved that Karen had come. They talked of small things while Karen stood by the registration table with Jim welcoming colleagues from across the state.

"This old hotel is still so beautiful, so full of charm, and history," she said.

"After the cocktail hour, I was going to eat in the hotel restaurant, but we can go out if you like?"

"Here is fine," she answered.

"The convocation starts tomorrow morning at ten. That will give some of the other judges time to drive over in the morning. The whole gang is here. It'll be good to see them all. I have some private meetings scheduled between the formal sessions. I'll be pretty busy, but there's an agenda and excursions for judge's wives, husbands, and significant others who came.

"After dinner we can take a stroll around the plaza. It will be cooler after sunset," he said.

They ate in the glass enclosed courtyard restaurant of La Fonda. Above the glass partition of the walls were bright colored hand painted Mexican murals. The dining room gave the feeling of being both outdoors and indoors simultaneously because the glass ceiling let in so much light.

Karen and Big Jim were enjoying their dinner. Jim still couldn't get over that Karen had given up school just to be with him. He thought to himself, *"I'm lucky to have a wife like this. She still surprises me after all these years,"* and he beamed at her.

In Albuquerque, Steve Light and his F.B.I. detail were also readying for dinner. Crystal had already left, heading back to Clovis. It had been a long day. Steve was tired and hungry. He'd be happy for sleep this night, he thought. Tomorrow started his de-briefing and counseling appointments on base.

Two agents and Steve walked out of the door of their base inn room and onto the outside walkway to the stairs.

They had to pass a maid's chart to reach the stairway. Just then the maid came out of the room.

"*Abogado* Light! *Abogado* Light!" She called. "It's me, Anna Sanchez, from Clovis. You helped my son Roberto when he got in trouble. Do you remember?"

"Hello Anna, yes I remember. It's nice to see you. How's your family?"

"We're doing much better. When we moved here, my husband got a job as a janitor in the schools and I work here at the inn. My son got married and got a job, and the other children are well. Things are good. It's good to see you again."

"Thank you Anna, it's good to see you too. My regards to your family."

The two agents stood by silently, unconcerned, but to Steve this spelled trouble, and indeed it did.

Anna went home that evening and there on the front page of her Spanish language newspaper was a picture of Steve Light, her son's former Legal Aid lawyer who had been killed in a car accident earlier in the day. *"Something is wrong,"* she thought.

"Patricia, this is Anna in Albuquerque," she said in Spanish. "Something's not right. I just saw and spoke with *Abogado* Light here in Albuquerque. Yes, I know him. He helped Roberto when he got into trouble over there. Anyway, the paper here says he died in a car crash this morning.

"He's fine. I tell you, I just spoke to him at the base inn, where I work, just before I came home."

Crystal Deland and the F.B.I. had not counted on this. Steve knew the power of the informal family networks that existed among Spanish families and crossed state lines. Within two hours Spanish Town Clovis had suspicions that Steve Light was not dead. And from Clovis to Santa Fe was only a phone call away.

"Margarita, this is Cousin Ida in Clovis. I have some news for you. Your husband works with Judge Light from Clovis, no?

"Well the papers say he was killed today outside of Albuquerque, but my friend Sylvia said she spoke to her cousin, who spoke to another cousin, who said she saw Judge Light tonight at the Air Force base in Albuquerque. That he spoke to this friend and he is alive."

"Thank you for the news. I'll call Len. He's not home from work yet. How's your family?"

Fifteen minutes later Len, George, and Vance were congratulating themselves in a local watering hole when Len's cell phone rang. "Rita, I'm having a drink with Vance and George".

Then there was quiet. Len's face drained of color; he tightened his grip on the phone; his finger turned white; his jaw clamped tight, contorting the muscles in his face. "Are you sure?

"Okay, thanks, I love you too. I'll be home when we finish."

Len looked sickened as he closed the phone. George saw the look, "What?"

"Steve Light is alive. He's at Kirtland Air Force Base in Albuquerque. The feds have him."

Silence seeped across their faces as the specter of a future in prison now rose before them.

"We've got to get Light," Vance said. "Let go back to the office."

Three blocks away from the office a white van with no windows was parked at the curb. On its sides were painted the logo: "Always Ready Cleaning Company" and a Santa Fe address and phone number. The janitors from Vance's office were inside testing their listening device when Vance, Len, and George entered the suite of offices that made up Vance's work area. The janitors started listening and recording the conversation taking place.

Upon entering the office, Vance said, "I don't like this. We've got to do something before they call a federal grand jury. I'm not spending the rest of my life in prison."

Vance was impetuous; he would act on instinct without thinking, and that made him like a shark: very dangerous and very unpredictable.

"George, what do you think?" asked Len, hoping to tamp down some of Vance's fire.

"We could surface a good portion of the money, return it and place it in the state's accounts, but the agency's records are on computer now, and a duplicate set is stored off site in a secure state vault—we'd be unable to destroy or alter them. We have copies of all the records at headquarters and other copies exist at the regional offices around the state. Even some case workers have some of the records on their personal computers; so we can't easily destroy all the records.

"I need to think about this alone. I'm going for a walk. I'll be back in a little while. Len, you stay with Vance. Don't let him shoot anyone until I get back," George said in mockery, but half seriously, knowing Vance's mercurial rages.

After George went out Vance left the rooms on the pretext of going to the restroom, and celled to set up a meeting in northern New Mexico. He would get away to keep the rendezvous during one of the breaks at the convocation. He was now beyond the point of sending messages.

George walked towards the cobblestone streets surrounding the plaza and the narrow streets in downtown Santa Fe. He was too absorbed in thought to take in the quintessential Spanish colonial architecture of the Palace of the Governors, the seat of Spanish power, where the timeless Native American jewelry sellers would sit each day with their silver and turquoise hand crafted goods.

He thought as he walked: *"Despite Vance's predisposition for violence, we can't kill anyone—least of all a judge. We can't destroy or alter all the computer records. The state already has a copy of them. But we could create a fall guy: Bill Losum. Make him deputy director in charge of finance and collection. We could then surface the money into an account with his name on it.*

"Or we could just wait it out and see what the feds come up with, but knowing them, if they convene a grand jury they'll have all their ducks in a row and marshal a strong case.

"The records go back, but with some effort by the feds, they'll be able to trace the money trail back to us—we weren't very deceptive or sophisticated in moving the money, even though we did use that bank in the Cayman Islands.

"No, we'll have to think of something."

Steve Light was terrified since seeing Anna Sanchez. He knew the power of Spanish family networks, the informal string of family members, cousins, and friends that extended across Arizona, New Mexico, Colorado, and Texas. Steve remembered how the janitors in city hall and the Police Department in Clovis used to report the political doings to his Hispanic support staff at Legal Aid. Steve knew things at city hall before the mayor did, all because a Spanish janitor had seen something in the trash and taken home the discarded draft of a letter for his English reading daughter to read, or took it by the Legal Aid office to have it deciphered.

Steve guessed rightly. Before the day was over his premature death would be known as a ruse in Clovis and beyond. The two agents left with him didn't believe it when he expressed his fear. They had just been recently posted to Albuquerque from Wisconsin and Michigan, and were unfamiliar with the folkways of the Hispanic culture in the American Southwest.

Steve was feeling very insecure about his protection and rightly so. Anna would see him again tomorrow, and the next day, and the day after that, and she would wonder who these men were around him. She would figure out something and share it.

The months of overwork and fear were taking their toll on Steve. Having gone it alone against a powerful department of state government, fear clouded his judgment. He again expressed his fear to the agents protecting him, but they minimized the threat: "She's only a maid."

Steve wanted to get as far away from the inn as he could. He wanted to run. He thought he had made the case easy for the bureau; all they had to do was connect the dots and Bart knew most of the information between the dots. Bart could fill them in.

Steve thought, "*I don't have a car. I have some cash and my credit cards. I need to get off base and as far away from here as possible. I can catch a bus or a train and head out of 'Dodge' to my sister in Ohio, her family and friends.*" Steve kept his thoughts to himself and kept off the phones. He figured that his room was wired for video and sound, but perhaps not the bathroom.

He could, during the course of the day, casually take the things he would need on a trip and put them in the bathroom. Dawn would be a good time to make his move.

At 5:00 a.m. Steve was up and within 15 minutes he was out the bathroom window and at the base guardhouse pretending to be jogging off base. He was alone, but free and, he thought, out of danger.

Now he had no protection, but he was anonymous, faceless. He took a city bus to the Interstate Bus Station and bought a ticket for Denver. It would stop in Santa Fe: that could be dangerous given Vance Arnold's connections.

Albuquerque to Denver was a straight shot about 440 miles through all of New Mexico and a good chunk of Colorado. Steve wandered around the bus station for a while, bought a baseball cap with the abbreviation ALBQ on it to hide his face, and boarded the bus. He walked half way down the aisle, and took a window seat on the driver's side of the bus. As the sun rose and he put on his sunglasses. He carried a shaving kit, but had no other luggage or food other than a half eaten breakfast burrito that he had purchased from a woman vendor outside the bus station.

A few minutes later the bus pulled out of the Albuquerque terminal and headed north to Denver, with quick stops in Santa Fe and Raton before crossing the Raton Pass into Colorado and on into Denver.

At 7:00 a.m. F.B.I. agent Todd Atkinson opened the adjoining door to Steve Light's room. He saw the bathroom door closed and heard the shower and went back to his room.

"He's already up," he told his partner Dan Morris. "He's in the shower."

It was another twenty minutes before they realized their charge had fled.

They drove quickly around the base, hoping Steve was jogging at the track like some of the servicemen stationed on base. Then they drove to the guardhouse.

"He left early this morning. Here's the video of him leaving the gate area jogging."

"We need to call Williams. He's running this operation."

When they reported Light missing there was an explosion on the other end of the phone. "You don't know where he is! You'd better get off you asses and find him pretty quick! If something happens to him I'll have you skinned, tanned, and tacked up on the barn wall! We've been working this case for nearly a year and you lose the star witness. I hope you like winter 'cause after this you're both headed to Nome!

"Check the airport, rail, and bus depots. What happened over there that made him run?"

"He saw a Spanish maid here at the inn last night who was a former client's mother and she recognized him. He got pretty scared after that."

"And you're just telling me about this now! You find him, and find him quick!

"I'll send Casey and Robinson back out to the base to help you. Check out before that maid sees you, and have her interviewed by Robinson. Find out who she talked to, and put the fear of God in her to keep her from talking."

Steve Light sat on the bus looking out at the Sandia Mountains just on the outskirts of Albuquerque. There was a grassy plain at the foot of the mountains. The mountains themselves looked like they had been pressed up by God from inside the earth and burst through the crust twenty million years ago to their staggering height. Now, however, the eyesore of a casino lay on the plain and marred the majestic view of the mountain range.

The bus arrived in Santa Fe at 6:45 a.m. A few passengers got off and one or two got on. No one sat next to Steve. He was free to be with his thoughts, but they were racing.

Who would Anna Sanchez call? When would they discover he was gone? Would they try to stop the bus en route and take him off? Could he get safely away to Colorado and then on to Ohio? He could take a plane from Denver to Toledo. He'd be with his older sister and her family then. He'd be safe.

Questions, doubts, fears clouded his mind, obscuring the facts and the reality. He had exposed the corruption in the Children's Department by a fluke. He stumbled into it unawares, just trying to do a good job and move the cases. But now there was little doubt that beyond the case backlog there was much more that was amiss in the Children's Department.

The bus rolled northward out of Santa Fe heading for the New Mexico city of Raton, the bus would stop there, and then go on up into the Raton Pass through the mountains and into Colorado.

"I need to relax," Steve thought. *"I can't go on like this. I must quiet my mind or sleep until we get to Denver."* And then his mind would start up racing again. *"What if I had done this? What if I had done that? What if I called a press conference and exposed them to the public? Calm down,"* he thought. *"You're leaving this all behind. Just make it to Denver. Denver's the first leg on the way to safety, if only I can keep myself from unraveling."*

Agents Atkinson and Morris had checked out of the inn. They had not seen Anna Sanchez and had met up with agents Casey and Robinson.

Robinson was in charge, "Okay. Todd you and Dan start at the airport and see if our boy has taken a flight out of New Mexico. Then check the train and bus depot downtown. Here's his picture from the newspaper."

An hour and a half later Atkinson and Morris contacted agent Robinson. "He's taken the bus to Denver. The ticket agent remembers him from this morning. He left at five-thirty. The bus arrived in Santa Fe at six forty-five a.m. and left again at seven. Do you want us to have the bus stopped?"

Robinson thought for a second, "No. Where does the bus make its next stop?"

"Raton, New Mexico at ten thirty a.m."

"Okay, put an agent on the bus at Raton. Let Light know he has some friends and we're concerned about him and need his help. Don't scare him! He's already been spooked by the maid recognizing him."

On the bus Steve continued debating with himself. *"If I had done this. Maybe I should've called him. Why didn't I see that?"* On and on went the interior debate, that was all his mind would allow him to focus on. That and getting safely to Toledo. He knew he was in trouble; he was restless and agitated in his seat. He tried sitting back, but shifted from one distracting position to another didn't calm him down.

Back in Albuquerque Casey and Robinson found the maid at the inn. The two well dressed men asked her if she was Anna Sanchez as they approached her while she was taking some sheets from her cart to make a bed in a guest's room.

"Yes, I'm Anna Sanchez."

"This is Agent Robinson and I'm Agent Casey of the F.B.I. We'd like to talk to you."

"I have done nothing. I was born here."

"No, it's not about your citizenship; we'd like to talk with you about lawyer Steve Light.

"The *abogado*?"

"Yes."

"You saw him here yesterday."

"Yes I recognized him; he was my son's lawyer in Clovis when we lived there. I don't know why the newspaper said he was dead. I saw him, and talked to him."

"Did you tell anyone that you saw Lawyer Light alive?"

"Yes, of course. I told my husband, Francisco, and I called my cousin Patricia in Clovis. I told her I saw *abogado* Light here where I work in Albuquerque. Is he in trouble? He helped our family; we like him."

"No," but we'd like you to tell no one else that you saw him. Can you do that?"

"Okay."

"If you can't do that, then we're going to have to take you downtown for questioning. You understand?"

"Yes, I understand. I will not speak of him again."

"Okay. Thank you," the two F.B.I. agents said then turned and walked away.

Anna wondered what kind of trouble *abogado* Light was in. "But I will not talk of him again. I have my own troubles," she said to herself.

Even when she talked to herself in English Anna spoke in the melodic cadence of the Hispanic Spanish speakers of the southwest, with a lilting upswing on the last word or syllable of each sentence. It was very pleasing to the ear, this English that took on the vowels and intonation of Spanish.

35

Vance Arnold was asleep at his home when Steve Light's bus stopped at the Santa Fe Bus Depot—not three mile from Vance's house. Had he known, Steve Light might never have made it across the state line of New Mexico into Colorado.

For Vance it was a big day. He, George, and Len, were to meet with the judges of Steve Light's quadrant in the afternoon, after the convocation had recessed for the day. The meeting was important and he knew that Steve Light was alive and providing the feds with information.

Vance also had a private meeting with Big Jim. Vance knew he was on the edge. So was Big Jim if the F.B.I. could string the evidence together and, with Steve Light helping them, that seemed probable.

After lunch, the judges of Clovis, Tucumcari, Las Vegas, Taos, and Raton were in a small conference room in La Fonda. Sitting across the room from them at another table were Vance Arnold, George Cody, Len Coffee, and Bill Losum, who had joined them that day.

Judge Aaron White chaired the meeting. "Mr. Arnold, as you know Steve Light died yesterday en route to this meeting. So to make a determination as to his effectiveness and of your or his grievances doesn't seem necessary. However, some of the information that Steve Light shared with us before his untimely death are of concern to us, and I speak for all the judges when I express these concerns.

"The cases are not being heard in a timely fashion. There is a backlog in all the districts in our part of the state. Cases have lingered in my judicial district for over two years before having a hearing set. Steve Light brought that to our attention. This is true not only in Tucumcari, but also in Clovis and the other cities in the region. Many children are hurt by these delays. What do you intend to do about the backlog?"

"Judge White, the Children's Department is working diligently to address this problem. We've added more staff to the regional office in San Miguel County to work exclusively on the backlog. These new workers are just coming up to speed to handle the old cases. We have fully computerized the entire office in San Miguel County which services all your courts. This will improve efficiency."

"Mr. Arnold, the federal government requires that all cases take no more than ninety days from time of initial filing to final disposition by the child support judge. Nowhere in our region is this being done. As a result, the federal government penalized New Mexico five hundred thousand dollars for failure to meet these deadlines. That money could have been better spent in New Mexico helping the people in our state.

"Steve Light made the first concerted effort to bring this to our attention, and it was obvious your department did not like that or him for his efforts to bring you into compliance. Instead of working with him to reduce the backlog you impeded him in his efforts."

"Judge, the problem with Steve Light was that he was too young. He didn't take into consideration the way state government works. He was a young man in a hurry, and that is not possible in a department of our size."

"But what about the law, Mr. Arnold?" Judge White asked. "What about the ninety day guidelines set by the federal government and the financial penalties imposed upon our state by your failure to meet them? You own a home in New Mexico, Mr. Arnold?"

"Yes, Judge."

"Do you pay your mortgage on time every month, or do you tell to the bank give me another six months or a year? Is that the way you do business?"

Vance was taking the brunt of the criticism and was feeling under siege. His face was grim and dark and his eyes focused on Judge White. He tried to contain his anger. Aaron White was not the man who caused this humiliation—it was Steve Light—and he would deal with Steve Light later.

Judge White continued, "Wasn't it Steve Light who instituted the use of private process servers to increase attendance at hearings? And didn't he also institute entering orders at the time of hearing instead of waiting for your office to type them, which took anywhere from two weeks to two months to circulate? Didn't Steve Light dictate the orders over the phone to his paralegal and have her type them and then fax them to him for his signature right at the time of hearing, when all the parties were present, so that collection could begin sooner, thus increasing your department's revenues and meeting the federal time guidelines? And lastly, didn't Steve Light want your attorney to start collecting money orders or certified checks from these fathers at the time of hearing when they felt the pressure of jail time before them? These were all Steve Light's ideas, Mr. Arnold, and your department fought him every step of the way in spite of the successes he was having in bringing the department into compliance."

Vance was coming unglued at Judge White's comments. He started to sweat visibly and stammer when he attempted to answer the stern accusations. "I don't know about all these details, but my deputy, George Cody, can best answer them."

"Judge White," Judge Bass said, "In defense of the department, Steve Light was trying to move heaven and earth and he wanted to do it all now. I agree there is a lot of inertia at the department, but Steve Light was young and needed more seasoning."

"Perhaps Judge Bass makes a point in your favor Mr. Arnold. But let me ask you, how many cases are currently filed and open in your office for our quadrant, including those not yet filed in the court clerk's offices and those that are in the court system?"

Vance knew that Light had tallied the number of cases, both the unfiled and filed, in the various courthouses of the region and felt certain Light had turned over the numbers to the judges. Vance was compelled to tell the truth, something he did not want to do.

"Judge, there are a total of twelve thousand open cases in all the districts in your region, with six hundred thirty-six currently in the various courthouses."

All the judges, including the sympathetic Judge Bass, glanced tellingly at each other.

"And how many new filings a month?"

"There are over four hundred new filings a month in your quadrant."

"So we have four thousand eight hundred new cases being filed a year. How do you propose we reduce this backlog if only two hundred sixty cases are heard a year?" Judge White asked.

Vance fell silent at this question. He had not been challenged like this for many years. He had always dealt from a position of strength and authority. Now his incompetence was revealed and he seethed with anger, but had to control it before the judges. Someone would pay, he promised himself.

"I think Steve Light's suggestions for reducing the backlog were positive and we intend to implement them."

"How many cases a month does your office set for hearing, Mr. Arnold?"

Vance also knew Light had sent the judges a census of the number of cases heard in their districts during the month.

"Approximately twenty cases per month were being set for hearing before Steve Light."

"So the backlog is interminable, Mr. Arnold? It will just spread on and out into the future without ever being addressed?" Judge White asked with some stridency in his voice. "Mr. Arnold, may I suggest you take the next thirty days to come up with a plan that will start to whittle away at our backlog."

"Yes, Judge."

"And get back to us with your plan."

The rest of the judges in the room sat stern and stone-faced. Judge Bass had thought the problems were just in the personalities or just in isolated counties. He never imagined it was pandemic throughout the region.

Now the scope of the problem was clearly set before them all. Even those one or two judges sympathetic to the department now took it seriously. Steve Light had been right, but Judicial Restraint had kept them from acting sooner.

What didn't occur to the judges now, as it didn't occur to Steve, was the possibility that the backlog was used to further their corruption. This was beyond the ken of their current horizon.

The bus sped northward up into the New Mexico highlands towards Raton. The weather had turned wet, the sky gray, promising a late season storm up in the mountains to the north. As the bus spun along the wet Interstate its tires made a wusssshing sound that filled the passenger compartment and drowned out all other noise with the exception of people sitting and talking next to each other. The driver came on the intercom. "Folks, we're ten minutes from Raton, New Mexico. We'll make a twenty minute stop there. Time enough for a cup of coffee and some eggs if you'd like. Then we're up into the pass and through this storm and on into Colorado and Denver."

When Steve got off the bus, the air smelled clean and fresh, cleansed by the rain and snow that continued to fall lightly, and the nearness of the mountain forests: Steve could smell them. The rain continued falling forming large puddles in the depot parking lot, the puddles had become iridescent with the rainbow colors of gasoline and oil residue lifted from the parking lot surface, loosened by the rain and snow, and as Steve carelessly walked through these puddles on his way to the restaurant drops of water splashed off his shoes and back into the puddles, and Steve thought, *"If only this whole affair would be like these drops of water, and just fall from my mind back into the large puddle of non-thinking so I can have peace."*

He ate some breakfast. The eggs, toast, and hot coffee warmed him inside. He was a little more relaxed now that he would be heading north into Colorado.

The station master announced over the loudspeaker re-boarding of the bus to Denver. Two new passengers boarded at Raton; one was an old woman carrying two large, old fashioned hat boxes, and Steve was glad she by-passed him and took a seat further back in the bus in an empty row of seats with plenty of room for her and her hat boxes. Next came an ordinary man of average weight and height about fifty-five years old. He wore a white shirt and light brown tweed sports coat and carried a small overnight bag and coat. He wore black framed glasses, was neatly groomed, and was looking for a place to sit. As he came to Steve's row he asked, "Mind if I sit here?"

"No," Steve answered.

And so the man settled into the aisle seat next to Steve. He put his small travel bag and coat in the rack above his seat, and as he sat down his sports coat separated and Steve saw a pistol in a shoulder holster. Steve became frightened, but had little choice but to stay put. His mind started racing again. Was this friend or foe he asked himself. But he reasoned it would be impossible for someone to shoot him on the bus. Then his fear took hold again and he felt he had to get away: to run, but there was nowhere to go. He was trapped in his seat on the bus, fear running like contagion through his mind.

The rain continued, and as they climbed the mountains north of Raton it started to snow—the wet snow that comes with the spring in the West. The bus slowed its speed. The flakes pelting the warm bus windows melted on contact. As the bus climbed higher, the snow intensified and started to stick to the windows and blanket the ground.

"Looks like a heavy spring storm," his seat mate said, turning and smiling.

"Yes," Steve answered tersely not wanting to start a conversation.

But his seat mate didn't give up. "I'm headed north on some business. Glad I didn't fly. How 'bout you?"

"Denver."

"Do you have business there?"

"No, just want to see the city."

"I went to law school in Denver," the man said, "really enjoyed the city. Great place to live and raise a family."

Steve thawed a little. They spoke the same language. "Did you practice in Denver?"

"For a short while I was in private practice. Then I took a job with the feds and stayed with them twenty-five years."

"What did you do?"

"I worked for the Department of Justice: The Federal Bureau of Investigation."

Steve now knew it was no chance occurrence that this man was sitting next to him.

"I retired last year after twenty-five years service, but I still do some work for the bureau. My wife and I moved down to Raton a year ago and I opened a small law office just to keep busy and help pay the bills. I like living in a small town. The people are friendly and I enjoy outdoor living: the fishing, hiking, and camping. It's been a good move for us. How 'bout you."

"I'm a lawyer too from Clovis, New Mexico."

"That's south near the Texas line. A lot warmer there than here," the man said.

"That it is—back home the farmers are laying in the crops about now. The days are warm and sunny and it smells of spring," Steve said.

"It won't be spring in Raton for another six weeks. Do you like farming?"

"I really want a small ranch some day. That's part of why I live in New Mexico. Anyway, why are you carrying a weapon on board an interstate bus? Isn't that illegal?" Steve asked pointedly.

"I'm here to protect someone. His new friends at the bureau are worried about him, and he could be in danger. The bureau called early this morning for emergency help."

"I see. And you're convinced he's in danger?"

"Yes, very much so. His enemies want him any way they can get him. He's learned too much and is in danger."

"And you're here to protect him?"

"Yes."

"What should this person do?"

"Stay off the telephone. Listen to his new friends; keep a low profile; don't contact anyone in New Mexico; and don't speak to the media."

"What happened that put him in so much danger?"

"He stumbled into something much bigger than he realized against very powerful men, who will stop at nothing to keep him from making disclosures. They don't want to go to prison."

"What would you do if you were in his place knowing what you do?"

"I would get to a metropolitan area, take a plane to somewhere I felt safe, cooperate in the investigation from afar, and not step foot in my state again until summoned by a federal grand jury or asked to testify in court by his new friends with guaranteed protection."

"What about his new friends' failure to protect him earlier on base?"

"That was a bad mistake made by rookies and senior people are sorry about that, but his help is essential, and the top people apologize for past errors and no more mistakes will be made in the future he can rest assured. He should come in, as the spies say, 'out of the cold.'"

"Would he be in danger on this bus?"

"No, it's not likely."

"What's your name?"

"Retired Special Agent John Woods of the F.B.I. Here is my I.D.," showing Steve his credentials and badge.

"I'm Steve Light, child support judge from Clovis."

"I know. Nice to meet you. I've heard about you."

"You're here to protect me?"

"Yes, I'm going to ride with you to Denver and accompany you to the airport so you can travel to somewhere where you'll be and feel safe, and where we can contact you. Agents will meet your plane and take you to your destination and work with you to establish what went on in New Mexico in the Children's Department. Does that sound okay?"

"Yes, that sounds fine."

"Before you fly out we'd like to get a statement from you about how you figured this out. This has been going on for a while and no one caught it but you."

"Okay."

"So where are you going?"

"To my sister's in Toledo, Ohio. I'll feel safe around her and her family."

"You're still going to need some counseling."

"I know that."

"If you want to testify, we want you strong during cross examination. We don't want some defense attorney tearing you apart piece-by-piece on the witness stand."

"I want those guys. They put me through hell. They did everything they could to de-rail me. I wanted to make this judgeship work so badly; to address the backlog; to get these funds to the kids and mothers faster. And those bastards in the department fought me every step of the way. And now I learn that it wasn't for principle or even department interest, but so they could steal the money. I'm angry all over again when I think about it."

"It's good that you're so passionate about this. Your indignation and anger will help you when you testify and will get you back on your feet faster. The bureau will get you to Ohio safely. We want you to get strong again so we can get these guys."

"What were they doing with the money? Where was it going?"

"I don't know exactly. My assignment was to locate you, befriend you, protect you, and get you safely to a place where you would be comfortable and the bureau could work with you at length. I don't have all the facts. We were scurrying around trying to find you this morning. But I'm certain the money was percolating into their personal accounts."

"Have they hired someone to kill me?"

"We don't know for certain, at least not yet. Why did you leave Albuquerque? You were safe on the base."

"One of the maids at the inn recognized me. I represented her son when I was a Legal Aid lawyer. It was only a matter of time before they would have found me."

"But why did you leave?"

"I got scared. The two agents with me didn't have a clue about the cultural network of Hispanic people here. They were rookies, and I felt I was in danger."

"Tell me about how you discovered the corruption?"

"At first I felt it was just institutional tension. The regional office of the Children's Department in San Miguel County hadn't had any scrutiny in ten years or more and then I came on the scene. So in the beginning I thought they'd get used to an independent judicial officer: impartial and civil to all parties. But what they wanted was a 'candy store' where they could get whatever they wanted; to run their cases at whatever pace they wanted and get everything they asked for in court.

"Cindy Dolant, their abysmally poor lawyer, was astonished once she didn't get everything she asked for at hearing and said to me angrily, 'You work for the department. How can you rule against me?' The statute was clear: I was appointed by the district court judges to serve as an independent judge. She hadn't even read the statute governing the hearings of her own job. She is the most unprepared, and slovenly lawyer I have ever encountered. She couldn't believe it was my sworn duty to be an independent judicial officer, or to impartially decide the facts of each case, and to bring the department's caseload into compliance with the statute and time guidelines established by the law of both the state and federal governments.

"So it wasn't institutional tension after all—it was corruption, and I was a judge trying to bring a rogue department into compliance which was kicking and screaming at every turn in the road. But I just stumbled into the corruption because of the backlog of cases."

Steve feeling vulnerable, and having the need to feel protected and assured turned to John Woods and asked, "Did you ever kill anyone John?"

There was a pause before John answered; it was a memory he neither gloried in nor wanted to relive. "Yes once," he answered softly. "I can still see it. I shouted at the perpetrator to drop his gun, but he just kept drawing a bead on me, and I squeezed the trigger twice. The world went into slow motion and became quiet. All my focus was on him and if my shots would get off before his. He kept raising his weapon almost to level. I can still see the snarling, defiant look of hatred in his face, the color of his shirt—it was tan. I barely heard the burst as my cartridges exploded in the chamber and ripped down the barrel. I saw the smoke, mine before his, and the bullets knocked him backwards to the ground. The shots hit his upper chest near the heart.

"His pistol fell from his grasp. He was gasping, his defiance replaced by a look of astonishment and disbelief. He couldn't believe he was dying, but he died right at my feet.

"He didn't have to die. I gave him a chance, but he made a choice. I took a little time off after that—the bureau requires you to. I went to the bureau's shrink in Denver and worked through it and then went back to work in about two weeks, but I still remember, not as vividly as in the days and weeks that followed, but I still remember."

"How old were you?"

"I was twenty-nine."

"It was not only evil that killed him Steve, but it was also my desire to live—self-preservation—that saved me, and his own belief that he was invincible that killed him."

The wussshing of the tires on the snow strewn highway muffled the sound of the conversation in the bus and left the passenger compartment quiet. Only Steve heard what John had said as they made their way to Denver.

36

I   t was nearing 7:00 a.m. in Santa Fe and the sun was rising toward the purple
sky and up over the mountains. As Vance awoke he thought, *"I need to meet with
Big Jim today. There's a lot to talk about."* They had to decide what to do about Steve
Light. It was a certainty he was in the hands of the F.B.I. and with a little digging
the feds would be able to trace the money. They had been only somewhat creative in
moving the money—it would be easy to follow its trail.

George had started a kitchen re-modeling business to quietly surface his
share. Vance, himself, buried black plastic garbage bags of currency with newly
planted trees in his backyard. And Len he just spent like a sailor on leave. His
neighbors wondered if he had come into money: a new car, solar panels on the house,
other high ticket items. His wife was happy too. "Len got a promotion," she told
neighbors.

At 7:30 a.m. Vance called Big Jim's home. In his anxiety Vance forgot the
customary 'Good morning' and blurted out, "We need to get together today."

"Sure, we can do that. How about 11:45 a.m. at the Guadalupe Café near the
'Roundhouse' (the capitol)? We have a break in the convocation then."

"Fine, I know the place, I'll meet you there."

At a quiet corner table, Jim appeared relaxed. He had had a convivial morning
among his colleagues at the convocation, learning and reviewing some new aspects
of the law. Learning the law still excited him, as it had in his days with Judge Reuben.

Vance, in contrast, was grim and intensely focused. "We have some decisions
to make about Steve Light. He's with the F.B.I. now. We don't have a lot of time.
The feds will be able to piece this together fast. We have to act now to stay out of
prison."

"What do you want to do?" Jim asked.

"I want to eliminate Steve Light before he testifies to a grand jury," said Vance.

"We can't do that! That's murder! If we go down now it's a jail sentence, but if you kill Steve Light, he's a judicial officer. You're looking at the death penalty. Aren't there other options?" Jim asked.

"We could set up someone else in the department. That would remove George, Len, and me from jeopardy, but the money would still trace back to you and your campaign."

"How would you set someone up?" Jim asked.

"We could put Bill Losum in charge of accounting and finance effective six months ago and set up a series of accounts in his relatives' names out of state and then create a money trail from the department to the accounts implicating him. That would leave Len, George, and me out. The feds would have a perpetrator when they audited, but that would still leave you," said Vance.

"How much am I in for as of now?" Big Jim asked.

"Two hundred eighty-five thousand with the promise of up to five hundred thousand total to come before the primary."

"Okay, I'm going to pay you back. I'll get a loan from the bank and pledge my pension for collateral. We'll treat it as a simple loan from you to me, with repayment back to you, and you can put the money back in the system."

As he then sat across from Vance, Jim couldn't believe that Vance would actually follow through with killing Steve Light, but Jim knew there was an icy corner in Vance's character, a part that had been hardened by years of police work; and now made Vance a criminal, and Jim pondered: so am I.

Vance didn't see himself that way. He felt he was only helping himself to funds like everyone else in state government, that's the way things worked in New Mexico. He had worked hard and been straight all those years. Now he felt entitled. It would make up for all those nights away from his family and those thankless years of dealing with those low lifes he had locked away.

Jim sat there going through his legal defenses. He could argue that he didn't always know where his contributions originated—he only knew the contributors' names. *"No,"* he thought, *"Vance would turn on me in an instant if it meant prison.*

"But I'm so close to the senate," he said to himself. "If I can only prevail in the primary, the general election will be easy. But now I've got to deal with Vance and his problem: Steve Light.

"How to make the problem go away? Murder? That was too far. He remembered his law school Dean telling his young group of students, with his southern drawl,

'Gentlemen, the trouble with tainted money is it tain't enough.'" Big Jim had forgotten that lesson. He had sold things that were beyond price, irreplaceable: his self-esteem, his integrity, and his self-respect. *"The United States senate was worth it,"* he thought. He was only borrowing the money; he would pay it back. He could help New Mexico and her people—he'd be able to get back his old self again and square things just as soon as he got elected.

Jim needed to jettison Vance, his crew, and his money. Murder was out of the question. He was back paddling in his mind so fast that he didn't touch his food. Jim knew that Vance was impulsive and knew that once he was set on a course it would be difficult to dissuade him from action. Even as far as he had fallen, Jim would not kill someone.

Vance was different, and said to himself, "I'm too old for prison. I'm a former cop; I know what they do to cops in prison. I'll take my stand on the outside. I can always run to Mexico or beyond, but Steve Light, that young punk, is not going to put me in prison, especially not a federal pen."

At the same moment Jim was thinking to himself, *"If Vance could kill Steve Light he could easily offer me up to a federal grand jury. I'm the 'fat cat' every young prosecutor chomps at the bit to get at: a career building case."*

Vance stopped talking, and looked to Big Jim for his suggestions. Jim said, "Why don't you name Losum as head of accounting and finance and start shifting the money into his accounts? I'll return the money I borrowed from you and you can pay back as much money as you can."

"What about Light?" asked Vance.

"From what you say, the feds already have him, so how are you going to get to him? It's a pretty good bet they already know what he has to say. They've just got to go back and put their case together: finding bank records, seizing computers, interviewing bank officers. They're already assembling their case. You'll have to move faster than them and cover your tracks. If we can return the money now, that will help us."

And Jim continued, "The F.B.I. is very thorough. They're not going to miss much. They only need Steve Light to tie the evidence together, to trace the money back from the branches to the main trunk and then to the roots: you and me, George, and Len."

"But you still think we ought to leave Steve Light alone?"

"Yes, the damage he could do has already been done. We need to move and counter punch. You can call a news conference and announce your department's own investigation due to money irregularities coming from the regional offices of the Children's Department and put Losum on administrative leave as head of accounting and finance pending the outcome of your investigation. Call in the media and give them some evidence and details when you make your announcement. This would throw a curve at the federal investigation and steal their thunder. It will also buy us time to put money back into the system."

What Big Jim and Vance didn't know was that Steve Light had fled before dotting the "i's" and crossing the "t's" for the bureau. They were still a long way off from convening a federal grand jury and needed Steve's testimony and knowledge about the workings of the Children's Department operations and corruption.

During their luncheon, Vance didn't tell Big Jim about two calls he had made, or a meeting he had had in northern New Mexico just outside the town of Chama a day earlier at a big cabin filled with animal trophies killed by a man who was a professional hunter and guide, known to a select few for his precise and immaculate work. He tracked and hunted game—all species—and provided his clients with clear, true shots of their quarry, and when necessary killed himself.

He worked alone and had the intelligence, tenacity, and perseverance of a tiger hunting. He talked little; listened much. Vance felt the grip of his eyes when they met, and held back nothing in their meeting.

"Here is a picture taken from the local newspaper when he was appointed. We know that two days ago he was on Kirtland Base in Albuquerque. He had a two man F.B.I. detail with him. We think he may still be on base, but we don't know. He is smart—figured things out by himself. He is resourceful and wouldn't stop—we tried to wave him off, we tried to buy him off, but he just kept on coming. He can make the case against us. He has to be eliminated before he can testify to a federal grand jury."

"My fee is one hundred fifty thousand."

"That's steep."

"He's a judge, guarded by the F.B.I. The cost is calibrated against the amount of risk assumed and the high profile of the quarry. You pay me in full now. Once you pay me and leave this room, there is no rescinding the arrangement. I will work until our agreement is fulfilled."

Vance went out to his car. In the trunk were two black plastic garbage bags folded and wrapped in gray duct tape. He took a small knife from his pocket, opened the blade, and cut the tape. He counted out a hundred and fifty thousand dollars, placed it in an empty attaché case, and carried it back into the cabin. "Here's the money," Vance said.

"You'll know when the quarry is taken," the hunter responded.

Vance felt the pull and power of the hunter's eyes; this was a man you didn't ask questions of. Vance drove away from the cabin convinced that Steve Light would not testify at any grand jury proceedings. None of the others knew anything of the meeting.

37

etired agent John Woods and Steve Light were nearing the outskirts of Denver, a large city with vast suburbs. The sun had started to set into the wall of the Rockies just west of the city.

"John, what are our plans when we arrive in Denver?"

"I'd like you to come with me to the bureau office downtown so we can get a statement. We need to know what you know if you want to put these guys away. Then we'll get you on a plane tonight or tomorrow morning for Toledo."

"I'll go, as long as you go with me. I trust you, and that's saying a lot for me right now. Everybody wants something from me, but the bureau has asked the least and provided me with protection. I still want to know if it was the bureau that was in my house in Clovis without a warrant two months ago."

"Yes Steve, off the record, it was us. You always left your back door open, I guess so your dogs could get back in and out of the house if they needed cover. So one of our men climbed the back fence with treats in his pockets for the dogs and walked into the open back door. The entry was necessary, but it shouldn't have happened without a warrant. I'm sorry."

They had reached the bus station. The bus pulled into one of the outdoor gates at the terminal.

"Ladies and gentlemen, this is Denver, thank you for traveling with us. We will be terminating our trip here today. Your baggage will be outside on the right hand side as you leave the bus."

John Woods and Steve walked out into the aisle to the steep, narrow steps. Steve went first, John followed, and the old lady with her two large hat boxes came behind them. A line of passengers were in front of them and behind.

A half block away from a top floor window of a small run down building Steve was sighted in the cross hairs of a rifle scope. The hunter saw his victim put on his baseball hat and sunglasses before taking the steps. He sighted the kill, inhaled, and squeezed the trigger ever so gently and firmly.

In just that instant, the old lady stumbled against her hat boxes, lurching into John Woods who ricocheted into Steve and down the steps they all tumbled. John Woods felt the bullet bite into his thigh. Because of a silencer there was no rifle report. He fell to the ground on top of Steve.

He yelled in pain, "I've been shot!" blood gushing from his wound. Still on the ground, Steve pulled the wounded man under the bus where they took refuge. John shouted, "Get away from here as fast as you can! Get to the bureau office—they'll protect you! Let them know what happened to me. Get going!"

Steve was spooked. No one was playing anymore. This wasn't just talk and embezzlement. This was killing.

Steve crawled out from beneath the bus on the other side, fearful that a second shot would find him. He was scared, but marshaled his faculties. There was a permanent police detail at the bus station, and in addition, responding to the shooting, cruisers were converging on the scene.

The top floor room of the small building half a block away was now empty, the window closed, the rifle broken down and placed in a lap top computer bag. Even the bullet casing had been picked up and finger prints wiped clean.

The shooter, wearing a light blue shirt and tie, looked every bit the business executive and fit easily into the downtown crowd leaving their offices, carrying his computer bag home at the end of the day. Just another nondescript office worker making his way from work.

Steve moved quickly also after the shot. He jumped into a taxi at the front of the bus station, "Take me to the F.B.I. office downtown," he told the cab driver. "This is an emergency!"

The cabbie smashed down the gas pedal, Steve was thrown back into his seat and in less than five minutes they were there.

Steve ran to the receptionist's desk, "I'm Steve Light! I was with Agent John Woods. He's just been shot at the bus station! I need to speak to the agent in charge!"

She picked up the telephone, "I have a man down here who said he was with Agent John Woods who's just been shot at the bus station. He says his name is Steve Light."

"Hold him there! We'll be down immediately!"

"Mr. Light, they're coming right down. Why don't you wait behind my desk in those chairs by the wall."

"Where is he?" an out of breath agent asked who had taken the stairs instead of waiting for the elevator.

"He's sitting right behind me," she turned in her swivel chair, but Steve Light was gone.

"He was just there."

Out on the street, fear clutched Steve again. He irrationally thought that if they can find him with the F.B.I. helping me this far from Clovis, they can find me anywhere. I need to keep moving.

Steve hopped another cab. "Take me to the nearest used car dealer."

"I know one not far from here."

"Good, get me there fast!"

Within forty-five minutes Steve was the owner of a 2001 big gray Olds Delta 88 that smoked oil sometimes, but could easily reach speeds over 95 m.p.h. if coaxed. She rode quietly for the most part, and would also serve as his hotel on wheels. He could easily sleep in the large back seat pulled off on the side of any road. "Basic transportation," Steve thought.

"Now where to?" he asked himself out loud.

"Easy," he answered, "get as far away from here and New Mexico as possible."

"Every time I get near the F.B.I. guys I put myself in danger. Is one of their own giving up information about me?" he asked himself.

"I'm being stalked and the bureau men stand out. They're too clean cut. Their hair is too short and neatly trimmed. They're like decoys and I'm the duck drawn to them—the quarry." He had learned in the last few weeks that talking out loud kept his mind focused and it didn't wander as much. "I've got to make tracks and keep moving, find somewhere safe where I can get some peace of mind. First I've got to find somewhere safe, then I can worry about my psyche. I need a map of the West. The gas station up ahead may have one. I'll fill up my chariot and buy a map."

Steve perused the map of the western United States and Canada. Where would he be safe and able to open up some distance between himself, the shooting, and New Mexico? "I could head north into Wyoming and Montana, cross into Canada, and take the Trans-Canadian Highway to Detroit, then drive down into Ohio and be with my sister in Toledo. That made sense, but could the car make the arduous journey?

"I could head northwest to Oregon and Washington; I have plenty of friends and contacts up there from law school days at Gonzaga. I'd be a lot safer that far from New Mexico and Colorado."

What Steve didn't know was that there were two interested parties in pursuit of him: the F.B.I. and the hunter.

Steve got on Interstate 70 and headed west. He was frantic; he couldn't tell friend from foe. He played over and over in his mind the events of the last seventy-two hours as he drove through the night across the mountains of Colorado and on into Utah—his destination: Salt Lake City.

At Salt Lake City, he stopped to call the local F.B.I. office. "My name is Steve Light. I'd like to talk to an agent about an incident in New Mexico and the shooting yesterday of retired agent John Woods in Denver."

"Please hold, I'll get an agent for you."

"This is Special Agent Ken Randall. How can I help you?"

"My name is Steve Light. I'm the child support judge from New Mexico. I was with retired Agent John Woods yesterday in Denver when he was shot. How is he?"

"We've heard about you. Do you want to come into our office here in Salt Lake? We'd like to help you."

"I don't want to be detained, but I'd like to meet with an agent. How about at the Sandwich Shoppe just off Highway fifteen about six miles south of town on the left hand side of the road as you head south."

"We'll send an agent out to meet you."

"How is John?"

"He's okay. He was wounded in the thigh and lost blood, but the bullet wasn't meant for him—you know that?"

"Yes, it was meant for me."

"We'd like to try to help you. If you let us."

"Right now I'm looking for a safe haven. Every time I'm with you guys I'm in greater danger, but I'll meet with your agents."

"They should be there in twenty minutes."

Twenty minutes later a late model white Marquis pulled up to the Sandwich Shoppe. A tall, well groomed, true to the mold, young man of about thirty stepped out of the driver's side, and an attractive blonde woman in slacks and a leather jacket stepped out of the passenger side. Steve and the agents assessed each other on opposite sides of an outdoor picnic table.

Steve asked, "Are you from the Salt Lake office?"

"Yes, I'm Special Agent Mark Barnes and this is Special Agent Lindsay Taylor."

Steve had shaved and cleaned up that morning in a truck stop south of Salt Lake. He looked clean and non-descript in a dark blue golf shirt and tan pants. He wore his sunglasses.

The agents were both casually dressed. They had 9mm weapons on their waistband, clearly visible. Steve was visibly nervous. He was fearful of the agents, but wanted to tell his story. He ran through the details again as he had a thousand times during the course of the night's drive into Salt Lake. "They're into the money. At first I thought it was just an institutional struggle of having a judge for the first time supervising the caseload, but then I started to feel differently. And when I wanted to increase the number of cases heard every month the resistance was so strong and persistent that I got curious. The intensity of their push back was in no way proportionate to my request. And that's when I started to ask more and more questions and stumbled on this: they're into the money."

When Steve finished his story he asked, "How is John Woods? Will he be okay? I trusted him."

"Yes, he got hit in the thigh. It didn't break the bone, but he lost a lot of blood. He'll be okay. Where are you headed?" Agent Barnes asked.

"To the Oregon coast. I'm going to try and get away from all this and find a safe place to relax and make sense of everything."

"We'd like to help you. We believe you're in danger."

"Every time I get hooked up with you guys I'm exposed to even more danger. I want to cooperate with you and I'd be happy to testify at the grand jury or at trial, but now I just want to get some peace of mind. Up on the Oregon coast I'll get my health back. I'll get back in touch with you after a while. Do you have a card?" Steve asked.

Reaching into his pocket Barnes pulled out his wallet and handed Steve his card.

"How about yours?" Barnes asked, and Steve exchanged his card.

"Give me a call in a week," Barnes said, "my direct dial number is on the card." With that the two men shook hands and Steve got back into his car and headed north on Interstate 15 to the junction of Interstate 80 in Salt Lake City; there he headed west, passing the Great Salt Lake and pushing westward beyond the salt flats. Staying back two miles, a late model American car with two men in it followed the trail Steve Light was taking from Utah into Northern Nevada and the town of Winnemucca, his jumping off point into eastern Oregon.

The men had a pair of field glasses on the dashboard and every so often the passenger would sight Steve's car up the road.

A few miles back behind the American car was a tan Camry with a single passenger, a lap top computer bag, and mobile police radio scanner turned on in the passenger seat following the two car procession in front of him, watching with skill and patience.

Steve took notice of the colors of Utah, yellow and brighter than the deep high desert's browns of New Mexico. Utah's brightness caused by an almost white sky and sun that seemed to absorb and then reflect back to the land the bright, light colors of the Great Salt Lake Flats and Basin. The Salt Lake Valley was expansive in all directions. The Latter Day Saints had built a beautiful showcase city in this arid land of Utah, by the shores of the Great Salt Lake.

Unbeknownst to him, the procession of cars behind Steve ambled along the highway. Steve drove just below the speed limit to view the scenery and small towns that punctuated the road. Reaching Winnemucca, Nevada Steve headed north and then northwest towards Klamath Falls, Oregon and from there to Ashland where a summer Shakespeare Festival was held.

Usually gray Oregon, sun drenched this time of year, gave Steve a free feeling, a feeling cleansed from the venal, corrosive graft of New Mexico. Oregon was free and fertile and moist, a land bringing forth a clean, fresh new harvest with the nourishing sun of the season. Steve felt alive again, felt he had left the past and the desert's audacious sun in the southwest.

The northwest, he remembered, grew tall forests and fruit orchards—Oregon was bountiful. Everywhere there were signs of water, green vegetation, and forests, in contrast to New Mexico.

After driving through eastern Oregon, Steve kept driving toward the Oregon coast, and the palisades that overlooked the Pacific Ocean. The town of Brookings caught his attention on the map. It was the first Oregon town just north of the California state line that was right on the coast.

Steve found Brookings a small pleasant town. The main street had real estate offices and banks, restaurants, and a new shopping center with a large modern supermarket just in the south of town. The town's library, a remodeled older home, was several blocks off the main street in a residential section.

In the library, Steve did his research about the town. The staff was friendly and helpful, introducing him to the local resources: the newspaper, the Chamber of Commerce Guide, the listing of local attorneys. Steve wanted to learn about the town if he intended to spend any time here. He looked at a map of the coast and the coastal highway.

After his library exploration, Steve drove north out of town on Highway 101, the coastal highway, the Pacific on his left below the palisades and the forest to his right. About seven miles outside of town he found a dirt road with heavily used tire tracks. He turned into the road and was on a plateau and there below from the heights of the palisades was the sapphire blue vista of the Pacific Ocean. Steve felt he was home. He was not moving another inch. This was his new paradise.

38

The blue Pacific lay outstretched to the horizon before him. Steve made his way down from the heights to the beach below. There on the beach undulating waves came every few seconds, rhythmically, continuously, small curls came, spewing their life onto the famished sand. Out in the ocean a series of rock formations jutted from the sea floor and rose nearly to the height of the high cliffs on the mainland. These stone monoliths were being etched into magnificent forms sculpted by an eternity of waves into solitary shapes, subdued by the onslaught of the sea. Like Michelangelo, the waves chipped piece by tiny piece away from the stone formations in the placid summer seas, then using the heavy chisels of winter storms to do the sculptor's real craving.

Steve sensed that here he would find peace, recover his former self, and make sense of what had gone on in New Mexico.

Here where the sea met the shore with its tranquil unceasing song—the song of the waves—he would be soothed back into harmony by the repetitive, hypnotic rhythm of the waves bringing peace and rest.

Daily Steve would open all the windows and doors of his Olds, lie down on the big back seat, and let the melody of the waves lull him for hours at a time.

Then he would awaken, eat a peanut butter and jelly sandwich, watch the azure ocean, smell the air, and listen to the chanting cadence of the sea. The recurrent metered accent soothed him and again he fell back to sleep. He needed the rest; he needed to restore his strength after months of depletion.

There were three cylindrical rock formations in the ocean just off the high plateau where Steve had parked. The largest lay just south of Steve's camp on the heights, and beside this formation was a small fishing runabout with four men aboard. They all wore orange rain slickers and pants against the morning fog that came across the ocean and collided with the cool air of the forest, forming a screen of mist.

Steve took no notice of them at first, but every morning they would be there, staying all through the day. At first Steve thought they were fishing, or doing field studies, but curious about the men, Steve took out some field glasses that he had bought in town to watch the ocean and trained it on the men in the runabout. They were definitely not fishing—at least not for fish from the sea. They had a large telescopic camera lens and kept it focused on Steve and his old car, that he had christened "Betsy."

Steve tried to pay no notice of them. He thought they could be law enforcement. He continued his routine of sleeping and lounging. He ate when he wanted to eat; slept when he needed to sleep; he followed no schedule. He was in one of the most serene places on earth, and Steve tried to draw in the peace and serenity of the place every day, just as he drew in breath, trusting that breathing and being in this paradise would sooth and restore his tranquility. In the evenings he would cook spaghetti and sauce on a Coleman stove he bought—a simple meal of carbohydrates.

It became Steve's routine to drive into town daily to do his shopping for fresh fruit and other items and the chance to socialize; swapping the constant surveillance of the men in the runabout for the young mothers and their children scurrying up and down the supermarket aisles filling their baskets with detergent and multi-colored cereal. He wanted to belong.

But he was an outsider in this community. Passing through. Recovering. A tourist come to see the famed orchids of Brookings and the coast. He had not put down roots. His mind was back in New Mexico, still trying to make some sense of all that happened there: tracking the money; yet his body was on the Oregon coast, pristine and peaceful.

He realized now there was no going back to his beloved life in New Mexico; that had come to an abrupt end. What was important was that he feel secure again—safe and at peace and able to start over.

One week after he arrived in Brookings, he called Mark Barnes, the F.B.I. agent he had met with outside Salt Lake City, as they had agreed.

"Where are you?" Barnes asked.

"I'm in Brookings, Oregon on the coast."

"Are you safe?"

"I think so. I'm as far away from New Mexico as possible."

"Well, keep your head down." Barnes said. "We've started tracking the money orders and bank checks. Actually, the New Mexico office is doing that. They're tracking bank deposits and withdrawals from the accounts of the Children's

Department. There are irregularities, and they're still working backwards up the money stream. I wouldn't be calling New Mexico or telling anyone where you are with the exception of your friend, Ed Wright, the United States magistrate. He's honest and you can trust him. His phone line has been tested and is clear of all taps except ours. You might want to give him a call. He has some news for you from the front page of the latest *New Mexico Bar Bulletin*—that's your lawyers' newspaper in New Mexico isn't it?"

"Yes, they print all the legal news and the recent cases decided by the supreme court and court of appeals."

"I'd give Ed a call if I were you. He's a good friend of yours and a good man."

"I'll do that right away," Steve said.

"Call me again next week and stay safe. Try to get some rest."

Steve hung up and then dialed Ed Wright's office number, but he was out of his office; Mark Barnes hung up and called the Medford, Oregon Field office of the F.B.I.

"This is Special Agent Mark Barnes in Salt Lake City. May I speak with the agent working the Steve Light case from New Mexico?"

"Please hold Barnes. I'll get Agent Vincent on the line."

"This is Agent Glen Vincent."

"I'm Agent Mark Barnes from the Salt Lake office."

"How can I help you Barnes?"

"I'm calling about Steve Light."

"Well he's in Brookings, on the coast, camping out about six miles north of town. He's under surveillance twenty-four seven. Any break in the case?"

"New Mexico is going over the money trail: the bank checks and money orders. They're finding irregularities. Some of the money has been diverted, but they don't know how much yet or to whom. Tracing the money orders will take time.

"Keep him safe up there. We need him. He cracked this alone. He's the key witness. They put him through a very rough time down there and he's afraid of everyone. He doesn't know who to trust."

"We have him covered out here."

"I asked him to call me next week. I'll call you again after I speak with him."

"Fine, look forward to hearing from you."

Two weeks passed, and Steve was still camped out on the Oregon coast outside of Brookings.

39

*L*ife had returned to normal in New Mexico. Big Jim and Karen were back at home from the convocation following their usual routine after seeing so many friends and colleagues. Jim resumed his responsibilities at the supreme court, continued campaigning around the state, and the F.B.I. was working feverishly.

During one of his campaign jaunts across the state, Jim alone, inconspicuously drove into Clovis late one afternoon and made his way to the Catholic Church graveyard in Spanish Town. He had come on a quiet, solemn pilgrimage to the grave of his mentor and guide Judge Reuben Fuentes. He sat alone on a bench in front of Judge Reuben's grave. Under his breath he started a conversation with his departed friend and master. Jim knew he was in over his head. He tried to blame Vance, but the trouble he knew was of his own making and he admitted it here before his old teacher and friend. "Reuben I have shamed your memory. I have done wrong. I have taken money to advance my own career. I have disgraced myself and lost my self-respect and don't know the way out. Now Vance wants to kill a young judge who is not much older than I was when I first came to learn from you. I can't let that happen. Tell me what to do Reuben, I need your help."

Tears wet Jim's cheeks. He was alone in his guilt, contrite, and sorrowful. He knew there was danger ahead. He knew he was guilty of stealing state funds, but killing this young man was murder. He knew he could not cross that line. Jim sat alone for an hour talking out loud to his old friend. "Reuben, what do I do? Do I resign? Do I fold my bid for the senate? Do I turn myself in? Tell me, old friend." A solitary gray cat walked through the graveyard brushing up against cool headstones here and there, not disturbing the sleeping occupants below, or paying any particular attention to the prominent chief justice of New Mexico sitting in his graveyard in the waning hours of the day. People came and people went, but he, the cat, stayed in his graveyard waiting for his dinner bowl of fresh milk from the parish cook. As Jim Richards sat there hoping for solace from his departed friend, the cat broke the spell, but in his heart Jim knew he couldn't or wouldn't turn back and quietly left Clovis without seeing family or friends or finding the peace he sought.

One morning, about four weeks after Big Jim's pilgrimage to Judge Reuben's grave he was in chambers in Santa Fe when the phone rang. "This is United States Attorney Leroy Clarkson's office. Is Chief Justice Richards in? Mr. Clarkson would like to speak with him?"

"Yes, the chief justice is in. Put Mr. Clarkson on and I'll get the judge," said Theresa, the judge's secretary.

"Leroy?"

"Yes, Judge."

"How are you?"

"Just fine. I wonder if you'll have some time to see me and Chief Agent Bill Kenly of the F.B.I. later this afternoon?"

"Sure, is three o'clock okay?"

"Yes that will be fine, I'll see you at three. Thank you, Judge."

At ten to three, two gentlemen walked into Chief Justice Richards chambers. The men approached Theresa's desk. The shorter man spoke to Theresa. As expected, he was immaculately dressed in a dark blue pin stripe suit and white shirt with a conservative tie. He wore black cowboy boots with stitching in the customary western fashion. The other man was taller and older. He looked harder and had a grim, firm facial appearance. He held an attaché case. His face showed signs of fatigue and overwork and both men looked serious and grave as they stood at Theresa's desk.

"I'm Leroy Clarkson. I have an appointment with Chief Justice Richards."

"Yes Mr. Clarkson, the judge is expecting you. I'll tell him you are here." Instead of buzzing the judge on the intercom, Theresa got up from her desk and walked into Big Jim's chamber office.

"Judge, Mr. Clarkson and another man are outside."

"Show them in Theresa, and hold all calls and visitors."

Theresa walked back into the ante-room. "Go right on in Mr. Clarkson, the judge is expecting you."

After Clarkson and the other man entered the inner office Theresa closed the door.

Big Jim stood up and extended his hand across to Leroy and they shook in greeting, but Agent Bill Kenly hung back.

"It's been a while Leroy. What brings you into state court?"

"Jim, we're here on sad and serious business. It concerns you and your associates at the Children's Department. For the past few months Bill here has tapped Vance Arnold's phone and has used listening devices at his office and recently in a restaurant here in Santa Fe during the New Mexico judges' convocation.

Leroy continued, "We have traced bank checks and money orders from the Children's Department. Some of the money was diverted to Vance Arnold and his 'friends' at the Children's Department for their personal use. Some of that money was directed to you, Jim, for your senatorial campaign with your knowledge."

Instantaneously blood drained from Jim's face, he turned ashen and gray, his expression became corpse-like, his heart racing and pounding, sweat pouring from his underarms. The moment he feared had arrived: he was exposed. Surveying the wreckage of his ambitions and dreams, he foresaw a twenty year prison term, and thought, *"How will I survive in a cell with violent men, some of whom I might well have sentenced to their confinement."* There would be no saving angel, no stay of execution, he would go to prison without hope or reprieve. His body collapsed from within, shriveled up like a dying cancer patient, eaten from the inside by the foul and fetid disease, but this cancer was of Jim's own making.

"Bill here has a tape of a conversation you had with Vance Arnold at the Guadalupe Café in Santa Fe."

Turning to the agent Leroy said, "Let him hear it, Bill." And Agent Kenly opened the attaché, took out a small cassette player and depressed the button. It was Vance Arnold's voice: "We have some decisions to make about Steve Light. He's with the F.B.I. now. We don't have a lot of time. The feds will be able to piece this together fast. We have to act now to stay out of prison."

"What do you want to do?"

"I want to eliminate Steve Light before he testifies to a grand jury."

"That's murder! If we go down now it's a jail sentence, but if you kill Steve Light, he's a judicial officer, you're looking at the death penalty."

While the tape was still playing Jim seemed to have aged twenty years and shrunk six inches.

"Turn it off Bill," Leroy said.

"There's more Jim. Lots more." The United States attorney said, dropping his voice sadly.

"What are you going to do?" Jim asked softly.

"My first inclination was to indict and try all of you and let a jury and federal judge decide your fate. Jim, how long have you been on the court now?"

"Thirteen years here in Santa Fe, and then another twelve in Clovis on the district court and magistrate court."

"You have been a good judge, Jim, fair, even-handed, and respected," Clarkson said. "How many criminal appeals were you involved in during the last thirteen years?"

"Probably thousands of them."

"And that's my problem, Jim. If I indict you, every criminal defendant in every case you ever took part in will be filing appeals in the federal courts claiming violation of their civil rights and seeking writs of habeas corpus for their release. The federal courts will be jammed for years trying to accommodate all the cases.

"No Jim, I'm using my prosecutorial discretion. I'm not going to try you. You're going to resign effective this Friday. You are to hear no cases from today until you leave the bench. You are to cooperate fully with my investigation. And you are to return all the monies taken from the Children's Department.

"You can continue your senatorial campaign, but we both know that without the funding for a media blitz before the primary your campaign is doomed. And there's one other thing."

"What's that?" Jim asked with complete despair in his voice surveying the ruins of his collapsed life, a voice at once hollow and bereft of all life, a voice that had diminished in size and sound to a puny whimper, as the man himself had in the last five minutes.

"If something happens to that kid out there, if he's murdered, all bets are off and you'll be tried as a co-conspirator in a murder case of a judicial officer and face the death penalty. Do you understand?"

"Yes."

"You may want to issue a press release that you're stepping down to devote your entire energy to your campaign."

"What if I win?"

"We'll cross that bridge down the road, but the operative word is 'IF.' An assistant United States attorney and the F.B.I. will set up a meeting with you for later this week. You are to cooperate with us fully. If you tip off Vance Arnold and his men you will be dealt with in the severest way.

"Jim, do you understand these conditions?"

Big Jim just sat at his desk, his head bowed, his shoulders drooped and heavy, his focus only on his desktop. He was lucky. He would be saved full disgrace, prosecution, and prison. But nothing else was salvaged. Without the money he could not hope to win the primary. It was all over. Now he had to hope Vance wouldn't kill Steve Light.

"I understand." Jim said without looking up.

"We'll see ourselves out," Clarkson said as he and Kenly got up from their chairs.

40

*L*uke and Blaze, Steve's dogs, were being fed every morning and evening by Barbara Chase from the district court clerk's office in Clovis. Crystal Deland had arranged it when Steve first went on base in Albuquerque. The dogs had the run of the fenced backyard and Luke would climb the six foot fence at will after he was fed in the morning, returning just before the sun started down in the sky. That's when Luke knew Barbara came back to Steve's house on her way home from work to feed and water them again and make sure everything was okay before going home.

Luke and Blaze were good natured dogs—after all, they were golden retrievers—loyal, friendly to a fault, and inquisitive. In Steve's absence, Blaze had a litter of six puppies—three males and three females. She nursed and nuzzled them all day. Luke walked around the backyard, the proud father, head and tail held high, asserting his prowess in his role as head of the family.

Barbara had fashioned a lean-to for Blaze and her puppies to keep cool and shaded. The puppies were frisky, some rust and some blonde colored, soft velvet balls of fur. Between nuzzling their mother for milk or warmth they would follow their father about the yard nipping at his legs, trying to climb on him, or chasing his tail.

When Luke would saunter around the yard the puppies would follow their papa. When he stopped all the puppies following behind in a line would careen into each other, falling and then rolling over onto one another, a mass of soft fur balls. Then they would circle up and Luke would lick their faces. Blaze, taking a welcomed break from her motherly duties, watched from the lean-to, glad for a few moments' rest. Luke gloried in his moments of fatherhood, watching over his family.

Sometimes when the pups were asleep between feedings and Blaze was resting in her shelter, Luke would think of Steve, his master: where had he gone? Why was he away so long? He had never left them in the past. Even in his proud moments of fatherhood, Luke longed for Steve. He missed his master's strong caress on his back or the cradling of his head and especially the back and forth shaking Steve would give him. He missed his master, but life was exploding before him every day. The memory of Steve consumed less and less of his time, as his duties with the new litter took precedence.

Barbara would play with the pups when she came to feed Luke and Blaze. Picking up one or two curlicues of fur with their innocent, sparkling brown eyes, she cradled the infant pups, cooing softly. The pups would wash her face with kisses until she laughed to herself at the ticklish tongues.

When Barbara came, the puppies paraded behind her as she made her way around the yard leaving several cool, fresh buckets of water and food for the evening and early morning. Luke and Blaze were used to her now—her comings and goings—and welcomed her twice daily visits. Blaze was grateful for the reprieve from her maternal duties, and Luke welcomed the human interaction in Steve's absence.

One afternoon at about two p.m., the hottest part of the day, a big man climbed the fence, as Steve did when he locked himself out, and as a stranger had done several months ago who gave them treats before the puppies were born.

Luke, in his good mannered way, went up to this new man to greet him and sniff him and make his acquaintance, as he had always done with humans. But this one reached beneath his shirt, and he pulled out a pistol with a silencer, put the muzzle to Luke's head, and fired a single shot. Luke crumpled, dead. Blaze, seeing this, growled, snarled, and charged the man, ripping into his leg before he could discharge the pistol a second time. But he managed to get off a shot after being bitten, and Blaze fell still, blood pouring from her fatal wound.

The man took a large pillow case from his back pocket; and one by one picked up the crying puppies and stuffed them in, tied the top, and dropped it into the small two foot deep pool Steve had dug for Luke to cool off in during the roaring hot summer days in Clovis. In less than five minutes all of Steve's golden retrievers, Luke, Blaze, and the puppies were dead.

The man climbed back over the fence, walked to his car parked two streets over, and drove away bleeding slightly from where Blaze had defended her family. Blood drippings marked his progression to his car. Vance Arnold's message had been sent, although it was late in being delivered.

When Barbara returned to Steve's house at 5:30 p.m. she screamed and started crying uncontrollably. Luke and Blaze lay sprawled where they had been shot. She pulled the pillow case from the pool and knew what was inside. She could see the outlines of the little lifeless bodies. She agonized bitterly over what kind of vicious person would kill puppies.

41

Some time later, after Steve spoke with Mark Barnes, he again called his friend and mentor, United States Magistrate Ed Wright in Clovis.

"Ed, this is Steve. How are you?"

"The big question is: how are you?"

"I'm doing better now that I'm out of state. One of the F.B.I. agents said you had news for me from the front page of the last *Bar Bulletin*."

"I have the latest copy of it right here," and Ed looked at it and all Steve heard over the line was, "Oh my God!"

"What is it Ed?"

"Chief Justice Richards steps down suddenly, resigns his post."

"Steve you'd better run deep and stay close to the bureau's men. They'll be coming after you. You can call me here any time. It's a secure line that's been cleared recently. The bureau just did a sweep of my office and phone so you're safe calling here. Don't call me at home."

"What does the article say, Ed?"

"'Chief Justice James 'Big Jim' Richards announced today that he is stepping down from the New Mexico Supreme Court effective this Friday. He will devote himself full time to his election campaign for the United States senate seat to be vacated by Senator Joe Templeton. This announcement took politically astute observers by surprise as Chief Justice Richards could have retained his office if he had lost the primary bid for the senate seat. Richards is the third candidate in the Democratic primary for the position. His resignation marks the first time in New Mexico history that a sitting chief justice has relinquished his seat to seek other political office.'

"Steve," Ed continued, "Richards' timing is very awkward. Without needing to do so he resigns, effective immediately. Why? Maybe now we know where the money trail ended. He's been buddies with Vance Arnold since the two of them started their careers here in Clovis thirty years ago. You'd better be very careful."

Steve's stomach seized. He turned silent. He had known Chief Justice

Richards when he was a young law clerk at the supreme court in Santa Fe after graduating from law school.

"I can't believe it Ed!" was all Steve could muster in a dazed and bewildered voice.

"What will happen to me?" he asked Ed.

"Steve, you're in way over your head. These are the big boys, they play hardball. They're not likely to want to go to prison."

"Let me go, Ed. I need time to think about all this and decide what my next move is."

"Remember you can call me any time here in my office. Take good care of yourself and keep in touch."

Steve was now in a different world. The luscious green and fertile beauty of Oregon fell away. The pristine waves of the Pacific didn't captivate. Now he had to decide how to stay alive. He was scared. He had already run from the F.B.I. twice. Were they likely to want to protect him? The pressure was now starting to build again. Now he knew a portion of what John Dean felt when he decided to testify against President Nixon.

After his call to Ed, Steve's mind transported him back to New Mexico. There the mesas and mountains formed geometric monuments and vistas extended for hundreds of miles in every direction; there the treeless landscape reached the horizon in other-worldly beauty and the mesas met the flat lines of the horizon; there the sun usurped the blue, near cloudless sky and roasted the land below with its incandescent white heat; there the shades of brown were many and varied and earth tone shadows were cast upon the desert floor by the rock formations and mountains. The only reprieve from the scalding heat was in the uplands and higher elevations of the mountains; there alpine green meadows and native wild flowers flourished and blossomed, fed by the melting snow pack sending clear pure rills down the mountainsides; and where the state's chief justice and the Children's Department were purulent and putridly involved in venal corrosive graft.

"No," Steve told himself, "I don't have time for the lush velvet beauty of Oregon now. I have to move and keep moving: 'A rolling stone gathers no moss.' Now I know who I'm up against—I'm in trouble. They could use not only bullets and murder, but also the authority and power of the state judiciary to deal with me. Chief Justice Richards will have a lot of favors due him and they could be called in now. Evidence could be conjured as a pretext to arrest, extradite, and dispose of me. I've got to make tracks."

He got into Old Betsy and started south. He had no plan. Uncertain of his next action, he just drove south heading into northern California, hoping that in its mega-cities he could lose himself and become difficult to find.

The F.B.I. detail assigned to Steve didn't realize he had left Brookings. They were waiting on the ocean in their boat below the Pacific palisades for Steve to return from shopping at the supermarket in town. They were caught short.

Steve had a fifty mile lead on them and was already well into California before they realized he was gone. He headed for the southlands of the Golden State hoping to get lost somewhere in its vast expanse.

An hour later the F.B.I. detail assigned to the case scrambled. They were now in chase mode again. The rabbit had fled again and they were once again in pursuit.

But there was something curious, if anyone had taken the time to notice. Sitting back ten miles from the F.B.I. chase team a late model Camry was also on the trail again. The driver had a police band radio receiver in his car and had been waiting in Brookings all this time. Now he listened to law enforcement chatter about their lost charge. He was patient. Now the hunt was on, he would let the F.B.I. "beaters" flush out the prey then he would snare the quarry at precisely the right moment.

All parties wanted Steve Light. The difference being some wanted him alive, some had other plans.

Down the coastal highway they drove into the most beautiful, treasured land in America. Into the giant sequoia redwood forests of California, these living, timeless, obelisks that were climbing skyward even before the landing of Columbus, the fall of Rome, or the birth of Christ.

These majestic trees had been witnesses to the founding of America: her colonization, her independence, her greatness. They would witness much more again than Steve Light and the sordid affairs of New Mexico's Children's Department, Steve was to them not even a filament of a fragile whisper of wind across their upper branches that swayed and danced to God's music. No, these giants took no notice of him at all as he drove through their forest.

The procession, hunted and hunters, moved through the redwood forest still heading south when Steve made a curious decision for no reason at all. Instead of continuing south to the cities (he had always mistrusted big cities), he turned east into the mountains. He had no goal. It was instinct. He just followed the lay of the land. Looking at a map of California roads, he took a secondary road towards Redding—just an arbitrary point he selected on the map south of Mount Shasta.

The land was bountiful. He had not seen its like before. Broad and expansive, its vastness was not desert or dry arroyos like New Mexico, but forest and fertile sun-quenched lands capable of growing anything. Her towns were new and clean— and they extended one into the other—small towns and larger towns, until he reached the mountains. *"California was an empire,"* he thought. *"The young American nation had to incorporate it into the United States or she would have been lost to another power. California was the crown jewel of the American West: rich in beauty, bounty, and resources."* Steve became fascinated by this vast and beautiful state.

His travel was aimless; he was just running without destination or goal. At night he would find a campground or a state park that permitted overnight camping and set up a small tent, put his sleeping bag inside and set up his Coleman stove to cook dinner. Sometimes he just skipped dinner and drove through the night stopping at an all night café if he felt hungry.

Steve felt pursued and terrified. He knew he had become the key witness to the corruption in the Children's Department and with the banking records there would be sufficient evidence to indict and prosecute Vance Arnold and his men. Steve could not feel safe anywhere. He knew what kind of man Vance Arnold was. Steve was having trouble distinguishing between his real fears and those he imagined. And now his fears intensified and took on frightening proportions in his mind with the inclusion of Chief Justice Richards in the scheme and the power of the state judiciary arrayed against him.

At first he did not notice a dark green Chevy riding four or five car lengths behind him. But becoming aware of the two men in casual dress and baseball hats he slowed down to a turtle-like pace so they would want to pass him. Instead, they slowed with him, trailing behind the same four to five car lengths. He slowed again; so did they. He accelerated; they did the same. They stuck to him like a fly in honey.

Neither Steve nor the two men in the green Chevy noticed the tan Camry now several miles behind just loping along easily like a determined wolf headed out for a night's hunt—an easy jaunt—but this driver had a goal, his loping was not aimless, he was in pursuit of prey.

Slowly, the two lead cars and the Camry made their way into the hills and mountains near Mount Shasta. Steve now fixed the notion in his mind of traveling southeast to Interstate 10 and riding it across country. But for tonight he would stay in Redding, California. He would rent a room in a motel and then continue his journey eastward in the morning.

Also checking into the same motel were the occupants of the dark green Chevy. It was Steve's chance to get a close look at the men following him. There were two desk clerks checking in customers. A young woman waited on Steve and a middle aged man waited on the occupants of the green Chevy. Steve strained to read the other man's name on his credit card as he presented it for payment, but was unsuccessful. Both parties completed their registration and moved off in the separate directions of their respective rooms for the night.

Steve ate a simple dinner at a local diner and then headed back to his room. He was tired and wanted to sleep. His plan now was to drive two thousand miles northeast to Ohio and his sister's. But he had the whole country before him to cross. Anything could happen. Especially with the power of New Mexico's highest judge posed against him.

The bureau didn't want Steve traveling aimlessly cross country; they had their own fears about his safety. They wanted to interview him at length over several days for extended periods of time to secure information that would tie all their evidence together, learn how he discovered the corruption, and to see if he could hold up to the demands of a strenuous cross examination if a trial developed. The bureau also knew Steve was in danger that could be imminent and would be lethal.

Unknown to either Steve or the bureau, the lone driver of the tan Camry registered at another motel in Redding just two blocks further down the main drag than Steve and his law enforcement escort.

When the lone hunter registered, the young college student motel clerk handed him back his credit card and started making conversation, "You're a long way from New Mexico. I've been through Albuquerque. Where do you live?"

The man was not adverse to friendly conversation; he had learned it was a good way to glean local information.

"I live north up near the Colorado border."

"What's it like?"

"Lots of green forests and snow in winter, with good trout fishing and camping in the summer and fall—the outdoor life."

It was a plain and friendly conversation, but the visitor soon excused himself on the grounds that he was tired after the long drive, and asked the way to his room.

He left his rifle securely packed in the trunk of his car, but parked just outside his first floor room, backing his car into the space so that the car trunk faced his motel room door if fast action was needed. Both he and the special agents slept well that night.

Steve slept fitfully in ragged bits and pieces. Twenty minutes here, then two hours and then he woke from a nightmare that he was being hunted and would get shot. There was no falling back to sleep. He was up for the day at 3:30 a.m. He was ready to move on, and so he drove away from the motel and into the night. All the others slept peacefully.

As Steve drove off, lured into the dark, he felt secure and safe, isolated in the ebony night. He was just two headlights and two red tail lights, unseen in the cool evening air, and it was pleasant to drive with the windows open, the heat of the day gone and dawn hours away. He was alone in the quiet, cool ease of night, where the scents of the hills and mountains mingled with the smell of the roadway and the aroma of the small town. Steve was on the road again making tracks.

He headed south and east. He took out his well-worn road map of the western United States. The next potential stop he decided on was Reno, Nevada: a city with plenty of tourists making it easy to fit in, and close to Lake Tahoe, straddling the California-Nevada state line.

It was 6:30 a.m. before the bureau men realized Steve was gone again. They scrambled and were ready for the road in fifteen minutes, but in which direction? They looked at the map.

"Where would he go?"

"He could have gone south towards the cities and the ocean again or across the state line into Nevada and down into Reno."

"We can start by heading south and then turn east or west. We're going to have to call out the chopper."

At daybreak a helicopter was scanning the roads south towards Sacramento and then over the secondary roads leading to Reno. It was approaching 9:30 and there below in a clump of fir trees obscured from the roadway was an old gray Olds with all her doors and windows open and an occupant asleep in the backseat.

Steve was startled awake by the helicopter churning the sky a hundred feet above and off to his left.

A Special Agent sat next to the pilot. He spoke into the radio, "We've found your boy. He's on Highway eighty-nine headed south, could be headed into Reno. He's pulled off the road in a stand of fir trees just south and east of Quincy. On the east side of the road, you probably won't be able to see him from the roadway.

"Over."

"Thanks," came back the reply.

"Just in a day's work."

Steve didn't know whether the helicopter was for him or not, but he was awake again feeling more rested than when he had pulled off the road just before dawn, when fatigue finally overtook him.

"Now," he said to himself, "get something to eat." He had peanut butter bread and jelly in the car and a plastic bottle of water. It would hold him until he had time for a proper meal in Reno. He knew casinos served good, cheap, hot food to keep the players at the gaming tables.

Steve had no problem with gambling. He knew how to hold himself in check. He would not squander his limited means at the gaming pits. He knew the casinos didn't stay in business because they were giving away money. He had the ability to detach himself from his immediate surroundings—greed was not a major motivator in his psyche. Steve could safely resist the temptation of the casinos and eat hearty and cheaply.

He washed from a five gallon container of water he carried on the floor in the back of his car. He wet a towel and scrubbed his face, soaped, washed, and then rinsed his hands. He brushed his teeth and rinsed his mouth. Now he was off to Reno.

Steve came down out of the Sierra Nevada's and crossed the state line into Nevada heading into Reno. It was afternoon when Steve arrived, and he drove through the downtown section. Tourists lined the streets in a Chinese dragon dance of curiosity and greed on the sidewalks of the downtown casinos. This was a tawdry, far cry from the natural beauty of New Mexico. Here everything was flashing. The whole atmosphere was geared to the sensory overload of the gambler to draw the moth to the candle.

During daylight the gambling halls showed like an old scarlet woman at noon—seedy and covered with warts. Only the black of night brought on the cloak that veiled her aged decrepitude.

The garish lights and lurid piles of money in the gambling casino windows enticed the greedy and attracted players to the tables. And the players came with thoughts and prayers: *"If I could just win a thousand I'd get Suzy that car for graduation." "If I could just win a couple of passes at the crap table I'd have enough to buy that new bass boat or send the folks on a trip to Europe for their fiftieth anniversary." "Please, Dear Jesus, help me win this hand. If I can beat the house Johnny will get his braces, and I promise I'll give up drinking." "Lord Jesus, no one has suffered more than Annie with her chemo; please let me win this hand for her so she can take that cruise she's always wanted before she leaves us."*

All these unanswered prayers, countless dashed wishes, and greed had built these glaring casinos dollar by dollar, year by year, decade by decade, 365 days a year, 24 hours a day, all day every day. No, there were no clocks on the walls in casinos. No time, and only a very small number of winners.

Steve stopped at one of the downtown casinos, bought himself two large hot-carved roast beef sandwiches, avoided the tumult of the gaming tables, and headed out of town. Looking at his map he found a state park near Carson City, the capital of Nevada about twenty miles south.

He turned in early that night. After seeing the bells and whistles of the casinos in Reno, the state park was a welcomed respite of quietude. Tomorrow Steve would drive to Carson City and up to Lake Tahoe.

On the other side of the campground, two men in a Ford pulled into one of the sites.

Fifteen minutes later, two more men in a small truck pulling a camper parked in another camp site. And then, just before the park ranger closed and locked the gates for the night, a tan Camry pulled into the park. All these late arrivers bedded down for the clear star-lit night just outside Carson City.

42

The dawn awoke royal purple, then lightened to violet and red with orange casts as the sun neared the rim of the horizon. The high clouds caught the first rays of the sun. Next the dark night sky came alive with color, as a lone bird streaked through the early morning shafts of light making its way to water. When the sun finally broke above the horizon, the land burst into a brilliant cascade of colors.

The waterfall of colors foretold a beautiful day in Nevada. The darkness was receding, but the crescent moon, silver and white, the last witness of night, still hung in the sky ready to salute her sister, the new day's sun, before she herself set.

The man in the tan Camry was the first to stir. He was setting out his coffee and watching the dawning sky; he had learned long ago how to read the day's weather from the sunrise. Steve was next to wake. The men in the Ford and camper were last to greet the new day.

Steve heated water for his instant coffee and oatmeal. The oatmeal was a hearty, filling breakfast. He watched as the oatmeal bubbled in the pot like the lava of a small volcano. It was soon finished, and he poured it into a bowl and added some milk from his cooler. He ate it with relish, then had his coffee and a small carton of orange juice he had purchased the day before.

He took out his map and studied the surrounding area. Steve decided he would drive into Carson City see the state buildings, and then drive up to Lake Tahoe. It was still early morning, and the Carson City streets were empty, except for the occasional citizen. Steve continued his drive around the streets just getting a feel for the city. He drove down the main streets for a while, then saw a sign that said Lake Tahoe, followed the arrow, and started the climb up the mountain.

The road had a heavy forest on both sides. The air was cooler than in the flats below and scented with mountain fir; the wind blew lightly and the aspen leaves whispered to each other as Steve, the indiscrete eavesdropper of their quiet conversation, drove higher up the mountain, anticipating seeing the famed lake.

Near the top Steve passed another state park, and thought that this would be a perfect stopover point. But first he wanted to see the lake. All through the West, Lake Tahoe was famed for its beauty and challenging skiing. The lake sat in the top of a dormant volcano with mountain peaks above it. The quartz blue sky rose over the lake and peaks.

It was an early morning at the end of August, autumn and winter still just hinted by the cool air. Steve reached the mountain top and there was the lake. He was awestruck by the deep blue of its water. The lake's surface reflected the billowy white clouds above, and a light wind played across the water, rippling the surface, cooling the shoreline. Steve drove the road around the lake shore, crossing the state line back into California. There was an immediate difference between the properties on each side of the lake.

The California side was more residential, less elaborate, and less lavish with no gambling. The Nevada side, where gambling was permitted, had larger, more opulent resorts and homes. Steve drove half-way around the lake and then doubled back to the state park he had seen on the Nevada side.

At the park, he registered and put his car in an assigned space. The park was empty on this weekday: the season was just about over, and the first storms were not far away. He had found serenity again, as on the Oregon coast. The mountain peaks surrounded the campground. On both sides of the mountain road was the forest. The small state park campgrounds had been cleared of most trees for the campsites, but the forest abutted the park.

Steve with his wanderlust set up his tent, aired his sleeping bag on the roof of the car and then took off into the forest and up the mountain where he hoped the crest's elevation would give him a pure unobstructed view of the entire lake from above. A flick of wind played across the aspen leaves, setting them to dance and beat against each other as Steve headed up the mountain for his lake view.

The man in the Camry followed the scent some distance behind the all too obvious caravan of the Ford and truck with camper in front of him. He waited with his radio scanner to head up to the lake. He knew with his hunter's instinct—as an observer of animal behavior—that now was the time. He would act today. Before the next sunrise he would snare his quarry on this mountain with the lake.

After Steve had started to make his ascent up the mountain, the truck with the camper attached and the Ford pulled into the campgrounds. Two men in sports shirts inquired of the attendant the whereabouts of the driver of the gray Olds. The attendant pointed in the direction Steve had taken up the mountain.

The men in the Ford decided to drive higher up the mountain road to observe Steve, while the two men in the camper headed up the mountain from the campgrounds by foot. When the men in the Ford had pulled further up the mountain road they saw the tan Camry parked into the shoulder of the road.

"Hank, get a make on that car. It's been with us before." They inspected the Camry, it was empty, but they saw the police scanner and their suspicions grew.

The Camry's occupant had already started up the mountain; he knew his quarry. He knew from observing his prey that the hunted man would want to ascend the mountain to see the lake. He set off in a line that would intersect Steve's course. He had his laptop computer bag over his shoulder and around his neck. In the forest, he stopped momentarily, when he could no longer be seen from the road, took out the barrel and butt of his German-made sniper's rifle, assembled it; and fitted the scope with ease as he had done many times before. He checked his ammunition. The cartridges he loaded were the special killing kind that fragmented on impact. Then he laid the computer bag in a tree, marked the spot in memory, notched the trunk with his pocket knife, and leaned two rocks against the tree trunk.

He headed up the mountain moving surely and steadily at a quick pace. He was no longer conserving his energy; the waiting was over. The pursuit was on to the crestline of the ridge.

Further down the mountain, now parked behind the Camry, was Mark Barnes, the young F.B.I. agent from Salt Lake City. He too headed up the mountain. In his earphone he heard, "Mark, we have a make on the driver of the Camry, one Richard Howlins from Chama, New Mexico. No criminal record." Mark continued his climb up the mountain, his legs churning, moving swiftly upward like the boy he had been in Wyoming. He knew the outdoor life. He also knew Steve Light was in danger. But he didn't know he was poised against an expert.

Steve stopped for a moment to take a drink from his canteen. He stood in a small clearing that had been made for a ski lift pylon as its chairs made their way up the mountain. *"On my next effort,"* Steve thought, *"I'll reach the crestline and have a spectacular view of the lake below."* The sun was in and out of some clouds. It was quiet; even the aspen leaves had stopped their fluttering. He stood and listened: a lone bird chirped, but all else was still and silent.

Steve felt at ease and at peace here on the mountain, alone in nature. The chaos of all night driving and running from enemies receded and seemed far away. The mountains surrounding Lake Tahoe, like the Oregon coast, were God-filled places of tranquility. Here was peace. But he was not alone.

Mark Barnes felt something too. It wasn't the serenity of nature or its ministering to his soul. He felt he had to get to Steve Light quickly.

Two other agents were heading up to the crestline from the campgrounds, and a third stayed behind where the Camry had been parked, knowing Howlins would have to return to it. The hood had been hot when Mark Barnes touched it so the occupant was not far ahead.

"Push yourself," Mark said to himself, "Move! Move! Move!" It was like he was an Eagle Scout again up in the Tetons. Now someone's life depended on his agility and endurance. It had come down to a simple footrace up the mountain.

Mark moved stealthily and with speed up the mountain. His youth and good conditioning were now being drawn upon, tapped, and tested. "A man's life depends upon it," he told himself.

About three hundred yards further up the mountain he saw Steve Light standing in a clearing, leaning against a ski lift pylon drinking from his canteen. What he didn't see immediately was a man on his left higher up the mountain propping his weapon against an aspen trunk for stability to draw a bead on Steve Light.

Then he made out Howlins. Mark pivoted to his left, automatically squared his stance, and fired three shots without taking careful aim. "Freeze! It's the F.B.I.!" What seemed like hours passed in those five seconds. Howlins kept the barrel of his rifle to the tree and turned to site Mark Barnes, through the scope. Barnes' face was in the cross hairs. At this distance there was no missing. Mark Barnes charged his pistol up, the rifleman well within range. The first one to get his shot off would survive.

Mark, stopped beside a tree, aimed. Howlins took a breath in preparation for his shot. Time stopped. Then Howlins did a curious thing: he dropped the rifle and put up his hands. He had not fired his weapon. He knew the penalty for killing an F.B.I. Agent. He would draw the death penalty. This way he had done very little and had information to trade. He'd risk the justice system. All this transpired in mil-instants of a second. *"They'll have a hard time linking me to any of the other murders,"*

Howlins thought to himself. *"I've always destroyed the weapon."* But he had forgotten about his shooting of retired agent John Woods with this weapon. Mark Barnes would have plenty of time to assemble a case against him.

Steve Light heard the shots coming from the forest below him and ducked down behind the cement pylon. Two men their 9mm pistols drawn emerged from the trees above him.

"Stay down," one shouted to him, "we're the F.B.I. Are you Steve Light?

"Yes."

"Where did the shots come from?" Steve pointed to the area below and into the trees. The two agents, guns drawn, ran for the tree line where the shots had come from.

Just then Mark Barnes emerged from the forest, marching out Richard Howlins who was handcuffed with his arms behind him and walking ahead of Mark into the clearing. Mark had his gun drawn and was carrying the sniper's rifle.

Howlins was taken to the federal holding facility in Reno. Within an hour Barnes had notified the agent in charge in New Mexico that Steve Light was okay and had barely escaped being killed.

"Hold onto him!" the voice said over the phone.

"We've arrested a Richard Howlins from Chama, New Mexico a 'real professional,' a hunter-guide. You'll want to search his residence," said Barnes.

43

owlins flipped easily and started trading information about Vance Arnold as the person who hired him to kill Steve Light.

That afternoon—a Tuesday—the United States attorney's office in Reno, Nevada contacted their counterparts in New Mexico and the wheels of justice started to turn. Vance Arnold, George Cody, and Len Coffee were quietly arrested at their homes that evening after dark in Santa Fe.

Mark Barnes and Steve Light had a conversation that Tuesday at dusk. "You're to stay here in Reno and cooperate with the United States attorney's office from New Mexico and the bureau. You're the chief witness. If you move even an eyebrow, I am going to lock you in a cell! Understand? New Mexico is sending an agent and assistant United States attorney here tomorrow to interview you.

"I have been ordered to hold you. I hope you have had enough of running. Your family has been notified that you're okay. We need your help to help us put together the pieces of how you figured this out. You are out of danger. Vance Arnold and his cohorts are going to be arrested tonight."

"I'll cooperate and stay put," was all Steve said in a subdued voice.

"Tonight you'll stay with a detail of agents in your room at a hotel. It's over now. No one is after you anymore. Your family will be here tomorrow. You'll be okay. One more thing: Vance Arnold and his men were powerful in New Mexico with powerful friends. We're going to try to get them to enter pleas so you won't have to testify as a witness. If I were you, and Leroy Clarkson, the United States Attorney sent this advice also, put New Mexico in your past. Your safety might be in jeopardy if the whole story got out and your role in it becomes widely known."

Steve listened intently to Mark Barnes, who had saved his life just a short while before. "An agent will take you to the hotel. I'll see you tomorrow morning. Stay with the agents tonight. They're there for your protection. Don't climb out of any bathroom windows."

Steve turned to Mark Barnes, slowly offered his hand, and said quietly, "Thank you for saving my life." And then walked away with the agents who were part of his detail.

The next morning, Steve ate breakfast with the two agents in his hotel room and worked on the investigation at the United States attorney's office in Reno. He met with the investigators from New Mexico through the week and into the weekend. He explained how he put his assumptions together and how he worked out the details. He was video taped and transcribed.

At a break for lunch, on the first day after the arrests, waiting in another office were his mother and sister. It was a tearful reunion.

Vance tried to trade Big Jim, but the assistant United States attorney didn't bite. He had been informed by his chief deputy to keep the former chief justice out of the case because he had been instrumental in resolving the matter.

Vance, George, and Len copped pleas. Vance drew the harshest sentence for the attempted murder for hire of a judicial officer—thirty years with an additional fifteen years stacked on top of that for the Children's Department embezzlement to be served consecutively, which meant he had to serve the first thirty years before he could begin serving the second fifteen year term. Vance would spend the rest of his life in prison: a cop doesn't do well in prison. George and Len both cooperated with the prosecutors in the case against Vance and each received an eight year sentence without the chance for early release. Richard Howlins received a fifteen year sentence for the shooting of John Woods and pled to life imprisonment for other murders that the bureau pieced together against him from evidence seized at his cabin.

Later that week in New Mexico between Tucumcari and Las Vegas, a big man was driving on a narrow road with no guard rail. The man drove his car at the usual New Mexico speed limit when no one was around: whatever the hell you feel like. Beside him on the passenger seat sat a case of Budweiser. He was drinking as he drove and had been so since getting off work. He talked to himself as he drove, "That bastard had me kill those puppies. Innocent, little puppies. All of them. You are a sorry bastard. Look at you. Go ahead, you sonofabitch. Look in the mirror." And just as he looked at himself in the mirror the car failed to negotiate a turn and catapulted from the road surface down the winding mountain road into a deep arroyo. He hadn't been wearing his seat belt and was partially ejected out of the driver's side window as the car rolled over and over again on its side. His foot wedged beneath the brake and gas pedal and instead of being thrown clear he was caught between the car and surface of the ground.

With each revolution of the car his body was pressed like dough beneath a rolling pin. But he was still alive when the car came to rest with the driver's door on the ground sideways up. His screams alerted the coyotes in the area, who mimicked his cries. One of his legs and both arms were pinned beneath the car. He could not move. The coyotes came to investigate. They were not averse to gnawing on a living man. He was their feast that night. They liked the belly meat best. With sun up the buzzards started circling overhead; they considered the liquid of the eyes a delicacy. He was still alive at mid-morning, the vultures and coyotes fighting for his tenders, while he howled in unendurable pain. Four days later the body, or what was left of it, was found. Even the big bones of the arms and legs had been cracked and the red, juicy pith of the marrow greedily sucked out by the famished pack that fought over the strewn remains.

Big Jim lost the primary decisively. He ran last. His message never got out. And the people of New Mexico considered it an oddity that their highest sitting judge should now want to be a politician. Instead voters cast their ballot for a young, energetic congressman from a rich, established New Mexico family. People were surprised that Big Jim didn't even mount a substantial media blitz before the election. It was a wholly mismanaged campaign, people thought.

After he lost the election, law firms considered Jim a liability and he was forced into retirement. The newly elected United States senator, who had power to steer business to a firm which had supported him, would also steer business away from a firm who had his primary opponent in the last election as a partner who would gain monetarily from the senator's connections. Politicians have the memory of elephants, especially the winners. Jim faded from the scene. He was through.

Jim became something of an oddity: too old to practice law and too young to die and be remembered. Instead, he helped Karen with her supermarket shopping, lifting groceries from the trunk of her car in the driveway and carrying them to the kitchen. He had become a "bag boy." He aged quickly and would continue to do so for the next twelve years as he stooped and shuffled from the driveway to the kitchen, a man old before his time, useless, unwanted, and used up.